The Quiet Part

The Quiet Part

by

Eric N. Solomont

Creative Epiphany

First paperback edition 2026.

ISBN: 979-8-9949480-0-2

Published by Creative Epiphany
Hyannis, Massachusetts

Cover design by Eric N. Solomont

Printed in the United States of America

For my father,
my wife,
and The Daily Paper
on West Main St. in Hyannis, MA
for the use of Table 12.

"Still waters run deep, but a good whiskey runs deeper."

Prologue
1888

He sat alone. Morning light pressed through warped glass panes, catching the dust that hung in the air in soft, slanting rays. Another day, he might have seen it as angelic.

They had walked from the jail just after sunrise. The deputy tried to make small talk, but he wasn't in the mood. He still wore yesterday's clothes. Still tried to wear yesterday's face, though it didn't seem to have the same fit.

He was deposited in the holding room. He'd become very familiar with it over the last several days. Always starting, and often ending, his days here. The room smelled like old paper and some type of sanitizer. The smell had gotten to him once or twice... bitter at the back of the nose, like cleaning fluid turned sour. But now it barely registered. It had folded itself into the background.

The hard-backed chair was less than comfortable. It wasn't meant to be. The table in front of him, darkened and dulled, remained pockmarked despite years of shellac.

In the silence of the room, echoes ran through his head.

His lawyer, sharp around the edges but perhaps green where he shouldn't be... always rehearsing the upside... sure it would be manslaughter at most. Time served, maybe. A few years with good behavior.

His wife, constantly bringing up the future. A shop of his own… children… after this bump in the road.

It had taken longer than expected for the jury to come back.

But then the paper was read aloud. Even the clerk had stumbled for a beat.

Second-degree.

He hadn't slept. Not really. Not last night, not much during the trial.

There had been a kind of brightness to him all the way through. Steady. Hopeful. He never lost his thin smile.

If only to keep her from falling apart.

Footsteps and muted voices approached. They stopped just outside the door. A brief back and forth, then the door opened with a soft groan.

The lawyer had entered first, already speaking.

"You have to understand, the family is very important. Anyone else, and it was manslaughter… probably no more than two years."

She followed close behind. Eyes red, she had been crying. She shook her head, her voice barely audible.

"Please… it no longer matters. What should we expect now?"

The lawyer rambled on as if not hearing her, "maybe even a suspended sentence, depending on the judge…" He trailed off again. He was pacing slowly, hands resting on his knees.

"But that family…" He let the words drift. "Someone on that jury knew the family… the name alone could have… there's no getting around them."

"Stop please…" she said, softer this time.

He paused mid-step. "They wanted a conviction…" the lawyer stated emphatically. "Probably wanted it to *look* merciful though. Second-degree gives them that. Gives the papers something neat to print, too."

Bang.

The sound cracked across the room. A sudden slam of a hand against the table.

From the corner of his eye, the lawyer saw his client, the man who until now had been silent at the table, looking at him.

The man spoke, low but firm.

"Wes. Let's focus. It doesn't matter anymore."

She stepped forward and placed her hand gently on his.

He turned and offered a weak smile.

The lawyer straightened. He cleared his throat. He reached into his briefcase and took out some papers, thumbing through them as if that might restore some confidence in his clients.

"Now look," he said, speaking carefully. "The verdict was harsh. No doubt. But that's often how these things balance out. The judge knows the weight of it. Second-degree gives the family what they wanted. But sentencing… sentencing is a different matter."

He looked like her—not quite smiling, but softer now.

"There's still a range. And I expect the court to lean low. Ten, maybe twelve. Good behavior… parole will bring it down. Could be five, six years before there's a hearing. I'd say that'll be it."

Her breath hitched just slightly. She began to nod. She raised her eyes, and some of the weight behind them seemed to loosen.

"I've got to think," the lawyer went on, "if they'd wanted to make an example, it would've been first-degree. That'd be rope or life. No choice. They didn't go that far. That tells me they're leaving room."

She nodded faintly, perhaps not entirely understanding. Her fingers brushed the man's, clearly her husband. He didn't move. His eyes were fixed on a place just past the wall.

The lawyer cleared his throat again. "We'll know soon. But I think there's reason for optimism."

There was a knock on the door. The bailiff stepped in and said, "They're calling you in now."

The lawyer, suddenly nervous, fumbled the papers as he hurried to stuff them back into his briefcase.

The man said, "Can we have a minute?"

The lawyer paused, then gave a brief nod.

"I'll wait in the hall."

The man turned to her. He took her hands in his and looked into her eyes. He forced a smile. It looked forced.

"This is it," the man said. "I don't know if Wes is right. But it doesn't matter. Ten days or ten years… we'll be okay."

She wanted to smile. She nodded, but she wasn't sure. She was already lonely, and they'd only been apart just under seven weeks. She hadn't told him, but she'd moved in with her parents.

He saw the look on her face... the struggle behind it. He squeezed her hands just slightly.

"We'll be a'right."

The courtroom was sparsely populated.

As he was walked in, he noticed his parents… his in-laws. She sat down next to them. The victim's family was there. They stared daggers. A lone reporter sat at the back.

His foot caught on an uneven floorboard and he stumbled. The lawyer caught his arm, steadying him, then guided him to his seat at the table near the front.

Seated, he let his eyes scan the room. He avoided the victim's family, quickly passing over their row and settling on his folks'. His father gave a small wave. He kept going, found her again. Gave the small nod. The forced smile.

Then he turned to face front.

The deputy who'd brought him in that morning stood off to the side. He'd been a constant presence since the beginning. He'd become a kind of friend… well as close as you could under the circumstances.

The deputy looked at his watch, then said, "Rise."

The word came flatly, and the air shifted. There was a clatter of movement as all came to their feet.

In a bit of a fog, he didn't register the command, or that everyone around him had already stood. The lawyer gave him a nudge. He shook his head and looked around, realizing his misstep. With a meek look on his face, he rose.

The judge entered through a simple door to the left of the large desk at the front of the room, the judge's bench.

He was a large man. Not obese. Solid, especially for his age. His presence commanded attention, but he was inconsistent. Sometimes he was fully engaged, sharp-eyed, asking questions, hanging on every word. Other times, he barely seemed present at all. Even flipping through the daily paper like it was any other morning.

The clatter resumed as people took their seats, then faded, replaced by the quiet creak of the judge's chair settling in.

Though the jury box was now empty, he could make out phantom shapes where they had sat. He could see the foreman's ghost rise to declare guilt. He could hear the collective gasp ripple through the gallery at the words "*murder in the second degree.*"

Without looking up, the judge pulled a page from a stack of papers and began to read.

"Having been duly tried and found guilty by a jury of your peers on the charge of murder in the second degree, it is the judgment of this court that you, the defendant, be committed to the custody of the Kentucky State Penitentiary.

You are hereby sentenced to a term of fifty years of confinement at hard labor, to be carried out in such manner and facility as the Department of Corrections shall determine.

Credit shall be given for time already served. You may become eligible for parole under the laws and regulations of this Commonwealth at such time as deemed appropriate by the parole board."

There was no outburst. Just a hush. It seemed to fall heavier than any silence.

The lawyer stared straight ahead, motionless. His lips parted slightly, but no words came. This wasn't what he'd expected.

She sat frozen, rows behind, between her parents and his. Her eyes searched the courtroom, blinking fast, looking for an indication that she'd heard wrong, or more was coming to make it all better. From where she sat, he looked impossibly far away.

The victim's family was still, but their eyes were fixed, unblinking. Then one of them exhaled. Another gave a slow nod, registering a quiet satisfaction.

Behind them all, the lone reporter scratched vigorously on a notepad.

The judge stared at the sentenced man. He stared back, though he didn't seem to see him.

The judge addressed the lawyer, but the words landed between them all.

"The sentence may seem harsh, Mr. Brooks," the judge said, addressing the lawyer, "but your client knows the truth of it. In any trial, there are things that come out and there are things that remain hidden. While you may not like it, it is the hidden things that may make the sentence justified."

The judge gave the prisoner one last look.

The gavel came down, sharp, final.

Chapter 1
1929

A loud clanging awoke Joseph Henry, the usual wake-up call. Sitting up, he scratched his close-cropped head of hair. All of the prisoners were required to have their heads shaved close on a weekly basis. Joseph Henry could tell the day of the week by the give of the morning stubble. This good scratch told him it was Tuesday. Tomorrow he'd be freshly shorn.

He could hear other inmates rousing in cells around him. "You awake, Crow?" he managed in a scratchy voice, still full of dust and grime inhaled while snoring through the night. Joseph Henry was normally up before wake-up call. Once up, inmates had 45 minutes to get washed, dressed, and ready for work detail. Joseph Henry took on the added responsibility of helping Old Crow get going. Most of the cell doors were opened at wake-up. Joseph Henry rolled out of his cot, stood up, and pulled on his linen overalls. He walked the short distance to Old Crow's cell and looked in.

"You awake, Crow?" Old Crow was still face down on his cot, his face stuffed in the crook of his arm, his back facing the door. Every morning, Joseph Henry would see him in a similar position. Every day he'd shudder at the sight, wondering if this was going to be the day that he'd find Old Crow stiff and dead, with no need to be roused. "Come on now, Crow!" Joseph Henry hastened to Old Crow's side. He put his hand on the ancient leathery skin of Old Crow's back. He let out the usual sigh of relief at still feeling the warmth of life, and he gently rocked the old man back and forth. "Come on now, the guards'll be by. Need to get moving."

Old Crow slowly turned in Joseph Henry's direction and opened one of his crusty eyes. Old Crow squinted, trying to focus on Joseph Henry's face inches from his own. Joseph Henry always wore a warm, closed-lipped smile… kind, but tinged with sadness. As Old Crow recognized Joseph Henry, he broke out a smile of his own. His was a big, toothy grin, though with far fewer teeth than he probably once had. "Alright, alright, I be ah comin'." Joseph Henry knew he still wouldn't without sufficient prodding.

"You'll have to do better than that, Crow." Joseph Henry put an arm under the old man and hefted him up to a sitting position. He looked around the cell and found a shirt and pants on the floor where they likely had fallen from Old Crow's body the night before. He helped the old man back into them.

With a bit more encouragement, Old Crow began to move on his own. He hoisted himself into a standing position. "Okay, okay, I can dress myself," though he was already mostly clothed by now.

Joseph Henry returned to his own cell and finished his dressing. He folded his thin blanket and placed it neatly over the end of his cot and made sure everything in the small room was in its place. A tidy cell was one of the few things a man could control in here. The guards didn't really care how neat the cell was. They'd usually only get on an inmate if a cell was dirty or messy enough to draw bugs or rodents or mites.

After making sure Old Crow was still up, the two walked towards the washrooms. The hallway smelled of bleach and cold metal. The floor was still damp from the early morning mopping, and Joseph Henry walked with his usual care, while making sure Old Crow avoided any remaining slick spots. Like always, Old Crow shuffled beside him, his bare feet scratching against the cold cement.

Every so often, a guard passed them by, usually not even offering a nod. Joseph Henry nodded regardless, and would often give a "g'd morning," sometimes just to see if he'd get one back. He knew most of the guards by name. Most were pretty amiable, some lazy, a few genuinely decent. It was infrequent that they'd act harshly without an inmate doing something to deserve it. Joseph Henry never was a problem, and most of the guards knew it, so Joseph Henry was given a lot of leeway. Time gave you a lot of knowledge about how you'd be treated, and Joseph Henry had more time than pretty much everyone else there.

"Mornin', Mister Henry. Mornin', Crow."

"Mornin', Walker," replied Joseph Henry as they approached a stout inmate with a scar through his left eye and half his nose. Most of the inmates referred to Joseph Henry as some form of Mister. Something about his long tenure gave the other inmates the impression that he had some official status. He wasn't in charge of anything or anyone, but he wasn't ignored, either. He carried a quiet authority earned by decades of surviving.

"Mornin', Mista' Henry… Mornin' Crow."

"Morning, Jimmy." Joseph Henry never stopped smiling. He was well liked, but gave as much respect as he got. Most of the inmates saw him as a steady presence, a man who'd become part of the prison's very architecture. You could lean on him, ask him something, or sit beside him without any worry. Joseph Henry didn't talk more than needed, but when he did, it could be worth hearing.

The washroom was already crowded. Cold water ran from darkened faucets, echoing off the long metal sinks. Joseph Henry guided Old Crow to their usual spot. The other inmates let the old man have the corner, where there was a small ledge to sit on. As Joseph washed his face and scrubbed his arms, he caught sight of himself in the dull warped mirror. His head stubble would be gone tomorrow, but the lines around his eyes, the slump of his shoulders—those weren't going anywhere. Joseph Henry gave a brief chuckle, wondering where the young man he remembered seeing in the same mirror for so long had gone.

He paused a moment and ran his hand over the basin, trailing his fingers along the edge. The metal was cold and smooth, worn down by decades of use. He always pictured others who had stood in the same spot, thinking their own thoughts and regrets, just like he did now. Joseph Henry always pushed aside the regrets. While he lost so much, he knew he had it better than most others in the penitentiary.

Someone bumped into his side. "Sorry, Mista' Henry," came a voice.

"No harm," Joseph replied. He dried his face and checked on Crow. Crow stared at Joseph Henry like a loyal dog waiting on his master. They made their way back to the cells and finished getting dressed, which usually entailed putting on shoes or boots, depending on which morning work detail they had.

Joseph Henry thought about the day ahead. Tuesday meant maintenance stockroom… a quiet job, mostly sorting tools and supplies for the week's projects. He didn't mind it. It kept him away from the younger inmates trying to prove themselves. He didn't have to sweep leaves in the yard or listen to men yell about football teams they hadn't seen play in decades.

He remembered one Tuesday, maybe fifteen years ago now, when a shipment of tools went missing. The guards were sure it was an inside job, and half the block was locked down for two days. Joseph Henry had nothing to do with it, but they questioned him anyway. After all, he knew the routines better than most. In the end, it turned out to be a clerical error. Boxes mislabeled. Still, for a time, the air had gone sour with suspicion.

Across the room, someone new caught his eye. A fresh inmate. Young. Jumpy. The kind who still looked at the walls like they might close in and swallow him. Joseph Henry made a note to keep an eye out. He remembered the look. He'd seen it in the mirror, long ago. When he still thought he might get out. When he still thought things mattered.

Old Crow was humming now, low and tuneless. Joseph Henry sat beside him and waited. He had over forty years of waiting behind him. He could manage another few minutes.

The morning bell would ring again soon. Then the shuffle would begin—boots on tile, guards shouting, doors clanging open and shut. Another Tuesday, another slow march through a life reduced to repetitions. But for now, in the humid stillness of the washroom, Joseph Henry sat in a silent calm. Not contentment, not joy, but calm—the kind a man earns through acceptance and routine rather than hope.

Chapter 2
1929… 1790…

JOSEPH Henry was feeling his age. He had recently turned sixty-four, older than most men around him, but not diminished. He was the longest-serving inmate at Frankfort. Most of the men he remembered had come and gone. Some were released, some transferred, some just died.

Old Crow was the oldest inmate, but Joseph Henry had been inside longer. Most of the long-termers didn't make it this far. Too many of the jobs inside wore a man down. Harvesting turpentine through wet winters or breathing noxious air in the leather shop would take years off a man's sentence just by taking the years off the man.

Joseph Henry had done his share of these, but in his later years he was fortunate. He'd been given more innocuous work, delivering products into town or driving Boss Van's wife and daughters on errands to Louisville or Lexington. Both jobs let him outside the walls, a rare privilege for someone convicted of killing another.

But Joseph Henry wasn't seen as a murderer. Not really. Not by the guards. Not by the inmates. Not even by the warden. No one did, except for the Kentucky Penal System.

The others all saw Joseph Henry for what he was: a good man.

"A victim of circumstance," they'd say.

Only he, and maybe Minnie, knew the real circumstance.

They had been married just over six months back then. Things were good. Joseph Henry had been working hard for several years to properly support Minnie and whatever little ones might come along.

He split time between working for his father as a lathe maker and apprenticing with Mr. Spears, distilling whiskey. Joseph Henry liked lathe making, but he loved crafting whiskey. He believed he could produce the finest whiskey Kentucky had to offer.

It wasn't some pipe dream. Joseph Henry had a talent, and he had the knowledge to back it up. It was a craft handed down like a keepsake, beginning with Baker Henry, his great-grandfather, and refined with each generation. Joseph Henry carried it now, determined to take it further than any of them had.

He'd tell Old Crow bits and pieces of stories sometimes, while folding laundry or sitting in the mess hall. When Joseph Henry spoke about his family, or the past, Old Crow knew to just let him talk. He liked to hear stories, any stories.

It all began with Baker Henry. He learned to distill alongside Elijah Craig himself, back before Craig's name meant anything.

Craig had moved to Kentucky just after 1780 and established a mill complex that included a grist mill, a fulling mill, and a paper mill. As a newcomer to the area, he brought on Baker Henry, who had previously run a carding mill near Georgetown, to help manage operations.

Distilling was a natural fit. Like many frontier millers, Craig also farmed, growing corn, rye, wheat, and barley to supply his grist mill. But grain didn't keep well in Kentucky's humid summers, and excess harvests often spoiled or went to waste. Distilling offered a practical solution. It preserved surplus grain and turned it into something stable, portable, and even profitable. For this reason, Elijah Craig and Baker Henry taught themselves distilling, and selling the product became an added business. But the product was rough, raw, and wildly inconsistent. It was often cut with fruit, molasses, tobacco, or spices just to make it drinkable.

Elijah Craig, ever the entrepreneur, saw potential. He and Baker scoured the region for better methods. They studied, experimented, and refined their craft until they believed they had something more valuable than the usual farmer's whiskey.

Business grew. As buyers sampled the new product, demand increased. Attention to the mill complex began to slip. At the same time, demand for textiles was rising in the fledgling state. In order to ensure profit from both, Baker Henry was reassigned to manage Craig's other holdings, specifically the fulling mill, while the whiskey operation became Craig's focus alone.

But that's not to say Baker Henry had no hand in Kentucky's rich whiskey history. Despite the simpler course his life took, legend had it that Baker Henry was, quite ironically, responsible for Elijah Craig's inventing bourbon and beginning Kentucky's great whiskey legacy.

Baker was to meet Elijah Craig to present new textile samples he hoped to produce in the fledgling fulling mill. Craig was too busy to meet properly, so he told Baker to leave the samples at the distillery, an old barn that had been converted to store whiskey barrels.

The locals say Craig was short with Baker and curtly told him to just leave the samples. Dejected, Baker dropped the pile of cloth squares, though he placed them too close to a lantern. At some point, the cloth combusted, burning down the barn.

Many of the barrels were a total loss, but some were only burned on the inside. Craig, ever frugal, decided to use them anyway.

Later, a shipment of whiskey sent to New Orleans included some of the charred barrels. During the long trip downriver, the charred wood imparted a darker color and richer taste not seen before. The buyers were uncertain at first, but soon praised it as "Kentucky's new Red Liquor."

From that time forward, Craig's process would always include aging whiskey in barrels that had been charred on the inside.

Much to Baker's dismay, Craig let him go, claiming the fire had been his fault. However, after his good fortune and improved whiskey, he rehired Baker, this time putting him in charge of his paper mill.

The locals joked that Craig was trying to create more good fortune by putting Baker near something even more combustible.

Since then, the Henrys always enjoyed producing whiskey, though other priorities had kept them in more mundane trades. While Joseph Henry felt the same responsibilities that kept whiskey merely a family hobby, he was going to be the first to use his talents in a more professional way.

His father had introduced Joseph Henry to Mr. Spears, a regular customer and friend of Samuel Henry. Having sampled some of the fruits of the Henry family hobby, after that Mr. Spears was more than happy to have Joseph Henry apprenticing.

Joseph Henry gained little in the apprenticeship, apart from ten cents an hour and the chance to be closer to his passion. There was little he didn't already know about the making of good whiskey. Mr. Spears, on the other hand, gained greatly. He quickly recognized the asset he had in Joseph Henry and took full advantage.

Joseph Henry didn't mind. He was making some money, and he was making some whiskey.

Old Crow didn't say much when the stories ended. He just gave a nod, and a smile, and sometimes he'd prod for another.

Chapter 3

1929

New inmates admitted to the Frankfort Penitentiary were all treated more or less the same. There was no drama based on the severity of crimes. Petty theft, larceny, robbery, even manslaughter were processed without distinction. Those guilty of more violent or malicious acts were typically sent elsewhere.

José "Ugly" Attics had been arrested alongside two other men after a robbery at a general store. Two men and a child were killed. His accomplices were sent to a different facility, maybe to get the rope. Ugly, though, wound up at Frankfort. It was determined he hadn't played a role in the deaths, and he testified against the others. In the end, he was given fifteen years.

Ugly was happy with that. He knew he'd had more to do with the outcome than anyone ever determined. It could have been life. Or worse.

"Name?" a guard behind a high counter asked, not looking up from the clipboard in his left hand. He rolled a pencil nub back and forth in his right.

When no answer came, the guard looked up over wire-rimmed spectacles. Ugly was taking in his surroundings.

Thick, oily hair sat atop his head, drooping leftward as if half-glued in place.

As Ugly looked around, the guard blinked, caught off guard by the man's odd face.

From the right, he saw a simple smile, the kind you might find on a small child in wonderment at his surroundings. Then Ugly turned his head.

The guard flinched.

The left side was stark. If the right side was a summer morning, the left was a gray winter.

Broad, faded scars stretched from his ear to the corner of his mouth, which wouldn't rise with the right side to complete the smile. The mouth itself wasn't frozen. It moved on both sides, but while the right side smiled, the left failed at the attempt, leaving not quite a sneer, but something just as unsettling.

The guard shook his head and forced his eyes back to the clipboard. He cleared his throat.

"Name?" he asked again, this time more firmly.

Ugly snapped his gaze forward. "Ooglay," he said in an accent the guard took to be Mexican.

The guard scanned the clipboard. No name came close.

"Ooglay?" he repeated. "Full given name?"

"Oh… sorry, Mister. José Attics."

Chapter 4
1929

The maintenance stockroom was quiet, but Joseph Henry had learned to appreciate his time there. This was his detail most Tuesdays as well as other days when the weather didn't agree with leaving the grounds. He'd been in the stockroom almost once a week going back as long as he could remember. Joseph Henry couldn't recall ever receiving any training or being told what was to be done in the stockroom, but he spent a lot of time in the lathing shop, and doing what was needed to maintain that shop was as good as anything.

He'd do a lot of counting and sorting. He'd log incoming shipments of tools, nails, screws, hinges, wire, and other maintenance supplies. He'd keep a ledger of stock levels. There wasn't any kind of ledger when he arrived. Joseph Henry couldn't remember where he got the ledger, but he'd been keeping it for the stockroom now for as long as he'd been there. He'd note shortages and the need for supplies as they came in from other areas of the penitentiary. Joseph Henry didn't do any ordering, so someone must be looking at the ledger because he'd always receive shipments of items that he noted needing in the ledger.

The things Joseph Henry really enjoyed doing in the stockroom were cleaning and repairing tools that were returned from work crews. He'd polish and shine hammers and shovels, sharpen blades, oil metal parts to prevent rust, re-handle broken tool shafts, and assemble simple equipment like wheelbarrows and pulley kits. He had to do similar work in the lathe shop. It made him feel good to make use of his old experience, like his life wasn't a total waste. Boss Van recognizing and making use of Joseph Henry's other skills though was what truly kept him alive.

Joseph Henry sat on the floor with his back against the wall. It was a busier day than normal in the stockroom. His hands ached and his eyes stung from the caustic tool cleaners. With his eyes closed, Joseph Henry listened to the low sounds of the penitentiary. The brick walls muted the constant ruckus. The clatter of the yard, the grumble of boilers, the barking of guards… all of it faded into a low hum this deep inside the prison. Here, it was just Joseph Henry and the slow dull rhythm of his life.

The door creaked.

Joseph Henry's eyes snapped open. The stockroom didn't get visitors, especially during mid-shift. He didn't like to be seen resting. He was a constant here and took pride in continuous activity. In one motion he was on his feet, a hammer and polishing rag in his hands, with fingers curled around the handle. He looked up to see the door suddenly ajar.

A figure slid in, slow and deliberate. Coal dust clung to him in thick blotches and bands across his face, arms, and the front of his shirt. The only clean thing about him was the cigarette hanging from his lip. He produced a wooden match, probably pilfered from the same source as the cigarette. Striking the match against the wall near the door, it flared with a brief snap of yellow and the stink of sulfur rose with a waft of pale gray smoke. The man cupped the flame with both hands, like he was shielding something precious. He brought the flame to the tip of his rollie and puffed gently, until the end glowed like a little angry eye.

The newcomer let the first drag curl from his mouth, slow and lazy. The end of the cigarette burned hot and steady. He tipped his head up just enough to take in his new surroundings. He realized he wasn't alone. His eyes took a quick scan of the stockroom before letting them rest on Joseph Henry.

"Nice little nest you got here, Mister. Mind if I take the edge off?"

Joseph Henry said nothing. He just watched the man take in the room, balancing equal amounts of confidence and unease, trying to determine which he should go with and trying to decide if he had stumbled into trouble or not. He finally settled on confident and formed a slight smirk on the right side of his face.

"This a cozy spot, Mister." He began to look around again as though assessing something... Maybe several somethings.

Joseph Henry gave a small nod, polite, cautious. "Just my work detail, just doing my job." He found himself suddenly feeling something that seemed out of his nature. Despite being incarcerated and living as a convict for what seemed like ages, Joseph Henry had always felt a level of comfort in his situation. All at once and for the first time in a long time, he didn't feel that. Like a warm blanket had suddenly been yanked off of his shoulders.

The man smiled. Or half of him did. The right side of his face curled into something resembling charm. The left dragged behind, as though still deciding whether to bother. "Sure. Your job. Nice work, if you can get it. Me, I've been shovelin' coal since first bell. How does a fella get a soft job like this?"

Joseph Henry shifted his grip on the hammer, set it gently on the shelf. "Been here a long time." He placed the man's accent south of the border, maybe Mexico or Panama. Truth to tell, Joseph Henry didn't know enough about the area down there to tell the difference.

The man took a slow pull from his cigarette, letting the smoke curl lazily from the corner of his mouth. "Course... A man don't stay in a place like this without learnin' the right handshakes. Maybe passin' around a few favors. Making the right friends." His eyes gleamed, sharp beneath the dirt. "Man like me could use a few friends too. Think you and me oughta be amigos."

Joseph Henry's throat felt dry. This was not an invitation. He unconsciously began looking around for help in an empty room, "Ah… Maybe."

The man chuckled. "That's right. Prison life's a long haul. I'm a good friend too. You want me as a friend, amigo. You want me watchin' your back. And you do things for your amigo Ugly too." He turned his hand and pointed his thumb at his face. "José… Attics… but folks been calling me Ugly. I'm ok with that."

Joseph Henry gave an involuntary nod. "Joseph Henry."

Ugly's smirk deepened. "Pleasure, Mister Henry. Like I said, you and me gonna be amigos."

The weight of his words through the thick accent settled heavy in the air. 'Ugly'? Did the man say that? Sounded like 'Oogly', but he had heard others talking about a new inmate, calling him 'Ugly'. This was him. Joseph Henry was pretty sure the new one was supposed to be a Mexican.

From the hallway, a guard's voice rang out, sharp and impatient. "Attics! Get your ass back to the chute before I toss you in it!"

Ugly's grin widened and flicked the rest of his cigarette onto the stockroom floor.

"Well, gotta go. But you don't worry, Mister Henry. I'll be back. Wouldn't want you missing your new amigo."

He turned, sauntered out as casually as he'd come. The door swung shut behind him with a quiet click.

Joseph Henry stood still for a long moment. Then he stepped forward and ground Ugly's cigarette into the concrete with the toe of his boot. His hands went back to the tools, but slower now. The quiet wasn't quite so comforting anymore.

Joseph Henry didn't move again until Ugly and the guard's footsteps could no longer be heard. He let out an audible sigh, turned back to his tools, and silently returned to his work.

A half-sharpened chisel lay on the table, one that he had begun sharpening early in the day but set aside to pack up a box of nails for a carpentry project in the yard. He picked it up with the intent of finishing the job, but for some reason his attention was drawn to the scuffed handle. He grabbed a rag already soaked with linseed oil and rubbed it into the wood, slowly and methodically.

Joseph Henry felt something stirring in his chest. He tried to name it. He'd felt it before. It wasn't dread. It wasn't fear.

His encounter with Ugly had unsettled him… but why? He wasn't afraid of Ugly, not exactly. Joseph Henry had seen all kinds in this place. Men who barked loud. Men who struck without warning. Ugly wasn't either of these.

Joseph Henry's mind wandered with the rhythmic motion of the linen.

He couldn't deny that he had it better than some others in the system. He paused and felt a slight smile develop. Actually, he had it better than just about anyone in the Frankfort Penitentiary. Most folks… guards and inmates alike… knew it. Part of it was circumstance… he was white, well-mannered, and carried himself with a quiet civility. But more than that, people didn't really believe he belonged there. Even the guards, who were not known for their kindness, treated Joseph Henry with a casual respect.

He scrutinized the newly polished handle and allowed himself the briefest flicker of pride, though such feelings didn't come naturally to him. He placed the oiled chisel in a box with a handful of polished screwdrivers and stood there, eyes unfocused.

Early on, Boss Van, the warden, knew Joseph Henry wasn't just another inmate. He was a man with skills, a man who made things work. Maybe he looked into Joseph Henry's background, but Boss Van didn't think there was much risk in trusting Joseph Henry with "special" work details, often off the grounds: driving the truck full of prison-made goods to local vendors, or even chauffeuring the warden's wife and daughters on errands into town. While other men would remain behind stone walls, Joseph Henry watched the seasons change from behind the wheel of a flatbed Ford.

Joseph Henry picked up a battered spade, its blade flecked with rust and old earth. He began scraping at it with a wire brush.

At first, the other inmates grumbled about his freedom, about the way he came and went, how the guards gave a knowing nod when he passed. But that didn't last. Joseph Henry never acted like he was entitled or better than anyone. In fact, most of the time he brought something back: a handful of tobacco, a worn copy of *Harper's Monthly* or *Western Story Magazine*, maybe a jar of liniment for a bad knee. Sometimes it was something a man had mentioned offhand weeks earlier. Over time, the others came to see him as *their* man, someone on the outside who still belonged to them. And in a way, it made them feel like they were getting out too.

He set down the spade, reached for another tool, and fervently began working it.

Joseph Henry never knew how Boss Van first learned about his talent for making whiskey. It was rumored that some kind of moonshine operation had long been connected to the penitentiaries, most of it barely drinkable rotgut, but people took what they could get. Boss Van saw an opportunity. If he could offer a product that *kicked it up a notch*, there was money to be made. He'd already begun staffing the operation, pulling in what talent he could from previous connections, but something was still missing. He had hands, but no master.

A sound outside, distant boots on tile, made him open his eyes. Shift change? No, not yet. He still had another hour. Maybe more.

When Boss Van summoned him, Joseph Henry couldn't fathom why. But the warden laid it out casually before him, almost like he was offering a management position or speaking to a new business partner, not an inmate. Joseph would run production, manage the customers, and oversee deliveries. Boss Van just wanted to see the profits. Joseph Henry was dumbfounded. He didn't know what to say. He had given up on his dreams the day he entered the penal system. But now, in a strange and unexpected way, prison was giving him everything he had once planned for: stability, purpose, and a quiet version of the life he'd longed for. It wasn't freedom but it was enough to make him forget, sometimes, that he didn't have it.

Joseph Henry stood up and put the tool in its place. He picked up the ledger and flipped to the most recent page. Two hammers noted as cracked. A request for more roofing nails. A tally of grease tins. He pressed his fingers to the paper, leaving behind a faint smudge. The handwriting was neat. Disciplined.

Someone knocked once on the door frame. Joseph Henry closed the ledger before looking up.

It was a new guard. A younger one. Cap pressed a bit too low. Nervous. Trying not to look uncertain… like he was reporting to a superior.

"Evening, Mr. Henry," the guard said.

Joseph Henry nodded. "Evening." He noticed the nervousness in his own voice was gone. He was himself again.

"Boss Van says he might have you riding out tomorrow. Delivery run. He said Gearalt's Leather Goods."

Joseph Henry paused. *Gearalt's* was a code. It meant the operation. He'd be leaving the grounds tomorrow to see to the still. The tension of the day eased from his shoulders. He didn't mean to, but he smiled.

"All right," he said.

The guard lingered a half second too long before nodding and moving on.

Chapter 5
1876

Joseph Henry had known Minnie Timmons since grade school. Her father worked in Samuel Henry's shop. Though schooling wasn't yet compulsory, Samuel insisted on it for his own children, and strongly encouraged the same for the families of his employees.

Samuel Henry believed a boy who could read, write, and reckon would always be of value to the community and would never be in want of work. He said it often. "Education is an investment," he'd say. "One that pays back in steady hands and clear thinking." And he was adamant that it wasn't just for the boys. "Girls ought to go, too. A well-read woman," he'd say, "will raise a better household, without foolish children." He put his money where his mouth was, making sure that employees who sent their children to school were never without what they needed. He kept a stash of slate boards, pencils, and paper for his workers to take, as well as wool mittens and scarves for the children to wear on colder days for the long walk to the schoolhouse.

Joseph Henry first met Minnie when his father volunteered him to walk her to and from the schoolhouse each day. She was a quiet girl with dove-pale skin and blonde hair that caught the light where it curled at the ends. He would walk a mile to her home, then the two of them would walk the three miles to the schoolhouse.

At first, the walk was silent. Both children were inherently shy. Most days, the only words Joseph Henry managed were a quiet

'Mornin', Minnie," or a soft *"Cold mornin',"* followed by three miles of silence.

They didn't quite walk together. Joseph Henry kept half a pace ahead or half a pace behind, always in a quiet quandary over whether it was ruder to lead or to follow the girl. Minnie kept her eyes on the road, though occasionally she'd peek up at Joseph Henry when he was in front or passing her. Joseph Henry would sometimes glance sideways, trying to guess whether she was bored or cold or just waiting for it all to be over. He'd always get an awkward feeling when their glances met. Mostly, though, he walked, and she walked.

Then one day, the class was tasked with bringing something to school that represented what their fathers did, or what their families enjoyed. Minnie brought a chair leg her father had crafted. Joseph Henry brought a glass flask of whiskey.

Minnie clutched the chair leg tightly as she walked. It wasn't heavy, but it was awkward alongside her slate board and lunch pail. She held the leg out in front of her with both hands, trying to keep it balanced.

Joseph Henry was slightly ahead of her that morning. He carried his slate board under one arm, his lunch pail in his left hand, and the whiskey flask gripped tightly in his right.

Minnie had her slate tucked under her left arm, the lunch pail under her right, and the chair leg resting lengthwise across both forearms. When her boot caught a rock, she stumbled, and everything went down.

She dropped to her knees, scrambling to check the slate first. It hadn't cracked. The pail had rolled into a ditch, and the chair leg lay at an odd angle in the dirt.

Joseph Henry turned at the sound and rushed back to help. He handed her the slate and the pail, then picked up the chair leg and gave it a quick, concerned look.

"I'll carry this," he said. "You take the flask." He hesitated, then handed it to her. "Careful, though."

She nodded and took the bottle, cradling it like something far more delicate than it was.

As they resumed walking, she looked over at it, brow furrowed.

"What is it?" she asked.

Joseph Henry lit up. Even at that age, he already knew quite a bit about whiskey-making, lessons given to him by his father.

He spent the next three miles talking without pause: how he made the mash, how he boiled the wort, what mash was, what wort was, how you brewed beer, what a still looked like. He went on and on.

And Minnie listened the whole way, eyes bright, her head slightly tilted, hanging on every word.

From then on, their walks were filled with conversation.

They talked about the weather first. Then the harvest. Minnie's sick dog. Even Harland Letcher, an older boy who had taken a shine to Minnie and clearly didn't care for Joseph Henry, likely on account of that friendship.

Later, they'd fill the miles with stories they made up for each other.

Minnie's stories were short and simple. Joseph Henry listened to every word, nodding along, sometimes asking questions just to keep her talking.

Joseph Henry's stories were long and winding. He'd spin them out as they walked, piling on details, inventing facts as he went. Some tales stretched across the full three miles to school and picked up again on the walk home.

Minnie delighted in them. She'd tell Joseph Henry how she retold his stories to her family in the evenings, just before they turned the lights down. Those retellings became new stories, ones shaped by her family's reactions and whatever happened to them that day. What went wrong in the lathe shop. How the wind blew the laundry straight off the line. How a fight between two of Minnie's brothers ended with the older getting a black eye from a surprise wallop by the younger.

Joseph Henry listened to it all. He laughed or showed concern, whatever seemed right. Anything to keep Minnie talking.

One morning, Minnie was unusually quiet when Joseph Henry arrived. She didn't greet him, didn't look up. Her slate was clutched tighter than usual, and her steps dragged.

Not long into the walk, she began to cry.

Joseph Henry prodded gently, recognizing something was wrong. He kept at it for a while. Just when he was about to give up, Minnie finally spoke.

Her dog had been badly mauled trying to chase off a pair of coyotes that had come too close to the barn. He wasn't expected to survive.

Joseph Henry had never so much as touched Minnie before. He hesitated, unsure what was allowed. Then he pulled her close, wrapped his arms around her, and kissed the top of her head.

He held her hand the rest of the way.

The next morning, they didn't go to the schoolhouse. Instead, Joseph Henry helped Minnie's brothers dig a large hole and bury the dog.

The brothers were impassive, their shovels moving silently. None of them cried. They just stayed stoic and kept digging. They were men. Minnie tried to be the same. She didn't cry either. She stood with her arms crossed, her face drawn tight.

Joseph Henry stayed. He helped Minnie make a cross and mark the grave. They spent the rest of the day beside it, and Joseph Henry listened as Minnie told stories about the dog. She told him how the dog once chased a rooster into the well and barked until someone pulled it out. How he'd slept at the foot of her bed when she had the fever. How he always growled at her uncle, even when the man wasn't doing anything wrong.

From then on, they held hands every day as they walked. It never felt strange. It felt like the most natural thing in the world, like something they'd always done.

Chapter 6
1878

The walk to the schoolhouse was a mandatory thing. School didn't care whether it was hot or cold, sunny or a drenching rain. Three miles each way was just a fact. It was the constant. Always the same road. Past the split-rail fence, the burned-out barn, and the hollow where the land dipped toward a small pond where the river birches' peeling bark cast a cinnamon hue across a clearing.

What changed was their routine upon arrival. By the time they reached the schoolhouse steps, they were flushed from the effort. On cold mornings their faces would be wind-bitten. Their shoes carried anything from a coating of dust to a thick layer of mud.

Before entering the one-room schoolhouse, Joseph Henry and Minnie would bang the mud or dust from their boots on the stoop, often laughing when it made more of a mess on the other than was on the boots. Inside, they'd hang their coats and satchels on a few crooked pegs. What gathered on the floor beneath was a testament to the kind of weather the children had braved. On the cold or wet mornings, there wasn't much effort spent trying to dry off. Just a hope that the stove was already going.

Most school days were the same. Not exactly verbatim, but predictable. It would begin with morning chores that each child was designated, such as bringing in firewood, starting the stove, or fetching water.

After settling in, the teacher would lead a reading, often a psalm or proverb, sometimes a patriotic verse. Occasionally a song. The morning lessons then would begin. The older children were called first, standing stiffly near the front to recite grammar rules or copy passages from the McGuffey Reader onto the slate board. The younger ones remained at their desks, working quietly. Some practicing arithmetic, others copying spelling words on their small slates. Then the groups would switch.

Sometimes the waiting group got restless, and things didn't always stay quiet. A loud whisper, a passed note, a dropped slate or pencil, or a sudden fit of giggles might break the calm. The teacher would pause and fix the room with a stern look, letting the silence do the rest. If that didn't solve the problem, sharp words might follow. Failing that, a ruler might rap on a desk, or more severely, across someone's knuckles. Most learned quickly, less from the punishment and more from the embarrassment.

At midday, the class filed outside to eat, unless rain or cold kept them indoors. Most children brought a packed lunch… biscuits wrapped in cloth, sometimes cold ham or leftover fried chicken, occasionally a slice of pie. A few children would arrive at school without, either due to a lack of means or a forgotten lunch pail. Some families had gotten into the habit of sending extras when they could, to be quietly shared.

The boys would kick at a hoop or chase each other with sticks, either playing tag or mocking swordplay. The girls played clapping games, singing little rhymes they'd known for years, while their hands smacked in rhythm. Joseph Henry and Minnie rarely joined in. They would sit at the edge of the yard, just near the fence line, talking or telling stories, sometimes with others, sometimes alone.

The afternoon wore on with geography, spelling, or history. A period for recitation was common, where children of any age would stand and read, sometimes from a book, other times a memorized poem or lesson. When the teacher rang the final bell, the children set about their end-of-day chores: sweeping the floor, wiping down the chalkboard, emptying the ashes from the stove. Then they packed their satchels and stepped out into whatever weather waited for the long walk home.

Joseph Henry and Minnie were a fixture among the other children. They didn't command attention, but they didn't fade into the background either. They were well liked and took part in both lessons and leisure time.

To the others, the affection between the two was plain to see, but it didn't matter. At first there were a few jokes. "Bet he'd churn butter with her if he could." "When's the wedding, Minnie? Should we bring pie or cobbler?" But their calm demeanor made them hard to bait. For the most part, the other children let it lie.

Not everyone was content to leave it alone. There was Harland Letcher. Harland took particular issue with the affection between the two. He was two years older and nearly a foot taller than Joseph Henry, and he had never liked him, though few could say why. Maybe it was just Joseph Henry's nature. He was so openly amiable, so ready to help without being asked. Some people can't stand polite. Or kind. Or generous. Harland was one of them. He couldn't be any of those things, and it tormented him to see it in someone else. He didn't know why. He only knew that unless he was harassing or tormenting someone, he didn't feel much of anything at all.

Harland was the kind of boy who never felt comfortable, not even in his own skin. And it only got worse when people were kind to one another. Worse still when they tried to be kind to him. He didn't know what to do with the feelings that stirred up. It made him feel raw and restless, like something under his skin was itching and he didn't know how to scratch it. Joseph Henry was like a giant patch of poison ivy on Harland's soul.

What Harland really couldn't shake was that he had a soft spot for Minnie. He never said it aloud, but it showed in how he hovered near her when no one else was looking. Around her, the usual harshness in his face softened, though he could never find the words to match it. Seeing her with Joseph Henry turned something in him sour. He watched them from a distance with a look caught somewhere between longing and hatred. It didn't seem right to him. He convinced himself Joseph Henry didn't deserve her. And in quiet moments, a darker corner of Harland's mind began to imagine ways to undo what had bloomed between them.

Harland was caught in a conflict he couldn't untangle. His nature pushed him to bully Joseph Henry, just as he did with others, but his feelings for Minnie complicated things. He hated Joseph Henry. That much wasn't the problem. But laying hands on him, or even mocking him, would displease Minnie, and that thought made Harland hesitate. His mind went in circles over what to do. He could leave them both alone, which was unnatural to him. Sometimes he turned his cruelty on Minnie, though never with more than cutting remarks. Most often, he gave in to his instincts and went after Joseph Henry anyway, with words, or blows, or both. That was what brought him the most satisfaction.

Another factor was that Joseph Henry was well liked by the other children. Harland Letcher was the outcast. Strength in numbers often led the others to come to Joseph Henry's defense. When Harland acted up, they pushed back as a group, sometimes even turning their own form of bullying on him, though never physically. They'd call him "Haystack," mocking the way his unkempt hair stuck out in every direction, or "Ox-boy," pointing out his lumbering size. They'd even mimic his classroom mistakes in exaggerated voices during the midday break. It didn't carry the same sting Harland was used to dishing out, but it left him red-faced and seething all the same.

Harland had a reputation for not being the sharpest knife in the drawer. The other children, behind his back, would say he was *slow as molasses in January* or that he had *a head full of feathers*. Even his own father had once said he *couldn't pour piss out of a boot with instructions on the heel*, while venting to the boys at the tavern. In fact Harland was not unintelligent at all. He struggled with speaking up in class, but when left to work on his own, he could be surprisingly sharp. The schoolhouse environment didn't play to his strengths, though, so most of the other children, and even the teacher, only saw the thinnest side of him.

Harland didn't care for the quiet, passive kind of persecution he came to face in the schoolyard. He was smart enough to know that he needed a better strategy to quell whatever it was that made him feel wrong inside. So he began targeting others when they were alone or in smaller groups, usually on the road to or from the schoolhouse. He'd come upon one child or another, and brutalize them, then threaten even worse if they told anyone. Cuts or bruises could always be blamed on a fall, and few adults thought to question a child who seemed hesitant to explain.

During the school day, he even became cordial, friendly, even to Joseph Henry. It was agony inside, but he took comfort in the thought of what might await him on the walk home.

It was a Thursday. That time of year, the school week ran only four days in their part of Kentucky, since it was planting season. Joseph Henry and Minnie had just left the schoolhouse, glad they wouldn't be returning again until Monday. Minnie didn't love planting, but she liked the break from the recitations and arithmetic. Joseph Henry usually spent those Fridays helping out in the lathe shop, which he didn't mind.

They walked the familiar road with their satchels slung over one shoulder, the late afternoon sun slanting between the trees. They played a simple game of tag as they made their way down the road. One trying to keep away from the other, leaving the dirt road and darting between trees.

Minnie was "it," and Joseph Henry didn't make it easy. He darted off the road and into the trees, weaving between trunks and hopping over roots, letting her get close before slipping away again with a laugh.

"You're dragging it out!" she called, both exasperated and amused.

Looping around a tree and ducking low, he burst out onto the road again, tapped her on the shoulder and darted back again as she swiped out at him. "You're just slow!" he laughed playfully.

That earned a sharper chase. Minnie charged after him with renewed energy, her skirt gathered up in her hands to keep from tripping, feet pounding hard against the packed dirt.

For only a moment, Joseph Henry caught a flash of her stockinged legs, more than he'd ever seen before. He looked away quick, face going warm. Something about it made his chest flutter, like he'd swallowed too much air. He pushed it down and leapt away again. Minnie gave a frustrated sigh and pouted. Sensing her frustration, he let out a dramatic gasp and stumbled, feigning a misstep. He flailed a little, then stood just long enough for Minnie to catch up.

"You did that on purpose!" she shouted, both hands slapping the middle of his chest.

He paused just a moment, then he scooped her into a hug before Minnie could think to stop him, lifting her clean off the ground.

Minnie squealed and twisted, laughing, then shoved at his chest until he let her go. Her smile lingered.

She tagged him hard in the middle of his chest. "You're it!" she said, breathless and pink-cheeked, already stepping back.

She turned on her heel and took off, but stopped short with a sharp inhale.

Harland Letcher was standing just off the road, shadowed beneath a tree. He was leaning back, arms folded tight across his chest, with a bemused sneer on his face. Watching.

He didn't move from his spot. He just shifted his weight and grinned, eyes flicking between the two of them.

"Minnie," he drawled, "you gonna give me a turn with you when you're done with this one?"

The words hung in the air too long. Minnie's brow furrowed, her mouth parting as if she wasn't sure she'd heard it right. Then the meaning settled, and her face flushed with embarrassment and alarm.

Joseph Henry stiffened. His jaw set and his hands curled, but he didn't step forward. He just stood there quiet and unreadable.

Minnie turned slightly toward him. She could feel a conflict inside him. She knew him. Knew how deep his restraint ran. "Turn the other cheek" didn't begin to cover it. Joseph Henry had always been the kind to bear it, to swallow it, no matter the weight. But Minnie always sensed that there was something else. Something harsh that might come forth if pushed.

And something she never wanted him to use, for fear he'd lose some part of himself afterwards.

Harland saw that Joseph Henry wasn't going to act. Whether it was restraint or fear, he couldn't tell, and he didn't care. It gave him confidence.

He left the tree and began walking toward them, slow and deliberate.

Joseph Henry stepped forward, unsteady, placing himself between Harland and Minnie.

Harland stopped for a beat. His eyes flicked to Minnie, then back to Joseph Henry. He smiled. It was filled with a giddy malice.

"Well now," he said. "Ain't that sweet. Mr. Protector. That's real nice. Real nice."

He stepped closer, nearly chest to chest with Joseph Henry. His extra two inches seemed more like a foot. "You think standing there makes you a man? You think she likes that? That she's gonna run off and be yours 'cause you play brave for her?"

Joseph Henry didn't answer. His face didn't shift. He just stood still, eyes locked on Harland.

Harland's smirk twitched. He pulled back one hand suddenly, feigning a punch to Joseph Henry's face.

Joseph Henry didn't flinch.

That did something. Harland's face twitched again, the grin falling flat for a breath before it returned… this time forced.

"Look at that. Stone man," Harland said, but his voice had lost something.

Then, with a sudden burst, he shoved Joseph Henry hard in the chest.

Joseph seemed surprised by this, like he didn't actually expect Harland to act. He stumbled backward, off balance. He felt Minnie behind him and reached out to stop himself, but too late. His back hit her, and she gave a small cry as she toppled over behind him.

He twisted unnaturally, trying to catch her, but his hand never caught her. She went down fast. There was an awkward thud, a sharp gasp, then silence.

Joseph turned fully and saw her on the ground. Her eyes were closed. Blood was running from the side of her head, a thin stream trickling into the dirt.

Harland's breath caught. His strut evaporated in an instant.

"I…" he said, stepping back.

Joseph Henry stared. His chest rose and fell. Everything inside him went quiet.

"Minnie?" he said.

She didn't answer.

Minnie's mother was hanging the laundry on the line when she saw Joseph Henry in the distance. Something was off. It took her a moment to realize he was carrying someone. Her heart caught… it was Minnie.

She gave a yell, and one of Minnie's brothers came out. He froze a moment, then ran to Joseph Henry and took Minnie from his arms. Without a word, he carried her into the house, their mother rushing behind.

A few minutes later, the brother came back out wondering why Joseph Henry hadn't followed.

He was still standing where he'd handed Minnie over. Unmoving. Arms by his sides. Hands open.

Minnie's brother guided Joseph Henry into the house. Their mother gave a loud gasp. At first, it wasn't clear if it was from the sight of her daughter or the state of Joseph Henry. He looked haggard and was streaked with blood. She was already kneeling beside Minnie with a wet cloth, tending to her quickly. Her eyes flicked between the two.

"Joseph, what happened? Was it an animal? What happened to Minnie…" She managed to curb her hysteria just enough to register his condition as well. "…and you?"

Joseph Henry didn't answer.

After a moment, Minnie's mother gave him a longer look. He seemed to be in a trance. She motioned to her son to bring over a chair, then asked him to fetch another cloth and tend to Joseph Henry while she returned to Minnie.

Eventually, Joseph Henry stirred. He blinked a few times, his eyes slowly coming into focus, like he was stepping in from a dark room. Seeing Minnie's mother bent over her daughter, Joseph Henry began to rise. Minnie's brother firmly pressed him back into the chair. Joseph

Henry didn't resist. He dropped his face into his hands and broke down.

Minnie's brother had been sent to find the doctor. Minnie seemed to be stable, but she had not yet come to. She'd been moved to her bed, and her mother had pressed a folded cloth to the wound on her head, firm and steady, swapping it out when it grew too wet and stained. She acted with urgency, but not panic. She had done this before. She packed the wound with spiderweb and honey, a remedy passed down from her grandmother, to help stem the bleeding until the doctor could arrive.

When she was satisfied she'd done what she could, she draped a quilt over Minnie's legs and tucked it in to keep her warm. Only then did she turn to Joseph Henry.

Minnie's mother pulled up a stool and squatted in front of where Joseph Henry sat. He gushed out the entire story, from the moment they left the schoolhouse to Minnie's fall, leaving out no detail. Throughout, their eyes stayed fixed on each other. When she prodded for more, he gave it.

She saw something in his eyes, like he didn't want to continue. Joseph Henry looked away, averting her gaze.

"Joseph…" she urged, "…and then?"

Joseph Henry paused, then stammered, "I don't remember anything else before arriving at the house." He rubbed his hands together without thinking.

Minnie's mother's expression shifted, something between concern and doubt. Throughout the conversation, Joseph Henry had looked her in the eyes. Now he looked down.

"And Harland?" she asked.

Joseph Henry's eyes turned toward the door.

"He… I think he ran into the woods after he realized what happened."

"You think?"

Joseph Henry didn't speak for a moment, which seemed to stretch long. "Yes, ma'am."

Minnie's mother looked at him for a long time. His eyes met hers again, then turned away.

Something had happened after the injury. Joseph Henry couldn't remember what… perhaps. She seemed to come to a decision.

"You've always been gentle," she said softly. "That's what folks say about you."

She didn't add the rest, just paused, then, "Thank you, Joseph. Thank you for taking care of Minnie."

Joseph Henry didn't seem to entirely hear her, but answered with a quiet, "Yes, ma'am."

Minnie woke late that evening, before the doctor arrived. When he did examine her, he had little to contribute to her recovery. It was several days past the weekend before the two returned to school. News of the events had spread quickly, but few talked about it.

Harland had not returned. In fact, he was missing. No one had seen him since he left the schoolhouse on that Thursday, except for Minnie and Joseph Henry. No one knew what had become of him. Though Joseph Henry and Minnie were both questioned, no one doubted their story. Joseph Henry said he remembered nothing after the injury, and Minnie had nothing more to offer. Minnie's mother confirmed what Joseph Henry had told her, and that was all.

Harland's disappearance became part of local folklore. A story emerged about "The Wild Man of the Woods", who protects children from bullies, pouncing on them and dragging them into the woods, never to be seen again.

Chapter 7
1878

Not long after the incident, Minnie and her family moved away. Her uncles made furniture near Scottsville, and her father, already skilled with a lathe, fell easily into their business. It was never said outright that the move had anything to do with what happened, and folks didn't speak Harland Letcher's name in connection with Minnie or Joseph Henry. But things were quieter around both families after that. Some neighbors kept a little more distance. Strangely, it seemed to fall more on Minnie's family than Joseph Henry's, though no one ever said why.

Harland Letcher's family, distraught and inconsolable, had tried to press the authorities to take action against Joseph Henry. But there was no proof of anything, and both Joseph Henry and Minnie were known as good, well-mannered children. The matter never went anywhere. Not long after, the Letcher house was found empty. Word around town was that they'd picked up and moved to Tennessee. No one knew for sure.

Joseph Henry was crushed by the news of Minnie's sudden move. He'd barely had time to speak with her.

Samuel Henry explained that Minnie's father had made arrangements to relocate some time ago. He'd given more than adequate notice. But in hindsight, it had always felt like just a possibility. The recent situation may have sealed the decision.

Minnie's father had thanked Samuel for the years of steady employment, and Samuel told him he'd be welcome back anytime.

Joseph Henry and Minnie walked slowly through the woods behind her family's house. Their hands swung lightly between them, fingers intertwined. They had walked the trail many times, but it felt suddenly unfamiliar.

There wasn't much talking. A few quiet, unimportant observations passed between them. The ground was soft from last night's rain. Minnie's hem was damp. A squirrel cut across their path and scurried up a tree.

"You remember when we found that turtle with the cracked shell?" Minnie asked. Her voice was quiet.

Joseph Henry nodded, knowing the words were only a distraction. "You kept it in a shoebox for weeks. Thought you could heal it with twine and paste."

"I still think we helped it…" she said with a frown.

"It floated downstream when you put it back in."

"I think it swam."

"No… I think it floated," he said with a slight laugh.

They passed the old cedar where they used to leave notes in a rusted tin for each other, back before Joseph Henry was a fixture at her house. The tin was still there. Minnie glanced toward it but didn't stop.

The trail opened onto the brook. They often ended up here during their walks down the same trail. Water moved steadily, splashing over stones. Joseph Henry sat first, as if something in him had gone slack. He brushed the dirt from a flat rock beside him, making room for Minnie.

She joined him, pulling her knees in close.

They sat like that for a long time.

The brook burbled and hummed, low and even.

Minnie picked up a small stone and tossed it into the water. She nudged another toward Joseph Henry with the toe of her shoe.

He looked at it, then at her. He picked it up and sent it skipping once before it plunked under.

They tossed a few more like that, back and forth. Between throws, they held hands, listening.

Joseph Henry knew it was only a distraction. He played along, but his heart wasn't in it. Minnie realized it too. After a while, she stopped and took his hand again, though she kept moving stones with her feet.

The rhythm of the current had a sad kind of song to it, like it knew what was coming.

Neither of them spoke now. It felt like something was coming to a close. Nothing seemed worth saying.

Minnie glanced over at Joseph Henry's still boyish face. He was watching the water, lost in the sound.

When she finally spoke, it startled him, like he'd expected silence right up until the moment they said goodbye.

"I'm sure this isn't the end," she said softly. "I can feel in my soul that we'll find each other again."

Joseph Henry turned toward her, thoughtful but uncertain. He didn't hide his doubt. Ninety miles felt impossibly far.

Minnie leaned forward and kissed him on the forehead. Her hand came beneath his chin, lifting his face. His eyes met hers.

Then Joseph Henry was surprised, pleasantly. She kissed him on the lips. A kiss usually reserved for the betrothed, or the married. The words weren't spoken, but Joseph Henry felt something pass between them. A promise.

A tear slipped down Joseph Henry's cheek. A smile followed, awkward and elated, still with a touch of sorrow.

Minnie caught the tear with two fingers. She rose slowly and kissed his forehead once more.

She turned to walk back toward the house, but Joseph Henry threw his arms around her in a sudden bear hug, more childlike than the acts just shared.

They walked hand in hand to the door, where Minnie gave Joseph Henry one last kiss before stepping inside and closing the door behind her.

He stood there for several minutes, staring at the door, then turned and walked home.

Chapter 8
1929

Downtime was something Joseph Henry didn't like. He preferred a full day of tasks. Wake with the bell. Get himself going. Get Old Crow going. Stand in line for morning headcount. Work through the day, whether inside or out. Chores. Cleanup. Maybe read. Maybe write. Evening roll call. Inspection. Lights out. Sleep.

Structure made the hours pass. Predictable. Smooth. Even on tumultuous days. It was the space between things, the unfilled minutes, where things could become unsettled.

Recreation Time, sometimes called Yard Time, wasn't a regular occurrence. It often took place in the late morning or early afternoon, when Joseph Henry was usually off grounds. Only occasionally did the schedule line up with one of his on-site days, usually on a Tuesday.

He'd heard that in other prison systems, like Auburn or Pennsylvania, the rules were harsher. Talking wasn't even allowed. Men walked in silence, eyes down, one behind the other, as if serving penance with every step.

But at the Frankfort Penitentiary, it was looser. Boss Van ran a tight ship, but his philosophy was different. Give the inmates a little space to breathe, and they were less likely to blow. Let them talk. Let them tell stories. Let them stretch their legs and remember they were still men.

It wasn't generous, exactly. It was more strategic. Joseph Henry saw the wisdom in it, sometimes participated and even enjoyed it. Though he still much preferred keeping his busy routine.

The yard wasn't much. A patchwork of dirt and worn grass, with concrete benches, slightly listed to one side. There was some new construction. Boss Van was adding some wooden tables to play some cards or checkers, and an exercise area with a pull-up bar and maybe a sit-up board.

The sun had cracked through the clouds, and the inmates mostly sat and tried to capture some of its warmth.

Joseph Henry would usually just lean against the wall. Routine. Same spot. Same lean.

Often, a few inmates like Nils, Duane, or Old Crow would pick a spot nearby. They'd swap stories, throw out jokes at another's expense. Joseph Henry would sometimes offer a laugh or a quiet, "Is that so…"

Rarely, he'd toss in a story or a barb of his own.

Something had shifted today.

He was still holding up the same wall, in the same place, with the same lean. But he stood there alone.

Ordinarily, he would've been just fine with that. Left to his thoughts, planning the next day, or several. But something itched at him in a way it usually wouldn't.

The group that would've been nearby Joseph Henry today was instead gathered at the benches. They formed a loose cluster, laughter coming in small bursts. At the center was Ugly Attics, talking fast, arms carving the air, emphasizing some story. The half-dozen around him hanging on his words.

It had been several weeks since Joseph Henry's encounter with Ugly in the stockroom. The two had barely come within 25 feet of each other since.

Joseph Henry had seen him from a distance, loud, animated, always with someone near for him to entertain. Ugly talked a lot.

Moved fast. But nothing had come of it. No stunts. No incidents. Just noise.

Joseph Henry tried to take a new measure of the man who'd once rattled him. Loud. Conniving. Probably not entirely harmless, but probably not entirely dangerous either.

Just another yard dog with an annoying bark and very little bite.

Joseph Henry was torn from his thoughts, surprised to find himself suddenly among the group. He hadn't meant to join, not really. Duane had caught his eye and waved him over with a half-smile, and Joseph Henry walked over, hands in his pockets, like a man in a trance.

Ugly was in mid-story, impersonating one of the guards with cruel precision and voice pitched high. The crowd cackled. Joseph Henry offered a faint smile and let out a laugh himself.

Ugly suddenly stopped and looked straight at Joseph Henry. Joseph Henry went cold. He could feel the hairs at the back of his neck rise. He couldn't tell which was the stunted side of Ugly's face.

The crowd had stopped their laughing, watching confused as something shifted between the two men.

Ugly slowly began a new story. He leaned forward a little. His voice didn't rise, but the sound around him faded as he began…

"Two men… they been traveling together for about a week. Through forest, over a narrow pass, across a riverbed. Same age, same shape. Not young, not old. Men with rough hands, hard shoulders."

No one said anything, but the air around the benches shifted.

"They kept off the main roads, moving early before sunrise and again near dusk. Days were hot. Nights colder than expected.

They didn't talk much. Not 'cause they didn't like each other… just didn't see a point. They were together outta necessity. Both needed to get north. Nobody asked questions. Nobody offered details."

Old Crow glanced at Joseph Henry. Just a flick of the eyes. Like he recognized this story wasn't meant for the group.

"They fell into a kind of rhythm. One starts the fire. The other cooks. One kept the compass. The other checks the map. Each night, they'd find the same kind of place to settle down… low ground, a stump or a rock. They'd bed down without a word… boots on, hats pulled low."

Duane smirked like he wanted to say something but didn't.

"After a while there was something like trust between them, not friendship, but a tolerance made smooth through repetition. The kind of closeness that comes not from talk, but from traveling the same miles."

He let that hang just long enough to mean something.

"Fifth or sixth morning, they find tracks. Big. Pushed into the soft trail. Four toes. Looked like claws.
'Bear,' one of them said.
The other don't answer. He only crouches to study the print, then looks up toward the hills.
That afternoon, they hear it. Sound of breath behind them… wet, dragging, deliberate. They both stop. No branches snap. No growl. Just a sense that something big and tireless was in the woods with them.

They don't run, not yet. They walk faster. Stay alert. Every so often, one of them glances back. Nothing there."

Someone exhaled... sharp... then quieted again.

"But by nightfall," Ugly said, quieter, "they knew it was closer.

They didn't eat. Didn't speak. They tied their food high in a tree and made no fire. Slept in turns, but only lightly.

In the morning, they were quiet again. The wind had shifted. They were sure the bear was tracking them now... not just wandering nearby. Always just out of sight, but close. They could feel it out there. Big. Slow. Watching."

Ugly paused and ran his tongue along his teeth before going on.

"They broke camp without a word and began climbing a steep rise that overlooked a gully to the west. The earth was soft near the top, and one of them slipped. The other caught his arm and steadied him without a word.

They moved on.

Midday, they reached the high ground. Below them stretched a long run of dense brush. Thick... might slow them, but open enough to maybe run through.

Then they heard it. Behind them. Close. Something big crashing through the undergrowth.

They didn't wait."

Nils, quiet at the back, swallowed hard.

"They ran.

First, they ran together… stride for stride, breath for breath, packs bouncing against their backs. Trees blurred past. Rocks shifted underfoot. A low roar rolled through the brush not far behind, and birds took to the sky."

Ugly's voice slowed.

"One man began to fall behind. Limping… slightly. Maybe from the slip that morning. Maybe from something older. He didn't call out. Didn't ask for help.

The other man looked back and sighed. A look of futility on his face… or maybe disappointment."

Ugly gave a small nod, just to himself.

"He slowed. Knelt behind a cluster of stones, and began retying his boots.

The limping man caught up, breath ragged, sweat clinging to his face. 'What are you doing?!' he gasped.

The man didn't look up. 'Tightening my laces.'

'What?' the other wheezed. 'We have to keep moving. It's too close.'

Now the man looked up. Calm. Composed. No urgency in his voice. An impassive look on his face."

Ugly leaned back slightly, still speaking low.

"'I know.'

'Then let's go!'

A pause.

'I don't need to outrun the bear,' the man said, standing slow. He turned his back. 'I only need to outrun you.'"

A few in the circle looked at each other, uneasy.

"It didn't register at first.

The words hung in the air a beat too long. The limping man stared at him. 'You're serious…'

The other gave a small shrug.

The limping man's mouth opened. Closed.

The other man ran.

Not a sprint. Not panicked. Just steady. Long-legged. Practiced. Like he'd been waiting for this. A plan…"

Ugly looked at Joseph Henry.

"The limping man stood there. Stunned. He heard the crashing behind him. The grunt. The weight of something massive closing the last stretch of ground. He just stood there. Tired.

He knew already he couldn't make it.

He looked once more toward the trees where the other man had vanished.

Then… the growl."

That last word hung in the air… then there was nothing.

No movement. No murmuring. The group sat frozen in silence, still held by Ugly's parable.

Then the bell rang.

Sharp. Sudden. It split the moment wide open.

Several flinched.

Duane leaped up with a "Goddamn!"

Boots scraped against dirt as the cluster around the benches began to break apart, scattered back to their routines.

Joseph Henry didn't move right away.

The echo of the bell faded. His thoughts were elsewhere. He knew Ugly was telling the story to him, but he wasn't sure if he was the one running or the one limping.

By the time he looked up, the crowd was gone. Ugly remained.

Joseph Henry gave Ugly a slight nod and turned to head in.

"Mister Henry," Ugly called.

Joseph Henry stopped but didn't turn.

Ugly walked up and in front of him. Slowly, the sly grin crept back on the right side of his face.

"Hell of a thing, that," Ugly said. "You standing there laughing with us. Looked almost natural."

Joseph met his eyes. "Almost…"

Ugly's tone was light, but carried an edge. The grin vanished.

"Just… it's like not real. Like a smiling snake. Looks wrong, you know? Like you're holding something back all the time."

"What are you trying to say?" Joseph Henry didn't like this conversation, but suddenly had no fear of Ugly Attics.

"You think you're noble," Ugly said. "But you're not noble. More like arrogant. You walk around like you're above all this. Like you're something better because you do your little jobs and come and go."

Joseph Henry didn't respond.

Ugly stepped closer.

"I could break you down," he whispered.

Joseph Henry suddenly felt afire, "Okay, let's…"

"Not with fists… I don't want to fight. I don't need to fight. With talk. With laughter. With the right words. You think those boys are yours, but they're just waiting for something more interesting. You ever feel irrelevant, amigo?"

The words hit like cold water. The fire had gone. Joseph Henry stiffened.

Ugly smiled, but it was flat. A dead thing.

"You're too comfortable, Mister Henry. You know that's dangerous. Comfort is for free men. You're not a free man. It's just another story."

Joseph Henry's voice was quiet. Without fear. Without anger.

"You don't know me. And truth to tell, you don't want to know me. But you do what you've gotta do."

Ugly tilted his head.

"Maybe I don't know you amigo," he said. "But I know your type. You're the kind of man who thinks quiet is safe. It's not. It's nothing."

He stepped back then. The moment passed. Ugly's grin returned as if nothing had happened. He nodded toward the building.

"See you later, Mister Henry. I've got plans."

Joseph didn't move until Ugly had walked away.

The new measure of Ugly was in.

Chapter 9
1902-1919

Ugly never saw himself as a bad man.

His mother always told him to do whatever it took to be happy, so long as it didn't stop anyone else from doing the same.

His memories of her were hazy but warm. Bright eyes. A tired smile. The sound of her voice when the day was over. She worked constantly. She had to, for him. For her little José.

He was very young, but already knew what it meant to be alone. Most mornings he woke to an empty room, though sometimes his father was still on the couch, passed out beside a bottle of cerveza or tequila.

The days were long and quiet. Even at five years old, he was used to fending for himself. He spent much of the day wandering through the village, watching people work or other children play. If he was lucky, he'd find something to eat.

Bedtime was different. It was the only time of day he'd look forward to. When the sun went down, he'd climb into bed and wait. Sometimes he fell asleep, but even then, the smallest sound would wake him. Often, he just lay still, listening for the door.

When it opened, when she finally came home, he could feel her before he even heard her voice.

She would sit beside him in the dark. Her hand might brush his hair from his forehead. She would whisper to him, or tell him a story. Nothing long. Nothing loud. Just her voice in the quiet, and the soft sound of her settling beside him. He was safe then. And then he would sleep.

He never knew what happened to her.

Ugly had no memories beyond those nights. One day, she was simply gone. His father never spoke of her. Any question about her ended in silence. Whenever the subject came up, Uncle Borissimo would only laugh, like a joke he knew Ugly wasn't in on.

That laugh confused José. It didn't sound amused. It didn't sound bitter. It was a flat, empty sound. Like he was filling space.

The absence of his mother didn't upset Ugly. She just wasn't there anymore. Just as she hadn't been there during the day, now she wasn't there at night either. He asked questions, but her place in his life began to feel more like a story he'd read long ago.

Later, as he stumbled his way through life, Ugly began to wonder if happiness was really as simple as his mother had made it sound. Maybe it wasn't just about doing what it took. Maybe it came at a cost, and someone always had to pay it. Maybe some people had to give up their happiness so others could have any at all. Ugly began to wonder why it so often seemed to be him going without.

He didn't know if that was fair, or if it was just the way things worked. But when he thought of his mother, and what she seemed to give up, it started to make sense.

And maybe that was what Uncle Borissimo's laugh had always meant.

Occasionally, Ugly would press him. Not like a detective on an investigation, he was just trying to find some missing pages in the old book.

"Oh, you don't really want to know," Uncle Borissimo would say with that same dry, mechanical chuckle. "Believe me. You should not ask."

Uncle Borissimo was a bad man. Ugly knew this.

He lived with Ugly and Ugly's father now. They didn't raise him. To say they did would be an insult to bad parents. Ugly never knew where food or money came from, but he was sure neither man was a shopkeeper, a carpenter, a hauler, or a miner.

They didn't sit down for dinner.

They didn't feed him.

They didn't clothe him.

They didn't give him money for clothes.

Ugly took what food he could, but not too much. If they noticed anything missing, the beatings were real.

When his father and uncle drank themselves to sleep, Ugly would take pesos from around the house. On bolder nights, when he was hungry or desperate, he would fish a copper or silver straight from their pockets.

He did what he had to do to be happy, like his mother said. And it wasn't like his father or uncle were using their happiness much anyway.

Over time, the house offered less. Loose pesos weren't always there, or simply weren't enough. And food didn't appear just because Ugly was hungry. The more he searched—under cushions, behind cabinets, beneath the mattress—the more he came up empty. Ugly began to understand that whatever he could scrape together was not enough.

He was clever, though, and he knew that the world wasn't confined to the house or to his father and uncle. So, he stopped relying on what was left behind and started thinking about what he could get outside. There were many other people and things just beyond the front door.

He saw people wearing shoes that fit and jackets without holes. There was no reason why they should have these while his shoes hurt his feet and his jacket was worn and barely wearable. He began watching closely, noticing how people moved through markets, how pockets sat loose, how a small purse might swing unattended. He learned what was easy to grab and what was worth the risk.

He always remembered what his mother taught him. "Always do what it took to be happy." He knew the other part, but he often pretended it wasn't there. He knew which part was important. His mother certainly wouldn't have wanted him to starve, or even to go without.

Ugly became adept at getting what he needed. He got better and better at lifting items from people in crowds, and he even figured out how to get around locks and enter residences for a bigger score. To Ugly, it became his job. Other people waited tables in shops or restaurants, tended market stalls, hauled freight, fixed shoes, or baked bread. He was earning a living just like everyone else.

To him, Ugly was the only real thing in his world. Everyone else was simply there to keep him fed or clothed. As time went by, like anyone else, Ugly began to think, why should I only be able to keep myself fed and clothed? The shopkeeper wanted more than a meager living. The carpenter wanted to build himself a bigger house. Why not Ugly?

In time, Ugly had enough. He could feed himself, clothe himself, even find a dry place to sleep. He no longer needed anything from his father and uncle, and he stopped going back. Whatever they were to him once, they weren't anymore.

He didn't know if they wondered where he was, or why he no longer showed up. He didn't care. He had figured out how to live.

For a while, he felt something like contentment. In truth, it was only the absence of need, but compared to what had come before, it was a life. And for a time, it was enough.

But it didn't last. Ugly began to think he should have more. He worked hard. He took risks. But other people had better coats, better food, better beds, better lives. Ugly saw no reason why they should have more than him.

So he began to think bigger.

Ugly met Edwardo de Cordova by chance. He had been passing near the edge of town, walking a shaded trail he rarely took. He noticed a man kneeling in the weeds just off the path, admiring a cluster of small yellow flowers with papery petals. The man stood slowly and brushed off his knees when he saw Ugly staring at him.

"They are quite striking, these," the man said, indicating the cluster. "Do you know what they are?"

Ugly didn't. Edwardo smiled.

"I think they are damiana. It's a medicinal. Maybe an aphrodisiac too I think." He gave a short laugh. "Here, smell."

Ugly suddenly felt very self-conscious, but he leaned in to the flowers and inhaled.

"A nice sweet herbal scent, no?" the man asked.

"Yes," said Ugly.

The man gave a small nod, still looking at the flowers. "I'm Edwardo," he said after a moment. He paused waiting for Ugly to reciprocate the introduction.

Ugly hesitated, then replied, "José."

Edwardo glanced at him. "José," he repeated, like he was trying it out. "Nice to meet you."

Ugly gave a slight nod.

"Do you walk this way often?"

"Not usually," Ugly said.

"Well," Edwardo said, brushing his hands off again, "if you find yourself needing shade or water, you're welcome to stop by. I'm just through those trees there. You'll see the gate."

Ugly looked past him, toward a barely visible path.

"I live alone," Edwardo added. "Not much company, but I can offer a seat and some conversation."

Ugly wasn't sure what to say, so he just nodded.

Edwardo gave a faint smile, like that was enough.

Ugly continued down the trail, unsure what just transpired. People didn't talk to him. It wasn't much, just a word from a quiet man. Ugly remembered it. A few days later, he decided to pass that way again.

This time he made his way through the path that Edwardo had indicated. He was startled to find a sprawling villa. Through the gate he could see Edwardo neatening up a garden. Edwardo looked up, smiled, and waved Ugly in.

They sat in the courtyard for a while, sharing cerveza and easy conversation.

It became a kind of ritual. Edwardo did not like to leave the property, but he would ask about the town, and Ugly would invent stories. Ugly didn't mind. For a while, he even liked it. Eventually, Edwardo began asking Ugly to run errands. It became a routine, an arrangement. Edwardo enjoyed the company, and had gained something like a manservant.

Ugly had liked the conversations at first, but he didn't care for being sent around, not by a man who seemed to have everything and never left his gate. Still, he began to see an opportunity. Edwardo lived alone in a beautiful home filled with things he barely touched. And no one else ever came. Ugly never saw any family. No servants. No friends. He decided no one would miss the man. What Edwardo had could belong to someone else. Could all of this be Ugly's?

He was terribly conflicted when he strangled Edwardo. The man hadn't even cried out. Ugly wrapped him in a rug, dragged him deep into the woods, and left him there beneath a fallen tree.

Now, the house and everything within belonged to Ugly.

Ugly hadn't spent much time inside the villa before. He began to explore it, slowly, room by room. Edwardo had much: cellars of good wine, shelves of fine artwork, and stashes of pesos hidden in drawers and in cabinets. Ugly wandered through it all, taking it in. He had never owned anything before that he couldn't carry. Now he had velvet curtains, oil lamps, silver cups and plates, a bed with a frame.

In town, Ugly made a show of things. He told anyone who asked that he was now Edwardo de Cordova's manservant. Edwardo's health, he explained, had taken a turn, and he now required full-time care. Most people had heard of Edwardo de Cordova, but few had ever seen him.

It was a warm morning when the man arrived. He wore a dark coat despite the heat and carried a leather satchel tucked close to his side. He stopped at the gate and looked up at the villa like he already knew it.

Ugly saw him from the garden. He considered slipping out of sight, but the man had already spotted him.

"Is Edwardo in?" the man asked.

Ugly wiped his forehead. "He's resting. Not well today."

The man nodded, though not with sympathy, more like an acknowledgment. "I see. I'm Arturo Saldaña. I handle some of Mr. de Cordova's affairs. I usually stop by once a season. Just a few documents for review, nothing too demanding."

Ugly said nothing.

"I'd written ahead," Saldaña continued, "but I suppose if he's unwell…"

"I can take a message," Ugly offered, realizing he may have said it a little too quickly.

Saldaña studied him. "And you are?"

"His manservant," Ugly said. "Been with him a while."

"I don't recall hearing about you," Saldaña said lightly. "But perhaps Edwardo mentioned you in one of his notes. I'll have to check."

He shifted the satchel under one arm.

"Well," he said, "tell Mr. de Cordova I'll return the day after tomorrow. These papers can wait a few days, but not forever. Please let him know I came."

Ugly gave a stiff nod. Saldaña didn't linger. He turned and walked back down the road.

Ugly had headed into town. He wanted to pick up some cerveza, and maybe some meats and cheese.

He saw Saldaña before Saldaña saw him. Across the square, the man stepped out of the post office with a small packet in hand. He paused, glanced around, then crossed toward the constable's office.

Ugly waited several minutes, motionless. The possibilities went through his mind.

Then he turned and walked back the way he came, steady at first, then faster. By the time he reached the edge of town, his shirt clung damp to his back.

At the villa, he paced the hall, thinking through his options. It could be nothing. He could talk his way past Saldaña. But what if he truly suspected… or worse, knew. Maybe Saldaña had expected letters from Edwardo. Maybe the visit was because they had stopped coming.

Ugly packed what he could carry: a satchel of pesos, some silver, a few pieces of jewelry he thought he could trade. One bottle of wine. A coat. He didn't eat. He didn't look back.

By nightfall, he was on the road north.

Chapter 10
1886

Joseph Henry entered the lathe shop. He'd spent an exhausting morning at Whilton Spear's distillery. A boiler wouldn't hold a proper draft, and Joseph Henry spent the better part of two hours shoveling damp, unseasoned wood into a sluggish fire that refused to catch. The air inside was thick with smoke and steam, and his shirt clung to him before the sun had fully cleared the ridge. Then the mash tun overflowed, a clog in the runoff pipe, and he'd had to drag the grate free and scoop out half-cooked grain with a bucket. His hands were raw from the heat.

By noon, he hadn't even gone home to wash. Just hung up his work apron, rinsed his face, and started walking to the lathe shop. He was supposed to be there before noon. He was late.

He expected a stern look from his father, but Samuel wasn't at one of the lathes. His office door was closed, and Joseph Henry heard light talk from the other side. He grabbed the chance to slip in unnoticed. He went to a lathe and began working a table leg.

The office door opened. Joseph Henry kept his head down. He had turned off the lathe and was checking his work. Footsteps approached. He assumed it was his father coming to give him grief.

"Hello, Joseph."

The voice was familiar, but it wasn't his father's.

Joseph Henry looked up.

His father was still in the doorway, a light smile on his face.

Standing in front of Joseph Henry was the man who'd spoken.

Joseph Henry blinked. His jaw dropped.

"Mr. Timmons?" Joseph Henry said. *Minnie's father.*

He looked older. It had been eight years. His hair was thinner, and all gray. His face had gathered deep lines Joseph Henry didn't remember.

But it was him. Minnie's father.

Joseph Henry couldn't say anything.

In the first couple of years, he had received letters. He'd respond, wait, respond again. It became a rhythm. Eventually it faded.

At first his mother would say *absence makes the heart grow fonder* to help him through the separation. Later, she'd say *distance dulls the heart* to explain the silence.

"How have you been, son?" Mr. Timmons asked.

Joseph Henry straightened. "Working full days. I apprentice at Spears's in the mornings and spend the rest here in the shop. Mostly lathe work."

Mr. Timmons gave a slight frown. He nodded, then gave Joseph Henry a pat on the shoulder. "Good to see you, boy." He began to turn.

Joseph Henry blurted, "How's your… family, sir?"

Mr. Timmons's eyes creased, and he smiled.

"Minnie is just fine, Joseph. She's looking forward to seeing you."

"I don't think so, sir," Joseph Henry said, then caught himself, hearing the words leave his mouth. "I mean…"

Mr. Timmons returned his hand to Joseph Henry's shoulder. "I know, son. Trust me though." He turned away and started walking towards the door. "Thank you, Samuel, I'll see you on Monday." Samuel Henry nodded, and Mr. Timmons walked out.

Joseph Henry was stunned. He stood with both hands pressed against the workbench, trying to make sense of what had just occurred. His father, seeing him like that, walked over.

He stood beside him for a moment without speaking.

"You know," he said finally, "I've worked in this shop most of my life. First with your grandfather, then on my own. Thought I understood a thing or two about things… like turning something raw into something worth keeping." He rested his hand on the table leg Joseph Henry was working on.

"But even the cleanest wood's got knots. And if you work it too hard, you'll split it. You learn, over time, where to lean in, and where to let it be."

He paused, letting the quiet settle.

"I saw your face just now. Heard what you said. And I don't think you meant it—not fully. You've been carrying things for a long while, son. That's clear enough. But not everything needs to stay heavy."

He turned to face Joseph Henry more directly.

"You did right by her. You stayed decent. You worked hard. And that girl… I'm sure she remembers all that."

Another pause. His voice softened a little.

"The Timmons family will be at the harvest festival. So will we. No expectations, son. Just a good evening, a little music, and pie." He smiled. "Gotta have pie."

He hesitated again. "If something's meant to happen, it'll happen."

He gave his son a small nod, then added, "But don't go waiting on fate to do all the work."

Joseph Henry remained still. Samuel leaned in and kissed his forehead, then turned back toward the office. Before entering, he paused. He glanced back at his son and said in a stern voice, "And next time you're late, you'll be docked a day's pay!" He gave a wink and a grin.

Joseph Henry broke into a smile as his father went into the office and closed the door. He went back to finishing the table leg.

Despite looking forward to the Harvest Festival for weeks, Joseph Henry had to be goaded into going. Ever since seeing Mr. Timmons in the lathe shop, he'd carried a knot in his stomach that wouldn't leave. His father had done his best, offering pointed looks and quiet wisdom, but nothing had settled Joseph Henry's nerves. The closer the hour came, the less he wanted to go.

The idea of running into Minnie, after all that time, all that silence… felt heavier than he could carry. He wasn't sure what scared him more: that she wouldn't want to see him, or that she would.

In the end, Joseph Henry joined his family and walked to the fields behind the church. Lanterns had been lit early, first for atmosphere and later for darkness, as the festival often stretched late into the night. Their soft orange flickers danced down the paths past quilt-covered picnic tables, leading toward stalls with games and food. Smoke from cook-fires curled into the sky, carrying the scent of hickory, roasted meat, and sweet molasses. Farther across the field stood the large barn, where the night's festivities would culminate with string music and dancing: reels, waltzes, and square sets called by the strong voice of Andy Barton, the blacksmith.

Joseph Henry stayed back, lingering near the wagons where the horses had been hitched and watered. He adjusted his collar nervously with one hand, the other tucked deep in his pocket. His family had already moved down the path toward the food stalls. He didn't follow, only slowed, letting them drift away. After they were sufficiently out of sight Joseph Henry meandered into the more crowded area himself, eyes scanning the crowd.

Children ran barefoot between booths, their shouts mingling with the fiddle music coming from a hay wagon bandstand. Joseph Henry had to sidestep as two boys barreled past him. Off to the side, other boys bounced across the field, racing in burlap sacks and toppling into each other at the finish line. Farther down, a pair of elderly women sold thick slices of vinegar pie, molasses cookies, and dried apple tarts from a table draped in faded gingham, a red-and-white checkered cloth that had seen many seasons of use. The pie and cookies looked dark, almost black, but they were going fast.

Joseph Henry walked on, past the quilt display. Strips of calico and muslin, sewn in a multitude of geometric patterns, hung from ropes stretched between saplings. A few were simple, but others had stitching so fine it looked painted. He ran a finger across one patch of faded red cotton. A young woman's laugh rose beside him. He turned, tentative and nervous, but saw only a brunette lass walking with her young man. It wasn't Minnie's blonde hair.

More laughter rolled from a circle of young folks near the apple press, where a stout man in suspenders pumped a wooden lever with theatrical effort. Juice poured out into a tin pail, foaming bright and golden.

And there she was.

Minnie brought a mug of cider to her lips. Joseph Henry stood frozen. He was stunned by the sight of her. She was no longer the adolescent girl he remembered from eight years ago, but a grown woman. Taller. Poised. Confident. Even buxom. And yet, undeniably Minnie.

She laughed as cider dribbled down from the mug onto her dress: bright red with black polka dots, a sash at the waist, and a large bow tied in the back. A young man with brown hair, perhaps the journeyman from the farrier shop, stepped forward and dabbed at the spill with a handkerchief.

Joseph Henry stepped back between two stalls. Behind him, at the edge of a clearing, a few lanterns swung gently from shepherd hooks. He looked forward again, and his eyes suddenly met Minnie's.

There was no surprise on her face, just a smile. Her mouth formed a simple, silent "Hi."

The young man beside her turned, following her gaze. Joseph Henry stumbled backward, out into the clearing.

Joseph Henry, abashed from fleeing, started walking home. He paused beside the road, angry at himself, though he wasn't sure if it was for running off or for letting himself be talked into going in the first place.

He could still hear the music, distant but clear. The high pitch of the fiddles carried. Laughter carried too, softer but unmistakable. Dusk had settled in. In the near darkness, he could make out the faint glow of fires and lanterns across the fields.

He turned and started walking again, only to stop after a few steps. Then he turned back toward the festival, hesitated, and turned once more. His head was spinning. He started again for home, then stopped. His feet couldn't keep up with his shifting thoughts.

He was perplexed. Minnie had smiled at him. Smiled, and mouthed *hi* like nothing had changed. Like it hadn't been eight years. Like he hadn't been left behind.

And the young man, the farrier's boy, was he a friend? More? It didn't matter. Or maybe it did. Joseph Henry didn't know, or didn't want to know.

He balled his fists and looked down the road. It didn't matter. He had other reasons to leave. He was tired. He had work early.

No… he was lying to himself.

After a point, he hadn't written either. She had written, and he had written back. Then the space between letters grew. Eventually, it all went quiet. She had stopped. But so had he. Life went on.

He looked back over his shoulder. His eyes followed the faint lantern glow across the field. By now, the people would be filing into the barn. They'd pair off. They'd dance. Maybe she already had. Or maybe she was waiting.

He told himself he had moved on. There had been stretches when he hadn't thought of her at all. He had worked hard. Buried himself in it. Lived simply. Focused on what was in front of him. Stopped looking back.

But now, seeing her, he felt something shift. It was new, and yet it wasn't. It had always been there. Every day, he worked to keep it down. He hadn't realized how tired that had made him, how tired he had become. Like a rope being pulled for years, fraying strand by strand, too slow to notice until it was ready to give.

She was still everything to him. Maybe she always had been.

Joseph Henry took a breath. He glanced once more down the road toward home.

Then he turned and walked back toward the festival.

Joseph Henry stood outside the barn. He stayed in the shadows, in a stand of trees several yards away, off to the side of the large open doors. He could hear the music but hoped he couldn't be seen. Light poured through the doors and cracks in the walls, flickering like fireflies.

Inside, Andy Barton's voice rose and fell in rhythm with the fiddle and banjo as he called out the square dance set.

"Swing your partner, don't be shy—round and round with a twinkle in your eye!"

Boots stomped on the old floorboards. Joseph Henry crept from the shadows and moved closer to the barn, trying to make himself look small.

"Bow to your partner, tip your hat—swing her once, but don't hit the cat!"

Laughter roared at Andy's improvisation. Joseph Henry stepped closer, just to the edge of the light. He could smell sawdust and cider.

He quickly ducked further back as a young couple exited through the doorway, though they didn't notice him.

"Duck your head and make that turn—or she'll switch you out for Old Man Vern!"

More laughter. Clapping.

He leaned forward slightly, peering through the doors, catching glimpses of dancers spinning under the rafters. For a moment, he thought he saw Minnie… but no, it was another girl in a similar dress.

He scanned the room again. There were Mr. and Mrs. Timmons. One of Minnie's brothers stood beside them. And just beyond… Minnie. The farrier stood beside her.

Minnie's face was lit with a smile.

Joseph Henry drew back, his breath short. His fingers curled at his sides. He felt out of place. And Minnie… she was smiling.

The band played on.

But something about the smile… *Polite? Cordial?*

He wiped his hands on his trousers, took one last breath to steady himself, then stepped into the barn.

Joseph Henry wove his way through the crowd. Minnie seemed impossibly far off. He nodded awkwardly at anyone who glanced his way or called out, but his eyes never left her.

A hand touched his shoulder. "Joseph?" his mother said softly.

He glanced at her, but it was like looking through fog.

Samuel stepped beside his wife and gently took her arm. She turned toward him, puzzled. He nodded toward Minnie across the room.

Joseph Henry's mother followed his gaze and let out a quiet, "Oh." Then she stepped back and let her son go.

He continued through the crowd, hesitating only briefly when Minnie finally noticed him. She gave an almost sly smile, then turned toward the farrier and spoke a few quick words. Before turning back, she seemed to take a breath. She brushed her hands down the front of her dress, then took a single step forward.

Joseph Henry stopped abruptly in front of her, closer than he intended. He wanted to talk, but the music was loud. Realizing how near he was, he flushed red.

Minnie glanced down the length of him, then back up. Their eyes met. She gave a faint smile.

"Hello, Joseph," she said, soft but sure. Her voice drifted easily over the music.

"Hello, Minnie." He paused. "I… we should talk."

A beat passed. He started to say more, but she beat him to it.

"You look older." Then, with a flicker of mischief, she glanced down and up again, "A little taller, too."

Joseph Henry followed her glance, then looked back at her, serious.

"Well… a bunch of years'll do that, you know."

Minnie studied him for a moment, her smile tempered now.

"You're very serious, Joseph," she said lightly. "If you get any more solemn, I might have to go dance with someone less intimidating."

She turned half toward the party, though her eyes never left him. "I didn't see this going this way. Maybe let's let it be. Talk in a day or so."

Joseph Henry blinked. He didn't mean to, but his voice rose.

"Now… now see here, Minnie…"

Just then the music stopped. His words carried across the floor, drawing every nearby eye. He froze, stunned by the silence.

His voice caught. He glanced around at the staring faces, then tried again, quieter this time. "I just mean… I didn't expect this. I didn't expect *you*. I was doing just fine until your father came in this morning. Now everything is upside down. I didn't…"

Her expression softened, just a touch.

"I thought maybe," he went on, "if we could talk, we could…"

He faltered again. "We could talk."

Minnie tilted her head. Softly, she said, "Then talk."

Music began to play again, and slowly the crowd returned to conversation and dancing.

"When I saw you with…" Joseph Henry glanced past her, toward the farrier.

Minnie turned to follow his gaze. When she realized what he meant, she laughed.

"That's Everett. He's my cousin. His family is helping us move back here. We're staying on his father's farm until we have a place of our own."

Joseph Henry's mouth hung open as he processed the information. Then, slowly, he smiled.

Minnie looked him straight in the eye.

"I've been waiting for you."

Joseph Henry's smile faded slightly.

"For the afternoon?"

"For eight years," she replied.

Chapter 11

1886

The sky was a dull gray, woolly clouds drifting across it in slow herds, letting through only the briefest wisps of sun. A brisk wind swept down from the ridge, tugging at collars and blowing more than a few hats from the heads of men making small repairs to picnic tables and raising the simple willow arbor. They worked with backs hunched and coats pulled close, spirits high despite the cold.

Long ribbons, left from another recent gathering, were still tied to the old white fence around the churchyard. They whipped angrily, threatening to tear themselves free and sail for the hills.

The women were up most of the night, and many continued working through the early morning. The kitchen was already warm when they began. By midnight, it felt like they were in the oven. Every window was wide open, but the breeze never seemed to come in, despite it howling through the trees outside.

Several lamps lit the room unevenly, along with the hearth fire and the flickering light from the wood-burning cookstove. The table was dusted with flour, and it seemed like every bowl, pot, wooden spoon, and piece of cutlery in the house was in use. Both Minnie's and Joseph Henry's mothers worked diligently, kneading biscuit dough or trussing birds, while barking orders to the handful of other women who had shown up to help. Once settled into their tasks, they moved with a quiet, practiced rhythm, working in a fervent silence that carried a weighty diligence.

Just after sun-up, the ladies stood surveying their work. The kitchen smelled of smoke, bread, and fried fat. The hearth fire smoldered, but no one felt it needed further feeding. Pies lined the bench in careful stacks: apple, peach, blackberry, molasses, and two vinegar pies Mrs. Timmons insisted on making. Several spice cakes and jam cakes rested on a countertop, alongside a larger decorated single white cake brought in by Mrs. Grieves, with a ribbon tied around each tier, and flowers adorning the top and sides. Hams had been sliced and laid out in a shallow crate lined with paper, and baskets of fried chicken were tied shut with twine. Biscuits were stacked high in towel-lined bowls near jars of fresh butter and a jug of sorghum. Jars of pickled beans and beets were packed between rolls of cloth to keep them from clinking together on the way to the churchyard. Potato salad and cabbage slaw were being kept cool in the root cellar and would be taken out at the last minute. A pot of baked beans still bubbled on the stove, nearly forgotten. Mrs. Henry caught an almost scorched-sweet smell from it, and hurried across the room to lift it off the surface with a groan.

All the ladies stood quietly for several moments, blinking as the new sunlight came through the windows, illuminating the flour dust that still floated through the air. They laughed lightly, seeing each other, soot and flour on their cheeks and grease and gravy stains across their aprons and exposed dresses. Everything smelled like effort. Mrs. Timmons muttered, "That'll do," and Mrs. Henry nodded.

Joseph Henry nervously milled around, trying to look like he had something to do. He had arrived at the churchyard in the early afternoon, wearing the same suit his father had worn years before on his wedding day.

He looked up and frowned as a fine mist began to fall from the sky.

"It'll be fine, Joseph," his father said, walking toward him. "The weather will break. I can feel it in my bones."

Joseph Henry just smiled. He gave the arbor a light push, as though making certain it was sturdy enough to last the day.

Though still an hour early, people had begun to drift into the churchyard and claim their seats. About seventy-five slat-back wooden chairs had been set out for the entire community. Some didn't even know the Henrys or the Timmonses well, but everyone enjoyed a gathering and would sit through the ceremony just for the food and the dance.

A horse and cart from Samuel's shop had pulled up and the foodstuffs were being unloaded from it and brought to tables at the edge of the field. Another larger cart, being pulled by two horses, came bouncing down the road, and almost took out a portion of the fence before it came to rest. Mr. Spears and one of his apprentices hopped off the cart, and Mr. Spears called over to several others to help unload. It seemed to be three large kegs of beer and what Joseph Henry reckoned was a cask of whiskey.

The minister came out of the church after the cart had rocked to a halt, the front wheel pressing up against the fence post causing it to lean awkwardly. A few guests looked over in surprise, but no one seemed particularly alarmed. Mr. Spears waved off the minister as if to dismiss the whole thing.

"Post needed moving anyway," he called out, grinning. His son was already untying the barrels with practiced speed.

"You planning to baptize the whole county when those things break open, Emmett?" someone shouted from across the yard.

"I will if someone wants to pay for it," Spears replied.

There was a ripple of laughter, and the near-miss was forgotten. The men Spears had drafted lifted the barrels and an unmistakable smell of oak and corn mash floated briefly on the breeze.

Joseph Henry shook his head and smiled. Samuel, seeing his son relaxing a bit, gave him a gentle pat on the shoulder.

More wagons rolled in from the lower road, along with families who arrived on foot, and the churchyard began to hum with conversation and motion. Children darted between the chairs chasing one another, their shoes, pant cuffs, and dress hems already muddy from the damp ground. Someone began plucking at a fiddle, coaxing out a few notes that might become a song later, and a group of older men gathered near the beer barrels, hoping one might be cracked open early. Many guests spoke in low tones, pointing nervously at the sky like it might open up on them at any moment.

The last of the guests trickled into the area.

The minister stepped out of the church and loudly clapped his hands for attention. As the guests settled into their chairs, he made his way to the arbor, carrying a worn black Bible in his left hand. Joseph Henry, already standing there waiting, suddenly felt stiff. His hands were folded in front of him, but he felt out of place at his own ceremony. He resisted the urge to adjust his collar for the third time. Beside him stood Samuel, looking entirely natural, as though he could have been the groom.

Then a murmur began, low at first, then rising, until all eyes turned toward the church. The rain had stopped, and almost as if on cue, the sun broke through the clouds. Minnie stepped out through the church doors, her father at her side. She wore a soft blue dress with a ribbon at the waist and a crown of wildflowers perfectly meshed in her blonde hair. Her mother had pinned frills of lace to her shoulders, and they danced in the breeze as she walked.

They crossed the grass slowly. No music played. No one spoke. Joseph Henry thought, *This must be what it would look like if angels walked instead of flew on wings.*

When they reached the arbor, Joseph took a step forward. Minnie's father gave a short nod, and pressed Minnie's hand into Joseph Henry's, holding it there for several seconds. A tear slowly meandered down his cheek. His lips parted like he meant to speak, but no words came. He gave her hand one final squeeze, then let them go and silently stepped back.

The minister opened his Bible.

"Dearly beloved, we are gathered here today in the sight of God and this community to witness the joining of this man and this woman in holy matrimony…"

He spoke plainly, with an easy rhythm, as though he were reading from memory. He talked of commitment, and patience. Then he gave a short sermon of how a good marriage was like a field, plowed deep, tended with care, never left unsown.

Joseph Henry repeated his vows with a sudden certainty. Minnie's voice trembled at first, but steadied when she looked into his eyes and saw the same boyish love she had seen all those years earlier.

There was no added pomp, no rings, just the simple vows, sealed with joined hands.

"I now pronounce you husband and wife," the minister said. "May the Lord bless and keep you both, all the days of your lives."

For a beat, no one moved. Then, the normally restrained Joseph Henry leaned in and kissed Minnie. It wasn't done, not in front of the whole churchyard, but he did it anyway. Minnie blinked, startled, then smiled against his lips. Someone gasped. Someone clapped. Then someone whistled. Suddenly the whole yard came back to life in a great cheer.

The food had been laid out in long rows under white cloths, held down with stones and jam jars. The smells of ham, baked beans, fried chicken, and fresh bread wafted across the field. Children running ahead reached under the cloths to steal a biscuit or a chunk of meat before the crowd arrived.

Mrs. Henry and Mrs. Timmons removed the cloths, then stood behind the tables with some of the other ladies who had spent the night preparing everything, like proud vendors at a fair. They handed out servings and urged seconds on anyone who so much as glanced their way. Mrs. Timmons was spooning slaw onto plates and smiling like she'd just married off her only daughter to royalty. Mrs. Henry fussed with the biscuit baskets, straightening the cloth linings even though they were already sitting neatly.

Most folks sat on picnic blankets or the grass itself. It didn't matter that the ground was still a bit damp. A few were caught dragging the slat-back chairs from the churchyard and were promptly scolded by the minister. The field was bathed in mid-afternoon sun and a lazy, warm breeze, with no hint of the morning weather that had threatened to spoil the day. Toasts began with mason jars filled with tea and lemonade. It wasn't long before someone tapped the first beer keg.

Joseph Henry and Minnie had their own blanket, set with a special basket prepared just for them. Inside were all of Minnie's favorites: cold fried chicken, soft rolls still warm in their towel, a jar of blackberry preserves, and two generous wedges of vinegar pie. Someone had even tucked in a small jar of pickled peaches with a bow tied around the lid. Joseph Henry poured her a glass of lemonade, spilling some on the blanket. Minnie gave a mock scolding but took the mason jar anyway, smiling as she did.

Near them, their parents shared another blanket, laughing and talking over the hum of the crowd. They occasionally called out to Joseph Henry and Minnie.

"You two got enough over there?" Mrs. Henry called. "We've got more if you need it."

Mr. Timmons, already into his second jar of beer, waved a drumstick in the air. "Just wait till tonight," he said, loud enough for half the yard to hear. "That boy'll be reelin' come morning."

His wife gasped and smacked his arm with her napkin. "Good Lord, Walter, hush!" she said, half-laughing but clearly not amused.

Samuel choked on his tea and looked up at the sky like he hadn't heard a thing. Mrs. Henry just shook her head and muttered something about men, giving Samuel a sideways look like he was the one who'd said it.

Mr. Timmons raised both hands like he was innocent. "I'm just sayin', they're adults now, aren't they?"

Minnie blushed and buried her face in Joseph Henry's shoulder. He just grinned at the grass, cheeks pink.

Mr. Timmons brought a jar of beer over to Joseph Henry. "Come on, boy, toast with me," he said, handing him the jar and clinking it against his own. He looked at Joseph Henry expectantly.

With a slight smile, Joseph Henry took a long draw, and Mr. Timmons gave a wide grin before emptying the rest of his second one. Joseph Henry started to follow suit, but Minnie reached over and took the jar from his hand.

Mr. Timmons began to protest, but Minnie abruptly said, "That's enough for now, Joseph, I'll be wanting a dance later."

The afternoon went on with more eating and drinking. Folks wandered past the family blankets offering congratulations, raising a toast, or sharing some well-worn piece of advice. As dusk approached and the shadows grew long, the sound of music drifted from the barn, and people began to gather themselves up and head inside.

The evening wore on, stretching late into the night. Joseph Henry and Minnie had lingered outside longer than most, still on their blanket,

Minnie resting her back against Joseph Henry. The blue-gray sky held faint traces of the morning's weather, but it gradually gave way to the colors of dusk. Low on the horizon, golden hues began to rise, soft amber, warm peach, pale orange, spreading gently as the sun slipped lower.

Around them, women moved quickly to gather up leftover food, fold linens, and repack baskets. Their children, only begrudgingly helping, kept glancing toward the barn where the music had already begun to play.

A square set had begun, though Andy Barton was nowhere to be found. His stand-in, Barney Tate, couldn't do it justice. A few of the calls drew chuckles, confusion, and visible cringes.

"Roll away, then turn to the right, let's make time with the preacher's wife!"

A few dancers paused mid-step. Someone snorted. Several couples peeled off toward the punch bowl instead. The minister did not look amused.

Joseph Henry and Minnie eventually made their way into the barn, just as a new reel was starting up. The crowd was already warm with drink, and a cheer rose up when someone spotted them near the doorway. Joseph Henry gave a thin smile and a modest wave. Minnie curtsied, laughing, and the two of them were roughly prodded toward the floor.

Joseph Henry was not a dancer. They joined for one full turn, but just one. The others on the floor gave way, and Joseph Henry and Minnie danced through them. They stepped light, hands clasped, eyes meeting now and then, doing their best to keep pace with the quick rhythm of the fiddles.

After the dance, the crowd tried to coax them into another, but they drifted toward the side of the barn where their parents and a handful of old friends had gathered. There were warm greetings, a few hugs, and some light teasing from neighbors who'd known them since they were children.

Later in the evening, when the music had slowed and families with younger children had gone home, Samuel stepped out onto the floor with a mason jar in his hand. The chatter faded as folks turned to watch. He cleared his throat.

"I just want to say a few words," he began, nodding toward Joseph Henry and Minnie. "You all know I'm not one for speeches, but… well…"

He turned to face his son directly. His pride was unmistakable, as he held back tears.

"I've always believed in hard work. In showing up, doing right, and keeping quiet about it. That's how I was raised, and that's how I tried to raise my boy."

He paused and gave a tight smile.

"But sometimes… sometimes you get lucky. You get a son who turns out better than you taught him to be. Someone who takes the best parts of you and lets them grow, builds on them."

His voice caught on that last part. He looked down, blinked a few times, then gave a short laugh to steady himself. He seemed to want to say more, but the words wouldn't come.

"Well…" he said, lifting his jar, "to Joseph and Minnie. May your days be gentle, your nights be long, and your hearts never know trouble."

He raised the jar high. The crowd followed suit.

"To a happy future!"

Samuel began to leave the floor, but he was stopped by Mr. Spears. Spears put a hand on his shoulder, shook his hand, and offered his congratulations. He then turned and said, "With Samuel's permission, I'd like to say something."

Samuel nodded and stepped back. Mr. Spears raised his own jar. His voice was loud, clear, and confident.

"When this young man started apprenticing with me, I thought I was doing him the favor." He looked over at Joseph Henry. "Sure, I knew Samuel had probably already taught him the trade, had him making good whiskey. But I never imagined that I'd be the one gettin' the better end of the arrangement."

There were several nods, quiet chuckles. "You ain't kiddin'," someone called out.

"Those who know me," Spears added, "know that isn't easy for me to say."

That brought real laughter.

"This cask here," he went on, pointing to the one resting near the beer kegs, "was drawn from the very first batch Joseph Henry saw through, start to finish, in my still. Thought it might come in handy someday."

He paused, clearing his throat.

"Truth is, Joseph Henry didn't just learn the trade. He improved it. More than once I've looked at a run and known it came out better because his hands were in it."

He looked at Joseph Henry. "Joseph, Monday morning you're going to be Journeyman." Joseph Henry looked stunned. The crowd applauded, and one person shouted out, "It's about time, Emmett!"

Spears smiled, then lifted his jar once more. "Tonight, we raise a glass not just to a fine young couple, but to the man who made my distillery just a bit better."

He walked over to the cask and pulled the cork with a soft pop. A warm, sharp scent drifted out into the air.

"To Joseph Henry and Minnie," he said.

"Joseph and Minnie," came the echo from around the barn.

The whiskey was poured. Even those who didn't usually partake took a small sip. Those who knew whiskey commented on the quality.

It went down smooth, full of depth and heat. Joseph Henry accepted his glass with a nod, a bit red in the cheeks. Minnie took his arm and leaned into him, her smile quiet and proud.

Mr. Spears stood near the cask and the beer kegs, where a couple of his younger apprentices were pouring for the guests. One of them was just finishing filling his jar when Joseph Henry approached.

"Thank you, Mr. Spears," Joseph Henry said.

"You know, Joseph, I meant every word," Spears replied. "This means longer hours. I know you spend time helping your father in the shop. Not sure how that'll work going forward. It also means more money."

"Thank you, sir," Joseph Henry said. "I'll make it work."

"There's something else we ought to talk about too. Come Monday."

"Sir?"

Spears glanced at him, voice softening. "You know I have no sons, Joseph."

Joseph Henry blinked. "I... sir?"

"Monday," Mr. Spears said, more firmly this time. "We'll talk Monday. Tonight's your night, my boy. Enjoy it."

He gave him a pat on the shoulder and walked off into the crowd, leaving the thought hanging for Joseph Henry to claw at.

Joseph Henry set his jar down and gave a polite nod to one of the apprentices for a fresh pour. But before the boy could move, Mr. Timmons stepped in, placing a firm hand over the rim of the jar. He was pink faced and swaying a little.

"Nope," he said. "I'm gettin' this one."

The apprentice hesitated, glancing between them. "Sir, there's no cost for the libations," he said, trying to sound polite.

Mr. Timmons blinked, confused. "I can't buy my new son-in-law a drink?" he asked, his voice rising.

"I…" The apprentice faltered, unsure, and looked to Joseph Henry for help.

"Of course you can, Mr. Timmons," Joseph Henry said, offering a knowing nod to the apprentice.

Mr. Timmons beamed. He fished a coin from his pocket and pressed it into the apprentice's hand.

The boy looked down, then lit up. He filled both jars generously. "Thank you, sir."

Mr. Timmons gave Joseph Henry a long, appraising look, nodded with satisfaction, and turned to amble back to his wife.

The crowd in the barn had thinned, but it hadn't emptied. A few couples still swayed in the corners. Laughter drifted from the punch table, and a circle of men stood arguing good-naturedly about horses or politics. The topics had tangled together, but they kept at it.

The band was long gone, save for a single fiddle and a boy tapping a washboard with the back of a spoon. Even so, they carried on, the music slow and aimless.

Joseph Henry and Minnie made their rounds, offering thanks, accepting lingering hugs and half-finished toasts. Mrs. Timmons was gathering up their gifts from the table. Samuel had fallen asleep sitting upright on a bench, hands folded across his belly. Mr. Spears gave one last handshake and a wink.

"Monday…" he said, but no more.

Eventually, the pair slipped out through the barn doors and into the open air. The night had cooled, but it wasn't cold. Fireflies blinked low over the fields. The last of the lanterns swayed gently in the breeze, throwing long shadows of the fence across the grass.

Minnie took Joseph Henry's arm, and for a long moment, neither of them spoke.

"This day…" she finally whispered, "I don't think it could've been better."

Joseph Henry nodded. "This is just the start."

Minnie smiled, leaning her head to his shoulder. "Maybe we'll get a hundred more."

He didn't answer, not right away. He looked out over the dark hills. Everything felt right, but something looked off… the way the light didn't quite reach the edge of the field. It was as if it was doing its best to hold back the night, which waited just beyond.

"I hope so," he said softly.

They walked on, the last notes of the fiddle drifting behind them, thinner and fainter with each step.

Chapter 12
1917

Boss Van didn't like being called Walter. His mother and his wife were the only ones who could use the name without trouble. But his last name, Vannoy, he liked even less.

Anyone not calling him Boss Van was just being disrespectful.

Folks said a lumberyard in Louisville burned to the ground after the owner kept calling him Mr. Vannoy. Maybe the fire was an accident. Maybe it wasn't.

Either way, the lore stuck.

Boss Van considered himself a businessman above all else. He didn't steal, and he'd never beg. He saw opportunities and took them. If a man was slow to realize how money could be made, Boss Van got there first. If a deal had multiple directions, he found the one that paid best.

He could also be ruthless in his endeavors, ensuring that competition often never left the gate.

Nobody said the word for what he was. They didn't have to. It was understood.

On the other side of the coin, if you worked with him, or more specifically for him, you could prosper. Politicians, sheriffs, county clerks, they all found ways to keep in his good graces. When an appointment opened up, Boss Van got it. Whether it came with a salary, a contract, or just a quiet advantage, he found ways to turn a position into profit.

The Warden's office was no different. The Frankfort Penitentiary made goods and provided services across the county. Boss Van made sure those resources flowed where he wanted, and that his name was tied to anything that mattered.

Near the beginning of 1917, when it became clear that Prohibition was coming, Boss Van set a plan in motion. He figured he had two, maybe three years at best to get it rolling.

The plan was to set up a clandestine whiskey operation, quiet and self-contained. It would have nothing to do with existing distilleries, which would be the first to face scrutiny once the crackdown began.

The goal would be to produce enough to supply what he figured would become a network of hidden drinking rooms. They didn't have a name yet, not officially, but Boss Van could already picture them: back rooms, basements, small halls with music and cash changing hands.

He would work with trusted local establishments to get them ready. Not taverns or barrooms — those were too obvious. Restaurants maybe, but even better, dry goods stores, warehouses, or service shops that had never dealt in alcohol before.

Anywhere with a cellar or a back room. Anywhere with the right kind of owner. Boss Van would arrange the shipments, handle the contracts, and of course, take his cut.

Boss Van found an old warehouse that had been lost to the forest years earlier and paid to have it fixed up, offering a good deal extra for discretion. He bought equipment from a distillery already shutting down and had it hauled to the new site. Then he brought in a crew of good old boys to get production going.

He even managed to hire a stillman from Old Taylor, which was already boarding up in anticipation of the Volstead Act.

The idea was solid. The outcome wasn't.

Despite paying for equipment, personnel, and even a few borrowed recipes, the final product was only a hair better than rotgut.

Boss Van didn't like failure. On any given day, he was certain where issues lay, and how to solve them.

He spent time and money draining and cleaning all the equipment.

He fired the entire staff and started from scratch, this time bringing in a former master distiller.

Then he blamed the barrels, so he swapped them out, every last one.

Then he thought it might be the water, so he paid to have it rerouted from a spring a mile away.

Then he thought it might be the yeast, so he had some shipped in special from Tennessee.

Then he thought maybe the grain was wrong, so he tried different wheats, then rye, then corn, then all three in rotation and combination. At one point, he had mash coming in from four counties just to see if anything stuck.

Then he blamed the weather, the heat and humidity. He put in new vents and flues and fans and louvers that would keep the mash from spoiling and let the yeast "breathe better."

Then he blamed the air itself and burned sulfur candles to "cleanse the room."

Then he changed the lighting. He repainted the walls. He even replaced the copper in one of the stills because it "looked off."

Then he switched out workers again. He made them wear gloves. Then he made them stop wearing gloves.

Then he made them sing old hymns during fermentation, because someone from the Brown-Forman Distillery told him the rhythm might help.

Then he banned singing altogether, and even had a man fired for whistling too near a barrel.

Month after month, the whiskey kept coming out the same… harsh, sour, and not worth another bottle to put it in.

***

It took Boss Van just under two weeks to make the journey from Kentucky to Bridgetown, Barbados. The train ride to the Port of New Orleans took two days, and the steamship added another ten, stopping in Havana and Kingston along the way. Fortunately, the weather held, and seas stayed calm.

His desperation to solve his quality issues had led him there. The Seale family had been exporting sugar and other commodities from Barbados since the early 1800s. But after the end of slavery on the island, they shifted focus, turned their attention to sugar processing and rum distillation, eventually forming the West Indies Rum Consortium.

Boss Van's family had done business with the Seales for generations, though face-to-face dealings had only occurred once during his lifetime. Still, the name carried weight.

George Seale had seven sons, all skilled in the distilling process. Deacon Seale was the youngest. And though he knew more about making rum than most, being the seventh son left him with little room to rise in the family business. George understood this, and the unfairness didn't escape him. It never sat quite right.

So when Boss Van came to the island seeking help with his venture in Kentucky, George was quick to suggest Deacon.

After interviewing Deacon, Boss Van immediately knew he had found the asset he was looking for. Deacon was knowledgeable and seemed to understand both the distilling process and the mechanics of the operation. He immediately offered him the position.

Deacon did not accept.

"I very much like what you're trying to do," he said, "and I believe I could be useful to you in the enterprise. But I have a requirement that may be beyond what you are willing to accept."

Boss Van was perplexed at what condition this man could possibly require. Still, he put his businessman hat on. He was certain he could negotiate something suitable to land this fish.

"What exactly do you require? This is an important venture to me, and while I won't say money is no object, I am willing to pay. You'll have good accommodations, meals, everything you need.

Now, there won't be any names on paper or formal arrangements. This can't be that kind of setup. I need someone who knows the craft but understands discretion too. This sort of thing won't be exactly legal in the States. That's why the money's good. Keeping things quiet is part of the job. I need someone who understands not just the whiskey, but the processes, and how to run a crew. From what I'm hearing, that's you.

So if there's a number you're thinking, say it. If it's something else you want, name it. I'm a reasonable man when the deal is right."

Deacon gave a slow nod. "It's not that Mr. Van."

"Boss Van is fine…"

"…Boss Van… There's a man I can't leave behind."

Boss Van leaned back slightly.

"He's nearly as skilled as I am… maybe better. Knows the still from the inside out. There's no part of the process he hasn't mastered. He'd be an asset to you as well. He'd fit in."

Boss Van studied him for a long moment. "This someone you're… um… close with, then?"

Deacon didn't catch the meaning at first, or maybe he did and gave Boss Van the benefit of the doubt.

Boss Van cleared his throat. "Look, I don't pry… and when it comes to money I try not to judge. What a man does in his private time isn't my concern. Far as I'm concerned, but…"

Deacon blinked. Then he gave a small, almost confused laugh.

"No. It's not like that," he said gently. "We're not… no. Giles and I… we're brothers."

Boss Van gave a tight nod, the kind a man gives when he doesn't quite understand but wants to. "Alright. Just surprised. George has seven sons, far as I heard. Thought they were all spoken for. Which one is it?"

Deacon smiled faintly. "You're right, the others aren't available. Giles isn't one of them."

Boss Van still looked puzzled.

"Let me bring him in."

Boss Van hesitated… just for a breath… then nodded. "All right son. Let's see what's going on."

Deacon left the room. Boss Van had no idea what to expect. When Deacon returned, he was followed by a colored man.

Boss Van suddenly understood.

Giles had the typical dark skin and coarse hair of a Barbadian of African descent, but in all other ways, he was the spitting image of Deacon. It was like looking at the negative of a photograph.

Deacon had a distinctive, almost British appearance: pale skin, freckles, mousy brown hair, sharp blue eyes, thin lips, a high hairline with the promise of rising higher. With the exception of the skin and hair, Giles matched him feature for feature.

Though no explanation was given, it was clear enough. George Seale had likely fathered a child with a woman who had once worked on the plantation… someone whose family had been indentured, or enslaved, or both.

Deacon certainly knew. And he held Giles as he would a full brother.

Boss Van had no real concept of the context of what it meant, or how it came to be, but strangely, he found himself feeling a deeper respect for the man he hoped to bring into his venture.

The cogs in Boss Van's head began to turn. An extra hand with real skills could be a great advantage… but Giles was colored.

That stuck in his craw.

The fact of Giles being colored didn't bother Boss Van personally. He was one of those rare types who saw the color of money more than the color of a man's skin. But appearances mattered. It probably wouldn't sit well for his venture to be employing a colored man, especially one who'd be paid more than most white men in Kentucky would ever see.

Still, Boss Van wasn't sure he could succeed without Deacon. The Seale family had been instrumental in growing Barbados's rum market, from small domestic batches to a scaled international business. He needed that kind of know-how. And Deacon seemed to be the man. But he clearly wouldn't budge.

Boss Van had come a long way to solve his problems, and he wasn't about to return empty handed. He hoped that Giles truly had the skills Deacon claimed. If so it was a bonus. If not, just an additional expense. And then there was the politics.

"Alright," Boss Van said slowly. "We'll try to make this work."

He hesitated, thinking through the dynamics.

"Surely you understand, the extra man will cut into your pay. And things may be a bit different for a colored man back home. Giles will have to live at the distillery."

Deacon's eyes lit up. "Yes sir, I could live there with him. That should save you a bit."

Boss Van was already impressed with Deacon. He gave a slow nod. "All right son, I'll make the arrangements."

He stood up and shook Deacon's hand, sealing the deal. Then he turned to Giles. There was a moment's pause. Then with a weak but genuine smile, he reached out and shook his hand too.

***

The idea was good, but Boss Van's knowledge of distillation was about as limited as Deacon and Giles's understanding of whiskey-making. They'd never claimed to be proficient in it, and Boss Van had never specifically asked. Apparently, the differences between distilling whiskey and rum were vast.

Both required heat, patience, and copper, but the similarities pretty much ended there. Boss Van certainly didn't know that. Truth be told, neither did Deacon or Giles. Not until they were well in it.

Rum, at its heart, was a sugar spirit. Back in Barbados, it started with molasses: dark, thick, plentiful, and cheap. If not molasses, then cane juice, syrup, or even raw sugar cane. All easy to come by on an island built around sugar. Fermentation was quick, the flavor forgiving, and the heat of the Caribbean helped everything move along. Deacon and Giles had grown up in that world. They knew when to cut the run, when to heat the wash, when to swap the coil. They could taste a barrel and tell you what month it came off the still.

None of that worked in Kentucky.

There was no sugarcane. No molasses. And bringing it in, especially by the barrel, would've been as good as hanging a sign on the road that said *illegal still this way*. Even if they could get the ingredients, it would cost a fortune and draw too many eyes. So rum was out.

And whiskey… whiskey was a different beast.

It started with grain… corn, rye, wheat, barley… all unfamiliar to Deacon and Giles. Instead of molasses, they had to cook mash, hit just the right consistency, watch for starch conversion, and manage temperatures with a precision that hadn't mattered much back home. The yeast behaved differently. It died off quicker in the cold. It didn't rise the same way. What was supposed to bubble and bloom came out thick and flat. The early batches were undercooked. The next ones, scorched. Then came infection. A week's worth of mash ruined from one fly in a cooling tank.

Even the barrels were different. Rum could take to nearly anything, used oak, new oak, charred, raw… but whiskey was picky. Deacon had Boss Van buy a stock of cheap barrels from a shuttered brandy outfit outside of Frankfort, thinking it'd save money. It didn't. The whiskey came out sharp and bitter, full of resin and smoke where there should have been caramel and spice.

Still, Deacon and Giles kept at it. They weren't allowed to quit.

The idea of switching to rum did come up. It was what they knew. But it wasn't an option… not in Kentucky. Molasses was expensive. Imported, taxed, and tracked. A single delivery could raise eyebrows fast... and possibly lead straight to the still. Sugarcane was out of the question entirely. The climate wasn't right, and the logistics of importing it were even worse than that of the molasses. Even if they could grow it, the process of extracting juice and boiling it down was far more conspicuous than milling corn or mashing grain. Too many wagons. Too many smells. Too many questions.

So they kept pushing forward with the whiskey.

Despite setback after setback, batch after batch came out wrong… harsh, flat, or soured. Boss Van's patience wore thinner with each cask. He still believed in the two men he'd brought up from the islands. And he had already sunk a fortune into them.

But something was missing. And Boss Van knew he had to find it.

Chapter 13
1919

Joseph Henry was never one to complain. He'd worked many details in the thirty-one years he'd been inside. This one was the longest, and maybe the harshest. Joseph Henry was pretty sure it was killing him.

The Lime Kiln.

A man didn't just sweat here… he burned. The dust got into your nose, your throat, your skin. Men coughed blood and came out looking like ghosts, coated head to toe in powder so fine even handkerchiefs over the face couldn't keep it out.

Each morning, the detail was marched in, handed crude shovels, and left to dig. It did no good to complain about the constant wet sting of the caustic air.

The terrible stuff they were digging was limestone. After they hauled it up, it got burned down to powder in the intense heat of the kiln. The result was *quicklime*, which was then bagged and hauled. It went into cement, mortar, whitewash, and other things. Some of it left the grounds, sold off by the state. A lot stayed inside. Other details needed it to make components used to patch walls, set stone, lay walkways, even paint the walls with that pale finish that covered the place. Most men never thought much about where it all came from. But Joseph Henry did, with every shovelful.

There were no walls, just piles of crushed stone, kiln smoke, and the slow groan of carts. No guards inside either. They didn't need them. The place punished with every step, every shovel, every movement.

Joseph Henry had learned to pace himself, when to breathe shallow, how to wrap his hands to hold the shovel without peeling the skin. But this wasn't a detail meant for decades. It wore a man down, layer by layer, and Joseph Henry was running out of layers.

Once shoveled, the lime was fed into the kiln, a great iron chamber sunk into a pit, stoked with coal and flame until it glowed hot from within. The heat didn't rise, it radiated sideways, soaking through boots and crawling up the legs.

Despite the misery of digging, Joseph Henry considered it a good day when he had a shovel in his hands. He'd seen men lose their eyebrows just leaning too close to the furnace. He had his share of burn scars on his arms, and even his forehead. Others had passed out in the smoke and had to be dragged clear.

He'd seen the kid, Bobby Getchel, drop dead right in front of him, his upper body folding into the firebox like it had been yanked.

That morning, Joseph Henry had drawn the worst detail in the yard. He and Carl Johnson were on the rakes.

The kiln burn was finished when the limestone crumbled like dry bone.

Then came the raking and the bagging.

The burned lime, quicklime they called it, was dragged out in clouds and funneled into canvas sacks, still steaming. When it touched wet skin, it ate through. No one got through without burns. It was worse in the rain. The dust turned to a slurry you couldn't avoid. They called it *milk of the devil*.

It wasn't raining that day, but the air felt wrong. Both men noticed. A low whine built in the kiln, like the air was trying to move but couldn't. The heat suddenly shifted, not up or out, but sideways. Joseph Henry knew what was happening, but didn't even have time to look at Carl.

Then it blew.

The pressure let go all at once, and a white cloud came roaring out of the pit, dry and angry, straight into them. It hit like sand and fire. The dust stuck to sweat on skin. It soaked through shirts and turned to paste.

And it started to burn.

Joseph sucked in a breath to scream, but his throat filled with the caustic cloud. His eyes went blind. The world turned white, then red, then nothing at all.

He woke several days later in the infirmary, wrapped in bandages, the pain still burning underneath. He didn't know who was luckier, himself or Carl Johnson, who had been put in the ground the day before.

***

Joseph Henry woke, forgetting he was in the infirmary. The walls were gray. The light was dim. The recollection of his whereabouts returned with the dull, endless pain and the constant itch that came with it.

He didn't speak for the first several days, and no one asked him to.

Somewhere to his left, a man coughed in wet, sharp fits until he quieted. Joseph Henry said a silent prayer that the man didn't have the consumption.

Farther away someone snored. It was nonstop. Short breaths and throat clicks.

The nurse was a plain woman. Black hair streaked gray along the sides, tied back in a bun. She didn't say much when she changed Joseph Henry's dressings, which was fine with him.

The doctor, an ancient-looking gentleman, stopped by once in the morning and once at night. Joseph Henry was pretty sure he said the same thing every time: "Healing well, could've been worse."

He already knew that.

Joseph Henry didn't know how long he'd been there. The days stretched and folded into each other. His only indicator was the pain becoming more dull and the itch more pronounced.

Some of the bandages had been removed. Joseph Henry hadn't seen his face since the accident.

Then he did.

He caught his reflection in the cracked steel of a meal tray. His face looked cooked. Not red, not raw. Just tight and wrong. Like something that had been boiled and then left out.

It was disturbing, but he didn't look away. It was hard to tell what was real and what was the distortion of the tray.

The nurse, seeing his scrutiny, said, "It may look bad now, but the doctor thinks it will mostly return to how it was. You're very lucky."

Joseph Henry looked up from the tray.

"Yes… lucky."

He realized that was the first thing he'd said since arriving.

During the latter days of his stay in the infirmary, the nurse would come by and slather a thick coat of something across his chest and back, and along his limbs. It helped with the itch, but the salve was thick and cold. Like lard left too long in a cellar. It dragged across his skin, settling into every crease and scar. The smell was faint but oily, like an empty kerosene lantern. He didn't like it, but it eased the tight pull of his cracked skin.

When they finally sent him back to his cell, he moved slowly. His skin was still tight, the skin along his arms pulling with each step. The hallway back to the cellblock felt longer than it had in years. His legs ached in a different way now, as much from the lack of movement as from the accident.

Back in his cell he collapsed onto his cot. Someone had cleared it and the linens had been replaced. His cup and bowl sat where he'd left them, but the floor had been mopped and the room had been sanitized. He closed his eyes, wondering who he had to thank.

The starched linens irritated his skin, but he was glad to be back in his own space. He chuckled at the irony.

Before dozing off he listened to the sounds of the block and realized he may have actually missed them.

A few cells down, someone whistled a tune. Someone else sneezed and swore. Voices carried like always. The noise was the same, but maybe he heard it differently now.

It was another two days before he joined his fellow inmates in the mess hall. Another before he ventured into the yard. At the end of the next week, a guard came by.

"Henry, back to work details tomorrow. Doctor signed off."

Joseph Henry tensed up and fought off a wave of nausea. He couldn't go back to the kiln. They wouldn't...

The next day, they sent him to the kitchen.

***

Joseph Henry didn't sleep well. Truth was, he didn't sleep at all. Since leaving the infirmary, life had felt almost like a vacation. His skin still itched, and there were stretches along his ribs and arms that still tugged with every breath. But most of the days he spent quietly, in his cell or out in the yard, resting, recovering. He hadn't had this much time to himself since his sentence began.

The cell block stayed quiet during those hours. The only sounds came from the men assigned to sanitizing duty, with mops slapping the floor and buckets rolling past, while the others were away on their work details.

When the guard stood outside his cell and delivered the news that he'd be returning to work detail, Joseph Henry felt the same hollow drop he had when they handed down his sentence and closed the door on the rest of his life.

That night, he lay awake, staring at the dark ceiling. He shook with a chill that didn't come from the cold. His chest rose in shallow lifts. He felt every tug of the tight skin stretching across his ribs.

The Lime Kiln… He wanted to think of anything else, but his mind dragged him back. The nasal breath of someone two cells down became the scrape of shovels on the stone. He rubbed at an itching scab and half-expected to find white dust clinging to his fingers.

Then came the carts… the sound of wooden wheels groaning under sacks of still-hot powder. The echo filled the block.

He clenched his eyes shut, trying to block it out, but then came the image again: Bobby Getchel folding into the firebox.

He shifted under the blanket. The linen scraped raw skin where the salve was thin. He opened his eyes again and tried to focus on something… anything. That morning. The yard. The crunch of grass underfoot. Blue sky. But it kept circling back.

The Lime Kiln…

He couldn't go back.

And for the first time since his sentence began, the thought crossed his mind. Could he end it? Was it really that bad?

He let the thought sit there, cold and still. It scared him.

Then something else came. His father's hands on the lathe. His mother's soft voice. The smell of the still. Then Minnie.

He couldn't. That wasn't who he was.

When the morning call came, Joseph Henry was already awake, sitting at the edge of his cot, head in his hands. He moved through the routine, joining the others as they filed into the washroom.

He stood under the cold water. It usually woke him, got him moving. Most didn't linger. This morning Joseph Henry did. He shivered as the water fell over him, but he knew stepping out meant moving forward with the day. He lost track of time.

"Let's go Henry!"

The guard's voice startled him. He opened his eyes and saw the washroom was empty now, except for him and now the guard.

Joseph Henry stepped out and stood before the man, naked, dripping water on the floor. He knew this guard well, even considered him a friend.

"I can't do it."

"Can't do what Henry?" The guard asked, confused.

"I can't go back to the Lime Kiln."

The guard gave a short laugh.

"They didn't tell you? You ain't goin' to the kiln, Henry. You've been reassigned. You're goin' to the kitchen."

Joseph Henry looked up, just to be sure he'd heard right. Then he smiled.

"Really? This ain't no joke, Marty?"

The guard smiled back.

"Let's go Henry. Can't be late."

Joseph Henry didn't know what to expect, and truth be told, he didn't care. The moment he stepped into the kitchen, it felt like he'd gotten out of prison. The heat was thick and damp, the air reeked of old grease and steam. But to him, it was like a cool spring day compared to the kiln.

Before midmorning, Joseph Henry was already mopping the floors. He whistled a tune as he pushed the mop across the floor, beneath the prep tables, along the back wall where years of stains had settled in. The other men worked in silence, sullen and slow. Joseph Henry didn't notice.

At lunchtime Joseph Henry was put on the serving line. He wore a simple smile as he found a rhythm. One scoop, one nod, one tray at a time. Sometimes he offered a quiet "Alright there?"

He didn't mind the stares or the grumbling. He liked watching the line move, liked the clatter of trays and even liked the smell of the food wafting up.

Next, he took to rinsing pans. You'd think he was scrubbing for gold. Burnt eggs, grease, dried hash; it was like a personal challenge. None of it bothered him. His hands were still healing, and he winced now and then, but he pushed through.

Joseph Henry noticed the other men muttering, cursing the cook, grumbling about the duty rosters. One quit mid-shift after a pot of gravy spilled across the floor. Joseph Henry just grabbed a mop, cleaned it up, and kept going.

He liked the sweat. He liked the noise. He liked the smell of the food.

He liked that no one yelled at him. No one watched him too closely.

No one got injured.

No one died.

Joseph Henry kept showing up with the same steady energy. It felt like a new beginning. What started as relief never wore off. In his mind this was the same as any honest work on the outside. The heat and the noise, the routine, even the endless scrubbing were probably on par with life in the lathe shop. He worked steady, nodded polite, and always found a rhythm. Joseph Henry was, for the first time in a long while, content.

Strangely, after a while, the others started to change. Men who used to groan through their shifts began working a little quicker. One or two even whistled. There were still complaints, still flare-ups now and then, but they didn't last. Joseph Henry didn't say much. He didn't try to lead anything. But somehow just by being there, he lifted the room.

The cook noticed first. Then the guards. By the end of the month, it was just known. The kitchen ran smoother now. Less griping. Fewer write-ups. No fights. It wasn't that the work got easier, but since Joseph Henry got there, everyone seemed a bit… happier. Life didn't feel quite so bad.

It went on like that for months. The work was good… mopping, serving, scrubbing. He never got bored and it never wore thin. It wasn't the life Joseph Henry had once imagined for himself, back before everything changed, but it was more than he could have asked for. Joseph Henry kept showing up early, kept his rhythm. He didn't count days anymore. They passed easily, marked by chores and meals, by small talk and the sounds of trays hitting the bins. Nothing about it stood out. But that was the point. It was steady. It was safe.

Even the guards stopped watching so closely. They still barked when they had to, but their eyes drifted elsewhere. The kitchen was just the kitchen, and everyone liked it that way. Joseph Henry stayed out of trouble, and trouble kept its distance.

Then came the shift. Quiet at first, just a word passed between guards, a paper handed off, a new name called. Joseph Henry didn't notice at first. But the change was coming. The life he'd built was about to be taken from him.

One morning, when the clanging came, a guard was standing outside his cell, and Joseph Henry knew it was all over.

Chapter 14
1919

Joseph Henry just looked at the guard. He didn't need to hear it. He already knew.

"Sorry Henry, it's back to the Kiln," the guard said flatly.

Joseph Henry gave a short chuckle.

"You've got to be shittin' me."

The guard's expression shifted, something sympathetic.

"You know me Henry, I'm just passin' it along. If it were up to me, you'd still be in the kitchen. This came from up higher."

Joseph Henry stared at him, dumbstruck.

"Up higher? Who the hell up higher would send me back? What grand design would have me back in the kiln?"

Joseph Henry took a step back from the bars.

"No. I'm not goin'."

The guard held up both hands. "Henry…"

"I mean it. I'm not steppin' foot near that place again. I'm not leavin' this cell. They'll have to drag me."

The guard glanced down the row, then back. "Don't make this hard. Not on me. Please. You know me."

Joseph Henry's jaw clenched. He looked at the man. Really looked at him. He wasn't a bad sort. Just another lifer in a different uniform. After a long pause, Joseph Henry let out a slow breath.

"Fine," he said. "But only 'cause it's you standin' there. But I ain't going to make it. This'll be the end of me."

Joseph Henry left the cell block, walking like a man on his way to the gallows. His steps were slow, like he was dragging a stone behind him. Other inmates offered the usual nods and greetings, but he didn't respond. Instead of taking a right and heading for the kitchen, he went through the doors and left the building.

The morning was overcast, and the light made everything look flat and washed out. He followed the path around the side of the main building, through a rusted gate he hadn't passed in months. He forced himself to be entirely numb. Suppressing all feelings so he didn't have to fight them. The gravel crunched underfoot.

When he approached the kiln yard, he stopped. Something was different. The acrid stench wasn't in the air. He had always been greeted by the sulfur, the smoke, the scorched-earth smell. But now there was only the scent of damp stone and old ash. The kiln had to be cold.

And there was no clatter of carts or scraping of shovels.

Joseph Henry quickened his step and approached the kiln yard. It was empty. No men. No guards. No one. The giant iron doors of the kiln sat closed. The walls were streaked white and gray, ghosted with yesterday's ash. He stepped forward slowly, scanning the space. He didn't understand.

Then he saw two chairs, and he understood even less.

There were two slat-back wooden chairs. In one sat a large man, though not fat. He wore an off-white linen dress shirt, sleeves neatly rolled. A darker-colored buttoned vest. A loose, solid tie. Two-tone leather shoes, well worn, but polished. And a Panama hat.

He looked entirely out of place.

Though Joseph Henry had only met the man once or twice, he immediately knew. This was the warden, Boss Van.

"Have a seat Mr. Henry."

Boss Van wore a wry smile. As he spoke, he gave the slightest nod toward the empty chair. The rest of his body remained still, like it wasn't worth the effort to move.

"Why do I feel like I've been set up, Warden?" Joseph Henry asked. The staging, the emptiness, the waiting, it all felt deliberate. He thought back wondering if everything since returning to his cell had been part of it.

He didn't feel anxious or nervous, though he was pretty certain that was the intent. He wasn't going to give this man the satisfaction.

"Please," Boss Van said, this time motioning to the chair with his hand, "just Boss Van, Mr. Henry. I'm not the warden today."

"Maybe I'm just imagining it Mr. Van."

"Boss Van," he said, with only the slightest irritation.

"Boss Van… You, or someone, gave me an easy life after the kiln accident. Let me settle into it. Let me get used to the new life. Then just pulled it out from under me. And now you bring me here," Joseph Henry made a sweeping gesture across the kiln yard, "thinking that the horror of it all would leave me in a state. A state for what Boss Van?" He put deliberate emphasis on the title.

Boss Van sighed heavily. He stared at the ground for several seconds, before looking up again.

"Please Mr. Henry, sit down." He seemed to be pleading now. "You are partially right. Please let's talk."

Joseph Henry had the impression that Boss Van didn't normally plead. He hesitated a moment, then sat down. He was about to speak again, but decided to wait.

They both sat in silence, each waiting for the other to speak. Boss Van was the type who always looked for an angle, always gauged how to control a situation. In this case, he figured having Joseph Henry speak first, he could steer the conversation from there. But Joseph Henry wasn't about to fall into that trap.

Boss Van's smile turned more genuine. He pointed a finger at Joseph Henry.

"You are a very clever man, Mr. Henry. I think that's a large part of why we're meeting."

"Mr. Van…" Joseph Henry stopped himself. "Boss… why am I here? What's going on?"

The chair creaked as Boss Van leaned back slightly, realizing just how much theater he'd staged.

"Mr. Henry… Joseph…" He sighed. "Sometimes I overdo things. I set an action in motion when I should just speak plain. I'm a man used to making things happen. Used to getting what I need. And sometimes, that makes me forget to simply ask."

He glanced toward the kiln before continuing.

"I didn't put you in the kitchen, but I heard how things changed once you got there. The calm. The order. I also learned something else about you around that same time. Something I need. Something that could help me."

Joseph Henry stayed quiet.

"I suppose I could've called you into my office, made a proper offer. But that's not always how I work. I tend to create conditions. Show a man what I can give. Let him feel what he stands to gain… or lose."

Joseph Henry still said nothing.

Boss Van's voice dropped a notch. It gained a slight edge.

"I don't talk like this to anyone, Joseph. That ought to tell you how badly I need this."

Joseph Henry let out a breath.

"Need what, Mr. Van? What is it you need from me?"

Boss Van seemed to relax. Joseph Henry felt him settling back into control.

"I understand you used to make whiskey."

Joseph Henry blinked, not sure he heard right.

"Whiskey, sir? I… what's this all about."

Boss Van gave a small nod. He smiled again, and this time it was full of confidence.

"Whiskey. I've heard your family had a hand in it going back some time. From what I understand you knew your way around a still."

Joseph Henry hesitated. Unsure where this was going. "I knew some."

"More than some," Boss Van said, brushing a speck of dust from his vest. "I recently purchased the remnants of a whiskey business from an old man named Whilton Spears. Somehow we got to talking about his early days. He mentioned an apprentice, said the name was Joseph Henry. Claimed this so-called apprentice was the one who actually taught him everything he needed to know. Said he never would've made it without you there at the start."

Joseph Henry looked away into the distance.

"That was a long time ago. Wasn't me."

Boss Van went serious.

"Of course it was Joseph."

He turned his gaze in the same direction.

"I'm at my wits' end. A couple of years ago, I came up with this plan. I was going to make a lot of money running whiskey during this prohibition thing."

His head turned back to Joseph Henry.

"It's a great plan. I ran the numbers. Goin' to make millions."

Joseph Henry kept his eyes on the distance.

"Sounds like a plan. So make your whiskey. Ain't so hard."

Boss Van gave a scoffing laugh.

"Believe me, I've tried. For years now. I've poured good money and good men into it. Gotten back nothing but headaches. Burned batches. Stuff that tastes like varnish. A waste."

He shook his head.

"Every solution I brought in turned into another problem. Every man I brought in turned out to be the wrong one."

He paused.

"I'm not in the habit of losing, Joseph."

Joseph Henry watched him closely. Boss Van's face was calm, but the frustration sat just beneath it. Then came a look of resolve.

"I'm going to offer you something, Joseph." Boss Van went on. "Something no one else on the inside has. Probably never will again."

Boss Van paused, letting the moment settle like it was his to shape.

Joseph Henry didn't buy it.

The calm, the confidence… it was a front. The control wasn't Boss Van's, not this time. Joseph Henry looked Boss Van in the eye and saw that Boss Van knew it too. For all his smooth delivery, he was the one who needed something.

Joseph Henry didn't plan to gloat, and he wasn't the kind to squeeze for more than was fair. But he understood the truth of it. He was in the driver's seat.

He kept his voice even.

"What is it you're offering, Boss Van?"

He tried not to sound as confident as he felt.

Boss Van seemed to sense something in the man across from him. Something he wasn't used to. Something he wasn't sure he liked. But he set it aside.

"You're done with the regular work details, Joseph. I'm going to need you outside, running this operation. From now on your assigned duties will include delivering penitentiary goods offsite. You can also run the personal errands for me, sometimes even driving around my wife and daughters into Lexington or Louisville… shopping and such."

He paused as if considering.

"This setup will allow you to come and go. I'll have passes signed ahead of time. No questions. You'll be covered."

He paused again.

"You'll need a regular work detail on the inside. Can't have you sitting around when there's nothing going on outside. Don't want to raise suspicion. Maybe the maintenance stockroom."

He looked Joseph Henry straight in the eye.

"Of course, all of this hinges on you being successful in our little venture."

There was another brief pause.

"You'll be everything but a free man. So… what do you think? Sound like a deal?"

Boss Van extended his hand to seal it.

Joseph Henry sat for a moment. Maybe a little too long, because he caught the faintest frown cross Boss Van's face.

"Not quite Boss Van."

It felt a little out of character, but Joseph Henry saw an opportunity. They didn't come, maybe not ever. And he felt something rare. He felt in control.

"You're right. I do know whiskey. Before everything happened that was the plan. It was going to be my life. And maybe it's vanity, but I didn't just think I was good. I knew I was real good. That kind of thing doesn't leave you."

He smiled. Not to mock. Not to gloat. It was just plain pride.

"I can do this for you. I know I can. And the life you're offering? It's good compensation."

He looked down, still smiling faintly. Boss Van did his best not to show his impatience.

"But…" Boss Van prompted.

"You see Boss Van, I don't intend to be a convict forever. Some day I'm going to be out for real."

"What are you trying to say, Joseph?"

"This is a lot of money for you," Joseph Henry said. He paused. "You want me to run your operation for next to nothing. Sure, there is value in a better life while serving my sentence. I'm not asking for anything unfair. But you need to figure out what you'd pay someone on the outside to do this job. I want that amount waiting for me when I'm done in here. You'll put it somewhere real. A bank. A name. Doesn't have to be mine on the paperwork, just so long as I can get it when I walk. It needs to be official somewhere. Managed by someone else."

Boss Van sat silent for several moments. Then he smiled. The man across from him was shrewd. He was also very intelligent. That's why this was going to work, he thought. Joseph Henry could see him crunching numbers behind his eyes.

"I can help you with those numbers, Boss Van."

Boss Van laughed out loud. "I'm sure you can, Joseph." He looked at Joseph Henry for several beats, then gave a slow nod, the corner of his mouth tightened. "Fair enough," he said. "I can arrange that. We'll put it in trust. Outside the system. We'll have a local law firm hold it. When the time comes, you say the word and it'll be yours. Clean and waiting. You have my word on that, and more importantly, you'll have someone else on the outside managing it."

Boss Van extended his hand once again.

"Now Joseph, do we have a deal?"

Joseph Henry looked at the hand before him. Everything was about to change. He presented one of his closed-mouth smiles and took his hand.

"Yes sir, we have a deal."

Chapter 15
1920

The still was quiet. A three-man operation didn't have the rush and racket of larger outfits, but Joseph Henry was certain it would be enough.

It had been two weeks since Boss Van brought him to the still. When they arrived the two men, introduced as Deacon and Giles, were mostly cleaning equipment, not mashing or fermenting or distilling. The air smelled more of vinegar and old copper than whiskey. Production had come to a halt. Boss Van had explained the string of failures they'd suffered and called for a pause to avoid wasting more good grain and other resources.

Joseph Henry had liked Giles immediately. He struck Joseph Henry as the kind of man who'd spent most of his life working with his hands and being overlooked for it. Maybe because of that, he was eager to achieve. He wasn't loud, but he listened sharp, always watching and learning, and always quick to nod when something made sense. There was no bluff in him, no hunger to impress, just a steady willingness to do the job right if someone showed him how.

Giles didn't say much, but when he understood something, or didn't, he would offer a quiet knowing smile that folks might take as harmless or slow. Joseph Henry knew it wasn't either. It carried a subtle weight to it, like it came from a place farther off than Kentucky, a kind of distance that didn't ask permission to be here. Giles was no fool. He just knew how to keep things easy on the surface.

Deacon was another matter, and Boss Van had warned Joseph Henry he might be. He'd been brought in because he had experience of his own. Boss Van had explained the Seale family's reputation, and Deacon's background. But neither Deacon nor Boss Van seemed to understand how different this operation would be, or the challenges that came with it. Deacon was clearly a proud man, and being knocked down a level, especially for something that wasn't entirely his fault, couldn't have come easy.

Deacon, though not aggressive, resisted every detail. He seemed to work halfheartedly, and had an air of quiet arrogance. Joseph Henry wasn't sure he'd ever come around, and wasn't sure how best to use him. But it seemed important to Boss Van that Deacon remain involved. So Joseph Henry would try to make use of the man.

Now, after two weeks, and a fair amount of prodding, they seemed to be making progress. The three men worked with little chatter, except when Joseph Henry gave direction or offered instruction. The subtle sounds of the still; the shifting grain, water sluicing from barrels, and the quiet chuff of the small furnace filled the space with a low, even hum.

Joseph Henry moved through the setup, checking on the product while keeping an eye on both Deacon and Giles. He gave the latest batch of mash a stir, then stepped over to another batch already well into fermentation. He was pleased to find Giles there ahead of him, checking the gravity with a hydrometer. The slender glass tool floated in the liquid, measuring how much sugar remained. The lower the reading, the closer the batch was to being ready for distilling.

Joseph Henry looked at the instrument. "What do you think?" he asked Giles.

Giles fumbled with the hydrometer under the scrutiny.

"I think it's about done. Mr. Joseph," he said, offering a slightly nervous smile.

Joseph Henry adjusted the glass slightly in the liquid.

"Oh… not quite," Giles said with a rare frown, spotting the difference.

"Probably about another day," Joseph Henry said.

Giles nodded and grinned. "Yes sir, Mr. Joseph."

He liked when Joseph Henry corrected him… never sharp, never enforcing. Just firm enough, and clear. In Barbados, Giles had worked under men who shouted at him, or even slapped the back of his head. They liked to give orders with their fists. Joseph Henry didn't do any of that. He explained things. And more than once, Giles had caught himself nodding before he even understood why. The man just made sense.

Joseph Henry gave a half laugh, "just Joseph, please, Giles."

"Yes sir, Mr. Joseph," Giles said, and gave him a wink.

Joseph Henry finished the laugh.

Deacon, across the room, lifted an eyebrow at the exchange. He didn't say anything, just wiped his hands on a rag and kept on adjusting some copper line. Joseph Henry didn't need to look to feel the skepticism coming from him.

Joseph Henry knew that Deacon came in convinced he was the smartest man in the room. Maybe he was. Joseph Henry didn't care. Deacon talked about chemical balances and heat indexes, quoted books by name. Joseph Henry didn't mind. Sometimes he'd give a chuckle. But he watched.

Deacon was meticulous. Joseph Henry had to give that to him. He didn't cut corners, didn't chase shortcuts. But he couldn't get beyond his own experience. He framed everything in terms of what he'd known, what he'd learned, what he'd done. But it didn't work that way.

"Whiskey," Joseph Henry had told him once, "wasn't chemistry. Not exactly. Not entirely. It was more like the weather. Something you had to feel."

Maybe Deacon didn't understand. But it didn't feel that way to Joseph Henry.

They didn't argue, but the air hung heavy with something unspoken. A tilt of the head here, a purposeful sigh there. Deacon had a way of pausing just long enough to suggest disagreement.

Of course Joseph Henry noticed, but he let it breathe. He remembered something his father had told him: Let a man's pride shrink on its own, or it'll grow twice the size of his hat.

Was that from the bible?

Joseph Henry took a moment to check the heat beneath one of the old copper pots. He ran his hand just above the flame, feeling the air ripple. "Not too hot, not too low," he muttered. Then he tapped the side of the pot with the back of his knuckle, listening for tone.

He realized Giles had come over to watch.

"When you're watching the temp gauge, remember it's slow to catch up. The coils don't warn you 'till it's too late. If you wait for the number, you've already waited too long."

Giles nodded, and even Deacon glanced up.

"Sometimes you listen. Sometimes you smell. Sometimes," Joseph Henry said, dipping a finger into a catch jar, "you just know."

Deacon was tweaking a batch of sour mash the next morning. Joseph Henry had not yet arrived. He was tied up with new inventory that had come early and had to be checked in to the maintenance stockroom.

When he walked in the smell stopped him cold.

Joseph Henry slid the door shut behind him and walked slowly toward the mash barrel. Giles stepped in from the back hallway, already sniffing the air. He looked puzzled.

"Something's off," Giles stated. "Smells sharp."

Deacon straightened up. "I adjusted the corn ratio. Slightly. Based on the retention we had yesterday, I figured we could get better draw with…"

Joseph Henry walked past him. He crouched, dipped a small tin cup, and swirled it under his nose. Then he took a sip. A tiny one.

He stood, nodded once, and set the cup down.

"It's off," he said simply. "Burned too hot, and too fast. The corn's gone bitter."

Deacon opened his mouth, then closed it, realizing what that meant.

Joseph Henry turned back to the still. "We'll dump it. Start over."

"That's half a day lost," Deacon muttered. "And four sacks of corn."

Joseph Henry nodded, with only the faintest agitation on his face. "That's right."

"I thought it would cut the cook time by an hour," Deacon said quietly. "I read…"

Joseph Henry nodded again. "Uh-huh," he said.

He didn't lecture or press the issue. He just walked over and grabbed a shovel.

Giles grabbed one too, keeping his eyes down, away from Deacon. He and Joseph Henry began scooping the spoiled mash into the waste trough. After a moment, Deacon joined them.

Later, Deacon left the still. Claimed he needed to get some air. Giles watched him go, wiping his hands, concern on his face.

"He'll be fine," Joseph Henry said.

Giles gave a little shrug. "He got plenty in that head. Lucky it's big enough to hold it."

Joseph Henry raised an eyebrow, then he laughed.

"Probably, this is just the thing Deacon needed. Back home," Giles added, "we'd call that *smartenin' the stubborn*. Not easy. Usually need a good knock to the head first."

Deacon didn't go far. Just outside near the pump house where the grass had grown tall. He sat down on a broken brick ledge and looked back at the old warehouse. He had his hands folded, fists clenched, like he was praying, but he wasn't. His jaw didn't move for a long time.

He'd never been talked to like that. Or rather, not talked to. Joseph Henry hadn't dressed him down, hadn't mocked him, hadn't even offered advice. Just let the truth walk by him like a street sweep taking care of his mess. That stung even more. He wanted to be yelled at, maybe even thrashed, but that wouldn't have gone over well.

He thought, for a moment, about walking away. But he couldn't picture the conversation with Boss Van.

So he sat there a while longer, watching nothing.

Then he stood, dusted his pants, and walked back. This had to end.

That evening, the three of them sat on overturned crates. A larger old shipping box served as a table. The makeshift kitchen sat in a corner near the hallway that led to the rooms where Deacon and Giles slept. The cracked concrete floor was stained dark in spots with grease. A small cast-iron stove squatted against the wall several feet away, its stovepipe vented through a rusted hole cut in the sheet-metal siding. A dented coffee pot sat simmering on top, and a battered skillet crackled with chopped meat and potatoes.

Deacon hadn't said a word since the incident, and neither Joseph Henry nor Giles attempted to get him to. Since it was often Deacon who made small talk, the table was uncomfortably silent.

He got up and spooned more food onto his plate, then sat again. He didn't commence eating. He held his utensils firmly in his hands looking at the plate.

"I learned a lot when I was in college," he said softly, eyes on his food. "Apparently, I didn't learn much about when to shut up and listen... and learn."

Joseph Henry kept chewing.

Deacon looked up at Joseph Henry. "You could've called me out," he added. "Could have made me look small, proved a point. Tried to drill it into me."

Joseph Henry kept chewing.

Giles snorted softly into his spoon. "I done told Mr. Henry you'd stop bein' an ass on your own."

Deacon got a stern look. Then gave a snort and a short laugh. "Fair enough," he finally said. "I do apologize. I have been an ass. I was brought here under certain pretenses. Those didn't work out. Fault doesn't matter, but it certainly isn't your fault Mr. Henry. Where I come from," he added quietly, "men don't admit error easily. Pride runs deep, sometimes deeper than good sense."

They all nodded and then sat in silence for a while.

Joseph Henry leaned back from the table. "My father once tried to push a hot mash through cheesecloth. Said he didn't have time to let it settle. Blew out an entire run trying to save time. Took three days to clean the damn thing out."

"What'd he do?"

"Blamed me. I was twelve."

Giles gave a low whistle.

"He wasn't wrong," Joseph Henry said. "But it stuck."

"You learn all this from him?" Deacon asked. "Or just from time?"

"Bit of both," Joseph Henry said. "But mostly from getting it wrong first."

Deacon looked at him a long moment, something softer in his eyes. "I can see it now, why Boss Van picked you."

Joseph Henry didn't respond.

Deacon stood, brushed his hands. "We'll get it right tomorrow."

"We will," Joseph Henry said.

Giles finished his stew and smiled. "Guess that's that, then. 'Bout time too."

They laughed, and realized they were doing it together.

The setback was behind them. Not forgotten, but absorbed. Like smoke in wood. So was the relationship.

As they scraped their bowls clean, Giles's head perked up. "Half past dusk now, Mr. Henry. Best you be headin' back."

"Don't need 'Mr.' or 'sir,' Giles. Just Joseph."

Deacon stood, but hesitated. "What you said about the coils… listening rather than waiting. That isn't something you find in a manual."

Joseph Henry tilted his head. "Lot of things you can't read your way into. Most of it actually."

"Quite right." Deacon rubbed his head. "I needed to be knocked down a peg… Joseph… thank you for not doing it with cricket bat."

Joseph Henry got a perplexed look, "a what now?"

Deacon and Giles laughed, then Deacon turned to Giles, "Thanks for shoveling out my mess."

Giles shrugged, grinning. "Didn't trouble me none. Was good seein' your clever self brought down a notch, I won't lie."

The three walked to the sliding door, which Deacon slid open. As Joseph headed towards the truck, Deacon and Giles lingered.

"You think folk ever believe good whiskey come from a place like this?" Giles said.

Joseph Henry let out a soft breath. "Don't care what they believe," he said as he climbed into the cab. "Long as they buy it."

Deacon and Giles watched the truck roll away.

Chapter 16
1929

The truck rattled over a stretch of gravel, the sound of it thinning as they crested the last rise before the county line. It wasn't often that deliveries were made on a Saturday, but it happened now and then. That morning Joseph Henry was off to deliver two loads. The first was to Eli Sparks's place, a feed store out near Perryville. It was about as far as they ever went, except for Louisville. Deacon came along for the ride.

Joseph Henry liked Saturday runs. They were quiet. That morning they hadn't passed more than three or four vehicles, even going through Lawrenceburg and Harrodsburg.

The delivery went well. Despite the long ride, Joseph Henry knew it was always an easy one. Eli never let him do any heavy lifting, instead sending his boys out to bring in the casks. Joseph Henry wasn't sure where the liquor finally wound up, but the feed store didn't look like it could be used as a speakeasy. It didn't matter to him. They were good people, and he was glad to see them doing well. As far as he knew, Eli was the only one in that part of the county supplying hooch to the locals, so business was probably good.

Joseph Henry eased off the throttle and brought the truck to the shoulder where a stand of poplars stood near a shallow ditch. Deacon climbed out and stretched his back, hands on his hips, squinting toward some cows in a field across the road.

They had left Eli Sparks's place about a half hour before, and both were ready for lunch. Joseph Henry had driven the route a dozen times and always made the stop there like clockwork. He cut the engine, let the ticking of the manifold fade, and reached behind the seat for his lunch sack.

Deacon joined him by the fender. They ate standing at first, then settled into the grass. Joseph Henry unwrapped a neat parcel of food from brown paper: two cold biscuits with ham and a boiled egg tucked between them. The bread was firm, but not stale, the meat salty with the tang of a week's age. He ate carefully, brushing away crumbs, habit more than need.

Deacon's lunch was looser, wrapped in waxed paper that smelled faintly of grease. He had a thigh of cold fried chicken, a biscuit broken in half, and a small jar of pickled okra. He speared one with his pocketknife and ate it slow, nodding to the flavor.

Joseph Henry poured coffee from the thermos, the steam curling against the chill breeze. They drank in turns, neither in a hurry.

For a while, they ate without talking. Deacon watched a redbird land on a fence post across the road. Somewhere a tractor coughed to life.

"You know," Deacon said at last with a soft smile, "I didn't like you much at first, Joseph."

Joseph Henry glanced up from his lunch. "Is that right?"

"Didn't care for the way you came in, looking as if you knew everything already. Thought you'd be another one of those men just trying to impress."

Joseph Henry chewed, nodded once. "Maybe I did know everything," he said, and laughed.

Deacon grinned a little. "Funny thing is, I didn't stop disliking you for quite a while. Even after I knew you were better at it than the rest of us."

Joseph Henry gave a quiet snort. "Didn't like you much either, Deacon."

Deacon's grin widened. "Yeah, I figured as much." He plucked a blade of grass, twirled it between his fingers. "One night, I remember it clear, the pressure line split under the lower coil. Giles went to pieces, the mash was everywhere. He thought you were going to take his head off. You didn't. You just grabbed a wrench and went down there yourself. Didn't have to. Could've let it blow and blamed me or Giles after."

Joseph Henry finished the last bite of biscuit and dusted his hands.

"After that," Deacon continued, "I realized it didn't much matter. It stopped feeling like we worked for you. Started feeling like three men running something together."

Joseph Henry smiled faintly.

Deacon took a drink from the coffee thermos and offered it back to Joseph Henry. "When did it turn for you?"

Joseph Henry met his eye, still smiling. "Didn't say it did."

Deacon laughed quietly and shook his head. They sat a while longer, the wind picking up and moving through the poplars. Then they got up and climbed back into the truck.

The second stop was closer to home, but it operated in the mornings, even on Saturdays, so fitting it in after lunch on the return trip was just fine.

The H-B Creamery sat along Benson Valley Road, a small dairy tucked between hills and pastures. The route took them off the main roads they had followed down to Perryville and onto the narrower trails that ran southwest of Frankfort.

Fields stretched out in both directions, fading toward the tree lines. Neither man had spoken for a while. Joseph Henry sipped what was left of the coffee. It had gone cold, and he tossed the rest out the window. He turned to Deacon, expecting a remark, but the other man just sat with one arm on the window frame and the other resting across his knee. His face had gone thoughtful, eyes fixed on the road, or maybe just on the hood.

"You okay there, Deacon?" Joseph Henry said, returning his eyes to the road.

Deacon blinked, as if waking. "Just thinking, Joseph."

"'bout anything in particular?"

Deacon's eyes stayed forward. He didn't say anything.

"Sorry. Don't mean to pry."

Deacon slowly turned and looked at him. "I've been thinking about going home."

Joseph Henry glanced over again. "To Barbados? Going to visit family?"

"No," he said. "Not for a visit."

Joseph Henry looked over at him, wondering if he was missing a joke. His gaze lingered a moment too long, and Deacon nodded toward the road ahead. Joseph Henry snapped his attention forward just in time to see the truck had drifted left. He tightened his grip on the wheel and eased it back into line.

Deacon gave a faint smile. "Don't wreck us, Joseph."

Joseph Henry steadied the wheel and glanced his way again. "Didn't expect that," he said.

"Yes, I understand," Deacon said. He leaned his head back and looked at the ceiling of the truck. He let out a long breath. "I don't have much of a life here."

Joseph Henry snuck another glance.

"Don't get me wrong, Joseph. I love the work, what the three of us built here… it's a good thing. Feels like it belongs to us more than to anyone else."

Joseph Henry nodded, saying nothing.

"But outside of it," Deacon went on, "there's not much. A man needs something to look forward to. Something to… go home to. I live at the still." He paused, eyes back on the road ahead. "And for Giles, it's worse."

Joseph Henry frowned. "How do you mean?"

Deacon was quiet a long moment before he answered. "You and me, we can move around. We can walk into town, buy a meal, talk to whoever we like. Giles doesn't get that."

Joseph Henry frowned. "I have'ta disagree, Deacon. Seems to me Giles has it better than most. He's got good work, respectable work, and he makes more than plenty of white men I've known. He's free to come and go as he pleases. Doesn't sound bad to me."

Deacon didn't answer right away. The road curved alongside a crick on the left, then crossed an old wooden bridge that creaked under the truck's weight.

"That's how it looks to you, and I understand," he said at last. "I don't fault you for thinking it."

"You think I'm wrong?"

Deacon paused and pressed his lips together, as though choosing his words with care. "You're not wrong, Joseph. You just cannot see it."

Joseph Henry's jaw tightened. "I do see it. I worked for what I've got, even where I am. Same as anyone could who works hard."

Deacon shook his head slowly. "That is the thing. You believe every man has the same chances. Joseph, you may be the most color-blind man I have met here, but that does not make it so. You and I, we can walk into town and be taken for men, nothing more. Nobody stops us. Nobody asks what right we've got to be there. Giles can't do that. It doesn't matter what he's earned, or how hard he's worked. He is still what they see when he walks through the door, and they will remind him of it, with words or worse… the moment they think he's forgotten his place."

Joseph Henry said nothing.

Deacon's voice stayed even, almost gentle. "Tell me this, Joseph. If Giles walked up to your front door and asked to see your sister…"

Joseph Henry began to object, but Deacon kept on. "It does not matter if you truly have a sister. What do you reckon would happen? What would your father have done? Your neighbor? Even if they did nothing, what would be in their minds?"

Joseph Henry blinked, still staring at the road ahead.

Deacon kept his tone low. "That is what I mean. You never had to actually think about it. Your world has done it for you."

The truck hit a rut, the jolt small but sharp. Joseph Henry's hands tightened on the wheel.

He opened his mouth slightly, but he couldn't find a thing to say.

Joseph Henry cleared his throat. "You and Giles, you'd be missed."

Deacon looked over and smiled.

Joseph Henry kept his eyes on the road. "I couldn't run the place half as well without you two." He paused a moment. "And I expect Boss Van might have a problem with the decision."

Deacon gave a low chuckle. "Boss Van doesn't think much about what happens below his line of sight. He will notice only when the barrels stop moving, not before."

Joseph Henry's brow furrowed. "Not sure about that. Even so, you've both been good for the still. It'd be hard to see it change."

Deacon looked back toward the fields. "For now it's only a thought, Joseph. Nothing more than that. If it ever happens, it won't be soon."

Joseph Henry said quietly, "I'm glad to hear that."

They rode on, the sound of the tires the only thing breaking the stillness. The road leveled, and through the trees ahead the white roof of the creamery came into view.

The truck slowed as they approached a wooden gate that stood open. The smell of milk and damp hay hung in the air, mixed with the earthiness of cows and manure. There was something clean in it, Joseph Henry thought, breathing through the open window, something natural. The milky, nutty scent of the place was nothing like the foul mix of coal smoke and wet brick in the city, or the sharp lime and sweat of the penitentiary. This was a newer stop for him, and he liked it. The air felt alive in a way many places no longer did.

They passed through the gate and saw a few wagons standing by a loading shed, horses still hitched, tails flicking at flies. Steam or light smoke drifted from vent pipes on the creamery roof, curling against the afternoon sun. Somewhere a churn was running, a steady rhythm low and hollow, like a heartbeat through the buildings around them, though not clear which ones.

Deacon was taking in the scenery. "Peaceful spot," he said.

Joseph Henry nodded, a content look on his face. He began to say something, then stopped. Deacon looked at him and saw his face change to a frown. He looked ahead to see the cause.

A dark car waited by the loading dock, a Packard, long and heavy, with the feel of the city on it, or money. It didn't belong here, not among the wagons and churns, and the sight of it was jarring.

Joseph Henry felt them before he even saw them, the men standing beside it.

There were two of them. One stood by the open bay door, talking to someone just inside. The other leaned against the front fender of the Packard, chewing on a toothpick.

The one at the door wore a dark suit that fit well enough but carried the dust of travel, his hat tilted back just enough to look casual without meaning to. The one by the car was dressed rougher, shirt sleeves rolled, vest unbuttoned, his hat likely left inside the Packard, looking ready to move something if the need came.

Joseph Henry slowed the truck and let it roll to a stop on the gravel across from the Packard.

"Listen carefully, Deacon," he said, watching the scene. "Take off your jacket and roll up your sleeves. Wait about two minutes, then get out. There's a Winchester behind the seat. Take it and come around to the other side. Lean against the fender and lay the rifle up beside you. Look casual. Stare across that field." He pointed off to the right.

Deacon suddenly looked nervous. His jaw flexed once, a habit from his father back on the island. Joseph Henry recognized it and gave him a confident smile.

"Don't worry," he said. "Just going to get rid of the riffraff."

Deacon returned a weaker smile and nodded. Joseph Henry opened the door and strode across the path. The man doing the talking turned, smiling as though he'd been waiting on them. The man against the Packard stood up straight.

"Afternoon," the first called. "Didn't mean to take up your man's time here. Just a little business talk."

"That business would be?" Joseph Henry said, a smile in his voice.

The man hesitated, not expecting a delivery driver to be asking about his business. Then he tipped his hat. "Name's Clem Rush. My partner, Virgil Pope," he said, indicating the other, who didn't nod. "We work under Ed Levinson. Big man in the trade. He's making sure folks along this road stay…" he paused and looked towards the sky, "safe. Wants to keep things running smooth."

Joseph Henry studied him. "Levinson… Isn't he out of Detroit? Long way from here."

Rush smiled but suddenly looked uncertain. A bead of sweat appeared on his brow. He hadn't expected the name to be known. "He's opening offices up in Newport. In Campbell County," he added as if needing to make it sound closer. "Across the Ohio from Cincinnati. Not so far."

Joseph Henry chuckled and folded his arms. "And what is it you're offering?"

The man inside the bay door finally stepped out and came to stand beside Joseph Henry, as though the conversation had become a negotiation and he needed to be part of it.

"Afternoon, Howard," Joseph Henry said, not taking his eyes off Rush.

Rush's smile returned, and he spoke with new confidence. "Nothing more than a little," he paused as if for effect, "insurance. Roads out this way can be rough. Trucks go missing. Deliveries delayed. Mr. Levinson likes to see good operations stay," he paused again, "protected."

Joseph Henry nodded once, as if considering it. Then he said, "I doubt Mr. Levinson knows where Harrodsburg is."

Rush's smile wavered. "Now, mister…"

As if on cue, Joseph Henry heard the truck door open. He saw Rush's face drop as Deacon walked around the truck with the rifle.

Joseph Henry took a slow step closer. "You come here throwing a name around and see who flinches. Next time, pick a name that won't make a man laugh if he hears you use it."

Virgil Pope straightened from the Packard, but Joseph Henry's calm stare stopped him cold. He looked at Rush, unsure what to do.

"Mr. Benson here has arrangements with Boss Van," Joseph Henry said. He saw Rush stiffen. "No trucks will go missing. No deliveries will be delayed." He looked back at Virgil Pope, then again at Rush. "Believe me, Clem Rush and Virgil Pope, it won't be Ed Levinson that Boss Van goes looking for."

Rush stammered, "Look mister, we don't…"

"Now, we've got a delivery to make," Joseph Henry cut him off. "You boys should be on your way."

Rush stood there for a moment, then adjusted his hat. He seemed to be trying to recover his grin. "Of course. You seem to already have what you need. We're really just offering our services, in case they're needed."

Joseph Henry laughed once. "Sure…" Then he turned dismissively and faced Howard Benson. "Where can we unload the truck, Howard?"

Howard Benson smiled, relief plain on his face. "Oh you don't need to worry about that Mr. Henry. I'll get my boys out here to take care of it." He looked at Rush and Pope for a moment, then turned and went back inside through the bay door.

After a moment, Rush touched his brim again, motioned to Virgil, and they both climbed back into the Packard. The engine coughed to life, and the car backed down the lane and out the gate.

Deacon let out a slow breath as it disappeared down the road. For a moment he watched the dust settle, then looked toward Joseph Henry.

"I don't believe I've ever seen you like that," he said.

Joseph Henry didn't answer, he just shrugged. Deacon saw a look on his face, like the last of a man's drive was melting away.

Deacon gave a brief nod, not entirely believing what he'd seen from Joseph Henry. "They seemed to take you at your word."

Joseph Henry looked up at him as if he just realized he was talking. He gauged the words. "Glad they did. Wouldn't have liked to go further."

Deacon wasn't sure he'd heard the last part right but was fine not knowing.

Howard Benson stepped out again through the bay door, wiping his hands on a rag. Two young men followed behind him and started for the truck.

"Mr. Henry," Benson said. "I can't thank you enough. Never seen folks like that before, though I'd heard stories. Didn't figure we had anyone really looking out for us."

Joseph Henry gave a short nod. "Well, you do. Just keep things steady. You'll do fine."

Benson smiled, still a little giddy now that the danger had passed. "We will. The creamery's doing fine, and we're opening the night room next week. Private hours. You and your man ought to come by. Boss Van too, if he cares to visit."

Deacon lifted an eyebrow. "A speakeasy? Here?"

Benson chuckled. "Nothing so fancy. This isn't Chicago, or even Louisville. More like just an after-hours place. Let some folks blow off a little steam. No harm in some good company when the doors are closed."

Joseph Henry's mouth curved faintly. "We'll see." Deacon seemed interested, a trace of amusement in his eyes.

Benson nodded, still smiling. "You really ought to."

In truth, Joseph Henry was very interested. He had been working the still and making deliveries for quite a time, but he had never seen the other side of things. He wondered if Boss Van would even allow it.

After the truck was unloaded, Joseph Henry and Deacon stood for a moment. The air smelled of milk and hay and cows and manure, as though nothing had happened at all. Howard Benson came out again and handed a large envelope to Joseph Henry. He thanked him. And the two men climbed back into the truck and headed back for the main road.

Chapter 17
1929

Joseph Henry steered the truck along the narrow lane that cut between dark fields, the engine giving a steady hum beneath him. The ride seemed entirely different from the ones he had made along the same route during daylight hours. The night was cool and empty, with only the occasional line of trees drifting by in silhouette. The vast fields swallowed what little light the moon and stars offered, turning everything beyond the reach of the headlights into a blanket of black. Joseph Henry looked at the silhouettes and wondered how they could stand out so sharply when there was so little light to cast them. Deacon sat silently on the passenger side with his hat low, watching the road ahead, just a narrow tunnel carved out by the headlamps.

A couple of days earlier Joseph Henry had left a note for Boss Van:

Delivered to new client H-B Creamery. They hold gatherings at night. Benson has asked us to visit. If agreeable, I would like to attend one evening. I think it would be good to better understand the places that buy from us. Please advise.

—JH

There had been no answer, but it wasn't the sort of thing that weighed on him. Boss Van replied when he saw fit, and silence often meant the matter did not concern him much. Joseph Henry decided it was simple enough to just go. If it turned out to be a mistake he would accept whatever followed.

Joseph Henry had asked Deacon and Giles to come along. Deacon already seemed interested after Howard Benson had asked them to come around. Joseph Henry hadn't noticed the slightest hesitation in him when Giles was invited. Giles, however, politely declined, offering a small smile and saying, "Thank you, sir. Long day today. Think I'll pass," as he rubbed his stiff hands. Joseph Henry thought nothing of it at the time. Giles did look worn, and the heat in the shop had been heavy that day.

As the truck rolled away from the still, Joseph Henry found himself thinking about the talk he had shared with Deacon on the road during their last visit to the creamery. It wasn't the words themselves, but the way they had settled in him afterward, uneven and uncomfortable, as though he had been looking at things with the wrong eyes, not seeing clearly what was in front of him. The thought stayed with him now, and it made Giles's decision to stay behind sit differently.

Fatigue could have been part of it, but Joseph Henry understood now that Giles saw things like he never could. The realization came quiet and unforced, like something he should have known already.

"Giles wasn't really all that tired," Joseph Henry said flatly. It wasn't a question.

Deacon glanced over. "No, he didn't think this was the right place for him."

Joseph Henry nodded, and Deacon gave a small nod of his own.

Far ahead, just visible between the branches, the outline of the creamery came into view, dark against the sky. For a moment Joseph Henry wondered if he was in the right place. Then he noticed a faint glow slipping through the vents near the roof. He saw the silhouettes of cars parked haphazardly in a wooded patch away from the main building. Deacon pointed toward a dark opening between the trees, and Joseph Henry eased the truck into it and shut off the engine.

The heaviness of his earlier thoughts fell back as they climbed out of the truck, replaced by a small spark of excitement. He hadn't thought much of what became of the work they did, and now he was eager to see it for himself.

The night air was cool for the time of year, and the smell of damp earth rose as Joseph Henry shut the door behind him. He picked up a faint sourness, no doubt the remnants of the morning's production beginning to turn. For a moment he stood still, letting his eyes adjust. The main building stood ahead, a long dark shape against the sky, broken only by a faint sliver of moonlight above the roof line. Somewhere inside there was the muted thrum of voices, distant and muffled, a sound that felt out of place in a building that looked otherwise abandoned for the night.

Deacon stepped around the front of the truck and joined him. Neither man spoke. The moment carried a quiet secrecy neither wanted to break. They moved with careful steps, avoiding gravel and dry leaves that might betray their presence. The sound of activity grew as they neared the building, though it stayed distant and muffled.

When they reached the side of the building, they paused. The bay door was shut tight, likely bolted from the inside. No light slipped through the seams. Other than the soft murmur coming from within, the place seemed as still as any empty warehouse.

Deacon gave a small nod toward the far corner, and Joseph Henry followed.

They rounded the far corner of the building. Its long side wall rose up beside them, a broad stretch of weathered boards. The moon caught the metal fixtures here and there, giving them a dull shine. Deacon pointed at the ground, where a mishmash of footprints littered the soft earth where rain had settled earlier that morning.

Joseph Henry's eyes followed them to a narrow door tucked back into a shallow recess, almost hidden by a stack of old milk crates and a boarded-up window. It was an entrance someone could walk past in daylight if they didn't know it was there.

A faint thread of light showed along the bottom edge of the door. Deacon's smile widened in the moonlight. He caught Joseph Henry looking at him and suddenly looked self-conscious.

"Forgive me, Joseph," Deacon whispered. "This is all too exciting."

Joseph Henry gave a soft laugh. "Not to worry, Deacon. It's too new to me also."

Joseph Henry went to rap on the door, but hesitated, listening. The murmur inside was strong here. It wasn't the wild sound of rowdy men but something steadier, low and warm; a blend of laughter, quiet talk, and the occasional scrape of a chair. Deeper in the building he was certain he could hear the thin, wavering edge of a fiddle trying to carry over the voices.

Deacon saw Joseph Henry hesitate. He stepped up beside him and reached out, rapping twice on the door with the back of his knuckles before stepping back behind Joseph Henry. Joseph Henry gave another laugh, seeing Deacon almost unable to contain his excitement.

Nothing stirred at first, though the building seemed to settle in front of them. The sound within did not cease, but it may have lulled the slightest bit. Joseph Henry felt the night air cool against his neck. He glanced back at Deacon, who only shifted his weight and gave a brief shrug.

Both men jumped when the latch clicked.

The door cracked open a finger's width. A sliver of bright lamplight spilled out, cutting a line across Joseph Henry's boots. Benson's voice came through before his face did.

"Who's there?"

Joseph Henry leaned closer. He whispered loudly, "Howard? It's Joseph Henry."

The gap widened, and Howard Benson's face came into view, brimming with a grin. His hat was pushed back on his head, and the glow from the light behind him threw soft shadows into the lines around his eyes. He broke into a toothy smile when he recognized the two at the door.

"Mr. Henry, well now," Benson said, pulling the door wider with one hand. "Didn't think you'd be taking me up on my invitation." He squinted past Joseph Henry. "Who's that with you? Did Boss Van come along?"

Joseph Henry was about to respond, but when Benson saw only Deacon behind him he waved a hand. "Oh, never mind, come on in." He began to open the door wider for them, then paused. "Hold on."

His face shifted into an exaggerated look of suspicion. With an almost theatrical motion he looked the two men over, then leaned in a bit, raising his eyebrows.

"Password?" he asked in a conspiratorial whisper.

Joseph Henry blinked and opened his mouth. "I…" He turned to see Deacon, who just stared back, deadpan, unsure of the protocol.

Benson held the moment a beat longer, then let out a bellowing laugh. He pushed the door wide open and motioned again for them to enter. "I'm only foolin' with you. This ain't no speakeasy. Come on in before somebody sees you standin' out there like you're tryin' to sell something."

He stepped aside, sweeping them in with an almost grand gesture.

As Joseph Henry crossed the threshold, the warmth inside washed over him, and he was assaulted by a mix of lamp heat, tobacco smoke, and the pungent smell of spilled whiskey. The murmur of voices unfolded into the fuller sound of laughter and conversation.

Benson closed the door behind them and guided them forward with a not-so-light touch on Joseph Henry's arm. Warm air met them at once. The heat from the lamps, mixed with the press of bodies, was mildly oppressive. Tobacco smoke hung in the air, thin at first, then thicker as they moved farther inside. The room carried the faint tang of whiskey that had worked its way into the floorboards over several nights since Benson had begun opening after hours.

Voices overlapped in steady waves. Nothing loud or unruly, more a comfortable sound of men letting the day fall away. The lamps cast uneven pools of light across tables and benches, leaving the far corners in quiet shadow. Most of the furnishings looked repurposed or borrowed from Benson's house. Few chairs matched, and the rest seemed to have been collected from wherever he could find them.

Benson led them through the crowd at an easy pace. Several men glanced their way, some curious, others giving Benson a familiar nod. Joseph Henry felt, more than saw, the way the room measured new arrivals. It was not suspicion so much as habit, a quiet acknowledgment that anyone who entered ought to fit in. The thought brought Giles to mind.

As they reached the far side of the room Joseph Henry saw that a plank had been set across two barrels to serve as a counter, with a line of jugs and bottles behind it, some stoppered and some not. A large cask sat back against the wall. A tin box rested near the middle of the plank. Behind it, the man tending the counter poured a drink as Benson approached with Joseph Henry and Deacon.

"First one is on me," Benson said, pride showing plainly in his face. He glanced at their empty hands and smiled. "Most folks bring their own jar or cup. We can't keep up with washing them, and I wouldn't try if I could." He bent down and pulled out two mason jars, placing them on the counter. "These will do you fine this time."

Joseph Henry accepted his with a quiet nod. Deacon lifted his jar and looked at it with a smile, as though somehow it made the moment more real for him.

"Five cents for most pours," Benson said, tapping the jugs to the left with his knuckles. "Ten for the good stuff, your stuff." He indicated the cask and some jugs to the right. "Folks don't mind paying for it."

Joseph Henry nodded, a faint tug of pride.

Benson reached for one of the jugs on the right and held it up a little. "This should seem familiar," he said, and poured a careful measure into Joseph Henry's and Deacon's mason jars. The whiskey shone a deep gold in the lamplight. Joseph Henry brought the jar to his nose before tasting it. The familiar scent met him at once, warm and clean, the way they worked for it to be. He took a sip and let it settle on his tongue before giving an appreciative nod.

"Now, help yourselves to some food if you like," Benson said. He pointed to a table near the wall where plates of biscuits, slices of cold ham, and pickled eggs had been set out. A metal can sat in the center with a handwritten note that simply said, *Help with cost.* "My wife made all that. Folks chip in."

They watched a few men drift up to the table, dropping coins in the can before helping themselves.

Over in the corner a man sat on a low stool, a fiddle tucked under his chin and resting against his shoulder. The bow moved in steady uneven strokes. His foot tapped in quick, rough beats as the tune worked its way through the room. Every so often a penny was left at his boot, and now and then someone would pour a splash of whiskey from their cup into his.

Nearby, at a table toward the center, several men were playing cards. It appeared to be five-card draw. Small stacks of coins sat in front of them. Their faces were intent but friendly, the stakes clearly modest. Deacon watched the game with a calm familiarity. He had played it often in Barbados long before coming to Kentucky, and the look on his face suggested he remembered the game well.

He leaned close to Joseph Henry. "If you do not mind, Joseph, I think I will try my hand."

Joseph Henry gave a small nod. "Don't lose too much," he said with a wry smile.

Deacon did not answer. He stepped toward the table, a focused look already on his face. One of the men slid a chair outward for him with his boot. Deacon sat and greeted them with a polite nod.

Joseph Henry turned as the fiddle music shifted. Another man had joined the first with a guitar. After a few bars the two of them moved into a tune he knew, "Cluck Old Hen." By the end of the first stanza several voices around the room had joined in.

"My old hen's a good old hen,

She lays eggs for the railroad men.

Sometimes eight and sometimes ten,

Cluck old hen, cluck and then."

Joseph Henry knew the song. He had not heard it since his wedding. All those years. Something in him went still at the memory.

Joseph Henry turned away, momentarily lost in thought, and walked straight into a man returning from the counter with a fresh refill. He struck him hard enough to slosh whiskey from the man's jar onto his shirt and the floor. Joseph Henry looked up to see the man, broad in the shoulders and unsteady on his feet, likely not needing the additional drink. The man's eyes narrowed as he looked at the whiskey on his shirt, then at Joseph Henry.

"Watch yourself," the man said, the words slurring into each other.

Joseph Henry steadied the man by the elbow without thinking. "My fault. My mind was elsewhere."

The man shook off his hand. "Mind it someplace else," he said, taking a half step forward, shoulders squaring as though he had not yet decided whether to swing or simply hold his balance.

Joseph Henry knew the look from the penitentiary. The man was sitting on the edge between bluster and something meaner.

The man made up his mind, and his right arm twitched forward, the beginning of a swing. Before it could move six inches Benson was suddenly at his side. He caught the man's arm lightly. "Easy now," Benson said, his voice light but firm. He pulled a cloth from his back pocket and began dabbing at the man's shirt. "Spill happens. No need to make more of it."

The man blinked and let him work, still glaring at Joseph Henry. "He ran into me."

"And he owned it," Benson said, still calm. "Come on. Let's step outside a minute."

For a moment it looked as though the man might push back, but then Joseph Henry saw the fight drain from his face. "Fine," he muttered.

Benson kept a steady hand on him as they moved toward the door, his tone gentle enough to keep the man from bristling again. At the threshold Benson opened the door and let him step out, then gave him a firmer push into the night before closing the door behind him.

He turned back to Joseph Henry, his expression composed. "Don't mind him. He's not a bad sort before he goes past his limit."

He stayed close to Joseph Henry the remainder of the night, guiding him from one knot of men to another with an easy, familiar manner. Joseph Henry could not tell whether Benson was keeping an eye on him after the trouble or simply taking pride in showing him around. Either way, he stayed at Joseph Henry's elbow, talking as though nothing at all had happened.

At each table Benson made introductions. "This here is Mr. Henry," he said more than once, a hand on Joseph Henry's shoulder. "Brings in the good stuff you all keep drinking." Men nodded, some with genuine interest. Some offered quiet handshakes, others just tipped their jars in acknowledgment. A few looked up when Benson mentioned Boss Van's name, the brief unspoken pause when a name with weight enters a conversation. Not exactly reverence, not quite caution, just a respectful awareness folks have around someone who can get things done but you don't want to cross. Joseph Henry sensed their regard settle on him as well. He knew it wasn't warranted, but he stayed silent.

Joseph Henry kept his responses modest, which seemed to please the room. The men treated him like a professional, not a spectacle. Benson never let the mood dip, keeping a steady thread of conversation going. He told small stories about work crews, weather complaints, and bits of local gossip. Nothing pointed, just easy.

As the night wound down the crowd thinned. Men drifted toward the exit with loose farewells, a few nods, and some murmured grunts. A few clapped Joseph Henry lightly on the back as they passed. Benson poured him one last drink, and Joseph Henry accepted it. He felt the warmth of the whiskey, but only a mild pull from it.

He started toward the card table to find Deacon. Deacon had gathered a modest pile of coins and looked thoroughly pleased. One of the players looked up and grinned. "Hope you're taking him home," he said to Joseph Henry, half-joking. Another man added with a laugh, "Good timing. He's been stealing our coin all night."

Deacon slid the coins into his pocket and stood, giving the table a small bow of the head. "Thank you, gentlemen. Perhaps we can do this again." The others grumbled in good humor, then laughed and said good night.

The two men crossed the room to where Benson stood near the door. Benson opened it for them, the night air drifting in cool and clean. "You two come around again," he said. "You're welcome any time."

Deacon gave a sincere nod. "Thank you. It was a pleasant night."

Joseph Henry hesitated, then said quietly, "Won't be something I can do often. But I'm glad we came."

Benson smiled in understanding. "Sometimes once in a while is enough."

Joseph Henry stepped out into the cool night, gave a look back and nodded, then let the door close behind him.

Chapter 18
1889 – 1898

The stone walls sweated with moisture. A narrow window, high above, let in a slanted beam of afternoon light. A small stove in the corner gave off less heat than was needed.

Minnie stood just outside the iron-barred door. She held a tin with both hands, wrapped in a dish cloth she'd had for some time, now faded to a color between cream and gray, with a light pink pattern that had once been red. A guard unlatched the door and motioned her inside. She stepped forward without speaking.

She was anxious. It had been more than three months since she'd last seen Joseph Henry. The first ninety days were often closed to visitors. Inmates had to earn the right through good behavior and steady work. After that, there were more delays. Letters exchanged. Permissions granted. Days lost to silence. Requests and communication were done through the mail, which moved brutally slow.

Now, finally, she was here.

Minnie saw that Joseph Henry was already seated on the other side of a mesh partition. The wire was taut, a dull gray darkened by age and flecked with rust. The openings were small, no more than half an inch, casting a faint haze across the person behind it. It wasn't meant for seeing. It was meant to keep anything from passing through. It separated two benches, each one bolted to the floor. A single guard leaned against the far wall, arms folded, watching.

She slowly walked to the bench and sat, stiffly. Her skirt rustled as she adjusted herself, and she cleared her throat. She tried to smile, but it didn't land. It looked practiced, unconvincing. Like a ribbon tied around an empty box.

Joseph Henry took in her visage. She looked tired, but upright. There were faint bags under her eyes, and a few strands of hair had worked loose near her temple. She wore no hat, though it looked as if she had until recently. Her gloves were mismatched, one white, the other a light cream. He wondered if she knew. She held the tin at her side, pressed against her skirt. She looked thinner than he remembered. But she was still Minnie.

Joseph Henry gave his thin smile. "Minnie…"

He instinctively reached toward her and was stopped by the mesh.

"Can't be doing that, Henry," said the guard. He didn't sound angry, only practical. Like someone reminding a child not to touch a hot stove.

Joseph Henry retracted his hand. "Sorry, Dennis."

Minnie wasn't surprised that Joseph Henry was already familiar with the guards.

They sat in silence for a moment. Minnie glanced back and forth between Joseph Henry and the guard.

"It's alright, Minnie," he said.

Minnie put her hands on her legs and squeezed. She breathed once and tried the smile again.

"I brought cornbread," she said quickly. "The sweet kind."

He made himself keep still. "Thank you."

She held up the tin awkwardly and glanced at the guard. He stepped forward, took it from her hands, opened it. He inspected the cloth, pinched the corner of a slice, and gave it a theatrical sniff.

"Smells good," he said, giving Minnie a friendly smile. "Might require a second opinion, though." He looked over at Joseph Henry with a half-grin.

Joseph Henry didn't return it.

"How's your mother?" he asked.

"She's well enough. Still fussing over the garden, though it's gone mostly to seed."

He nodded.

"Your ma and pa are managing," she continued, as though he had asked the question. "Samuel's been keeping busy with the shop."

Joseph Henry glanced at the guard, then back to Minnie. "They've got me in laundry for now. Not bad, really. Warm enough. I don't expect it to last."

Minnie nodded. "That sounds fine."

The words sounded strange in the air. She wasn't sure what she meant by them.

He continued. "Food's passable. Company's quiet. I've been trying to meet people."

Minnie smoothed the cloth on her lap. "That sounds like you."

They both gave the smallest of smiles, and then they were quiet again.

A voice called from the far end of the room. One of the guards was letting someone else know their time was up. Minnie felt a sudden urgency. She pressed her hands tighter.

Joseph Henry seemed to sense it too.

"I know. It's alright."

The room was colder now. The warmth from the stove seemed to have stopped trying at all.

Dennis coughed softly, still leaning against the wall. "Time's winding down, folks."

Minnie stood. She leaned toward the mesh, then thought better of it. She looked at Joseph Henry.

"I'll write," she said.

"I know."

"I'll be back next month."

Joseph Henry gave another thin smile.

She adjusted her gloves, suddenly noticing they didn't match. She blushed, almost smiled, then looked away.

Joseph Henry gave a short laugh.

Minnie turned and walked toward the exit. Her boots echoed on the stone floor, each step ringing slightly behind her. She didn't look back.

Joseph Henry sat still, watching for a while after she went through the door. The guard didn't say anything else.

***

By the third visit, the room had become familiar. So had the process. Minnie began mailing requests for several visits ahead almost as soon as she returned from the first visit.

She wore the same shawl each time. Joseph Henry began to recognize its color in the doorway before he saw her face. Her gloves were always matching.

The tin of baked goods had become expected, especially by the guard on duty. Often it was Dennis, though sometimes it was someone else. Either way, there would be a comment, just light enough to pass as a joke, usually about keeping it for themselves. Minnie would respond by telling them to go ahead and take a piece. She had started packing extra after the first visit.

Minnie sat a little easier, though her hands remained clasped in her lap when she wasn't speaking. Joseph Henry kept his down too, careful not to reach toward the mesh again.

He would ask about the weather. She might tell him about a fox that got into the neighbor's chickens.

They never talked about the future. They rarely talked about the past.

Joseph Henry only gave his thin smile when her voice sometimes caught in the middle of a sentence and didn't come back.

***

In the second year it had become a kind of happy rhythm.

Minnie got good at writing ahead to schedule visits. The office clerks now recognized her name before they opened the envelope. The guards greeted her when she arrived, as if she were a piece of their routine too. She often made up the tins days in advance, sometimes as part of larger batches she could share with her parents or the Henrys. She wrapped them in newer dishcloths now, ones she'd been given over the holidays.

Some visits she came with her hair pinned up in ways Joseph Henry hadn't seen before. Some days she brought something different in the tin, lemon shortcake or rhubarb squares.

Joseph Henry noticed all of it, though he rarely said so.

Their conversation became a light and comfortable pattern. She would ask what jobs he was doing. He would ask about the Timmonses or the neighbor's new roof. He asked once about the henhouse he used to help build. She laughed and told him it collapsed under that big snow last winter. He gave a quiet chuckle and said "Heh, that's why I was never a carpenter."

They both smiled a bit more, mostly at little things. Occasionally, they spoke like they used to.

Joseph Henry noticed that the visits had become more natural. The pause between the first hello and the first topic was shorter now. Her smile, still small, came more easily. His voice no longer cracked when he answered. She didn't always clasp her hands in her lap, and she managed to relax her shoulders. Minnie even got a couple of warnings for reaching toward the mesh herself, and they'd both laugh.

Sometimes she brought a newspaper, and they'd discuss the stories. She'd occasionally throw in something local about people he used to know.

"Andy Barton passed. His son runs the blacksmith shop now. I don't think that boy knows what he's doing yet, but he's trying. And, he certainly can't call a square dance."

She laughed, then wondered if Joseph Henry minded her still going to the festivals. But Joseph Henry still nodded and smiled, only saying "That's a shame. A good man."

Some visits she'd just be full of questions.

"Have you read anything lately?"

"Do they give you things to read?"

"Do they let you outside much?"

"Do you play cards or checkers or anything like that?"

He liked to listen much more than he liked to talk, but he'd answer honestly, and sometimes even shared more than he meant to.

He told her once that a fellow named Redding could play the harmonica decently, and that he'd play it in the yard sometimes. But recently, another inmate didn't like it and gave him a bit of a beating before smashing the harmonica.

Minnie was horrified, and Joseph Henry realized his mistake, quickly changing the subject after saying that almost never happens.

The silences weren't strained anymore. Though the time was short, it was alright if they didn't fill it. Sometimes she would sit quietly and look around, or look at him, and he was just fine with that.

He'd study her scarf or the pin on her collar and try to remember if it was one she used to wear or something new. Sometimes he'd ask, sometimes he wouldn't.

Dennis or another guard would even occasionally enter a conversation. Once, Dennis had asked Minnie what she put in the cornbread that made it taste so good. She told him it was nutmeg.

Joseph Henry knew that wasn't true but said nothing, though he wondered why Minnie said it.

On the way out, Minnie would turn to Dennis, or whichever guard was on duty, and say she hoped he'd enjoy the baked goods. They'd smile and say, "Thank you ma'am."

The visits had slowly become a part of Joseph Henry's pattern. Sleep. Work. Eat. Sleep. Work. Eat. Visit. He hoped it wasn't so for Minnie.

It wasn't exactly joy, but it brought something steady. Something quiet and comforting they could both hold on to.

***

By the fifth year, the visits had settled into something different. They weren't cold or unpleasant, but there was an empty weight to them now, like furniture in a room no one used. They came, they talked, they smiled, and then they left. Each a little eager to return to something else.

Minnie missed several months. She didn't come in May. When she returned in June, she apologized before sitting down, saying there had been a washout on the tracks. The train couldn't get through. In October, she said the penitentiary office hadn't responded in time to approve the visit.

Each time Joseph Henry would nod and say, "alright."

Once or twice, he added, "Not your fault."

Minnie still baked. Still wrapped the tins neatly. Still made sure her gloves matched and her shawl was pinned in place. But sometimes the scarf slipped loose, or her hair wasn't pinned as carefully. The baked goods were often repeats, with no new recipes. The guards noticed, mostly, though only occasionally made a light-hearted comment.

She still smiled when she greeted him, but the smile came later and faded sooner. Sometimes she talked more than usual, asking quick questions and jumping between topics, as if trying to keep a rhythm alive that had started to drag. Other times she fell quiet and let him carry more of it, only realizing partway through a story that she hadn't heard a word.

"Do you still work laundry?" she asked one week. "Or are you back in... where was it?"

Joseph Henry gave a slight shake of the head. "I'm on whitewash detail now."

"Oh," she said, then paused. "That seems better."

He hesitated. "It's not my favorite. By the end of the day my back hurts, and it can burn my hands sometimes."

She looked past him, up toward the window, "Well, it could be worse I suppose."

He gave another pause. "I suppose."

They still shared a few laughs, still slipped into their old rhythm now and again, but it took more effort to get there. They were older now. Not by much, but in ways that mattered.

The space between them hadn't changed, but it felt farther. Like a book left in the kitchen.

Minnie occasionally brought up people from town. But it wasn't just news.

"Do you remember Lucy Carter?" she asked once. "She married one of the Murphy boys. They've got four now, all with that same red hair. They took the cart down to Glasgow to stay with her family."

She let out a short breath, part laugh, part something else. "Imagine that. It must have taken days."

Joseph Henry smiled politely. "Sounds like a handful."

But he noticed the tiniest trace of longing in her voice.

"Yes, I'd imagine it was," she said, finishing with a sigh.

Another time she mentioned she'd been spending afternoons helping Mrs. Truett organize church records.

"She calls me her dependable spinster," Minnie said, smiling like it was a joke, though her voice gave away something unsettled. "I think it's meant kindly, but…" she finished quietly.

Joseph Henry paused, his voice quiet. "I imagine that's not easy."

She only looked at him slightly when she added, "Course, there's two of us now. Mr. Darnell helps on occasion. He's a widower. Older. Lost his wife some years ago. Not much of a help," she laughed, "but he's sweet."

She brushed a thread off her skirt. "Talks a lot, but that's o'kay."

Joseph Henry didn't flinch. He didn't change expression. "Sounds like you enjoy the company."

Minnie didn't answer right away. "It's different than this," she said softly. It wasn't clear what she meant.

One month, Joseph Henry had seemed quieter than usual. Not withdrawn, exactly, but something was dimmer. His eyes looked more sunken, his hands more stiff. It even seemed to pain him to keep up with conversation. Minnie noticed, but didn't mention it at first.

After several visits, seeing the same thing in her husband, she couldn't help asking. "Are you alright? You seem off lately. Maybe tired?"

Joseph Henry gave a shrug, then shifted in his seat. "It's nothing," he said, almost begrudgingly. "They've had me on some new details."

"What kind?"

He hesitated. "Tanning shop, mostly. Lime kiln, here and there."

Minnie frowned. "That sounds…"

He gave a small nod. "It is."

She looked down. "Is it dangerous?"

Joseph Henry didn't answer right away. "You get used to the heat. And the smell. Mostly. I'll be fine."

He flexed his hands on the table in front of him. They were red at the knuckles, the skin rougher than she remembered. She reached up as if to gesture toward them, but stopped short of the wire mesh.

After that, Joseph Henry tried to keep more upbeat.

On a particularly rainy day, after they sat down, Minnie looked across the mesh. She stared at Joseph Henry for several moments.

He noticed and asked, "What is it?"

She hesitated a little longer. "Sometimes I don't know what we're doing. It's like we're trying to keep something alive by remembering what it used to be."

She blinked, as if surprised by what she'd just said. Then she sat up straighter. "I didn't mean that the way it sounds. It's the weather. I'm just tired today."

Joseph Henry gave her a long, soft look. "It's alright."

***

During the ninth year, in late spring, the trees outside the window had barely leafed out. The year was, so far, undecided about whether to let it be spring yet. The days were brightening, but the chill wouldn't leave.

Joseph Henry sat still, watching Minnie as she made her way to her place on the opposite side of the mesh, her hands clinging to the cloth-wrapped tin. She smiled right away, but it was the empty smile. The one she began trying to wear before leaving the train.

"Just shortbread this time," she said, indicating the tin. "Didn't have the right ingredients for anything else."

"It's fine, thank you," Joseph Henry said. He saw Dennis stepping forward to take the tin, as he usually did. Joseph Henry raised a hand, stopping him. Minnie glanced between them, uncertain.

"Would you mind holding onto it for now?" he asked, gently.

Minnie blinked. "Alright. If you'd rather." She settled it in her lap and smoothed the cloth with her fingers. She glanced at Dennis, who shrugged.

"I just want to talk a bit first," he continued.

She gave a small nod, uncertain now. "Of course."

He folded his hands and rubbed his thumbs together, the way he did when he was working something out. She waited, but he didn't begin right away.

"Minnie," he said at last, "you know how grateful I am. For every visit. For everything you've done."

"I don't do anything," she said, softly.

"Yes, you do." He looked at her carefully. "You've given up years of your life to keep seeing me."

"I never saw it that way."

"I know." He paused again. "But I do."

She tilted her head. "Why are you saying this now?"

Joseph Henry looked down. "Because I've been thinking. I'm not sure it's fair to keep asking you to come."

"You're not asking," she said, her voice suddenly firm.

He met her eyes. "You deserve more."

Minnie froze. She knew Joseph Henry. She knew she could argue, but he had made a decision, and he would not relent. Tears welled. She reached for a handkerchief, but her fingers came up empty.

Joseph Henry spoke again, quieter, but more direct. "You told me once that Mrs. Truett calls you her dependable spinster."

Minnie blinked. "I was only… I didn't mean…"

"I know," he said. "But it stayed with me. The way you said it. The way you looked down after."

She said nothing.

"And Mr. Darnell, too. Helping at the church. Said he wasn't much help, but he was sweet. Talked a lot. That's okay." He smiled, but shifted slightly. "Maybe there was something there… It's alright."

Minnie's mouth parted, but no sound came.

Joseph Henry went on. "Lucy Carter, and the cart ride to Glasgow with her red-headed boys. You laughed, but you sighed after. I heard that, too."

Minnie couldn't believe it. He was pulling things from years ago. Tiny details she barely remembered.

He looked at her gently. She searched his face.

"You've got a life out there. Even if it's not what you thought it would be. Even if it's quiet. I want you to live it. You can't, not with… whatever this is. You stretch yourself too thin trying to keep this going."

Minnie began to say something, but she saw Joseph Henry's hands. They were clenched tightly together, knuckled white.

"If I don't do this now, I never will," he said.

"No, don't…" Minnie said, fear in her voice.

"I'm telling the warden I won't have any more visitors. Requests will be denied."

Her mouth opened, but no words came. Then finally, "I've never asked you for anything, Joseph. Just this."

He spoke quickly, sternly. "I've held onto it, but I shouldn't have. It's all for you."

Silence settled over them, broken only by the distant sound of a guard's keys. Minnie stood up, doing everything not to break down. She turned away but reached back for the mesh without looking.

"I never stopped loving you," she said.

"I know."

Her voice cracked. "You could've waited."

"I did," he said softly.

She lingered, just for a breath longer, then turned away.

Joseph Henry watched her go, not blinking, not breathing, until she was gone. He looked down at her bench, where she'd left the ribboned tin.

Chapter 19
1929

Alfred Earl Sanders, people called him Earl, spent most afternoons hanging around Cletus Hall's garage. He wore a pair of mechanic's overalls, same as Cletus, but only took the small jobs: oil changes, tire patches, things that didn't take much sweat. He was Cletus's wife's brother, so Cletus didn't have much choice but to keep him on. Family.

Cletus was the workhorse. It was his garage, and at any given time there were three to seven cars in various states of repair, either inside or scattered around the yard.

Cletus made more money off barrels than he ever did turning wrenches. During Prohibition, folks found all sorts of ways to skirt the law, and this was one of the better ones. The idea hadn't been Cletus's. Joseph Henry had worked it out, and Boss Van saw the opportunity. Together, they offered the setup to a few trusted customers. It was a clean little system that stayed just on the right side of legal.

Cletus didn't sell hooch. That would be a problem. He sold barrels. Plain oak ones, provided by Van, each with a generous smear of malt syrup caked at the bottom. Folks knew what to do. They added water, threw in some yeast, and waited a couple of weeks. It wasn't good, but it was beer. Drinkable enough. Van took a percentage, plus the cost of the barrels, and left the rest to Cletus.

Later in the day, and on through the night, Cletus's garage turned into what the locals in the know called the Oil Can Club. The Can was a relatively safe speakeasy. Cletus kept the local authorities well taken care of. Most of them were regulars anyway. It kept things running smooth.

He had a good relationship with Boss Van and Joseph Henry. Joseph Henry made sure quality product showed up often enough to keep the place stocked, but never so much that it raised suspicion. The locals looked the other way. They liked their drinks, and they liked their envelopes. The Feds were another matter. They didn't take your money, at least not directly, and if they came around, it wasn't to be friendly.

But they didn't come around often. Boss Van had a way of keeping things quiet, even at that level. How he did it wasn't something Cletus asked about. He was just glad the shipments kept coming and the doors stayed open.

Most days, Joseph Henry made the deliveries. Now and then, though, it didn't work out. On these rare occasions, Deacon had to fill in.

This time, Joseph Henry was in Louisville, handling a shipment for some of Boss Van's more refined customers, folks who expected proper Mint Juleps during a particular horse race. Normally, Deacon could have managed things on his own. But this time, he'd been knocked flat by a late-season influenza. He could barely stand, let alone carry out a full run.

For the first time, Giles had to leave the warehouse. He wasn't experienced, but he could drive the truck. The problem was, he had no idea where the deliveries needed to go. So Deacon, pale and sweating, rode shotgun. His fever had broken the night before, but he had no strength. He did his best to steer Giles toward the four stops scheduled for that day.

The early deliveries were uneventful. Most places along a route were quiet during the day, still running their regular business. In this case, Cletus's was an auto garage, same as always. One stop was a lumber yard, another a tobacco warehouse. The last had no daytime business at all. Just an old iron furnace, long since shut down. These days, it was used exclusively for saucing up locals after dark.

By the time Giles and Deacon arrived at Cletus's, it was late afternoon, and the garage had already been converted for the night's activities. Earl was sitting at a table with three others. Cletus didn't open for business until much later, but on Fridays he let his garage workers finish early and relax after setting up for the night.

When Boss Van's deliveries came in, it was generally expected that someone would help unload the product. Giles checked on Deacon, who had nodded off and was breathing in a labored way, then knocked twice on the garage door and let himself in.

***

Earl paused mid-sentence at the sound of the dull knock on the door. It swung open, and a figure stepped inside. With the sun behind him, Earl couldn't make out the face, but he was sure it was Fry Morrow.

Fry's family had worked for the Halls for generations. First as slaves, later as paid help. Fry came by most evenings to sweep up the garage. On weekends, he did a more thorough cleaning.

Earl didn't like Fry Morrow. He didn't like any Black man. But he loved tormenting them. Some days he stayed after work just to give Fry a good tongue-lashing. And sometimes, a beating.

"Well, looky here, boys. Fry's here!" Earl had already had his share of hooch, and he'd been looking forward to Fry's arrival.

He stood up. As he went to set his glass down, he missed the edge of the table. The half-full glass tipped and landed on its side, spilling dark brown liquid across the surface. The delivery hadn't come in yet, so Cletus was serving his usual bathtub gin. A sharp, foul concoction that only passed as drinkable when cut with Coca-Cola or ginger ale. In this case, it was the Coke.

The acrid liquid rushed toward Harris Philmore, who jumped back from the table. His chair went out from under him and hit the floor backside first. The other two, Howard George and Fred Weigler, laughed. One at Harris. The other at Earl.

Earl scowled at Howard, who clearly was the one laughing in his direction. He swiped the glass off the table. It shattered against the floor.

Then he turned toward "Fry." His face twisted into something cruel and tight. Clouded by drink and whatever passed for thought in Earl's hayseed mind, he managed to fix blame on the Black man who had just walked through the door.

Earl took a few deliberate steps toward Giles before realizing the man in the doorway wasn't Fry Morrow. He squinted, trying to make sense of what he was seeing. The man's skin was lighter than most, but still clearly Black. Earl froze. The angles of the face… the jawline… the thin lips… blue eyes.

He couldn't make sense of it. A white man? No. A Black man? Maybe. Something in between? That wasn't something Earl had words for. It didn't fit. Not with what he knew. People were one thing or the other, and you could tell which just by looking. But this was different. And it was clear. Earl Sanders didn't like different.

His brain stalled. He stood blinking, mouth slightly open, still trying to decide how to act.

Giles saw what had just happened at the table and felt a flicker of fear as the angry man started toward him. But then the man stopped short, wearing a blank, slack-jawed look, like a confused animal.

Giles grinned. "You having a moment there, boss?"

Earl blinked.

Giles stepped forward, just a few inches into the room. "Need a minute? I can come back later. Just here to bring in the delivery. Was told the boys'd be helping."

Howard chuckled quietly. Fred smirked into his drink.

Earl heard the words, but all he saw was the grin. Earl's eyes narrowed. Whatever confusion he'd felt a second earlier was gone. All that remained was heat and something else.

"Nigger bastard."

Sweat beaded on Earl's forehead. His jaw hung loose, eyes flat. He stepped toward Giles with slow, deliberate motion, like a locomotive building its momentum.

Giles straightened slightly, the grin falling away. He didn't step back. He knew what was coming, and braced for the impact.

Earl's fist plowed forward, almost without warning, low and fast, driving straight into Giles's stomach. Giles doubled over with a soft grunt, more breath than sound. Despite bracing for it, his face flickered with surprise, less from the impact than what it did to him.

Giles knew it was coming, he'd been hit before. He'd learned how to take it. But this time it was followed by another. Then another.

Earl wasn't trying to teach him a lesson. He was delivering a punishment.

The table behind Earl scraped slightly as someone shifted. Fred or Howard. But no one spoke.

Giles was on one knee now. He raised his hands, surrendering. Earl shoved them aside and grabbed the front of his shirt, yanking him back upright just long enough to drive a fist into the side of his face.

Giles slumped sideways. On his way down Earl slammed a knee into his ribs. As he hit the floor, Earl kicked him hard in the same spot. Once. Then again.

The room was quiet except for the dull rhythm of the beating. Fred stared, eyes wide. Howard had stopped chewing... whatever he'd been chewing. No one moved.

Earl stepped in again and drove his knee down hard into Giles's back. The sound wasn't loud, but it was solid. Harris Philmore gasped, then turned away.

Earl hesitated. Giles didn't cry out. He didn't beg. That only seemed to make Earl angrier.

He dropped to a knee and hit Giles again. Closed fist. Head, neck, shoulder. Quick, brutal shots, like he was trying to dig something out of him.

The door opened. Earl didn't notice the sound, or the sudden spill of sunlight that spread over him like it was something divine.

Deacon filled the doorway. He hesitated, taking in the scene. He had woken to a bang and grabbed the shotgun on his way to the door. His eyes lit with something feral. He didn't speak. Just raised the shotgun and fired into the ceiling.

Splinters and dust rained down across the room. The sound rolled through the rafters, like thunder trapped in a jar.

Earl jerked back, half falling as he scrambled to his feet. The silence that followed was sharp-edged and uneven, like everyone was afraid to breathe.

Giles lay on the floor.

Deacon leveled the shotgun at Earl.

"Step behind the table with your friends please."

Earl looked between Deacon and the end of the barrel, fear suddenly written plain on his face. He scurried behind the table like a dog trying to vanish under the porch.

Deacon stepped over, knelt beside Giles, and began checking him. Giles looked up, confused to see Deacon's face hovering above his.

"I think I lost a fight," he said, managing a weak smile.

Deacon gave a half smile of his own, though it was tight with concern. "Yes. I'd say you came out the worse for it. Come along."

Giles pushed himself up onto all fours. Blood dripped from his nose and mouth, pooling slowly on the floor beneath him. He got one foot under him, then the other, but stumbled as he rose. Deacon reached in and steadied him, keeping him upright.

He started to guide Giles toward the door, but Giles stopped him and turned back toward Earl. One of his eyes was swollen shut. He squinted through the other, found Earl, and managed his usual full grin.

"Not sure you'll be seein' any whiskey this time, friend." He gave Earl a wink from the good eye.

Earl scowled and started to take a step back around the table. Deacon leveled the shotgun again.

"Come on now, bossman," Giles said. "I think I've had enough."

He turned back toward the door, still leaning on Deacon, who kept one arm around him while trying to keep the shotgun trained on Earl.

Before stepping outside, Giles turned one more time. The grin hadn't left his face. "And I don't know this Fry you talkin' 'bout, but I think you gotta leave that boy alone too."

Deacon added, "I don't think Mr. Hall will be pleased, going without his whiskey."

Earl's mouth opened. His eyes darted. He heard the threat but looked like he was still working out the seriousness.

Deacon helped Giles into the cab of the truck. Despite his condition, he took the wheel. Giles was in no shape to cover for him anymore.

Chapter 20
1929

Joseph Henry had just about had it. Driving the Ford Model AA flatbed long distances could be exhausting on a normal day, but driving after dusk in a rainstorm was grueling. The truck was loud and stubborn, every bump in the road rattling through the floorboards and up his spine. The wheel fought him on the curves, slick with rain. It felt frigid in his hand. The loud engine gave off plenty of noise, but little warmth in the damp cab.

He wiped the inside of the windshield with the sleeve of his coat… again. Outside was just as bad. The windshield wiper wasn't automatic—not in a truck like this. A small metal crank jutted down above the glass. Joseph Henry had to work it by hand, back and forth, every few seconds, just to clear a thin strip to peer through. His left arm ached from working the lever, his right from holding the wheel steady.

The rain didn't fall; it hammered.

The headlights gave off a sick yellow glow, barely shining 10 feet past the hood. The road ahead seemed less a road and more a strip of dark mud that parted the trees like a scythe. But Joseph Henry knew this area… intimately. He knew every bend in the road, every stretch of leaning fence, every place where the land dropped off if you weren't careful. He gripped the wheel until his knuckles were white, worked the wiper crank, and fought his way through the storm.

Up until the storm it had been a good day. A productive day.

Joseph Henry had been up and ready to go at 5:00 AM. While he never liked leaving Old Crow to get himself up, Duane had offered to take over his duties in that area if Joseph Henry brought him back a sack of Bull Durham and a fresh pack of rolling papers.

Boss Van was on the grounds early. Stocking Louisville this time of year was big business, and no small risk.

Joseph Henry stepped out and gave him a wave. Boss Van stood alone beneath the overhang in his heavy coat, collar turned up, with a cigarette burning low. He had the truck running before Joseph Henry came through the door.

"Boss," Joseph Henry said, pulling his gloves tight, "this is a big run… Louisville. I'll see to it. Though I'm a bit concerned about today's regular deliveries. There's three more drop-offs 'supposed to go today… Tobacco house, Cletus's place, and the furnace outside Danville."

Boss Van barely looked up, a hint of annoyance in his voice. "Just get yourself goin'. Deacon'll have to take care of the rest."

"That's just it sir. Deacon's been under it lately. He's still pale from that spring fever. If he's got to run the whole route while I'm out…"

"Then he'll run it!" Boss Van snapped. He looked up, jaw set. Joseph Henry didn't see Boss Van get rigid often. "You think I don't know how tight this operation is? I picked Deacon. He'll manage. You just get to Louisville and back without anyone sniffing around your tailgate."

Joseph Henry nodded slow. "Yes, sir."

"Good. Truck's gassed and packed. You get the load, get there and back. You've got till dusk. Move."

Boss Van turned back toward the door, tossing the last inch of cigarette, still glowing, into the dirt.

Joseph Henry made the distillery in just under half an hour. The truck couldn't go very fast, but it held to the road pretty well. Covering the five miles at that pace wasn't bad. Joseph Henry was happy with the day's start.

That feeling didn't last.

Joseph Henry honked the horn. The heavy plank door slid aside, iron rollers groaned on the track above. Giles waved to Joseph Henry who backed the truck in, just clearing the threshold. Joseph Henry hopped out of the cab. The smile on his face fled just as quick. In front of him Deacon braced himself against a crate of corn mash, white as chalk and sweating through his undershirt. His chest rose in shallow bursts. He didn't even look up.

"Hell, Deacon," Joseph Henry said, stepping in fast. "You dying on me?"

Deacon blinked a few times before answering. "The fever came on again last night. Hard. I thought I'd shaken it last week, but it came right back."

He trailed off, mouth dry. He reached for a cloth on the workbench but came up short.

"Feels like it's broken again, but Lord… I can barely move."

Joseph Henry grabbed the cloth and pressed it into his hand. "Boss Van's countin' on you to cover today's local deliveries while I make Louisville. That still possible?"

Deacon gave a hollow laugh. "That depends on what you mean by possible."

"I don't like this." Joseph Henry looked him over. "You're barely upright."

"I'll manage," Deacon said, straightening as best he could. "I'll pull Giles in."

Joseph Henry frowned. "Giles?"

"He's been keeping the stores in order. Knows the routes well enough from the maps. I'll ride along, try to rest where I can. Quiet stops, short handoffs. We'll manage."

Joseph Henry didn't answer right away. He moved to the window and stared out at the graying sky.

"You sure about that?" he asked, voice low. "You know why Boss Van keeps him inside."

Deacon nodded. "Folk in these parts haven't moved past the last century. I know it well. But we've no other way."

Joseph Henry turned. "He's not even from here. This isn't Barbados. Folks only see skin. It's not like down there… It may be bad, but down there it's about class, about money and lineage. Here, it's black and white. Simple and stupid."

"We're not going far. Just Tobacco's, The Oil Can, The Yard, and The Furnace. One road, four stops. He hands the goods over, and we head straight back. No need for him to say a word."

Joseph Henry shook his head slowly. "Boss Van won't like it if there's trouble."

"And if we skip the run, Boss Van'll be even less pleased."

Joseph Henry didn't argue. It was clear Deacon couldn't make the deliveries himself.

"Alright," he said at last. "Give him the route. I'll get to Louisville. Keep him safe."

Deacon eased himself onto a bench with a groan. "That's the plan."

Deacon was no help in loading the two trucks. Joseph Henry and Giles had to do the loading themselves. It cost them an hour.

The rest of the day was a whirlwind. Joseph Henry pushed the truck as fast as it would go, but that wasn't much over 40 MPH. Still, he liked the hustle, and liked the work. His mood was back in the positive halfway to Louisville.

The route wasn't difficult. He liked most of the customers, and they were excited to see him. The Derby was a big deal, and all of the locals were geared up. Louisville had a lot of stops. Joseph Henry was well ready when time came for the return trip. He cleared the city limits at about three. At that pace, he'd be home before dusk.

Then the storm hit.

The gates of the penitentiary loomed ahead, a pair of dark shapes in the rain. The guard at the booth waved him in without comment. Joseph Henry would have returned the gesture, but his hands remained occupied with the wheel and the wiper crank. He managed a small nod.

Inside, he parked the truck in the covered loading area and killed the engine. The pistons seemed to cough a last couple of times before going silent. There was no real silence though. The storm pressed against every surface. Outside the water ran down the gutters in loud torrents as the rain battered the metal over-hang.

Joseph Henry stepped down from the cab, joints aching, and made his way to the rear door. He trudged through the back corridors, passing some of the night shift. A few nods. No conversation.

He passed Duane's cell. "Here ya go, Duane." He tossed a bag with the tobacco and papers over to his bed. "Thanks for the help."

Duane was lying on his cot. Propped up on one arm reading a magazine. "Thanks Mista' Henry!"

Joseph Henry reached his cell. He was soaked through. He stripped off the heavy clothes, letting them drop to the floor. He'd take care of them in the morning. A shudder remaining from the chill of the evening found its way up his back and through his shoulders. The blanket was folded at the foot of the cot, just as he'd left it. He gave a deep sigh, looking forward to the small comfort.

As he reached for the blanket, a knock came on the bars of his still open cell.

Joseph Henry turned, too tired to care about modesty. A younger guard, Joseph Henry thought his name might be Dunley, was holding out a folded slip of paper.

"Note came for you Mister Henry. Said it's urgent."

Joseph Henry nodded and took the paper. The guard, trying to avert his eyes from the naked white man, walked off without waiting for thanks.

The note was brief. Just a few lines. Joseph Henry recognized it as Deacon's tidy, angular script.

Giles is injured bad. Bring a doctor. Don't delay. – D

Joseph Henry folded the paper. He paused and thought for a minute. The storm outside seemed to press harder against the stone walls.

"Guard!"

The same guard, Dunley, came back to his cell. Before he could say anything, Joseph Henry said quickly, "Have a problem. Need to get to the Warden's office."

Dunley hesitated. He knew Joseph Henry was given more latitude, but he wasn't used to answering to a prisoner. Seeing the hesitation, Joseph Henry barked, "This has to happen now."

Dunley jumped as if making a sudden decision, "Let's go." Joseph Henry threw on some dry cloths and headed down the corridor.

Boss Van wasn't in his office. Joseph Henry hadn't expected him to be. But he knocked anyway. No answer. He opened the door.

The room was dark. Light from the hall cast long narrow shadows, just enough for Joseph Henry to find the switch to the desk lamp. The bulb gave off a dull orange glow… dim, but better than none.

Dunley stood in the doorway behind him.

Boss Van's desk sat square to the window, papers stacked neat, inkwell capped, ledger closed. The phone sat in the far corner, an old candlestick model, black and upright, with a separate earpiece receiver resting in a cradle, a small rotary crank on the side.

Joseph Henry stepped over and lifted the receiver from the cradle. He lifted it to his ear, but paused.

"Close the door and wait in the hall."

His voice carried more hesitation than he liked. Giving an order to a guard felt unnatural, and was not like Joseph Henry. Dunley clearly didn't like it either.

"Boss Van will want privacy for our call."

The name did its work. Dunley flinched. He gave a short nod, then stepped out and closed the door… still not liking it.

Joseph Henry took a breath, lifted the receiver to his ear again.

Dead silence.

Joseph Henry had little experience with a telephone. While they were becoming more common, residents of penitentiaries had few opportunities to use one. Joseph Henry had more than most due to his extraneous role, but it was still limited.

He tried to think how it worked. He reached for the crank, gave it two full turns, and waited.

A faint *click*, then static, then a voice… flat… maybe bored.

"Operator."

He cleared his throat. "Frankfort three-one-seven, please. Vannoy residence."

A pause.

"One moment."

Joseph Henry waited, hand gripping the metal stand, the receiver cold against his ear. In the distance he could hear the faint metallic clacks as the operator plugged cords into a switchboard.

click… click… ring…

The line came alive with a dull *burr-burr… burr-burr…* the distant ring of a household phone, somewhere else in the city, miles away.

The third ring was interrupted by the sound of a receiver being lifted on the other end.

"…Hello?" The voice was a woman's… soft, cautious. Tired.

Joseph Henry hesitated. "Evening, ma'am. Sorry to disturb you. Is Mr. Vannoy available?"

A pause. Then, "One moment."

He heard the faint sound of the receiver being set down, then… muffled steps. A door creaked. Then silence.

Another voice came on. Lower, but strong. Unmistakably Boss Van's.

"This better be good."

"It's Joseph Henry."

A pause.

"Go ahead."

"I just got back. Deacon had a note sent to me. Says Giles is in bad shape. Real bad. Says I need to bring a doctor."

Silence. Joseph Henry pictured Boss Van standing in the hallway where they kept the phone, maybe rubbing his temple.

"How bad?"

"Doesn't say. But Deacon don't overstate things. And he's never reached out before."

Another pause. Then a long exhale.

"All right. Listen. Is the Doc McCray still there?"

"I don't know. Could be."

"Go find him," dismissing the possibility that he might not be, "Don't make a show of it. You understand?"

"Yes, sir."

"McCray don't think he answers to anyone…" Boss Van paused again. Then, "In the right-hand desk drawer, there's a false back. Push in from the left, you'll find a bunch of bills. Take what you need to make him agreeable."

Joseph Henry said nothing.

"And that money isn't just for the ride. It's for his silence. Make sure that's understood. You take him to the distillery, he'll see things. I don't want him talking."

"I'll do it."

Another pause.

"Right… do it quiet, and do it fast."

Click.

Dr. McCray was just leaving from the infirmary when Joseph Henry… Dunley trailing behind… caught him in the corridor. McCray had a narrow rat-like face and a weary slump to his posture, maybe from a crooked back or leftovers of rickets as a child.

Joseph Henry grabbed his arm and steered him back into the infirmary, shutting the door behind them and leaving Dunley on the other side.

"What the..." McCray started.

"Look, doc, I'm gonna need you to come with me. Someone's hurt. Bad."

McCray narrowed his eyes. "Someone here?"

Joseph Henry shook his head. He glanced back at the door. "Off the grounds."

"Then it's not my concern. I don't make house calls… especially not in a monsoon."

Joseph Henry stepped closer, voice low. "This comes from Boss Van. You'll get paid."

"Boss Van pays me to be here. To work here."

Joseph Henry reached into his pocket and pulled out the wad of bills, thumbing through it. "Twenty do it?"

The doctor exhaled through his nose. "Fifty. You driving?"

"Yes."

"Give me five minutes to get what I need."

The rain hadn't let up.

Joseph Henry guided the truck onto the muddy road, the tires barely holding to the slick earth. Beside him, McCray sat stiff-backed, medical bag tucked between his boots. The moment they rolled out of the yard, he had reached up and began working the wiper crank. The glass was already thick with water, and although begrudgingly, the doctor understood it was partly self preservation… without his help, the driver would be nearly blind.

"Much obliged," Joseph Henry said, eyes on the road.

McCray didn't respond. The wiper squeaked with each pass, barely clearing enough to make him feel safer.

It was slow going, but for Joseph Henry, it was better than the ride back from Louisville.

After a stretch of silence, Joseph Henry spoke.

"There's something you need to understand before we get there."

McCray gave a sidelong glance but didn't stop cranking.

"What you're going to see… none of it leaves your mouth. Not to the guards. Not to your wife. Not to anyone."

McCray unconsciously let go of the crank. Joseph Henry nodded towards the glass.

"Come on…"

He resumed, working the crank harder, as if to catch up. He managed a sideways glance at Joseph Henry.

"That all part of the fifty?"

"And then some."

The cranking settled into a rhythm with the dull rumble of the engine.

"Guessing you ain't taking me to church."

"No…"

In the weather, Joseph Henry almost missed the turnoff, despite having driven it dozens of times. It was always hard to spot, the slight break in the trees where a narrow path veered from the road.

McCray lost the crank and slid towards Joseph Henry as the truck suddenly lurched to the side of the road. The turnoff was half concealed by hanging limbs and thick brush.

Joseph Henry climbed out into the storm and dragged the brush aside. It came away wet and heavy.

Through habit now, McCray kept the wiper going as Joseph Henry cleared the way. Then Joseph Henry was back in, coat and boots dripping, and prodded the truck forward down the hidden track.

The truck bounced along the uneven path, branches scraping the sides and roof. After a short ways, the silhouette of the old warehouse emerged through the trees.

McCray squinted through the windshield. "Where the hell are we?"

Joseph Henry honked once and waited. A moment later, the heavy plank door slid aside. The truck lumbered through before Joseph Henry cut the engine and opened the cab door.

McCray watched as Joseph Henry joined a tall white man to pull the wooden door closed again. The storm faded to a soft patter on the metal roof.

Dr. McCray climbed out of the cab and stepped forward, eyes adjusting to the low light. The air inside was warm and thick… rich with the bite of fermented mash, old wood, copper, and something metallic beneath it all. His gaze swept over the stills, the coiled piping, the rows of barrels stacked with care. Everything gleamed with function.

He stopped short halfway into the space.

"Well, I'll be damned…"

Joseph Henry glanced at the doctor but said nothing. He let him take it in.

McCray turned a slow circle. "I'd heard rumors. Thought Boss Van was cooking up some backwoods mess in rusted drums. Stuff that would strip paint off a barn… or just as surely make you go blind…" He gestured at the setup. "This is a proper operation. Hell, it's cleaner than some clinics I've worked in."

"Doctor."

The voice came sharp from the far side of the room. It was the tall white man.

Joseph Henry did a quick introduction, "McCray… Deacon".

"A pleasure," Deacon said. The words carried no warmth. "But this is not the time to be impressed."

He was already walking, motioning McCray to follow. "He is in the back room. If you please."

McCray lingered a second longer, but Joseph Henry gave him a gentle nudge forward.

Deacon led them through a narrow corridor stacked with supplies, racks, and coils of tubing.

A door opened into a smaller room in the back. Low ceiling. Bare walls. Just a cot, a chair, and a single hanging bulb casting a sickly yellow glow.

On the cot lay a black man, an unusual-looking one, McCray thought. His skin was dark, but his features mirrored Deacon's in strange ways. It gave him pause.

Even from the threshold, McCray could see the damage… bruises mottled across his ribs, one arm bent just wrong, swelling around one eye.

Deacon stepped aside.

"See to him. Quickly."

McCray knelt next to the cot, his hands already opening the bag.

He laid out a few supplies… bottle of spirits, gauze, cloth strips, a small roll of linen. He pressed gently along Giles's ribs. Giles flinched. His eyes fluttered open.

He looked around, dazed. His gaze found Deacon and Joseph Henry. A crooked grin formed beneath a swollen lip.

"Well now," he murmured. "I be dead, or jus' broke?"

McCray didn't look up. "If you're talking, you're doing better than I'd expected."

Giles gave a rough chuckle. "You the doc? Am I gon' live, doc?"

McCray leaned in. He raised two fingers and waved them side to side in front of Giles's eyes. Giles followed the motion, slow but steady.

"You know where you are?"

Giles blinked. "Ain't sure. Don't smell like no clinic. Back at he 'stillery?"

McCray grunted. "Pupils are a little slow, but they're moving. Bit of a concussion, if that. The ribs'll be worse. Could be cracked… I'd bet on it. Left side. I'll wrap them, but I wouldn't move for a while."

He shifted down the cot, gently lifting Giles's arm. Giles sucked in air through his teeth.

"This one's off," McCray muttered. He ran a hand down the forearm, probing at the wrist, then back toward the elbow.

"Elbow's dislocated. Bad angle. Must've taken a hard fall."

He looked at Deacon.

"I'll need some help. Need to hold him steady… shoulders and chest. Watch the left side though. This'll hurt. A lot… It'll be much worse if he twists or jerks.

Deacon nodded once, serious.

McCray turned back to Giles and folded a strip of cloth. "You'll want this between your teeth. Bite down, it'll help… a bit."

Giles accepted the cloth, jaw tightening as he bit down.

Deacon knelt behind him, arms bracing across Giles's upper body. McCray repositioned his hands along the forearm and wrist.

"Ready?" he asked, more to Deacon than Giles.

Deacon tightened his grip. Nodded.

McCray pulled and rotated in one swift, practiced motion.

The joint gave a muted pop.

Giles bucked against Deacon's arms, a muffled cry breaking through the cloth. Then his body sagged, the tension drained. His body relaxed, tears running down his cheeks.

McCray held the wrist a moment longer. Then he nodded and began to wrap the arm in linen, binding it to Giles's chest.

"He'll need to keep it still. But it's back where it belongs."

Deacon gently released Giles. His expression hadn't changed.

"He will recover?"

McCray nodded once. "If he rests. And stays out of trouble."

Giles gave a soft laugh that turned into a cough. "Ain't no trouble round here, man. Though too much to be done to stay still."

No one spoke for a while.

McCray packed up slowly. Then he and Joseph Henry walked back towards the truck.

McCray paused before climbing in. Without turning, he said, "You know, I've kept my nose out of others' business for years now. In my position, you learn to turn your back on things. Inmates come in clearly having been beaten, sometimes by other inmates, sometimes by guards. I just do my job. Never crossed Boss Van. Never asked questions."

Joseph Henry didn't look at him, just listened, wondering where this was going.

"I know what this is. Knew it wasn't just some warehouse when we pulled up."

Joseph Henry still said nothing.

"You want to keep it quiet? Fine. Part of what you paid for. But it'd be good for Boss Van to remember what I did here. What he needed done. Might be useful… having someone like me a little closer to the operation."

Joseph Henry gave a tired smile. "Sure, I'll mention it."

"You do that."

Just then they heard the sound of a horn outside. Joseph Henry stiffened, glanced towards the sliding door. Deacon appeared behind them.

"Who is that?!"

Joseph Henry crossed the room and slid open the heavy door, not sure what to expect. He was blinded for a moment from the headlamps of a Buick Master Six. The engine was running, but the driver was already out standing at the threshold as the door opened.

"Alright, how's Giles, and whose ass is going to be kicked?"

Boss Van stepped through the door before it was half open, rain slicking off his coat like it knew better than to cling to him.

Joseph Henry was past exhaustion. He wanted to be back in his cell… asleep. Instead, he found himself sitting at a heavy oak table in the distillery with Deacon and Boss Van.

Boss Van had told Dr. McCray to wait in the truck.

Deacon, still worn from the fever but animated by the night's events, recounted what had happened at The Can.

"I don't know this 'Earl'… Cletus is the one we do business with." Boss Van was calm, his words measured. He turned to Joseph Henry, ignoring the exhaustion on his face.

"I need you to deal with this. Handle Earl in a way that leaves no doubt. Our men are untouchable, regardless of color. And Cletus needs to make reparations."

Joseph Henry didn't like it. He ran the operation, oversaw production, ensured deliveries… but he wasn't the kind of man who handled beatings or blood.

Chapter 21
1929

Dr. McCray didn't like the look on Joseph Henry's face when he climbed back into the truck. He didn't know him well yet, but there was something coiled behind his eyes — a man caught in an argument with himself. Like a horse prodded one time too many, ready to buck.

"You okay there…?" McCray asked.

He noticed Joseph Henry's hands gripping the steering wheel, though the engine remained off, his knuckles turning white against the dark metal.

Joseph Henry didn't seem to hear him. After a moment, he let go of the wheel and stepped out of the cab.

McCray watched through the windshield as he walked into the rain, heading toward Boss Van, who was making his way to his car.

***

"Mr. Vannoy… a word."

Boss Van flinched at the name. He turned, ready to offer a rebuke — but stopped short when he saw Joseph Henry's face.

A beat passed.

He gave a short nod and gestured toward the Buick.

"In the car," he said, firm.

Joseph Henry opened the passenger door and climbed in. Confidence flickered… not entirely gone… but dulled. Boss Van slid behind the wheel.

"What is it, boy?"

Boy?

Age-wise, Joseph Henry was probably even with him, maybe older. The word wasn't casual. It was calculated… meant to put him in his place. Or maybe in a broom closet.

Joseph watched the wipers slide back and forth… automatically.

Boss Van would never turn a crank.

"I do a lot for you," he said. "Probably make you a lot of money. I make your whiskey. I get it where it needs to go. I get good money from the customers for you."

He paused, watching the wipers trace their arc across the glass.

"I don't threaten people. I don't hurt people."

Another beat. A slight scowl.

"I'm sure you've got people to do those things."

Boss Van looked out into the rain, a firm set to his jaw. The silence sent a tense ache through Joseph Henry's neck and shoulders.

Then Boss Van smiled… just a little… like a father ready to talk to his young child. He rested both hands on the wheel like they were settling onto a young man's shoulders.

"You're a good man, Joseph," he said softly. "Not many like you. That's why you get to sit here. In the front seat. Free as anyone can be, considering."

He let the word *free* hang, just long enough to emphasize the irony.

"You walk in and out of Frankfort Penitentiary. You make something valuable. You talk to people. Not many men in your position can say the same. I was happy to give you that."

He let the last part linger.

Boss Van met Joseph Henry's eyes… voice still level. "You don't hurt people? Maybe… You are in for a reason, Joseph."

A pause.

"You're a good man, Joseph. That's why you get to sit here."

Joseph Henry went ashen. *Boss Van knows…*

"You've done a lot for me. No doubt about it…" Boss Van's tone sharpened. "But this? This is part of it. You own this operation. I let you own this operation. And we take care of our own."

His voice gentled again. "That boy laid hands on one of ours. You make sure that never happens again."

He didn't press. Just looked back through the windshield.

His tone firmed once more. "This Earl has to be the example. Cletus just has to learn the lesson."

After a moment he turned back toward Joseph Henry. The soft voice again: "You understand?"

Joseph Henry understood. He had never seen this side of Boss Van, but he'd always known it was there.

He had no choice.

"Yes, sir…"

"That-a-boy," Boss Van said gently. "Now, is there anything else?"

Joseph Henry sat a moment, then cleared his throat softly… nervously.

"There's one more thing. Before we left the still… McCray said something."

Boss Van raised an eyebrow but didn't speak.

"He didn't say it outright, but… wasn't threatening anything. Seemed like he wanted in. Said it could be useful, having someone like him in the know. Said the setup impressed him."

He glanced sideways. "Didn't feel like a man about to report anything."

Boss Van paused, weighing his response.

"It's your operation. What do you think?"

Joseph Henry gave it a moment.

"Was good to have him there tonight. Would also allow us to keep him under wraps."

"Good," Boss Van replied. "I'll speak to him back at the penitentiary."

"Alright…" Joseph Henry suddenly felt a bit better. He opened the door to get out.

"One more thing…" Boss Van said. "You won't like the next time you call me anything but Boss Van."

He gave a dismissing nod.

Joseph Henry stepped out into the rain.

Chapter 22
1929

The truck bounced down the road. Joseph Henry had too many things to solve. Too much coming at him at once.

Ugly Attics was a flea, one he couldn't quite scratch. It wasn't clear what the man wanted, or why he kept circling. This wasn't just bullying. Ugly had something in mind. Joseph Henry just couldn't figure what.

And at this point, he wasn't sure Ugly was worth the effort. Might never be.

For now, the task at hand was Cletus and Earl. Boss Van had made himself clear. He wanted the matter handled.

Joseph Henry needed another way.

Boss Van was right—he could end Earl, clean and final. He could do it in a way that made Cletus straighten up, made sure his boys never disrespected Boss Van's holdings again. Hell, Cletus might even spread the word himself, make sure no one else got ideas.

But that wasn't Joseph Henry.

Joseph Henry needed to give them a way out. Earl had to go. No doubt about that. Boss Van wouldn't be ok with any solution that left Earl hanging around. And Cletus just needed to understand. Cletus may not even know there's a problem. These were reasonable men. It wouldn't be easy for Earl to up and leave, but he'd sure understand that it's better than the alternative. Cletus would probably have to help him out. Give him some moving money, and maybe a truck.

That's it. Joseph Henry would go in. Be calm. Talk. He'd even help them come up with a plan. In the end everyone would be happy, well except maybe Earl, but he'd be alive.

Maybe Joseph Henry would even cut Cletus a discount on the next delivery.

***

Joseph Henry stepped through the side door into Cletus's Garage.

He let it click shut behind him and stood still a moment, waiting for his eyes to adjust. The late morning sun had been bright. Inside the light was dim and the air was still and warm. The garage smelled of oil, metal, old rags, and something faintly burnt.

A car sat in the middle of the floor, hood up, a jack propping up the rear side where a tire was missing. The big garage door was shut. A few flies buzzed around some kind of food left on a plate sitting on a cluttered table.

Joseph Henry moved in hoping to find Cletus under the hood. He hadn't taken more than two steps when a voice called from deeper inside.

"That you, Mr. Henry?"

A figure stepped into better light near the workbench, wiping his hands on a rag. The voice was nasal, lightly twanged, and louder than it needed to be.

Joseph Henry gave a subtle groan, realizing it was Earl. He'd hoped to run into Cletus first.

Earl gave a wide, easy grin.

"Ain't nobody else here right now, Mr. Henry," he said. "But I can give ya a hand bringin' in the delivery. No trouble at all."

Joseph stopped. His eyes were still adjusting, but he could see Earl clearly now. The man was heavy, but with wiry arms, a bit fidgety… but not in a suspicious way. Just his nature.

"No delivery today," Joseph said evenly.

Earl's grin faltered for just a second… more confusion than anything… then it was back.

"Right, right. Not the right day. Never seen you here on another day before."

He tossed the rag onto the bench behind him and leaned against it, arms crossed. But his shoulders were a bit too tight. His eyes didn't quite settle. He was trying to look confident.

Joseph Henry knew the type. Earl might be the big man among his friends, but when it came to Cletus, or someone like Joseph Henry, he dropped a tier.

Joseph Henry took another step forward, letting the silence stretch just a little longer.

"Where's Mr. Hall?"

"Mr. Cletus ran down to the junkyard… said he was lookin' for a manifold for this here ol' T. Been fightin' with it since yesterday. He, uh… should be back soon."

Joseph Henry nodded, thought for a minute.

Reasonable men…

Calm…

Talk…

"That's fine Earl. I've got some time."

There was a low stool next to the car. Joseph Henry took a few quiet steps toward it and sat down.

He continued, voice still even.

"Say, Earl, can you tell me what happened with our man Giles who was by here the other day?"

Earl went silent.

His mouth opened, then closed again.

He stammered for a second, eyes darting… not quite sure where to land.

"I… he…"

"Hey… we're just gonna talk Earl. Things happen. I just want to know what those things were."

Earl swallowed, shifted his weight, rubbed the back of his neck with a dirty hand. Joseph Henry thought he was going to continue to stammer but say nothing… then:

"He come in here like he could tell me an' the boys what to do."

His voice started low, but it rose as he went.

"Walkin' through like I was supposed to be workin' for him or somethin'. Talkin' slick. Grinnin' like he thought it was all funny. Like had one over on me. In front of the fellas."

Joseph said nothing.

Earl looked at him, then away.

"I couldn't let that stand," he said. "Damn nigger comes in here, showin' me up? Naw. I ain't gonna be made a fool of by one of *them*. Didn't have a choice. You understand. 'Course you do."

His voice was steadier now. Wary, but resolved—like he knew he was on thin ice, but was in the right, standing by every word.

"What's goin on here?"

Cletus Hall had walked in through his office door… no doubt through the front entrance beyond.

"Hey there Cletus," Joseph Henry said, not looking away from Earl.

"We need to talk."

***

Cletus's office wasn't much, just a small room walled off from the main garage with a door that stuck when it got humid and a window that probably hadn't been washed in years.

There was a desk, old and scarred, probably scavenged from a schoolhouse or a bank. Papers were stacked unevenly across the top…

handwritten notes, parts invoices, and a few oil-stained ledgers. Cletus sat in a wooden chair behind it.

A faded calendar hung crooked on the wall, still turned to the wrong month. The picture showed a dark-haired woman in heels and a silk blouse, leaning against the fender of a Packard Eight. Joseph Henry looked at it a moment longer than necessary.

A dented filing cabinet leaned in the corner. There was a half-full coffee mug, along with several rings from where the mug had previously sat. A faint smell of stale cigarette smoke clung to everything, though Joseph Henry couldn't see any cigarettes—or even an ashtray.

In the back, a second door stood half-open. It led to a corridor, which led to a living area and another exit out of the building.

Joseph Henry sat on the same stool he'd used out in the garage. Cletus had grabbed it and brought it into the office for him.

The door to the garage was now closed.

Through the wall, they could hear Earl kicking something around, followed by a few muttered curses.

Joseph Henry's intent to handle things peacefully hadn't changed… though hearing Earl talk hadn't helped.

"We've got a problem, Cletus, and I'm really hoping we can come up with a solution."

Cletus fidgeted in his seat.

"Yeah, I figured this was comin'. The boys really put a beatin' on your black man. What was you thinkin', sendin' him over to do the delivery? No good coulda come of it."

Joseph Henry hesitated, carefully choosing his words.

"Well, it couldn't be helped. I was in Louisville, and Deacon had the flu. But that's beside the point. Giles, the black man, did what we told him to do. And you were getting your delivery."

Joseph Henry kept his voice steady.

"Earl should've let it happen. If he and his boys didn't want to help unload the truck, that's fine. But going after Giles shouldn't have happened. And you know Giles didn't talk shit to Earl and his boys."

Cletus rubbed his jaw, then shrugged like it should've been obvious.

"Look… he's a colored man. You send him in here like he's—"

Joseph Henry cut him off, but his voice still calm.

"Doesn't matter if he was Black, white, Mexican, or Chinese. He was doing the delivery. Should have been seen same as if it were me. Same as if it were Deacon."

Cletus opened his mouth, already shaking his head.

"Now hold on…"

"No," Joseph said, louder than before, but not by much. He raised a hand slightly, then let it fall. A touch of frustration crossed his face, but his voice still calm.

"Look. This is how it's going to be."

Joseph Henry leaned forward slightly on the stool. His hands rested on his knees, voice measured, even thoughtful.

"There's a way through this, Cletus. Earl's gotta go. He's gonna go. I know that's not an easy thing, but it's the only thing."

Cletus didn't speak, just looked at him, face unreadable.

Joseph Henry went on.

"Doesn't have to be ugly. Give him some cash. Help him get set up somewhere far from here. Maybe Memphis or St. Louis. Just far enough he won't be seen, and he won't come back."

He paused, watching Cletus for any sign of agreement.

"And going forward… doesn't matter who's making the deliveries. Black, white, anyone. If the truck shows up, it gets unloaded. No more trouble. You and me—we both know that's how this has to work. You've been a good customer. No reason for that to change."

Cletus scratched the side of his face and gave a little snort. It might've passed for a chuckle if it hadn't carried that edge.

"Well now," he said, drawing out the words, "you sure got it all sorted out, don't ya?"

Joseph Henry didn't catch the sarcasm. He nodded once, serious.

"I think it's fair. Earl's pride might be hurt, but it beats the alternative."

Cletus leaned back in his chair, the wood creaking beneath him.

"You want me to go get him? Bring him in? Let's all talk it through, man to man to man?"

Joseph Henry nodded again. "I think that's a good idea."

Cletus stood, stretched his back like he was working out a kink. Joseph Henry saw a half-smile on Cletus's face, and had a moment of doubt. Cletus stepped out the office door. A few seconds later, the door creaked open again and Earl stepped inside... tension tight through his back. Cletus had already told him.

Joseph Henry didn't rise.

"Earl," he said evenly.

Earl didn't answer. Just stared at him. Then the words came... sharp and loud, full of contempt.

"You think you can come in here and tell folks how it's gonna be?" he said. "Tell us how this place is supposed to run?! That gets me. You're owed somethin'?! You think your word carries weight?!"

He took a slow step forward, voice rising. Joseph Henry didn't look away from his eyes.

"You sent a colored boy in here like it's normal. Like that's fine. Like he had the right. That boy can tell us what to do?! Tell us to unload his truck?! And we're all supposed to stand up and say yessir."

Another step. Joseph Henry wondered if he was about to get hit.

"You wanna talk about what he said or didn't say? I don't give a damn. This ain't about that!"

Another step. His jaw clenched. The smirk had vanished. Joseph Henry's hands tightened, ready to react.

"You think I'm gonna stand by while a nigger walks in here like he belongs? Hell no. Not now. Not ever."

His eyes burned, and he spat the words without hesitation.

"Hell no!"

He paused, then leaned forward slightly—just enough.

"You want me gone? Want me to pack up and disappear 'cause I didn't bow to some Black boy struttin' around? 'Cause I stood my ground?!" He snorted. "I don't run. Not for you, and not for some damned buck."

Joseph Henry blinked once. There was the slightest release of tension, and he slightly relaxed, no longer expecting something physical. But something inside him went still.

Behind Earl, Cletus let out a dry, honest laugh.

"Well," he said, spreading his hands. "Guess that's that."

His face held no apology.

"We don't owe you nothin', Henry. Not you, not your operation. Not even your Boss Van. You want to make a delivery, fine. This thing's gotta end, well that's the way it'll be. But we don't take orders from you. And we sure as hell don't run off one of our own just 'cause you got a soft spot for them folk."

Joseph Henry didn't speak right away.

Earl and Cletus saw a shift in his face... so subtle it might've been missed if they weren't already on edge. Then Joseph gave a quiet laugh… soft, without humor. Earl glanced toward Cletus, uneasy.

Earl's posture shifted under Joseph Henry's gaze. Then Joseph Henry turned to Cletus. When he spoke, his voice was calm... calmer than before, but it carried an edge, like angry steel.

"I thought you were decent men."

He let the words settle. Not angry. Not wounded. Just matter-of-fact. A man just calculating the sum of things. Cletus stiffened, wondering if the voice came from the same man.

"I tried to make it easy," he said, still to Cletus. "I liked y'all, no one needed to get hurt. You've been a good customer. Reliable. Smoother than some. That's why I gave you a way out. I gave you a chance."

He paused again, letting it breathe. His eyes were locked on Cletus's, and Cletus could see daggers in them.

"But you made your choice. And now I'll make mine."

His voice didn't rise. He leaned forward on the stool, elbows to his knees, a menacing look on his face, yet still calm.

"I don't give a damn what you think about Mr. Giles, or Black men, or Mexicans, or Chinese... You want to hate folks, hate 'em. But you don't touch mine. You don't lay hands on one of my men and expect the world to keep turning like nothing happened."

He looked at Earl, but it was like he was staring through him.

"I was going to let you walk. Now I don't care. Earl's done. He's either gone or dead. I don't much care which."

Joseph Henry shifted his eyes back to Cletus.

"You'll beat him half to death yourself. Then you'll send him so far off he won't come crawling back. Else I'll come back here. And then it won't be just half to death… and it'll be your garage… and it'll be your family."

His tone never changed. Not once. Just that same measured certainty.

"And if you think I'm bluffing," he added, eyes locked with Cletus, "you go ahead and keep him here. Let's see what comes through that garage door next time."

He stood slowly.

Behind him, the stool made a faint scrape against the floor.

"And, one more thing. You let people know how well we treat you. We're the best of partners… No more trouble, Cletus. Or you'll know trouble."

Joseph Henry looked down at his knees and paused, not expecting a response. He stood, brushed something non-existent from his sleeve, and walked out through the garage.

His hand trembled as he reached for the cab door.

As the truck pulled away, Joseph Henry's breathing turned ragged… sharp… uncontrollable. He fought it for half a mile before slamming the brakes and skidding to the shoulder, narrowly missing a rotted sycamore. He flung the door open, stumbled out, and vomited.

Chapter 23
1924

Joseph Henry sat in the cab of the truck, engine off, hands resting on the wheel. He'd been there a quarter of an hour, eyes fixed on the sign: *Law Offices of Denton & Harbison.*

He'd left the penitentiary early that morning so he could visit the still, run his routes, and still have time for this visit. Now it was late in the afternoon.

At last, he wiped his brow with a handkerchief, opened the door, and stepped out. The crushed-stone drive crunched under his boots.

He paused to brush the dust from his coat.

The building sat halfway up a hill, red brick, ivy climbing up the front. It seemed to watch the town below. Joseph Henry gave a slight nod to no one in particular and climbed the steps to the oaken door.

The door made more noise than he expected. He gave a small wave of apology to the woman behind the reception desk, who looked up over a pair of spectacles resting low on her nose, a thin chain looping behind her neck.

The reception area was quiet. Afternoon light filtered through tall windows, casting long beams across polished wood floors. Joseph Henry stood for a few moments, taking in the room. He was struck by the heavy furniture and the overwhelming smell of paper and pipe smoke.

The woman looked amused, but only just.

"May I help you, sir?"

"I…" Joseph Henry pulled a wrinkled piece of paper from his pocket and glanced at it. "I'm looking for Mr. Denton."

"Is he expecting you Mr.…"

"I'm sorry. Henry… Joseph Henry." He extended his hand.

She paused, her expression shifting. There was a flicker of recognition, a trace of surprise. She looked at his outstretched hand, then rose quickly.

"One moment."

She turned and disappeared down the hall. Joseph Henry looked around awkwardly, and folded his hands behind his back. He turned and stared at a large painting of a tall ship.

After a moment, a man appeared. He wore the same flicker of surprise the woman had.

"Mister Henry," he said, his expression brightening. "I'm Walt Denton. Would you please come in?"

He led Joseph Henry down the hallway and into an office.

Joseph Henry paused at the doorway. The office was deeper than it seemed from the outside. Books lined the walls. A decanter sat untouched on a sideboard. An elegantly framed diploma hung beside the window: *University of Virginia School of Law, 1908.*

"Please, sit."

Denton took the seat behind the desk, his usual place, back to the window. Two identical chairs faced him from the other side. Joseph Henry looked at one of them for a moment, then lowered himself into it without a word.

Denton had a curious smile on his face. He leaned forward and rested his elbows on the desk.

"You know, I never thought I'd actually meet you," he said. He hesitated a moment, then let out a thin laugh. "Knowing Boss Van, I wasn't even certain you existed."

Joseph Henry seemed about to respond when the door abruptly opened. The woman from the reception area entered carrying a small tray. Two cups sat atop it, steaming gently. She placed one in front of Denton, the other near Joseph Henry. He nodded a quiet thanks, not quite sure whether to reach for it. He had coffee in the penitentiary, but was not fond of it. He picked it up carefully and took a tentative sip. It was dark, rich, and sharp on the tongue. Stronger than what he was used to, but he liked it. It was far superior to the pale and harsh brew back in the penitentiary, often scorched and always tasting of the metal pot it had been boiled in.

The woman exited, closing the door behind her. Joseph Henry took a longer sip from his cup.

Returning to the conversation, as though it had never paused, he gave a short laugh.

"Oh, I exist, Mr. Denton."

Denton gave Joseph Henry an appraising stare.

"So, I take it your confinement has concluded. Are you here about the funds we've been holding?"

"No…" Joseph Henry gave another short laugh. "I'm still under the care of the Commonwealth." He tried to match Denton's cadence, giving the phrase an official tone.

Denton suddenly looked nervous, unsure how this man could be on the outside.

"It's nothing like that," Joseph Henry said, catching the shift in Denton's expression. He gave a slight shake of the head. "This may take some time, but let me explain."

He didn't go into detail. He just said that certain arrangements had been made, unofficial ones, and that his skills in managing particular operations had earned him a degree of trust. Enough, at least, to move with some freedom when needed.

"It's all quiet," he said. "Nothing public. Nothing permanent. But it seems to work."

Denton listened without interrupting. When Joseph Henry finished, the lawyer gave a slow nod. Not approval, but more understanding.

"All right, Mr. Henry. So what exactly are you here for?"

Joseph Henry paused, as though carefully choosing his words.

"It has been some time now, and it's not that I don't trust Boss Van. I just want to… confirm the funds."

Denton stood up and crossed to the file cabinet.

"Boss Van may be many things, Mr. Henry, but he is most certainly trustworthy. I've written a great many contracts for him over the years. He's a man of his word."

He opened a long drawer, riffled through some files, and removed a folder. Returned to his seat, he laid the folder flat and opened it on the desk in front of him.

"Beginning in November of 1919, two hundred dollars has been added each month."

Joseph Henry had just taken another sip of his coffee when the words landed. He choked, coughing hard, and nearly dropped the cup, then set it down with both hands like it might explode. He coughed once more into his sleeve, eyes wide, trying to catch his breath. *"I beg your pardon?"* he managed, still blinking.

"Forgive me, Mr. Henry, but did you not know the terms of the arrangement you and Boss Van agreed to?"

Joseph Henry looked sheepish. The truth was, he didn't. At the time, he felt bold and shrewd just asking for money to be provided at the end of his incarceration. He'd been overly pleased with himself, certain he had won a great concession.

He figured if he had a couple of thousand dollars when he got out, he'd be able to make his way.

"In truth," he said, self-consciously, "we never really talked about the actual dollar amount."

"I see, two hundred dollars a month, beginning November of 1919," Denton repeated. "As with Boss Van's other accounts we added an ongoing four percent interest, compounded monthly. As of this month, the account stands at just under thirteen thousand, three hundred and fifty dollars."

Joseph Henry's mouth parted, but no sound came.

***

Denton waited patiently for Joseph Henry to come to his senses.

"I understand. It is a considerable amount of money."

"I had no idea," Joseph Henry said wistfully. "I knew that Boss Van intended to provide compensation, as we discussed, but..."

"I've known Boss Van for a long time, Mr. Henry. He is a man of, shall we say, complex scruples. But one thing that I can tell you is that he can be extremely generous and rewarding to those he values. This does not surprise me in the least."

Joseph Henry nodded, still in partial disbelief. The two sat in silence for a moment. Then Denton spoke.

"Now, is there anything else, Mr. Henry?"

Joseph Henry blinked and came back to himself. He looked at Denton.

"Yes. Yes, there is, Mr. Denton."

Denton leaned back slightly, waiting for him to continue.

"I'd like to arrange for a sum of money to be delivered to a Minnie Timmons Henry."

"I see, your wife?" said Denton.

"I don't exactly know where she currently lives."

Denton frowned.

"I'm afraid I'm not certain I can help you if we don't have a way to..."

"I can furnish you with information on where she was," Joseph Henry interrupted, "where her parents lived. I understand that there will be costs involved. These can be paid out of the funds you hold for me."

Denton gave a slow nod, but did not reach for his pen.

"And the amount, Mr. Henry? What would you like us to send?"

Joseph Henry hesitated. "After your fees, I'd like half of the remaining amount delivered."

"Mr. Henry, that is a considerable amount," Denton responded.

"Yes. And ongoing, I want half of what comes in sent. Monthly."

Denton looked at him for a long moment.

"And is this a charitable gift," he asked carefully, "or something in the nature of support or obligation?"

Joseph Henry's mouth twitched. "Fair question. It's not charity. But it also isn't anything she asked for."

Denton said nothing.

"I want her to have it," Joseph said. "No strings."

"All right," Denton said, finally reaching for his notepad. "We'll draft the necessary contract and gather whatever details you can provide regarding Minnie Timmons Henry, her history, and where she might be now." He looked up. "Now, is there anything else?"

"Yes," Joseph Henry said quickly. "I'd like you to put together divorce papers. Or whatever's required for that."

Denton paused, then frowned again.

"I can draw up the paperwork, Mr. Henry," he said slowly. "But you understand, it's unusual to provide any kind of financial support before a divorce has gone through. In fact, doing so might raise questions about your intent. Whether this is part of a settlement, or an attempt at influence."

Joseph Henry shook his head. "It isn't."

"You're certain you want to proceed this way?"

"I am."

Denton studied him. "Then may I suggest, formally, that we tie the payments to the divorce proceeding? Make them contingent, or at least connected?"

"No."

Denton raised an eyebrow.

"Mr. Henry…"

"No."

Joseph Henry's voice was quiet but firm. "The money is hers, Denton. It has nothing to do with the divorce. There will be no papers for the money. I want the papers drawn for the divorce. I'll sign them. You'll deliver them to her. She'll sign them."

"And if she doesn't sign?"

"Doesn't matter. She will. The money goes to her either way. Monthly. No strings."

Denton gave a slow, thoughtful nod. "Very well. I'll draw up both sets of documents."

Joseph Henry said nothing. The room settled into silence.

Chapter 24

1929

Joseph Henry entered the mess through the side door, the one nearest the kitchen. He was halted by the wave of sound. It hit him like a hammer striking stone. Just for a beat, it stopped him at the threshold.

The run had taken longer than it should have. The deliveries went fine. It was a cool day, which made the truck ride more bearable. But not five minutes out from the last stop, the carburetor flooded, like it sometimes did when the choke stuck. Joseph Henry had to sit there about fifteen minutes with the hood up, waiting for it to catch its breath again.

It wasn't uncommon for Joseph Henry to arrive past the start of mess time. The line had cleared out by then, and someone usually had a seat for him.

The noise met him in layers. Closest was the scrape of spoons against tin, a steady rasp broken now and then by the sharper clink of a mug or the thud of bread hitting a plate. Beneath it came the creak and groan of benches, boots shifting over the concrete, the hollow bump of a knee or elbow against the table. Over all of it was the churn of voices, talk rising and falling, sometimes pierced by a bark of laughter or a disgruntled shout. Somewhere toward the back, the pattern of a guard's boots struck in slow, even beats, each one pulling a brief dip in the noise before the room filled again.

Joseph Henry didn't realize how hungry he was. As he tried to recall his last meal, he was struck by the smell of beans boiled with salt pork, the grease no doubt cooling on top in a thin skin. The aroma was much more appealing than it should have been, though it was hampered by the woolly smell of the men crowded close. Underneath it all was the faint bite of lye from the morning's scrub.

He moved toward the counter. An inmate, someone new by the look of him, stood behind the steaming tubs with a ladle in one hand and the other resting on the edge of the bin. He dropped a heavy mound of the beans into the center of the plate. Then sliced potatoes, pale and wet, the edges sagging. At the end of the counter was what was left of some cornbread, the basket nearly empty, just the last few broken pieces. He took a palmful, not bothering to shake the crumbs free.

Plate in hand, Joseph Henry looked toward the usual spots. One of the tables would have had a seat saved for him. It always did.

Near the far wall, where the light didn't reach as sharp, a knot of men were gathered close. He recognized Jimmy, Duane, Walker, Old Crow, and Nils. Milton was there too, and one they just called Shortstack, a pair newer to the group.

Old Crow looked disturbed, his attention fixed on the conversation. Joseph Henry began walking toward the table, but he stopped.

At the center of the group was Ugly Attics, one elbow on the table, his head bent toward the men. He was speaking just loud enough to be a buzz above the throng to Joseph Henry. The ones nearest him leaned in, their shoulders nearly touching his, clearly hanging on his words. A couple wore faint, knowing smiles, like they'd just heard something worth repeating. Others looked uncertain. Old Crow, solely, had a belligerent look on his face.

Jimmy looked up and caught Joseph Henry. He quickly looked away, his mouth pulling with doubt as he bent back toward the others.

Old Crow was sitting upright at the edge of the group, his plate untouched. His jaw was set, his gaze locked on Ugly the way a man might watch a snake cross the floor, not because it was coming his way, but just because it was there. He seemed to say something, his face tight with restrained anger. Ugly stopped talking and looked at Old Crow for a moment, then responded calmly with subtle hand gestures. Old Crow scowled.

Joseph Henry started toward them, the noise of the room pressing in on him. The voices becoming clear. Then he noticed there was no seat.

It had always been there before. Not officially his, of course. But routine had its own order. It wasn't about vanity, or some unwritten hierarchy. Joseph Henry never gave it much thought, never noticed whether someone was keeping it open for him. It was just always there. Which worked out well after some of his long days.

Now it was different, and for a moment Joseph Henry didn't know what to do. So he stood there, as if still looking for the seat.

Shortstack, sitting across from Ugly with his back to Joseph Henry, laughed at something, his broad shoulders bouncing on his low stocky frame. Nils laughed too, then he saw Joseph Henry and he smirked in that sideways way he did when unsure. Jimmy and Duane went silent, the slightest look of uncertain guilt on their faces.

Ugly Attics was mid-sentence, but slowed as if sensing the shift. His gaze slid up to Joseph Henry. Then back. He didn't speak to Joseph Henry. Didn't gesture. He just kept talking.

Joseph Henry stood still a moment longer. Then he began to turn.

"No, don't go, Mister Henry." Only Joseph Henry picked up on faint mockery in Ugly's voice. "Shortstack, give Mister Henry your seat. You're finished, and Mister Henry must have had such a long day."

Shortstack paused, clearly shocked by the request. Ugly gave his lopsided smile and nodded. Shortstack slid back his seat and rose, lifting his tray from the table. He shot Joseph Henry a glare before heading to the collection station to deposit it.

Joseph Henry looked around the table. Most of the faces avoided his, looking some degree of discomfort. Only Old Crow met his eyes. He gave a small, almost pleading nod toward the empty seat. Joseph Henry forced a weak smile, set his tray down, and sat.

No one spoke for several minutes. Joseph Henry could feel Ugly Attics watching him, though he kept his own eyes on the plate. The beans had settled into a shallow ring around the cornbread. He wasn't hungry anymore. His fork moved absently through the food, just enough to keep his hand busy.

Ugly was watching him through his left eye, the ruined side of his face turned toward him. It wasn't careless. Joseph Henry had already noticed the habit. Ugly did it on purpose, as if to unnerve.

Ugly finally spoke, voice casual, though with a hint of caustic. Like he was remarking on the weather on a foul day.

"Funny how a man can walk into a room and the whole shape of it changes."

He dipped a piece of bread into the remains of his beans and brought it to his mouth. He chewed slowly. "Sometimes it's because he brings something with him." He paused for half a beat. "Other times, maybe something got dropped while he was gone."

He smiled, but didn't look up. "Hard to say which it was."

Joseph Henry didn't reply. Now that he'd had some time, he let go of the fork and leaned back in his seat. He gave Ugly his thin smile, indicating he was ready to hear the rest of what Ugly was going to say.

Ugly lifted his eyes without lifting his head. He caught Henry's expression and gave a short, empty laugh. "Course," he said, "folks talk. That's what they do. Fill the air. They don't always mean harm. But then again, they don't always know where the harm started. Not really."

Jimmy shifted beside him, sensing something he couldn't quite place. Duane's spoon stalled halfway to his mouth before he went on eating. Shortstack had returned by then and leaned against the wall, watching.

Ugly leaned back slightly. His eyes dropped back to his tray as his fingertips edged around the tin plate. His voice came soft, thoughtful, like he was musing more to himself than anyone else.

"Some men earn their place one honest day at a time. Hard days. Hard work. Earn every inch with the skin off their knuckles. Folks remember that kind of man. Trust him for it. Respect him, even if they don't like him."

He brought his eyes back to Joseph Henry.

"Then there's the other kind. Quiet. Maybe clever. Knows where to stand, when to speak. Knows how to look useful. Not always for the good of the work. Not for the workers, either. Just knows where the ground's a little softer, where the shade's a bit thicker. And after enough years of that, a man might sit himself down and not even realize where he got the seat. Just seemed to be his instead of someone else's."

Without looking away, he dipped the last bit of cornbread into his plate, sopped up the last of the beans, and ate it slowly. The others glanced around, unsure what he meant. But Joseph Henry knew.

Joseph Henry gave a wry smile as he prepared to speak. But an angry Crow beat him to it.

He had just heard Old Crow's fork strike the edge of the table, then hit the floor. Then…

"You talk a lot for someone nobody knew two months ago," Crow said. "Seems like every time your mouth opens, it's about someone else's business. And if you can't find a thing worth sayin', you make it up just the same."

His voice was right on the edge of rising.

"You want to talk about how a man gets his place? You go ahead. But don't sit here tryin' to measure another man's worth when you ain't even finished your own supper."

Then he seemed to run out of steam. He paused. Then he reached down and picked up his fork.

Ugly kept his eyes on Joseph Henry, slow and steady. He heard Old Crow, but it only hit him with the weight of a light breeze.

"Friends are a good thing. Real good… sometimes…" His voice came in an almost sleepy drawl. "The thing about friends is, sometimes you care about them."

He shifted slightly.

"I had a dog once, back when I was small. A little chico. He was my best amigo. I'd do anything for that dog. One day, some bigger chicos come to me. They wanted something. I don't remember what. Maybe pesos. I say no."

He gave an exaggerated sigh.

"They kicked my dog. I gave them the pesos."

He ran a finger through a smear of bean sauce on his plate, then slowly licked it clean.

"Not always fair. Just happens. Right place, wrong time."

His eyes slid to Old Crow.

"Poor Dog."

He let the words hang a moment, like smoke that hadn't found the ceiling yet. Then, in a flat tone, "The dog probably never knew why he was kicked."

Shortstack, still leaning against the wall, chuckled. Nils wore a look of disbelief, like he'd just realized what might have been said.

Ugly turned back to Joseph Henry with a new energy behind his eyes.

"Mister Henry... you know what I mean? You understand, eh?"

He tapped the table once with his index finger.

"Sometimes when things are going against you, it ain't just you who gets it. Sometimes you gotta wait and see who else limps away after."

Joseph Henry shot up. In one quick motion, he shoved his tray forward, the beans and cornbread splattering across Ugly's chest and chin. Ugly barely flinched.

There was a look on Joseph Henry's face, not quite rage, but something colder, more deliberate. It wasn't wild. It was measured.

To anyone watching, it might have looked like he'd lost control, like he was lunging across the table in a fit of fury. But it wasn't that. With a single, fluid movement, he turned the chair sideways and stepped onto it, ready to cross the table.

He felt a hand on his shoulder. Firm, but calm.

He turned slightly. Ronnie, one of the more seasoned guards, was standing behind him.

"Settle down, Mr. Henry," Ronnie said gently. "You don't want to do that."

Joseph Henry held still for a beat, then exhaled and stepped back down.

Ugly casually flicked food from his face.

"Well… well. There's the loud part, amigo."

Everyone at the table was struck. Ugly, for the first time since they'd met him, had almost managed a smile across his entire face. But it was a cold smile. A knowing smile. A satisfied smile.

Ronnie's hand lingered on Joseph Henry's shoulder a moment longer than necessary. Not gripping, not restraining, just steady and guiding.

"Come on, Mr. Henry," he said, like a friend walking another home after one too many. His voice was calm, almost warm. "Let's get you away from here."

Joseph Henry didn't resist. His jaw was tight, his eyes fixed on Ugly, but he let Ronnie nudge him gently back from the table.

They had barely taken two steps when Ugly's voice floated across the din, piercing. There was a kind of glee in his voice. Like a boy who just won his first game of marbles.

"I sure do like to see how nice these guards can be when they want to, don't you think?"

The noise at the table died. Ronnie slowed. Joseph Henry stopped altogether, and glanced back.

Ugly was still seated. He hadn't moved. He hadn't even wiped the rest of the beans from his shirt. But he had his eyes on Joseph Henry, flat, direct. And still that smile.

"See that, amigos?" Ugly's voice was the same. "You flip a tray. You step up like you're about to fly across the table, maybe hurt somebody. You make a mess on somebody. And what happens?"

With an exaggerated gesture he swept some beans from his shirt onto the table and floor. Glancing up at Joseph Henry with a mocking glare.

"Friendly Mister Guard here gives you a pat and walks you out like he's takin' you out to the yard for fresh air."

There was a small shift at the table, like they knew a line was being crossed and wanted to show they weren't part of it. Even by just moving inches. One or two men glanced at Ronnie, then quickly away.

"But let's say one of you did that amigos," he went on. "Shortstack, maybe. Or Nils. Or Milton. Hell, Jimmy. You think it would've gone that way?"

He turned his face slightly now, still angled toward Joseph Henry, but addressing the others. Nils and Jimmy looked away sheepishly, not wanting to be called out. Shortstack and Milton's faces suddenly developed belligerent looks.

"You think Mister Guard would have come up and helped you away? Maybe whispered in your ear like the mama hen?" He gave a laugh, dry as dust. "No. That's not how it goes, hermanos. Not for us."

Now he looked directly at Jimmy. Then at Duane. Seeing them trying to distance themselves, he stopped smiling.

His voice gained an edge. "You'd be on the ground by now, Jimmy. Face in the beans, Duane. Arm wrenched up so tight you'd hear your own shoulder pop. And then you'd be cooling off in the can for a day. Maybe two. Maybe three."

He looked back to Joseph Henry.

"But not him. Not the quiet boy. Not their favorite."

Now Ugly leaned forward, resting an elbow on the table. Not caring that it fell into the beans.

His voice became suddenly calm, almost kindly, like he was addressing a child after a scolding. "That's what we talked about earlier. Some folks are treated better than others. Maybe some people are better than others."

He finally looked up at Ronnie, like he'd just realized the man was there.

"No offense, Mister Guard. We all got our jobs."

Ronnie shifted slightly. He looked uncertain now, like he'd been drawn into something he didn't quite mean to be part of.

Ugly sat back.

"That's enough for today, amigos," he said cheerfully, as if the conversation had only been about the weather.

Joseph Henry flinched, like for a moment he might go back across the table. Then he allowed Ronnie to nudge him away, leaving the table behind.

Old Crow got up slowly, looked at the inmates at the table, then stepped in behind Ronnie and Joseph Henry.

"You go on, puppy dog," Ugly called after him. "You follow your master home." He snorted another laugh.

Ronnie escorted Joseph Henry back to the cell block, with Old Crow following close behind.

"Mr. Henry, you shouldn't do stuff like that," Ronnie said. "I know you and Boss Van are tight, but it don't do us guards no good bein' put in a situation like that."

Joseph Henry had returned to his usual self, as if the earlier events hadn't happened. He turned to Ronnie and stopped.

"I know, Ronnie. And I'm truly sorry." A thin smile touched his lips. "That's not me. Long day."

"I know, Mr. Henry. Never seen you like that before. You were like another man." He gave a short, uneasy laugh.

Joseph Henry stood a moment, staring at the floor. A faraway look passed over his face. Then he looked up again, reached out, and gave Ronnie's hand a brief shake.

"Goodnight, Ronnie. I appreciate your help."

Ronnie smiled, like he was getting a compliment from his boss.

"Thanks, Mr. Henry." He turned and walked back the way they'd come.

Joseph Henry turned and walked with Old Crow the rest of the way down the corridor.

Crow glanced up at him. "I don't understand what all that was about. I don't understand at all. Why don't that man like you none?"

"I don't know," Joseph Henry said quietly. "You don't need any of this. It's my mess."

They walked in silence a few more steps.

"I just don't like the way he looks at you. Like he knows something nobody else does."

Joseph Henry gave a soft exhale, something like a laugh but it wasn't. "He likes to stir things up, that's all. I don't know why exactly. He wants folks looking at me different."

Old Crow nodded, but it was clear he didn't understand.

Joseph Henry stopped at Crow's cell and guided him in. "Get some sleep, old man. You did more good than you know."

Crow stepped inside. He looked back once, eyes clouded. "You sure you're alright?"

"I'm alright."

Joseph Henry gave his shoulder a gentle pat, then turned and walked back down the row without looking back.

Chapter 25
1929

The run wasn't a long one, and it had nothing to do with the whiskey operation. As much as the penitentiary work sometimes felt like a cover, it was real work that took real time.

Joseph Henry had taken the truck out that morning with a load of leather for a shoe factory just outside of Frankfort. The foreman counted the bundles, signed the slip with a stub of pencil, then Joseph Henry turned the truck around and headed back to the penitentiary.

The mess hall run-in from the day before still hung on him. He didn't care what Ugly said or did to him. But he was pulling at the others now, and Joseph Henry liked a good many of them. Some he'd known a long time. Maybe not the sharpest, but they knew each other.

Ugly was good. Joseph Henry had to give him that. It wasn't fair that the others were being pulled into whatever this was.

Still, he figured it wouldn't stick. He went too far back with most of them. It was the new ones he didn't know. No telling what Ugly could do with them.

He pulled through the vehicle yard. The mid-afternoon air had that hollow quality it sometimes carried. A lot happening, but noise without shape. Men doing busy work that meant nothing to them. Eyes low, steps quick, not much talk. He parked where the truck always goes and set the brake. A pair of inmates who usually nodded as he passed didn't lift their heads. One of them looked like he might, then just didn't. Joseph Henry actually chuckled.

As he stepped down from the cab, Joseph Henry noticed the guard, Reeves, standing off to the side. Reeves wasn't often in the yard, but when he was, he'd usually make small talk, sometimes more. Now and then he'd pull Joseph Henry aside for a longer word or a quick story. Joseph Henry had the sense Reeves knew, from the other guards, about his standing with the warden, and maybe that he sometimes brought things back from Louisville for them. Joseph Henry would smile to himself at times, thinking Reeves a little overeager, like a pup jumping for attention.

This time Reeves didn't approach. He stayed where he was and gave Joseph Henry a small frown. A weight dropped in the pit of Joseph Henry's stomach. *Bad news,* he thought.

He walked over. Reeves looked at him, then away, as if about to impart some secret. Then, keeping it low, he said, "Your old man spent time in the infirmary this morning. Says he took a fall." Reeves shifted the keys in his hand. "Think there was more to it."

Joseph Henry felt a pinch in his gut. "More?"

Reeves glanced back at him. "Didn't see it. But there was a scuffle between Nils and that other one, they call him Short Stack, at about the same time."

Joseph Henry chewed on it for a moment. "Thanks. Appreciate it."

Reeves nodded, a faint, maybe satisfied smile at the corner of his mouth.

Joseph Henry walked the corridor toward the cell blocks, dreading what he would find. The mess hall from the night before kept running through his head. A mop bucket sat at rest by the door. Inside the block he heard a guard's voice snapping at an inmate. He walked on.

Halfway down on the left, near a pillar where the paint flaked in ribbons, Old Crow's cell sat open. Crow lay on the bunk with his hands crossed over his belly. His eyes seemed to be fixed on his hat that hung from a nail by the window. Joseph Henry stopped at the bars.

"You sleeping?" he said, trying to put a lightness to his voice.

Crow turned his head and smiled. A small line, but solid. "Just doing what could pass for it," he said. "If I lie still long enough I think it counts."

Joseph Henry gave a short laugh. "You hurt?"

"Old bones," Crow answered. "The floor makes a habit of meeting me more sudden than it used to."

"Heard the Infirmary had you for a spell. You took a fall…"

Crow shifted his eyes to the ceiling. "That's what I told them," he said.

Joseph Henry's jaw went tight. "Who?" Though he already knew the answer.

Crow's eyes narrowed. "I just took a fall, like I said." His voice didn't carry much conviction. He gave a small noise that might've been a laugh. "Maybe it was the stairs. My shoe met the step wrong. I met the wall."

Joseph Henry stepped in closer. A bruise ran from Crow's cheekbone into the cropped hair at the side of his head. His shoulder showed a stiffness too. He winced as he shifted to look at Joseph Henry.

"Stairs…" Joseph Henry said back to him.

Crow breathed out slow, resigned. "I've had worse," he said. "Don't just stand there like a doctor. I am all right."

Joseph Henry stood a moment longer, then nodded once. "You need anything?"

"You go on. Surely still things to do today."

He lingered one more beat, then turned and left the block. Outside the door, he let out a breath. A stream of light from a high window caught the mop bucket, casting a pale line across the floor. A smear of grease marked the concrete a few feet away. He didn't know why, but he took the mop and swiped it once across the mark, leaving the floor clean.

He studied his handiwork, then set off to find Nils.

Nils worked the afternoon in the laundry. The room was always louder than Joseph Henry expected. He stepped into the room and was met by the clatter of presses and the wet slap of fabric. Steam hung thick in the air like a wet wool blanket. The big roller irons gave off a steady churn, wheezing with each rotation, and the long folding tables were cluttered with half-sorted bundles. Everything smelled of lye soap and damp linen, cut now and then by the sharper scent of scorched cotton. A line of shirts hung over the back rail, sleeves limp and swaying with the draft from a wall vent.

More men than seemed necessary moved through it all in a kind of chaotic shuffle. The steam clung to everything, like a damp sheet left overnight on the line. The air was thick with it. Steam, effort, and the weight of repetition.

Joseph Henry scanned the room. In the far corner, away from the press tables, he found Nils. He stood next to Jimmy, the two working in tandem folding sheets. Jimmy saw him first. He gave him a look that slid away fast, like he'd been caught holding something he shouldn't. He finished folding the current sheet, then stepped away to another station without meeting Joseph Henry's eyes.

Joseph Henry followed him. "You hear about Crow?" he asked to Jimmy's back.

"Man falls," he said, not turning. "Old men fall more."

"Come on, Jimmy, he's one of us. You know he didn't just fall."

Jimmy looked toward Joseph Henry over his left shoulder, a bead of sweat running down and gathering at the end of his nose. "One of you... he's one of you... not us." There was a tinge of anger in his voice. "Attics isn't wrong 'bout that, is he?"

Joseph Henry leaned a knuckle against the bench and looked Jimmy square in the eye. His voice came firmer than he'd expected. "I have always done right by you, by all of you," he said. "When tools went missing, I found them for you. When you were late for a detail, who gave an excuse? You remember the day they moved you off the kiln? Who put in the word for you."

Jimmy looked down, a slight look of shame on his face, but he held on to his malice. He wiped his hands on his apron. His eyes rose slightly, but not enough to meet Joseph Henry's. "You have your liberties," he said. "We all see them."

"I have what Boss Van puts in my hands," Joseph Henry said. "But I don't stand above anyone. If I ever used any of it against you, you tell me. Right now."

Nils came up behind Joseph Henry. "You got things other men don't here," he said, and Joseph Henry craned his head over his shoulder to look at him.

"You go out the gate. You come back. You have a way with guards. They say you speak to the warden as if he knows your name. That makes a man look at you different."

Joseph Henry took a long breath and let it out slow and steady.

"I go out and do things because I do something for him," he said. "That's not for talk. It's something he needs, and something I can give. It's clean work and I don't boast. But I also use it for all of you when I can. I keep trouble off men who maybe couldn't carry it. I bring things in from the outside whenever I can. Get y'all magazines or food, or cigarettes. Anything to give y'all a little bit of the outside. I know it ain't fair that I go out and others don't. So I try to make it a little more fair. Remember that time you heard your brother got the fever and maybe wouldn't make it. You needed that day's quiet, and I got you off your details. I don't do any of that to own you. I don't want anything. I do it because it's right. I do it because we're like family."

Nils worked his jaw side to side and looked up at the ceiling. He knew they were steered wrong by Ugly Attics. He lowered his gaze back to Joseph Henry.

"He should not have said it."

"Who?" Joseph Henry said.

"Short Stack," Nils answered. "He started in on Crow. Said old men should keep their mouths closed. Said you didn't deserve anything you got, and he shouldn't be speaking up for you. Said you needed to answer for everything. But since you were always someplace else, maybe somebody else needed to answer for you. Crow just turned his back on Short Stack. Then Crow hit the stone and didn't get right back up. We all saw it. Short Stack pushed him when he'd turned away. Just pushed the old man. Ugly has a long arm, and somehow he's got it around us. I don't even know when it started. But Old Crow, he's one of us. I took Short Stack to task. And he's not as much of a man when the other fella ain't seventy. I pulled him away from Crow. He shoved me pretty good. Then I put a fist into his nose. He went down and was bleeding from it. That was about the end of it. Nobody else really moved, but me and Jimmy got Crow up and to the infirmary."

Joseph Henry weighed what Nils just said then nodded, "Well… thanks for that, Nils." He turned back to Jimmy, "Thank you too, Jimmy."

Jimmy's eyes were moist. "I'm sorry, Joseph," he said. "I don't know what that Ugly has. It's like a spell or something. This is over for us though. I ain't listening to a word from him no more."

Short Stack was still pretty new. He'd only been in the penitentiary a couple of months, but he seemed to know his way around. You could tell it wasn't his first go-round.

Joseph Henry had to ask around to find what detail Short Stack was on. Turned out he was with a group breaking up rock in the far corner of the yard, where a foundation was going to be laid for a new shed.

Most of them looked to be leaning on their sledgehammers, jawing more than swinging. The guard, Moneymaker, stood against the fence, laughing at something Short Stack or one of the others had said.

He spotted Joseph Henry crossing the yard, tensed up, and barked for the group to get back to work.

Short Stack looked up to see what had changed with Moneymaker. He probably expected to see another guard, maybe even the warden. He let out an exaggerated laugh when he saw who it was.

"Well now," he said, loud and slow, "look who's come to check on his crew. Thought maybe the *boss man* would be too busy runnin' the place to grace us with a visit."

Moneymaker snapped his head around. "That's enough, get them sledges swinging."

Short Stack gave a sideways grin at the guard, but kept his mouth shut. He laughed again as he picked up a sledge hammer.

Moneymaker straightened, wiping his hands on his belt. "Afternoon, Mr. Henry. Anything I can help you with?"

Joseph Henry tensed, realizing this interaction was part of the problem. Looking at Short Stack he felt ire rise within him, but pushed it to the back. This was going to be a civil conversation.

"Hey, Billy," he responded, not taking his eyes off of Short Stack. "Just need a word with one of your crew."

Short Stack suddenly got a nervous look on his face when Joseph Henry addressed the guard by his first name.

"Can I borrow Short Stack?" Joseph Henry continued.

"Sure thing, Mr. Henry, though not for too long. Or they won't be able to pour the floor tomorrow," Billy laughed.

Short Stack wiped his palms on his pants and walked over slow, knowing Joseph Henry had come for him. His eyes flicked to

Moneymaker, then back again. He stopped a few feet off, a wry smile sat on his face.

"You want a word?"

Joseph Henry gave a nod and gestured for them to walk. They stepped away from the others, past a wheelbarrow stacked with gravel. When they were out of earshot, Joseph Henry stopped.

"You know why I'm here," he said flatly.

Short Stack raised both eyebrows in mock surprise. "What, the old man took a tumble? Can't blame me if he trips over his own damn feet."

"'Course he did." Joseph Henry forced a similar mocking grin on his own face. "Then you took a bit of a tumble yourself… into someone's fist."

Short Stack frowned, his hand drifting up, almost unconsciously, to touch his nose. A dull shadow beneath his eyes showed more damage from Nils than just a nosebleed.

Joseph Henry let that pass. "You said some things," he went on. "Things that didn't sit right with Crow. Things about me, that have nothing to do with Crow. I don't care what you say about me. You and Ugly can do what you like to me." Joseph Henry's voice was calm, without malice. "Crow's just an old man. You're gonna leave him alone."

Short Stack's face slackened and he snorted. "Your Crow's part of it all, though. All I said's the truth. Ugly just points out what everyone else ought to be seein'. You come and go. You don't get the worst jobs. Heck, you probably eat and sleep better than the rest of us. Some of us wonder why you even belong in here. Maybe they should just open the gate and let you go." He smiled thin. "Seems to me Ugly's just the first one with the guts to call you out."

Joseph Henry nodded slowly. "You're not wrong that I've got things others don't. No point arguing it. I go out that gate because I do work the warden, *Boss Van*, needs done." He wasn't sure if using Boss

Van's name meant anything to Short Stack, but if it added weight it couldn't hurt. "I have something that helps him, and he uses it. He uses me. Can't talk much about it, but it matters to him. Sure, it makes my life a bit better. And every time I can, I try to use it to help the rest of you. I bring things back for the boys. I get folks off the hook when I can. I don't hold it over anyone."

He fixed Short Stack with his eyes, his voice steady and sincere.

"You think Crow and the others stick their necks out because I give them things? Or because I threatened them? No. They do it because I've had their backs. Because we've always had each other's backs."

Short Stack tilted his head and let out a laugh. "You're so noble? They should make you the Mayor of this place. A little bread for the birds. Tossing it from your warm spot on a park bench." He leaned in a touch. "Mr. Henry, I'm sure you're believing your own myth. Maybe the old man thinks he earned your kindness. But the rest of us are just characters in your story."

Short Stack's thin smile lingered as he straightened up. "This place ain't just your yard to stroll across. Men listen to Ugly. Heck, they hear him clearer than they hear you now." He jabbed a finger toward Joseph Henry's chest. "And me? I'm right here, carrying his word."

Now he let out a dry gravelly laugh. "Old Crow, and anybody who stands too close to you, they're gonna feel it. A push here, a shove there. Accidents happen. A man slips on the steps, a man don't get up so quick. Maybe don't get up at all. You know how it goes."

His eyes narrowed, voice dropping lower, harsher. "You like making things easier for all them? You best just move on. Find yourself a hole and crawl in it. Or better yet, next time you're outside, just keep going. Don't find your way back. Ugly's got a long arm..." Short Stack's laugh was genuine now. "...And I ain't afraid to use it. You, Crow, any other idiots that call you friend. They're all fair game."

Joseph Henry let the calm fall out of his face. What he put on in its place made Short Stack flinch. The air seemed to tighten, heavy and close, and Short Stack's eyes darted around as if something else had suddenly approached.

"You like to talk," Joseph Henry said. "You like to threaten. You like to strut around, flex your muscles. But I don't think you've thought this through." He stepped in close, his breath hot across Short Stack's face. "All these things that you say I have, all these strings you think I pull. What if I can do them with the snap of my fingers? What if I do have a thing with the guards… or the warden? I can have you in the lime kiln by the morning. Not for a day, for the whole season. I can cut your meals to once a day. I can take your sleep and break it into pieces so small that you will think you never closed your eyes. And your friends? They'll have the same, and they'll know it was because of you. Let's see who's getting a push and a shove then? Accidents happen…"

Short Stack's grin held a heartbeat, then slipped. He gave a laugh anyway, but he looked to his left as he did. Joseph Henry knew he'd gotten through.

"Think it over," Joseph Henry said. "A bit better than you have."

Short Stack licked his lips, the fight clearly gone from him. He shifted his weight and gave a half-shrug, refusing to meet Joseph Henry's eyes.

"All right, maybe you've made your point." His voice was thin, but he tried to layer it with indifference. It didn't work. "Don't know what it is Ugly's got against you, and truth be told, I guess I won't care any more. But Ugly? He ain't goin' to back off. It's not in him."

He rubbed his nose again where Nils had bloodied it, then let his hand drop. "I guess I can step aside. But Ugly? He's not going anywhere. That much you can count on."

Chapter 26
1929

Joseph Henry had been in the maintenance stockroom a couple of hours that morning. His mind kept circling back to the trouble Old Crow had, and the talk he had with Short Stack the day before. He felt confident Short Stack wouldn't be a problem anymore, but he was right about one thing, Ugly Attics. Joseph Henry had sat on his hands long enough, telling himself he didn't care what Ugly did to him. But now it had spread past him to Crow, and maybe the others. That changed things.

The open ledger sat in front of him, untouched. He had stared at it nearly half an hour. Not reading. Not jotting. Waiting. His eyes drifted to the clock every few minutes. He'd already spoken with Ephraim, a guard he knew from his trips through the vehicle yard. They had an unspoken understanding. Joseph Henry would bring him a jar or two of Lorillard's Scotch Sweet Snuff from Louisville, a favorite of Ephraim, and something that never made it out to the local country stores. Ephraim swore it was better than anything he could get in Frankfort. In return he would see to a favor now and again.

This time, he'd see that the guard who oversaw the boiler room detail took the other inmate assigned there away for a while, leaving Ugly Attics alone.

By then, the boiler room guard should be collecting the other inmate. Joseph Henry thought it might be Virgil. He was a thin, wiry man everyone called Red for the shot of hair on his head, though it had gone gray at the sides over the last year.

Joseph Henry shut the ledger and slid it into the drawer. He stepped out and eased the door closed behind him, as though the sound alone might compromise his plan. He gave a soft chuckle and shook his head at his own over-caution.

No one was in the hallways, but he kept to the shadows along the side, feeling as if he were on a mission no one was meant to see. Given his standing with the guards, it was unlikely anyone would question him if they saw him, but wasn't that the very heart of the issue? Joseph Henry began to wonder if he should do something to change that in the future.

He left the stockroom and followed the hallway. It soon narrowed into a service hall. The walls became close and bare. Pipes rose from the floor at the edges and ran along the ceiling overhead. A dim bulb hung every ten feet, each one humming faintly and leaving stretches of shadow where the pipes crossed.

Ahead on the right was a heavy door leading to the basement stairs. Though still fifteen feet off, Joseph Henry started when it swung open. Out came the guard from the boiler room, Virgil trailing behind.

The guard gave a nod. "Afternoon, Mr. Henry."

Joseph Henry recognized the face, though he couldn't place the name. He nodded back. "Afternoon…" Then to Virgil: "Red."

Virgil nodded back. He looked uneasy, likely from not knowing where the guard was taking him.

Joseph Henry slowed, waiting for the two to go out of sight before stepping into the stairwell. He started down and was immediately struck by how the air grew warmer with each step. The dull throb of machinery carried up from below, joined by the hiss of steam and the occasional clank of iron. As he reached the lower landing, the heat thickened, wisps of coal dust hanging in the air. By the time he turned toward the boiler room, he could smell the smoke and feel the dry burn in his throat. With each step closer to the door, his momentum ebbed, until he could scarcely take the last one.

He swallowed hard and reached for the handle. The iron was hot under his palm. He gave a steady pull, willing the door to move without a sound. If it made one, he didn't hear it. The noise came from within instead. The roar of the boilers and the hiss of steam spilled through the opening as the door gave way.

Joseph Henry had never seen the boiler room before. His early details had never taken him down to the bowels of the penitentiary. The chamber stretched longer than he expected, low and built of brick and concrete. The air pressed down on him like a pair of rough hands. Two great iron boilers sat side by side along the far wall twenty feet away, the heat from their firebox doors welling out and the glow of the fire seeping through the seams.

Wheelbarrow tracks and boot prints cut through months of coal dust that lay heavy on the floor. Beside the boilers a dark mound of coal waited to be fed into the fires, freshly spilled from the metal chute slanting down from the ceiling above.

Pipes ran overhead, some as thick as his torso, others no wider than an arm, hissing and dripping where the heat forced steam through the joints. Fist-sized bulbs in wire cages gave little light, leaving the glow of the fireboxes to throw an angry, restless flicker across the walls.

Joseph Henry hadn't known what to expect. Though not as bad as the lime kiln, the smell of smoke and scorched iron stung his throat, and the heat carried a dry weight that made every breath an effort.

Through the haze Joseph Henry spotted Ugly Attics. Left on his own, he leaned against the wall beside the chute, a cigarette glowing between his lips and a coal shovel at his feet. The memory of the lime kiln crossed Joseph Henry's mind, smoke and fire and dust, but he let it pass. Whatever the risk, he decided he didn't care.

Ugly glanced down at the shovel, then at the firebox doors, as if weighing whether to go back to work with no taskmaster watching. His eyes lifted toward the boiler-room door, where he had last seen the guard depart. There stood Joseph Henry. Ugly blinked, as though doubting what he saw. He brushed a hand across his face, as if to clear away the coal dust. Then, realizing Joseph Henry was truly there, he smiled a thin sneer.

Ugly leaned down slowly and lifted the shovel, resting the spade end on the floor, his eyes never leaving Joseph Henry. He straightened, then let his gaze drift around the room, feigning surprise at noticing the guard and the other inmate were gone. He gave a short laugh.

"Well now," he said, the cigarette still glowing at his lips. "Didn't figure your strings pulled that far. Thought you were just a favorite child… an errand boy. Seems I was wrong, amigo."

He let the smile fade, replacing it with a lopsided frown, the left side of his mouth slow to follow.

"Are you going to kill me, Mister Henry? Was that the plan?" He tightened his grip on the shovel, just in case. "Put my body in the firebox?"

"Don't want to fight, Ugly. Not here to kill anyone," Joseph Henry said, raising his hands in front of him in a calming gesture. "Just want to talk. Settle things."

Ugly's face went flat. He eased a little on the shovel handle. "Talk?"

Joseph Henry lowered his hands. His face tightened, and when he spoke his voice was firm and steady.

"When you started this," he said, "I didn't know what to make of it. It threw me a little. But it didn't bother me the way you think it did."

Ugly squinted at him through the haze, cigarette still clinging to his lip. He gave the slightest snort.

Joseph Henry took a step closer. "Then you pressed deeper. That bear story. Other things. Like you were feeling around for the right buttons to press."

Ugly grinned faintly. "I found a few."

"You did," Joseph Henry said. "Some good ones. That's when I knew there was something behind it. Not just talk. Not just bullying. You were after something." He paused. "But I still didn't care. You could work on me all day, it didn't matter. I don't care how it affects me."

The boiler gurgled and a shot of steam sent a hot breath across the room. Ugly took the cigarette from his mouth and flicked the ash, then he spit on the floor. Joseph Henry took another step forward. Ugly's grip stayed fixed on the shovel handle.

Joseph Henry gritted his teeth together. "But then you pressed the wrong buttons. Or maybe the right ones. You brought in others… Old Crow." His voice caught just enough for Ugly to notice a palpable restraint. He took one more step closer. His shadow stretched toward Ugly across the coal-dusted floor. "That crossed a line. You knew it would. And now I do care."

Ugly's smirk faltered. He shifted, easing again on the handle, though his eyes stayed sharp. "Careful, Mister Henry. A man says he don't care, then says he does. Hard to tell which man he is."

Joseph Henry shook his head once. "No. You wanted me to care. That's what you were pushing for. Well, you got it. Now I do care. Which means this ends here."

He let the words settle, the noise of the room filling the silence. Then he fixed Ugly with a hard look.

"Now you're going to tell me what you want. What this is all about. Why me."

Ugly studied him a long moment. He brought the cigarette back to his lips and drew deeply. Then he let the smoke curl from his lips. The sneer threatened to return, but it didn't.

"So… now we're amigos, Mister Henry."

Joseph Henry's brow tightened. "I think you know better than that, Ugly."

Ugly chuckled low, dropping the nub of his cigarette and grinding it out beneath his boot. "Course I do… amigo. Men like us don't trade friendship. We trade other things."

Joseph Henry watched him carefully. The heat and steam pressed in, sweat breaking across his brow. "Let's get down to it then. What do you want."

Ugly's eyes narrowed. "Saying maybe I don't have to keep after you. Or that old crow of yours. Maybe I let it all go." He leaned a little heavier on the shovel handle.

Joseph Henry said nothing at first. He weighed the words. The ground beneath them felt suddenly fragile.

"You're telling me the trouble stops," he said slowly, "so what do I have to give."

Ugly gave a raspy laugh. "Smart man. I knew you'd get there."

He wiped his forehead with the back of his hand, cutting a pale streak through the black of the coal dust. He dropped the shovel onto the coal pile beneath the chute and walked past Joseph Henry toward the door. Looking back, he motioned with his head for Joseph Henry to follow.

They stepped through the door, and Ugly led him halfway up the stairs before sitting down on the stone step. He gestured for Joseph Henry to do the same. Joseph Henry was glad to. The heat had gotten to him. Even at the halfway point, the air was already cooler, the difference sharp and bearable.

Ugly ran the back of his hand across his nose, the sweat smearing the soot into black clumps. He drew in a long breath, the cooler stairwell air easing him as well. Joseph Henry pulled a handkerchief from his pocket and offered it. Ugly studied it a moment, suspicion in his eyes. Then he nodded with a faint smile and took it.

Wiping his face, he spoke. "You asked what I want." Joseph Henry noticed something different in his tone, still strong but touched with wistfulness. "I want out of here." He swept his hand in a loose gesture, indicating the penitentiary itself.

"What?" Joseph Henry said suddenly, the word sounding wrong in his ears.

"Out of this place. Out of these walls. Out where I can breathe." He motioned toward the boiler-room door. "I've got something waiting out there for me. And it won't wait forever."

He tilted his head, studying Joseph Henry, showing the marred right side of his face.

Joseph Henry leaned back against the cooler stone of the stairwell. The thought of escape had never entered his mind. He had entertained many ideas about why Ugly was harassing him, but asking for his help was not one of them. And escape... he had heard men talk about it often enough, boasting in the yard, whispering in the dark. But this was different.

A strange agitation rose in Joseph Henry. All of this, just so Ugly could ask for... for help? And Joseph Henry had no intent of escaping. He was doing his time, and his life was steady enough.

Ugly was taken aback by the sudden heat in Joseph Henry's voice. "You've got the wrong man," Joseph Henry almost spat. "I don't know what you think I can do. I've no hand in the gates, no key in my pocket."

Ugly's face hardened, and he chuckled softly. Joseph Henry noticed his voice had returned to what it was before, the tone he'd come to know.

"Don't play small with me, Mister Henry. I've seen how you move. Guards don't trouble you. You walk in, you walk out, places the rest of us never see. Deliveries, errands, talks with men outside. You've got connections."

Joseph Henry's eyes narrowed.

"A man looking to get free don't watch the warden, don't even watch the guards. He watches the one who's already freer than most."

Ugly reached over and tapped Joseph Henry's chest with a sooty finger. "You've got what I need… resources, ideas. That's what I need. Not your fists. Not your pity. Your reach."

Joseph Henry was silent a long while. Ugly figured he was considering, but Joseph Henry was simply at a loss for words. The stairwell felt smaller, the air seemed to become still, flat. The roar of the boilers below filled in the silence. He rubbed his palms over his knees.

"Even if I had what you think…there's no walkaway here. They check the vehicles before letting me out the gate. The walls are solid. A man tries to get out, and he's shot. How do you think I can help?"

Ugly leaned back against the wall, his eyes glinting in the dim light. "A man tries it wrong though," Ugly said. "I don't plan on trying it wrong. I plan to have a plan. And you'll be part of that plan."

Joseph Henry let out a breath, more a sigh than resignation. "It ain't that easy."

Ugly's mouth twisted, getting tired of the conversation. "Nothing's easy. But you're going to help make it happen."

Joseph Henry studied him, the way the firelight from below cut a shadow across his face. Ugly looked calm, like there was no doubt to any of this, and that unsettled him more than the sneer on Ugly's face ever did. "No…"

Ugly tilted his head, as though expecting the answer. "Then we go back to what we had. Worse. And that old crow of yours… I've got patience, Mister Henry, but you're the one that came here, didn't you? Means you're already at the end. You care… for your Crow… probably for others too."

Joseph Henry swallowed, his throat dry. Ugly was right. He cared. He didn't want to. But he did, more than he'd admit.

He went back and tried again. "I don't have a key, Ugly. No maps… no blueprints. I don't even know what you're asking me to do."

Ugly leaned forward. His voice dropped low, almost a whisper under the hiss of steam. "I don't need maps. I don't need a key. I need a man who can reach further than I can. A man who gets favors, like what you did down here. To move things quiet like. That's you."

Joseph Henry shook his head, more to clear his thoughts than in refusal. "And if I do? You think there's a chance? You think you can make it?"

Ugly's smile returned, faint but certain. "I don't think. I know. I've lived my whole life getting out of places I wasn't meant to be. This one's no different. And not me… we. You're coming with me."

The words fell flat on Joseph Henry at first, then the realization hit him.

The stairwell went quieter. Ugly looked up. The boiler needed feeding. Joseph Henry leaned hard against the wall, staring at the man across from him. He didn't speak. He was still weighing it, taking it in. Ugly didn't press further. He stood up.

"You think on it. But not too long. I can't let things go for too long. Old Crow will get bored."

Joseph Henry glared, as Ugly turned and slipped back through the door.

Chapter 27
1927

The lamps had gone over in the scuffle. Only one remained, hanging from a rafter in the far corner, its glow mixing with the slanted shafts of late-afternoon sun that pushed through the warped panes of the storefront. Together they were all that lit the room.

Powder smoke lingered in the air, drifting in thin threads that caught the meager light. Near the front, a shelf lay broken across the floor where a clerk had gone down, also smashing a barrel of flour and scattering the white dust across the floor boards. Boot prints scattered every which way through the mess.

Two bodies lay still on the ground. One near the door, eyes and mouth open, a look of surprise fixed on his face. The other lay by the fallen shelf, slumped against a crate of nails. The sawdust around him was clumped with blood.

One of the men was already at the register, rifling through its drawer and the shelves beneath. The other raked tobacco pouches, boxes of ammunition, and whatever else might fetch a price into a sack. They moved with frantic haste, breath coming hard, nerves still raw from the violence.

"Goddamn waste," one spat. "All this trouble for a till that won't buy us a week of meals."

The other muttered a curse. "We should've been gone already. Somebody's bound to have heard the shots."

The one at the register paused, then let out a hoot. "Now this is better. Found a stash down here behind the counter. Couple of nice pistols, a gold watch, and some silver coin. This'll make it worthwhile."

Ugly stepped over the bodies without pause. He didn't seem to hear his accomplices. He moved slow, head turning as if listening. From behind another counter came a faint whimper.

He crouched and pushed aside a box. A girl sat pressed into the corner, no more than seven or eight. Her knees were pulled tight to her chest, eyes wide, dust streaked across her cheeks where the tears had run.

Ugly rested his arm on his knee and bent close enough to look her in the face, angling himself so she saw only his good side. "Hush now," he said softly. The tone was gentle, almost like a father to a child. "It's all right. Nobody gonna hurt you."

She blinked, breath quick through her nose. He pulled a handkerchief from his coat pocket and dabbed at her cheek with a folded corner, a faint smile on his face. Her breathing eased.

"Is my daddy dead?"

"No…" he said, drawing the word out. "He just fine. Those boys just need to do their work."

Ugly's eyes moved over the store until they caught a door toward the back.

"You come with me now," he said. "I get you cleaned up."

He helped the girl to her feet and guided her toward the rear, shifting his body so she couldn't see the scene at the front of the store. He opened the door revealing a back room… an office, and pulled the door shut behind them. A lamp on a wide desk lit the space better than the front. He sat the girl down in the big desk chair in front of the desk.

"Let me see what I can find around here," Ugly said, giving her another smile.

He began opening the drawers, pulling papers from out onto the desk and floor. Then he paused looking at a small strong box.

"Maybe there's something in here I can clean you up better with," Ugly said, smiling again. He glanced back at her. "What's your name little girl?"

"Elsie," she said with a sniff.

"That's a pretty name," Ugly said. "That's my momma's name too."

The girl gave a thin smile, wiping her cheek with the back of her hand.

Ugly pulled the box closer and, finding a sturdy letter opener on the desk, worked it into the latch. He gave a sharp twist. The iron groaned, then split with a loud crack.

The girl jumped, hands clapped over her ears.

"Easy now," Ugly murmured, glancing at her only slightly. He folded the lid back and riffled through the contents. Papers flipped between his fingers. Deeds, insurance slips, letters with their seals still intact. Beneath them lay a small leather billfold, thick with cash in various denominations, and an identification card tucked inside. A passport stamped in fading ink. Names. Property. Accounts.

Ugly's eyes lingered. Wheels turned quick in his head. This was it. What he'd been looking for. What he needed. A life laid out neat as a deck of cards, waiting for his hand to play them.

He thought back to Edwardo de Cordova. He'd been close then, but he hadn't thought of everything. He wouldn't make the same mistakes again. Now he would be… His gaze fixed on the passport. Henry Caldwell. He rolled the name once under his breath. He could work the accent, shift over a county or two. Who would ever know.

He paused, then turned and looked at Elsie.

She was still perched in the big chair, her feet not touching the floor. She watched him, wide-eyed. The tears had stopped.

Ugly's jaw worked once. He drew a breath through his nose and let it out slow.

His gaze stayed on the girl. A bit of sadness curled into his eyes.

He managed to give her a faint smile and he rose. Standing in before her he still angled his head to only show the good side. Then, slowly, he turned it and showed the other.

Elsie flinched, pressing back into the chair.

Ugly moved quick. He caught her up in his arms and lifted her against his chest. He cupped her small head in his hand and gently pressed her face into him, like a father comforting his daughter.

She struggled.

"Easy now," he whispered. "Easy."

She pushed back against his grip, and whimpered. He held her firm. "There you go… There you go." Her face stayed buried in his chest. She struggled only once more, her fists curling at his coat, then slackened.

Ugly rocked her as he held on, shushing her in low tones, stroking her hair. When she was still, he laid her back in the big chair.

The First & Farmers National Bank of Somerset sat quiet on the corner. The two-story building sat opposite the courthouse. Its brick front and limestone trim catching the midmorning sun.

Ugly had purchased a suit the day before from a small clothing shop on Main Street. Cumberland's Haberdasher had only recently begun stocking ready-to-wear suits. Alterations took far less time than cutting and stitching a suit from cloth.

The racks in the store still looked out of place. Until recently there had only been a few mannequins to show what a finished product might look like. Now a dozen jackets hung in different sizes, with trousers folded beneath. The tailor, who also served as clerk, measured his chest, waist, and inseam, then had him try on several jackets and pants. He frowned. Ugly was an odd size. Even with quick tailoring, the suit hung on his frame as if it had been borrowed from a larger man. Ugly didn't notice the difference, and the clerk chose not to point it out. He set Ugly up with a pair of equally ill-fitting shoes, and Ugly paid for it all with a couple of bills from the old billfold.

He entered the bank and was struck by the high ceilings, plaster walls, and dark wood wainscoting. His new shoes slid awkwardly on the marble floor. At the far end stood a large steel door with a round wheel handle. Near the top, stenciled in dark red paint, were the words *Diebold Safe & Lock Co.* Ugly gave only a passing thought to what it would take to get inside before snapping his focus back to the task at hand.

Ugly inhaled and caught the scents of ink, tobacco, fresh paper, and something else he couldn't put his finger on… maybe floor wax. A clerk at the counter looked up. His face stiffened at the sight of the small man in the ill-fitting suit before he remembered to smile.

"Can I help you, sir?"

The smile faltered as Ugly turned fully toward him, the scarred side of his face now in plain view.

"Good morning, sir, I am…" He paused, shaping the unfamiliar name carefully. "…Henry Caldwell." He tried to remove his accent, but failed. "I need of a safe deposit box."

The clerk paused only a moment before regaining his smile. "Of course, sir." He slid a form across the counter, along with a pen. "I'll need your mark here," he said, indicating the space at the bottom. His brows lifted, genuinely surprised, when Ugly picked up the form and seemed to study it. Then Ugly set it back down and scrawled *H. Caldwell.*

"The box will cost three dollars per year, Mr. Caldwell," the clerk said, not expecting the man before him to be able to pay.

Ugly drew three five-dollar bills from the billfold and laid them on the counter. "Five years," he said.

The clerk's eyes lingered on the money as if uncertain it was real. Then his fingers snapped shut on the bills and pulled them away. "Very good, sir."

For a moment he stood there, until Ugly looked expectantly.

"Ah, of course," the clerk said, "right this way."

Ugly followed the clerk to the large steel door. It looked built to outlast the century. The clerk worked the great handle, metal groaned, and it swung wide.

Inside, rows of narrow drawers stood stacked from floor to ceiling, each with two keyholes. The clerk handed Ugly a small key. He felt the weight of it in his palm. "You do not want to lose that," the clerk said. "It is a costly procedural nightmare, one that could take a very long time to resolve, should you."

The clerk held up another key, then slid it into one of the two keyholes of a box marked 617. He indicated for Ugly to do the same in the other with his key. Together they turned, and the box slid free, a long, shallow steel drawer. The clerk nodded toward a small table set off to the side with nothing but a chair and a lamp.

Ugly stepped to the table and set the drawer down. He glanced over his shoulder, suspecting the clerk was watching him, but the man had already turned away, facing the opposite wall. Ugly placed the small stack of papers he had taken from the general store into the box.

When he was finished, he carried the drawer back to its slot. It slid in with a hollow scrape that echoed through the quiet room. The clerk stepped forward. He raised his key again. "All right, sir. Together now." They inserted and turned their keys. There was a sharp click.

The clerk withdrew his key first, slipping it into his vest pocket. "Secure, sir."

Ugly gave the drawer a small pull, testing that it was locked, then smiled and removed his key, tucking it into his own pocket.

Ugly and his accomplices had planned to stash the items they'd gotten along with the money from the register. One of them had said, "We oughta split it up now." But Ugly shook his head. "Best let it sit till things blow over."

Ugly had his own plans, and they didn't include the other two.

They'd found a shack on the south edge of town, a one-room place with a couple of beds and a stove, left from some tenant who'd moved on. It was cramped with the three of them, but more comfortable than some places they'd been, and they wouldn't be there for long.

By late evening Ugly had come to the old barn. It wasn't entirely abandoned, but it was probably long out of use. A few farm implements leaned in the corners, rusted and forgotten, likely untouched for several seasons. The hay in the loft was matted and sour with water that leaked through holes in the roof. This was where they had hidden the loot. They had wrapped everything in oiled linens to keep out the damp, then dug a hole through the hay down to the floorboards.

Now Ugly retrieved it. He pulled his shirt up over his nose and mouth, then dug through the foul hay. The last time he'd made the other two do the digging, and he knew why.

Ugly pulled the bundle free, the oiled linens already rank with mildew from the straw. He stuffed the parcels into a burlap sack he'd brought and slung it over his shoulder.

When he stepped out of the barn the weather had turned. Rain sheeted down, running cold over his hat brim and soaking him through. He swore and set off, plodding nearly a mile along the muddy lane until he reached the cemetery.

In the rainy twilight the stones loomed dark gray, silhouettes leaning at odd angles. He found one older than the rest, its base cracked but otherwise intact. The spade he'd left there earlier leaned against the stone. He bent in the rain, worked the blade into the earth, and cleared a space beneath the marker. One by one he set the bundles inside, then slid the small safe deposit box key between them.

He pressed the earth back into place, tamping it firm with the spade. Rain quickly washed the dirt smooth. Ugly leaned close and read the name carved faint on the stone… Josiah Tuttle. He repeated it to himself, once, twice, then again, fixing it in his mind.

He rose, gave the grave a last look, and walked on into the wet night.

Ugly spent the next couple of hours trudging through the rain. When he first imagined his plan, he hadn't pictured such misery. The center of town was nearly four miles away.

From the moment Ugly found the papers and the passport, the wheels began to turn. He would be Henry Caldwell. He would start again. But the other two were a problem.

He thought about killing them. It was the most straightforward solution. Just the night before he had come close to setting a fire while they slept. But that would be too messy, and too much could go wrong. He thought again of Edwardo de Cordova. "No more mistakes," he told himself.

As he lay in the dark, listening to the other two snore, another thought came. What they'd done in the store would likely bring the rope. Why should he kill them, when the State of Kentucky would do it for him?

By morning his mind was made.

Ugly came into town with the rain still driving. Along the main street electric lamps burned weak and yellow. Water ran down the globes, bending the light at odd angles. Now and then one would dim, give a faint buzz, then flare back again.

He stopped to watch a lamp flicker, as if the storm itself were blowing at. Like there was a flame. There was no flame, no wick. He had no notion how such a thing worked. He'd seen some gas lamps when he went through New Orleans. These weren't like those either.

He lowered his gaze from the lamps to the square where he'd stood that morning. The bank and the courthouse loomed as shadows in the dark and rain. A block further on stood the sheriff's office, a narrow brick building with a single window black against the night. A wooden stoop led up to a plain wooden door. Unlike the streetlamps, over the step hung a gas lamp, sputtering and coughing in the wind. Ugly stopped short, bundling himself as deep as he could into his inadequate coat, the cold leaking in.

He came up to the step and stood a moment. A slight overhang gave him the briefest respite from the weather. The door was unremarkable. Just below the knob he found a narrow slot cut into the wood with a tin flap hanging loose on its hinges. He drew the folded scrap of paper from his pocket and looked at it, somewhat surprised it had stayed dry.

Ugly felt it said what it needed to say. *Two men holed up in a shack on the south edge of town, near the old wagon road. One tall, black hair, narrow through the shoulders. The other heavy in the chest, scar through the left eyebrow, a limp in his left leg. Both carry pistols. Both have silver coins and tobacco tins from the store in Tateville, where they killed two men and a small girl.*

Ugly slid the note into the slot. The flap clattered shut after the paper slipped through.

He tightened his coat around him again and stepped back into the rain.

Chapter 28
1927

Ugly was beginning to get concerned. Two days had passed, and there was still no sign the law was moving on his accomplices. The other two were growing restless. He had managed to keep them from bolting so far, but he knew he couldn't hold them much longer.

"Got someone settin' up a place for us up in Henryville," Ugly told them. "Just over the border in Indiana. We stay put three more days, then head up there. Outta the way. We'll be all right once we get there."

Ugly had no idea where Henryville was. Earlier that day he had stopped by the library and asked for the name of a small rural town in Indiana that might need farm hands. The librarian pulled out a huge atlas, flipped through its pages, and finally gave him the name Henryville, along with some general directions. Ugly hadn't bothered to listen to the directions. He only wanted a destination that sounded right.

The name, and the promise they would soon be moving on, seemed to calm the men.

Ugly lay on the small bed and stared at the ceiling. The three days were gone. Now it was over. This part of his plan had fallen apart. He had a choice now: leave the other two and hope he never saw them again, or finish it himself. Edwardo de Cordova. Ugly could not leave them alive. *Cortar por lo sano*, cut it clean, he told himself.

He was getting thin-jawed from watching them pace. They had grown restless, trading curses and occasionally kicking the stove or a wall.

"It's been three days, Ugly, you said three days. We goin' now or not?" one of them said.

Ugly rose and put his jacket on, slow, as if he had planned every motion.

"Listen," he said. The other two shut up quick, eager for anything. "My amigo cross the border, I told ya, settin' things up for us. He gettin' us harvest work. We get paid, we lay low. I'm goin' now, see where he's at. Said three days, it's been three days. Won't take long. I been talkin' by telegraph down at the depot. Bet there's a wire waitin' for me now."

The taller one looked uncertain.

"Hey, amigo, it'll all be good. If there's no wire we leave tomorrow mornin', either way."

They grumbled, but the pacing stopped. The promise of a place and a time settled over them. One even gave a weak smile. Ugly buttoned his coat, fingers steady though his jaw twitched. He paused after stepping through the door and closing it, listening. No griping inside. No sound but the stove groaning. He tightened his jaw and gave a single nod to himself, then walked toward town. Three days, he thought. That was long enough. This had to end.

Ugly chuckled as he walked. He didn't know if there really was a telegraph at the depot. He thought he'd heard a train, so he expected there'd be a depot.

The road lay open and gray before him and his mind kept turning over the same thought. The other two had to go, and he couldn't rely on others to do it. He had to finish them himself, simple and final. He'd considered doing it himself before… fire while they slept. Fire was quiet and could look like an accident, but it was not certain. He couldn't be there when it happened. They might wake before it got them, maybe get out.

Thoughts spun through options: gun, knife, rope, even shovel. Every one carried its own danger. In the end the blunt answer won out. A gun was crude and loud, but it offered the cleanest certainty. He did not like guns. He had not even carried one when they did the store. He had buried those nice ones from the loot with the other things, and wasn't going back to dig them up now.

When he got into town he walked the streets until he found a small shop. A sign in the window said *Second-hand Goods*. A pawn shop. He walked up and looked through the window, then went and pushed open the door. A bell gave a thin, tired jangle. The shop smelled of oil, damp wood, and something metallic. A single bulb hung from the ceiling, its light barely reaching the room's corners. Dust floated in the air, as if it couldn't find an empty place to settle. The counters were crowded with watches in velvet boxes, a row of old boots, coils of rope, and a heap of battered tools.

Behind the counter a man in a threadbare vest looked up and wiped his hands on a rag. The man had a natural smile, but it faded when he saw Ugly's face. He was used to seeing all sorts come and go from his shop, but what he saw now was unsettling.

"Morning, sir. Can I help you find something?" the clerk asked.

Ugly kept his head low, raising his eyes to meet the clerk.

"You got any cheap iron?" he asked. The words fell flat, like a trade term he wasn't sure applied.

The clerk's eyes flicked to the door then back to Ugly's face. "Depends what you call cheap. What do you need it for?"

Ugly paused. "Travelin'," he said. Short. Useful. He didn't want the man to think too hard. "Protection. Long roads, ya know."

The man reached under the counter and produced a small box. He opened it with a practiced motion and laid an old revolver on the counter. Nothing showy, the sort of thing someone might keep for peace of mind. It had scuffs and a dull finish, but it seemed whole and serviceable. ".32 top-break," he said. "Clean, works fine, shoots straight."

Ugly picked it up and felt the weight. He turned it in his hand, then glanced down the barrel, trying to act like he knew anything about guns. The clerk's mouth tightened as he watched, thankful he'd left the cylinder empty. Ugly set it back on the counter. "How much?"

"Seven," the man said. "Take it for five and some trade, maybe."

Ugly fished in his coat for the old billfold. He laid three bills on the counter, and as if considering, held a fourth in his hand. "Four," he said. His voice stayed low, not certain if it was needed.

The clerk considered the bills, then the scarred face. He frowned, seemed to do a quick calculation, then reached under the counter and came up with a small box of loose shells. "Five for the gun and a full load."

Ugly stared for a moment, as if not fully understanding, then smiled slightly.

"All right. Deal." He added one more bill. The clerk put six shells next to the gun, then looked up. "Want me to load it for you?"

Ugly hesitated looking at the gun, then the shells. "Yeah. Good idea."

The clerk picked up the gun and a couple of shells. Ugly leaned in closer than the counter allowed, watching the clerk slip the shells into the pistol's chambers, his own fingers twitching as if to copy a motion he'd never learned. The clerk paused and looked over his glasses at him. Ugly gave a weak grin and eased back.

The clerk handed the gun to Ugly. "You be careful with that."

"Sure." Ugly took it. He held it for a moment and frowned. It didn't quite feel right in his hand, but he seemed to make a decision that it would do, and he slid it into his coat pocket. The weight at his side felt different, something solid, final.

He didn't linger or care to test it. He gave the briefest nod to the clerk, and stepped toward and out the door. He took a step then paused. He looked down at his coat pocket. The revolver's weight sat warm against the fabric and felt surprisingly comfortable. He smiled. The sun had come out fully, and he felt it warm on his face. He felt good, and noticed it. For the first time in days he felt something close to things being right again. His plan was clear. The world suddenly had a kind of simple order. No more waiting on lawmen or luck. He could handle things himself. He should have done it from the start.

He paused, still smiling, and looked up and down Main Street. A pair of mules clattered past pulling a wagon stacked with tightly bound hay bales. Across the way a boy swept the front of a hardware store. Ugly inhaled deeply. The air smelled faintly of baked bread and maybe just a little coal smoke. For a moment he simply stood there, hands in his pockets, taking it all in, almost feeling like he might belong among all of it. A man just going about his business on a fine day.

He began walking without hurry, letting the sunlight soak in. A dog trotted ahead of him, nose to the ground. Two women passed, carrying parcels and talking softly. One looked up, met his eyes for a moment, then quickly looked away. Ugly barely noticed. He hadn't eaten since the day before. He found he was famished.

On the corner a narrow storefront bore a painted sign: *SOMERSET DRUG CO. — SODA FOUNTAIN AND LUNCHES.* Through the window he could see a marble counter, fronted by a row of round stools. Glass syrup bottles glinted on a shelf in front of a large mirror. Ugly nodded to himself and pushed through the door.

Inside it was cooler. The scent of coffee, sweet syrup, and the sharp edge of disinfectant mingled. A man behind the counter, wearing a white apron and round spectacles, looked up and gave a polite nod. It was still early for lunch, but a few customers sat along the counter: a young woman with her hat tipped forward as she stirred her drink, and a pair of men, perhaps farmers.

Ugly slid onto a stool halfway down. "Afternoon," he said, almost cheerful.

The man behind the counter cleared his throat and glanced up at the clock on the wall. "Morning." His expression dropped when he saw Ugly's face. "What'll it be?" he asked flatly.

"Ham sandwich and a Coca-Cola," Ugly said. He grinned faintly, tapping the counter. "Good day for it…"

"Reckon so," the man said, turning away.

Ugly rested his elbows on the counter and watched the street through the window. He felt a lightness he did not often feel. When the soda glass was set before him the sound of the fizz reached his ears. He lifted it as if making a small toast to the new order. He took a long pull through the straw. The bubbles tickled his nose.

"Busy town," he said after a moment, glancing at the others. "Always something going on, I bet."

No one answered. The young woman looked up only briefly, then shifted on her stool and returned to her straw. One of the men mumbled to the other and looked down at his plate.

Ugly went on anyway, smiling. "I knew a place like this years ago. Fine place. Lot of good people."

The man behind the counter gave a quick nod but didn't look up again. The room had gone quieter, but Ugly didn't feel it. He chewed his sandwich, thinking of the road ahead and how simple things would be now. He didn't see the other clerk near the door give a small shake of the head and turn away.

When he finished, he left a few coins on the counter and stepped back out into the sunlight. The brightness met him full in the face, and he squinted. He had his gun, his plan, and a clear path again. The world seemed to open before him again, simple and wide.

He walked on, enjoying the sun as he passed the blocks. As the town thinned behind him, the street sounds fell away. He felt the weight of what needed to be done, yet the lightness that rode with him didn't fade. There was no turning back now. His fingers stayed near the pocket where the revolver sat, tracing its shape through the wool. The day had been perfect; the end he planned would be no less so.

By late afternoon Ugly was near the edge of town where they'd been staying. The sun had dropped lower, and the air had cooled just enough to make the walk pleasant. He had a spring in his step as his plans turned over in his head. The end was almost in sight, and he could start his new life. He'd be a kinder man. Maybe open a store of his own. Maybe a wife… a little girl like that Elsie. Maybe he wouldn't kill anyone again, either.

He could see the line of the old wagon road bending ahead toward the shack where they were staying. Then saw it.

Ahead, a wagon stood crossways in the road, its wheels settled in the soft ruts left by the recent rain. The two mules still hitched stood patient, tails flicking. The sheriff waited near the door, hands on his hips, the star on his vest catching the low sun. One of the men from the shack stood beside the wagon, head down, wrists bound with cord looped through his belt to keep him still. A deputy hauled the second man out of the shack by the arms while another prodded him forward into the light. No one hurried. The talking was quiet, the kind that came when everything was already done.

Ugly was stunned. The entire morning, every piece of it, was gone. He just watched the scene in front of him without it registering what it meant: the lawmen, the wagon, his accomplices already being taken. He didn't even realize his feet kept moving on their own, carrying him forward slow and steady until he could smell the earthiness of the mules.

Then it struck him. He wouldn't have to do a thing. The state was doing its job, and his. After all he had put into it over the past day, the thought made him almost giddy, and before he knew it he was laughing.

Ugly noticed one of the deputies stop and look his way. He tried to stifle the laugh, but still smiling faintly. They had no reason to bother him, he thought. Just another man walking a road.

The deputy said something low to the sheriff. The sheriff's head turned, eyes narrowing slightly beneath the brim of his hat. For a moment nothing happened. Then the sheriff looked at a small pad of paper, then again at Ugly. He took a few steps forward, his boots heavy in the dirt. One of the others followed behind.

Ugly's smile stayed, but wavered. He nodded when they got closer, as though to say he meant no harm, but the sheriff didn't nod back. He stopped a few paces off.

"Afternoon," the sheriff said.

Ugly tipped his head. "Afternoon, mister."

The sheriff studied him for a moment, gaze steady, traveling across his face. His eyes lingered on the left side of Ugly's face, the side where the smile didn't reach. Something in his jaw tightened.

"Where you headed?" the sheriff asked.

Ugly glanced past them toward the wagon. "Just walking. Headin' north."

The deputy leaned in closer to the sheriff and murmured something. The sheriff's eyes lifted, and Ugly saw a change in them.

"Step over here a minute," the sheriff said.

Ugly hesitated, confusion flickering in his eyes. He looked from one man to the next, saw their hands lowering toward their belts, and felt something inside him sink.

The next several weeks were a whirlwind. Ugly found himself in the county jail, kept separate from the other two. The first days blurred together, full of questions, sleep, meals, and then more questions. He was caught off guard when they took him in, but found his footing soon enough. He knew he could get out of this. He knew he didn't have to hang.

He knew his story before the questions even started. He told them how they had planned to rob the general store. They needed money. They had not eaten in days. But nobody was supposed to get hurt. He did not even have a gun, barely knew how to use one.

He said he was shocked when he heard the gunshots, and more so when he saw the shopkeepers on the floor. He could not tell if they were dead, but he thought they might be. He wanted to run then, but he was afraid for his own life.

Then it happened. He saw one of the others, he couldn't remember which, smother the little girl. He kept still, terrified. But he knew he could not let it go. When it was done, he said he was the one who wrote the note and left it for the sheriff in the middle of the night.

They grilled Ugly for hours, but he was always ready with an answer. When they asked about the gun found in his coat, Ugly said he had waited three days for the sheriff to come, but he never did. He couldn't shake the image of the little girl. So finally he went into town to buy a gun himself, thinking he could bring the others in and make things right. He told them to check with the shopkeeper in the secondhand store. The man would remember Ugly buying the gun.

A lawyer had been appointed to Ugly. He sat beside him the whole time. He had nothing to add, only nodding and agreeing with whatever Ugly said, and that suited Ugly just fine.

When it finally went to court Ugly testified against the other two. He kept his tone soft, his eyes lowered, and kept the good side of his face in the light. The jury hung on his every word, and he even managed the hint of a tear when he talked about the little girl. His two accomplices sat dumbstruck. It seemed like even they believed his story might be true.

The shopkeeper from the secondhand store was called in and testified as to Ugly buying the gun the same day the sheriff caught the lot of them. He seemed to remember Ugly being a mostly harmless man looking for a gun, he said for protection.

Ugly's lawyer finally added some value in the end when he presented a closing that made Ugly out to be a victim, if not a hero.

Ugly was sentenced separately from the other two. He assumed that they would hang. He hoped they would hang. That was the plan from the start.

When the judge asked Ugly and his lawyer to rise as he pronounced sentence, Ugly once again felt giddy. Part of him thought he would just be let go. But the judge expressed that in Kentucky the law was firm, and while his intentions were admirable, Ugly must still pay for his part in the crime.

Ugly was sentenced to seven years in the Frankfort Penitentiary. He let his face drop when the sentence was read, but inside he was just fine. Five years, not bad, and maybe it could be even less than that. His new life was waiting in a pre-paid safe deposit box at *The First & Farmers National Bank of Somerset*, and would be for the five years he'd paid for.

When it was done they led him out and Ugly smiled as the door shut behind him.

Chapter 29
1929

The truck bounced down the road, hitting every rut and stone along the way. Joseph Henry sat in a daze behind the wheel, barely noticing the road go by. It wasn't his nature to give up, least of all to a man like Ugly Attics. He turned the problem over and over, but no matter how he worked it, he couldn't see a way to keep Old Crow safe. The others weighed on him too; Ugly would use anyone he could reach against him.

The branch across the road seemed to leap up in front of the truck. Joseph Henry didn't see it until he was on it. He threw the wheel and swerved, jolting the truck as it lurched sideways toward a ditch. He fought the wheel straight and let it roll to a stop on the shoulder. For a moment he just sat there, both hands clamped on the wheel, his chest tight. Then he dropped his head against the wheel, the air leaking out of him in a low sound somewhere between a groan and a laugh.

He got out and paced a few steps around the truck. The trees on either side swayed in the breeze. A crow cried out just overhead, sharp and close, causing him to jerk upright. He stared up at the crow and gave a hollow laugh. With his back to the truck, he slid down beside the rear tire and sank forward, elbows on his knees, head in his hands.

He sat there a long while, the engine ticking as it cooled. Dust settled around him in slow spirals, the air suddenly still. A feeling crept through him. It wasn't fear, or anger, or even exhaustion, but something heavier and quieter. He could name it. He knew what futility was. He had seen it in other men's eyes often enough, but he had never felt it in his own bones before.

He thought of the years spent finding himself and a measure of meaning since he lost his old life: the work, the deliveries, the careful tending of what he could control. It had always been enough to keep him steady. But now he could see no line forward. Every path ended with a sacrifice, or someone hurt. The thought of doing nothing felt as cowardly as doing the wrong thing, yet the right thing eluded him.

Ugly Attics had taken something from him, something Joseph Henry never knew could be taken. It wasn't his place or his pride, but the quiet conviction that his efforts mattered. Sitting there in the dust, Joseph Henry couldn't feel it. He wanted to fight for it, to wrestle it back, but for the first time, he couldn't find the energy.

He pressed the heels of his palms against his eyes and drew a breath, deep and rough. He told himself that it would pass, it always did, that there was a way through. But the thoughts had no weight this time. They hung in the air like smoke and were gone.

Joseph Henry left the truck outside the heavy plank sliding door. It was open wide when he arrived, letting in the warmth of the late morning. He stepped into the large room of the still and was glad for the fresh air being let in. As usual on hot days, the heat and smell hit him at once: mash, copper, damp wood. Giles was already doing his morning work, sleeves rolled, wiping down lengths of pipe.

"Morning, boss," Giles called over the slow gurgle from the nearby vats.

Joseph Henry didn't answer. He kept walking, a blank look on his face, eyes distant, boots scuffing the boards.

Giles tried again, lighter this time. "Got some coffee over here if you want it. Still almost hot."

Nothing. Joseph Henry moved past him without so much as a glance, heading toward the far end where some tools lay scattered, ready for him to finish the repairs he had started two days before.

Giles watched him a moment, a small frown on his face, his rag hanging limp in his hand. Then he gave a small shrug. "Well, all right then. No worries, boss."

He turned back to his work and began humming under his breath as Joseph Henry settled down by the copper lines at the back of the room, where he'd been replacing a section of pipe.

Joseph Henry sat for a while, looking at the tools as though they didn't make sense, then stared at the length of copper he had cut and fitted the day before. The section still needed to be sealed and reconnected to the feed line that ran along the wall. He nodded once, remembering where he was in the project.

He picked up a wrench and began working on the lower flange, drawing the bolts tight one at a time. The work was second nature, but his mind wasn't in it. He had replaced the cracked section the day before; all that remained was to finish sealing the joint and test the line. When he loosened the clamp at the far end to fit the gasket, the pipe gave a short shudder. A moment later a heavy burst of mash shot from the open joint, splattering across the floor. A sour smell filled the room as the copper hissed under the pressure.

Joseph Henry cursed under his breath, as he realized he should have checked that the valve feeding the pipe was still shut. He jerked back, trying to stand, his boot sliding in the wet mess. The wrench slipped from his hand and clattered away. He reached and closed the valve, then stood still, staring at the spreading mash, a warm haze rising around him.

For a long moment he stood there, just staring at the mess. The air was thick and close, and the smell felt sharp in his nose and throat. A sound came from behind him, the slow tread of boots on wood. He looked over his shoulder, and there was Giles. Without a word, he passed Joseph Henry, a rag in one hand and a bucket in the other. He knelt and began sweeping the mess toward a drain in the floor.

Joseph Henry watched him for a few beats, then bent down beside him and started to help. They worked in silence, the room filled only with the low hum from the vats and the faint scrape of wet cloth against the boards.

They worked that way for a while, neither speaking. The worst of the spill was gone, but the boards still shone wet in the light, highlighting the remaining smears of mash. Giles dipped the rag into the bucket, wrung it out, and began again, slower this time.

After a while he stopped and looked at Joseph Henry. "Had a friend back home," he said, his voice calm, easy, almost casual. "Good man. Reminds me of you some. Name was Desmond. He was quick with his hands, not easily flustered. Would never abide when something got in his way. Liked to figure things out."

"He worked with me at the mill down in St. Philip. Good job, steady hours. Desmond could set a belt or oil a bearing better than anyone. He'd clear a jam quick, or if a line broke loose he'd have it back in place in seconds. Man had nerves like a Bajan donkey. Seemed like nothin' rattled him."

"One day, though, the feed belt come clear off the pulley. No one's fault, just worn thin. Made a noise like a rifle shot, and Desmond went pale as chalk. Thought he was done. But he grabbed the nearest wrench and started at it. The belt was still moving though, whipping around the spindle. Caught his sleeve, pulled him in. Nearly tore his arm off. After that, he weren't the same. Couldn't walk into that room without flinching. Every creak, every hiss of steam, to him it all sounded like that belt snapping again."

"After that he couldn't go back near the mill. Tried taking smaller jobs around the yard, things he could do in quiet. Ya see, it was the noise. And the noise always found him. The hammer, the saw, gears turning. If they was about, you could see it building up in him till his hands would shake. Folks stopped calling him for work, not because he wasn't good, but because he couldn't start. Spent more time staring at a job than doing it."

"Last time I saw him, he was sitting out by the docks. Said he'd come to watch the tide. He told me the noises had finally left him alone, though he looked hollow saying it. Man just couldn't get past what had gone wrong. Couldn't take control again."

Giles wrung the rag out again, the water was now running dark between his fingers. "Shame, too," he said quietly. "He was a smart one. Just never found a way out of it."

He went quiet for a while after that, getting up the last bits of mash. Still looking at the floor he finally said, "You're not like Desmond, boss. You don't freeze when things turn sideways. You think. You find your way through. Whatever's got hold of you now, it must be just the noise. Gets between you and what you are."

He paused, then looked up at Joseph Henry. "Thing is, I see more of you than you show most folks. There's a part of you in there a hair darker than you let the rest of us even know. I've seen it now and then. Truth be told, it's given me a chill when it shows. You just don't like to use it."

He looked over then, not waiting for an answer, just letting the words hang there. "Don't really know what's gotten to you, but maybe that's what you need here. Maybe you need to use it. Brush away the noise."

Joseph Henry was quiet a long while. His face gave nothing, but his eyes stayed on Giles. For a moment it looked like he might take offense, then he let out a breath that could have been a sigh or even a laugh.

"You got all that from a man walking by you in a state and then dumping a ton of mash across the floor?" Joseph Henry said. "I couldn't even see it myself. Don't know if that says more about your eyes or my state of mind."

Giles looked up, half-smiling. "Just calling what I see, boss. A man can't see straight himself sometimes."

"No," Joseph Henry said, letting out a low laugh. "He can't."

He realized it was the first sound close to ease he'd made since he'd left Ugly. "You're right, though," he said looking square at Giles. "I've been circling the thing so close I couldn't see it. Guess it takes a full-on mash flood and a man with a mop to point it out."

Giles chuckled, shaking his head. "Could be worse ways to learn it, boss."

Joseph Henry nodded, smiling faintly. "Could be," he said. "Could be at that."

They finished the cleanup and stood for a moment, looking over the floor. The boards were damp but clean, the air still heavy with the smell of grain, but the sourness didn't bother Joseph Henry now.

He turned to Giles. "You've got a good head on you," he said. "You see things plain. That's a talent not many have."

Giles gave a modest shrug. "Old habit, I guess. Easier to spot a thing when it's not yours to carry."

Joseph Henry nodded. "Maybe so." He looked down at his hands, flexed them once, and wiped them on his trousers. "But you said something right. I've let things run me in circles."

He fell quiet then, his thoughts shifting. Ugly Attics… his face, his voice, the small grin when he thought he had the upper hand… it all seemed smaller now, like a machine rattling because a single bolt was loose. Something that he could fix, if he just decided to fix it.

For a long moment Joseph Henry stood still, the heat pressing against him, the hum of the vats steady in his ears. The weight that had been on him earlier was gone. In its place was a calm that felt sharper than before, almost cold and tempered.

He looked out the sliding door, the light falling on the truck in a hard white line. "You're right, Giles," he said quietly. "Sometimes you have to use what's in you."

Giles said something that Joseph Henry didn't hear. He felt a direction now, a focus. He stepped outside, toward the light, the faint smell of mash still lingering behind him, like something was burnt off and left behind.

Chapter 30
1929

Joseph Henry woke before the morning bell. He had slept like the dead that night, for the first time he could remember. The weight that had held him for months was gone.

He swung his legs off the bed and stretched, slow and deliberate, rolling his neck and shoulders. A small smile tugged at his mouth.

"Thanks, Giles," he said under his breath, then gave a quiet laugh. He felt almost giddy. He pulled on his clothes, humming an old tune.

The bell clanged just as he was tying his shoes. The sound rang through the block, iron against iron, echoing down the corridor. Joseph Henry stood and stepped to the bars.

"Time to get up, Crow," he called.

Down the corridor he heard boots on concrete and the jangle of keys. A guard was moving along the range, unlocking each cell in turn. When he reached Joseph Henry's he saw it was Mackey.

Joseph Henry gave a short nod. "Morning, Mackey."

The guard gave him a bleary look, still half asleep, then nodded. He slid the bolt and swung the door open. The hinges gave a familiar groan.

Joseph Henry stepped out and crossed to Old Crow's cell.

He was surprised to see Old Crow was sitting up on the edge of his bed by the time Joseph Henry reached him. He was rubbing the sleep from his eyes. His hands trembled slightly, the way they did most mornings.

"You're up early," Joseph Henry said.

"Couldn't sleep any longer," Crow said. His voice was rough, half a whisper. "Was up before the bell. Don't know why."

"Well you could've gotten dressed," Joseph Henry said with his thin smile.

"Wouldn't want to put you out of a job," Crow replied, giving a smile of his own.

Joseph Henry grabbed Crow's shirt and pants and tossed them in his direction. The shirt draped over Crow's head and left shoulder. He straightened it and forced his arms and body in, then grabbed the pants that had settled on the bed next to him, and slid them on.

"Come on. Let's get to the washroom before the line," Joseph Henry said, handing Crow his shoes.

Crow studied him as he rose. "You look different this morning."

"Do I?"

"Can't say what it is," Crow said, "Just different. Like something's settled."

Joseph Henry smiled at that and didn't answer.

They stepped into the corridor, joining the slow line of men heading toward the washroom. The air was thick with the sound of boots scraping over the concrete and the murmur of morning voices rising and falling.

As they approached the washroom doorway Nils was ahead of them in line, shoulders hunched, his towel slung over one arm. He glanced back, ready with his usual half-grin, but it faltered when he saw Joseph Henry's expression.

"Morning, Joseph," he said, a small smile forming for some reason.

"Morning, Nils," Joseph Henry said evenly. His tone carried no weight, no strain, but something in it made the others straighten up a little.

In the washroom Jimmy was at one of the basins, splashing water over his face. He caught sight of Joseph Henry in the mirror and gave a small nod.

"What's with you?" he said, "You look a lot better than last time I saw you. Someone send you flowers?"

Joseph Henry gave an audible laugh. "World didn't stop turning after all," he said, rolling up his sleeves and stepping to the basin beside him.

Short Stack came in behind them, slower than the rest, his eyes sharp and watchful. He stopped short when he saw Joseph Henry, as if he'd walked into the wrong room. The man standing at the basin looked too calm, too sure. Short Stack's mouth opened, then closed again. He dropped his gaze and moved on without a word.

The room filled with the sound of running water, towels slapping against wet stone, and the low hum of men beginning another day. Joseph Henry moved among them easily, his motions unhurried, his voice calm when he spoke. He began to help Old Crow with his morning. The tension that had followed him through the past weeks seemed to have drained away, leaving something else in its place, something steady, contained, and harder to name.

Old Crow sat in his usual spot. He glanced up at Joseph Henry, half a smile on his face. "You sure you're all right?"

"Better than that," Joseph Henry said. "I'm fine."

Now that Joseph Henry felt back in control, his mind worked with precision. His days were split between his penitentiary details and Boss Van's operation, and he gave both his full attention. The still was running at peak efficiency, every valve tuned to perfection. At the same time, his thoughts ran ceaselessly, shaping his plans around Ugly Attics, and the delivery runs gave him long miles of road to think.

At night, when the others had settled in their blocks and the air cooled the evening, Joseph Henry lay in his bunk with a ledger open across his knees. He had taken it from the maintenance stockroom. No one would miss a few blank pages. In his hand he thumbed a worn pencil, the point dulled from use.

He had been staring at the page for some time. The faint light from a small flashlight rested across his lap, the only illumination. He kept his ear tuned for any sound remotely like a boot fall, when he would quickly switch it off. He turned the pencil in his fingers, then began to write in a slow, steady hand.

Crow first.

Keep him close. Have him assigned to details with me, Jimmy, or Nils. Never leave him alone.

He paused, picturing the old man's face that morning, the tremor in his hands, the quiet humor. Ugly would use him again if anything went wrong. That couldn't happen.

A sound interrupted his thoughts. A slow step on concrete. Joseph Henry switched off the flashlight and waited. A guard walked the hallway outside, paused, then moved on. When the sound faded, Joseph Henry turned the light back on. He tapped the pencil once against the page and went on writing.

Nils... talk to him. He's still uneasy. Wants to make things right. Jimmy follows him.

Stack — watch him. Still a problem.

He hesitated, then added in smaller writing beneath:

> *Ugly uses Stack to talk. Cut that line. Maybe use a favor. Put him in the kiln.*

He leaned his head back, the pencil resting between his fingers. The words looked plain on the page, but they carried a weight. A purpose.

He turned to a fresh page.

Crow would be safe. The others could be managed. Ugly was still the question.

He wrote slowly, the tip of the pencil pressing deep into the paper.

> *Know how he moves. Who he leans on. Who listens when he talks.*
> *What are his real motivations?*

He stopped for a moment, the pencil hovering, his thoughts settling into order.

> *Don't give him a reason to suspect.*
> *Let him think he's steering everything.*
> *Let him think you're following.*

He pressed harder as he wrote the next line, each letter deliberate and even.

> *Make him think he's winning.*

He studied the words for a long time. That was the key. Ugly needs to be winning, living for control, feeding on it, needing it. Let him feel it. Let him hold it, right up to the moment it turns to dust in his hands.

He leaned back, breathing slow. The faint sound of snoring in a nearby cell came through the walls, then a brief cough.

He pushed it aside. There wasn't any noise now. Everything was clear, sharp, and simple.

He turned to the bottom of the page and wrote one last line.

When the time comes, end it. End him.

He closed the ledger and set it on the floor next to the bed. He dropped the pencil next to it. He smiled, it felt good again.

Joseph Henry lay there and looked at the ceiling. He saw images in the flickering light, then he switched it off, closed his eyes and drifted off to sleep.

Joseph Henry waited outside Boss Van's office. The small room smelled of stale smoke and paper. Though two wooden chairs sat against the wall, he remained standing just inside the doorway, cap in hand.

Behind a narrow oak desk sat a woman, perhaps in her forties, typing steadily. The keys of her Underwood clattered like rain on a tin roof. Every so often she glanced up to see if Joseph Henry had moved.

"Just another few minutes, Mr. Henry," she would say, and then return to her work. She'd said it six times now.

It had been nearly a week since Joseph Henry requested the meeting. He knew Boss Van didn't spend much time here. Warden or not, Boss Van's real business was elsewhere, and it clearly came first.

"Joseph..." came a voice from the doorway behind him.

Joseph Henry turned, startled, to see Boss Van stepping in from the corridor. He glanced toward the closed office door, realizing Van hadn't been inside at all.

The secretary looked up from her typing, offering a weak smile and a shrug.

Boss Van crossed the room, opened the office door, and went inside. Joseph Henry watched as Van set his briefcase on the desk, hung his hat on the rack, and settled into the large leather chair.

"He'll see you now, Mr. Henry," the secretary said, her tone businesslike as she resumed typing.

Joseph Henry gave her a perturbed look she didn't notice. He shifted his cap in his hands and stepped into the office.

Joseph Henry looked around the office. Dust hung in the beams of light that slanted through the blinds. A map of Kentucky covered one wall, dotted with pins. On the desk sat two ledgers, a glass ashtray beside a can of pipe tobacco, and a cup of coffee gone cold since the day before.

Boss Van leaned back, lighting his pipe, eyes fixed on Joseph Henry as he stepped in. He blew some smoke into the air.

"Morning, Joseph," he said. "It's usually not a good thing when you come see me... or call." He gave a wry smile. "You're looking better than the last time I saw you."

He motioned toward the seat across from him. "Sit down."

Joseph Henry nodded, took the chair, and rested his cap in his lap.

"Appreciate you making the time, sir."

Van puffed once, the smoke drifting toward Joseph Henry before curling up toward the ceiling. "You've earned a bit of my time. The still's running clean, the numbers look right, and I haven't heard a complaint in weeks." He leaned back slightly. "So, what's the matter?"

Joseph Henry hesitated. "There's an inmate causing trouble in the block."

Van cut him off almost immediately. "José Attics." A self-amused look flickered across his face.

Joseph Henry couldn't hide a brief look of surprise.

"I know everything that goes on in my penitentiary, Joseph," Van said, clearly pleased with himself.

Joseph Henry gave a small, doubtful smile, and Van laughed. "Well… maybe not everything. But the guards make their reports. I read about that dust-up in the mess hall. What do you need, Joseph? Want him moved to another block? Another facility?"

Joseph Henry shook his head. "No, sir. I know you could… would… but I need to deal with this myself."

Van's expression shifted, serious. "What did this man do to you, Joseph?"

Joseph Henry hesitated. He knew that a question like that from Boss Van needed an answer. He was quiet too long.

"Joseph?" Van said again, his voice lower now.

Something stirred in Joseph Henry. He sat a little straighter, a firmness settling behind his eyes. Boss Van noticed.

"Attics took something from me," Joseph Henry said. "I let him take it. I've been here a long time. I'll be here longer. But it's been all right. My penance took everything from me, but I've managed a kind of life. The work I do for you, that's something. And what I have in here, it's… well, it's a life too. I've got friends, maybe even family."

He drew a breath. "Attics has been trying to take that from me. He wants to use me, wants me to do things for him. He knows I can get things done, that I've got pull here, and he wants me to use it to help him."

Joseph Henry hesitated, weighing how much to say, then said, "He wants me to help him get out."

He looked at Boss Van, watching his reaction.

"I see," Boss Van said at last. He steepled his fingers, the pipe resting on the desk between them. "You know I'm going to have to do something about this, Joseph."

"With respect, sir," Joseph Henry said, pushing forward. "This one has to be mine. Attics pulled me apart, and I'm going to see him pay. He's going to know his mistake… and the cost of it. And he will know exactly who put down."

Boss Van regarded him through the thin veil of smoke. "That's not really like you, Joseph," he said slowly, regarding him. Then a faint smile formed. "Or maybe it is."

Joseph Henry let out a quiet laugh. "Yes, sir," he said. "Actually, it is."

Boss Van nodded knowingly. "So, Joseph, what are you asking me for?"

Joseph Henry held Boss Van's gaze a long moment, then leaned slightly forward, placing one hand on the desk. He spoke with even, measured clarity, explaining what he needed: the authority to alter work details and schedules for certain inmates, to keep Crow where he could watch him, or, if Joseph Henry was outside, to have Crow on details with Nils, Jimmy, or someone else he trusted. He needed the freedom to have guards nearby when he required them, and just as importantly, to have them elsewhere when he needed Attics to believe they had private time to talk or plan. It would settle some things down, though he admitted he would be kicking a hornet's nest for a few inmates.

Boss Van sat silently as Joseph Henry laid out his needs, then laughed out loud. "So basically, Joseph, you want to run the place."

Joseph Henry looked momentarily deflated, sensing it was not going his way.

Van sighed, then said, "Very well. Lord knows you could run this place better than most of the staff." He paused, considering. "I want to know what is going on, every step. I may even find this entertaining." He chuckled softly, then his tone hardened. "This little thing of yours cannot interfere with our operation or the running of this penitentiary. If it does, we pull the plug."

He leaned back in his chair, still serious. Then, just as suddenly, he laughed again. "Things have been too boring around here anyway."

Sensing the conversation was winding down, and not wanting to push his luck, Joseph Henry stood. "I appreciate it all, sir."

Boss Van nodded, still smiling faintly. Joseph Henry backed toward the door, turned, and stepped out into the hall.

Chapter 31
1929

The noon bell had just sounded when Joseph Henry stepped into the mess hall. The room was bright, the sun filtering through the high windows. It was busy with the lunchtime rush and nearly every bench was crowded. The scrape of tin utensils, trays hitting tables, and the roll of voices rising toward the rafters met him as he crossed the threshold. Until recently this sort of noise would have put Joseph Henry on edge, but now it washed over him without notice. It felt sharper, every sound landing with clear edges, and Joseph Henry seemed to take it in with ease. He moved through the throng with a steady gait, eyes forward, not looking at anyone, yet not avoiding anyone either.

Ugly Attics sat at a table closer to the left wall than the center of the room, a half dozen of the men around him. He was talking with his usual quick hands, throwing little cuts of humor or short anecdotes that made the men lean in, eager for more. Joseph Henry couldn't deny Ugly had skill. His voice had a rhythm to it, easy and quick.

Ugly saw Joseph Henry making his way across the room long before the others did, though he kept right on talking. Only his eyes shifted, narrowing a little as Joseph Henry approached. He raised an eyebrow when he noticed Joseph Henry was not carrying a tray. He wasn't here for lunch.

Joseph Henry stopped at the end of the table.

Ugly finished the sentence he was in the middle of, and the two men remained silent until the laughter died down. He looked Joseph Henry over, as though looking for something.

"Well now," Ugly said. "Here you are. Thought maybe you got lost or decided to crawl in a hole. Good thing you came now, for Crow's sake. And for some others too."

The threat floated under the words like a leaf moving on slow water. The men around the table did not seem to hear it. Joseph Henry did.

He didn't flinch. He didn't even shift his weight or lift his chin. He stood there waiting for Ugly's talk to wind down.

"Had some things to deal with," Joseph Henry said. "I'm done now."

Ugly studied him. Something in Joseph Henry's eyes made him pause. "You look different," Ugly said. "You get a good night's sleep? Strange time for that."

Joseph Henry gave a small laugh, without emotion. Ugly waited a moment, scratched at his jaw, then waved the moment away, like he decided what he thought he saw was nothing.

A commotion rose nearby. Both men looked up as someone pushed between the tables. Short Stack stumbled into view, his face lined with panic.

"You…" Short Stack said, breath high in his chest. "I know it. I know it was you."

Joseph Henry turned back toward Ugly, as though Short Stack held no importance.

Short Stack reached halfway toward Joseph Henry's shoulder, then slowed, thinking better of it. "Lime Kiln," he said, as though that explained everything. When no one reacted, he continued. "They moved me to the Lime Kiln. You know. You did this. I don't know how, but you put me there."

The words came fast, almost tripping over themselves. Short Stack was angry, but fear sat just behind it, quick and sharp.

Ugly looked amused. "Hey now Stack. Maybe you just had the bad luck."

Short Stack glared at him, then turned back to Joseph Henry. "You think you can do that to me? You think you had me bad before?"

Joseph Henry didn't move. All of his attention was on Ugly. Short Stack saw that. He blinked and lost his bluster. His face shifted from anger to something more like pleading.

He tried again, weaker. "Look… maybe we can talk on it. I didn't mean all that. Just… the Kiln is rough. You been there. You know. I can't stay there. It will be the end of me inside a month."

He waited for Joseph Henry to show some give. There was none.

The silence pressed in. Men nearby began to drift away, sensing something they did not want to be close to. Short Stack looked around and swallowed.

"I am just saying…" he stammered on, "…if you still got any sort of… pull… maybe you can… I don't know…"

Joseph Henry still kept his eyes on Ugly, ignoring Short Stack. The look was quiet and measured. It carried something that was not boast and not threat, but understanding. It said plainly: you know what I can manage. But at the same time Joseph Henry knew that was what Ugly wanted him for.

Ugly's one sided grin curled at the edge. He leaned back just a fraction, impressed but unwilling to show it fully.

"Nice trick," Ugly murmured. "But it's all the same."

Joseph Henry nodded. "I know." There was no resignation in it.

Their voices stayed low, meant for no one but each other. They talked as if they were alone in the room.

"I'll come down as before," Joseph Henry said. "We'll talk down there."

Ugly gave a small nod. It said more than it seemed. He rose and brushed crumbs from his hands. He gave a short chuckle and patted Short Stack on the shoulder, then slipped into the crowd without another word. The men who had been sitting with him followed his departure with their eyes, unsure what had just taken place.

Short Stack stayed where he was. His shoulders were slumped. He looked emptied out. Hollow.

Joseph Henry finally turned to him. His voice was even.

"You be a better friend to everyone in here. That will go further than anything else."

Short Stack opened his mouth but said nothing.

Joseph Henry leaned in just enough for only him to hear.

"Do that, and maybe you'll find yourself in a better place after a time."

Short Stack stared, realizing this was all the mercy he would get.

Joseph Henry turned and walked away. The noise of the mess hall filled the space around him again, but none of it touched him.

Joseph Henry stepped into the Boiler Room just after the noon work change. The air was cooler than before, less stifling, and the glow was lower. An acrid dark smoke seeped out of the seams and brought a stinging dryness to his throat. His own experience told him that Ugly hadn't fed the furnace in a while.

The guard assigned to the area was nowhere to be found. Ugly stood alone, leaning against the hopper with a cigarette at his lips.

"See you got us alone again, Mister Henry," Ugly said looking up as Joseph Henry approached. "You really do run things around here, don't you?"

It was clear to Joseph Henry that Ugly had been in that position for a while, probably since the guard left, not even pretending to work. Now he watched Joseph Henry with that easy grin. He motioned his head toward the shovel. "One of us should probably put a couple scoops in before the whole building goes cold."

Ugly was not moving. Joseph Henry looked at him, then at the shovel, knowing Ugly was prodding him to do his job. Joseph Henry wouldn't bite, not this time.

Ugly frowned. "Is this the time you get bold, Mister Henry?"

Joseph Henry ignored the comment. "We need to talk."

Ugly lifted his chin a little. "We are talking."

Joseph Henry held his gaze, calm and unbothered. "No games today."

Ugly's smile came back, but tighter at the edges. He took a long pull from the cigarette. "I do not play games. You know me. You know what I do. No games there."

Joseph Henry shook his head once. "You are already getting what you want. No need to posture anymore. Are we going to talk business or should I come back later?"

Ugly was not expecting that. His grin faded again, not fully, but enough to show the pause behind it. He rubbed the bad side of his face and studied Joseph Henry, measuring the change.

"Fine," Ugly said, trying to keep strength behind it. "But you know what will happen if you trick me."

"You don't need to say it," Joseph Henry replied. "You wanted a way out. I have given it some time, some thought. You are getting out of here."

Ugly watched him, his eyes narrowing with a mixture of respect and something colder. "You walk different now," he said. "Like a man who grew up between breakfast and lunch."

Joseph Henry did not react.

Ugly let out a small breath, accepting that his words wouldn't rile the man today. He nodded, "Tell me what you have."

Joseph Henry sat down on a metal drum, his voice steady and even. "I ran through every way I could think of. The obvious ones.

Hiding in a supply truck. Digging a tunnel. Slipping out with a delivery crew. None of that works. Too many eyes. Too many guards who know the patterns."

Ugly nodded slowly, as if waiting for the real part.

Joseph Henry continued. "I have been looking at the work details. Which ones get the men far from the yard. Which ones run through rough ground. Which ones lose sight of the main walls. There is only one that works."

He waited for Ugly to speak, but Ugly did not, watching him instead.

"Harvesting turpentine," Joseph Henry said.

Ugly's face tightened. Not much, but enough. He had done that detail before, if only briefly. He did not like it.

Joseph Henry went on. "It is outside the main grounds. Forest. Smoke. Tools. Fewer guards than there should be. It gives cover. You can disappear into the trees when the timing is right."

Ugly shook his head. "It is terrible work. Dangerous. Miserable. No man would ask for it."

"Right," Joseph Henry said. "Which is why you cannot ask for it directly. You will need to be placed on that detail weeks ahead. If it happens too fast, it will draw attention."

Ugly frowned. "Weeks? I cannot wait weeks... cannot do that work for weeks."

"It cannot be helped," Joseph Henry said. A quiet satisfaction rose within him, though he kept it well hidden. "This is the only way it works."

Ugly stared at him, measuring the firmness in Joseph Henry's voice. He counted his choices, and the number was low. He did not like this Joseph Henry. He was not as easy to tilt.

"So, what happens?" Ugly asked. "I just run into the trees while they watch you stand there?"

Joseph Henry shook his head. "No. There will be a distraction. Something that pulls the guards toward the truck. Something that does not involve you. When they move, you go. It is simple."

Ugly leaned forward. "And you come with me."

Joseph Henry paused for a breath, and Ugly saw it. "If that is what you need."

Ugly grinned. "It is what I need. You know, a man runs better with company. I trust a plan more when the other man stays close. No one is left to speak."

Joseph Henry gave a single nod. Ugly thought he saw a slight break in the man's new confidence.

Ugly watched him closely. "And Crow."

That caught Joseph Henry, he kept still for a beat. "He isn't part of it."

"He is part of it," Ugly said, like it was nothing. "Crow knows you. Crow trusts you. If you cross me, he will feel it first. That is all. If everything goes well, we leave him behind."

Joseph Henry took a slow breath. He was about to refuse, but then he thought that if everything went right it would not matter. "If that is what it takes."

Ugly leaned back again, satisfied. "Good. Good plan. We will do it."

Joseph Henry stood. "I will handle the rotations. Your details will be switched by the end of the week. Keep quiet. Keep steady. No trouble for the few weeks."

Ugly nodded, then tilted his head, his eyes brightening with a new amusement. "Tell me something, Mister Henry. You remember the bear story?"

Joseph Henry sighed but said nothing.

Ugly smiled, soft, thinking himself clever. "The one I told in the yard. The two men running from a bear. It was a good story, no? The first man does not need to outrun the bear. He only needs to outrun the amigo." He laughed and let the words drift in the smoky air. "Stories like that, they teach things."

Joseph Henry held the gaze without blinking.

Ugly's smile stayed. He looked like a man who believed he had the upper hand.

Joseph Henry did not correct him.

He turned and walked toward the door, leaving the heat and the smoke behind him. Ugly gave a chuckle as Joseph Henry stepped through the doorway.

The stairwell felt cooler as the door shut behind him. Joseph Henry gave a chuckle of his own. He looked back at the closed door and let out a long breath, then turned and took the steps at an easy pace, one hand on the rail, the other loose at his side, almost with a spring in his step. He felt good, in control. And he felt an incredible satisfaction. His plan was moving forward, and Ugly was going to suffer a bit before it even finished.

Joseph Henry knew that Ugly wouldn't like the turpentine detail idea. When he saw it in the tightening around Ugly's mouth and the way his eyes shifted as soon as the words left him, Joseph Henry had a difficult time not smiling. It pleased him more than he thought it would. Ugly had a way of getting under a man's skin, pulling at nerves without ever lifting a hand. To turn that back on him, to watch him face a detail he despised or even feared, gave Joseph Henry a satisfaction that felt clean and earned. Weeks on that detail was more than the plan required. A few days would have done it. But Joseph Henry wanted the extra time, almost like twisting a blunt knife in Ugly's side. He wanted Ugly to feel every morning of it, every strain in his muscles and joints, every breath of resin-heavy air.

The matter of Crow weighed on him more than he was comfortable with. Ugly's easy cruelty in naming him had cut through the satisfaction for a moment, and Joseph Henry felt that echo now. Crow did not need any of this, and it was something that could throw a wrench in the plans. Joseph Henry would have to make sure he was watched, guarded in whatever quiet way the situation allowed. Jimmy or Nils could help with that, though they would not like being put on that detail either. At least it would not need to be as long. They would be okay with it.

Joseph Henry reached the landing and paused. The light from the small window above cast a thin bar across the steps, pale against the shadowed walls. He let thoughts of Crow fade and felt the steadiness in him grow again. It was a calm that was part of him. One that Ugly had rattled for quite a time. Now Ugly thought he understood the ground they stood on.

"Let him think it," Joseph Henry said out loud. He knew better.

He climbed the last steps with growing certainty. It was only a matter of time now before this would be over.

Chapter 32
1929

Joseph Henry felt a stillness around him as he lay in bed before the bell the next morning. He had slept well these past several nights since Giles had set him right again. That talk had steadied him, settled something in him that had rattled loose.

But now, since facing Ugly the day before, something even sharper had taken hold. He felt completely in control of himself and of the situation.

That night he had slept like a stone, and he woke more refreshed than he'd felt in years. He tried to place the last time he'd felt anything close to it, but nothing came. He finally decided he hadn't slept that well in all the time he'd been in the penitentiary.

He gave a brief laugh and stretched. His thinking was crystal clear. He could see the plan in front of him and had no doubts. He did not expect everything to go entirely smooth, but whatever trouble came, he knew he could manage it.

He pulled himself out of the bed and took a few minutes to straighten up the cell. When the bell finally rang, he began the regular routine with Crow in the washroom. He did not always shave, but this morning he felt the need to.

At breakfast call everything seemed better than it should have. The coffee did not seem like the usual sludge. The bread had a touch of flavor. Even the Indian mush tasted better. Joseph Henry mused that it almost reminded him of the grits he'd had when he was younger.

He had an early delivery to make, bringing some leather to one of the newer shoe factories that had opened a town over. After that he planned to stop by the still and spend the rest of the day working with Deacon and Giles.

He walked across the yard toward the gate that led to the loading area. The sky was pale and low, holding the coolness of the morning. Joseph Henry moved with a steady, unhurried gait. His shoulders were set, his eyes level. He gave no outward sign of anything, but something in the way he carried himself made the others he passed shift a little, maybe straighten themselves to match. They lifted their heads, blinked once, maybe gave a small nod. Joseph Henry returned nothing more than a faint inclination of his own. It traveled across the space like a calm statement. This was the Joseph Henry they knew. The steady presence.

Joseph Henry caught sight of Ugly across the yard, standing by the far wall with a few men around him. Ugly said something that made one of them laugh, but his eyes weren't on them. They were fixed on Joseph Henry, narrowed in thin calculation. Ugly tilted his head a fraction, studying him, trying to read him. When their eyes met, Ugly gave a small nod. Joseph Henry smiled to himself, knowing it would be only days before Ugly was out harvesting turpentine. He wondered if the smile had any of the slyness he always saw in Ugly.

Joseph Henry did not change his pace. He did not even give the satisfaction of a nod back. Whatever Ugly thought he saw, he could keep thinking it.

He went through the gate into the loading area and made his way toward the truck.

The space was quiet. Joseph Henry looked across the yard and saw a single guard leaning against the loading dock, his chin low, eyes half-closed as though dozing. The man had a narrow face, and Joseph Henry recognized him as Gerald, a guard usually on the night shift. He wondered if Gerald's shift was nearing its end or if his relief was late.

Joseph Henry stepped a little heavier on the gravel, and Gerald's eyes opened. He jerked himself upright, then, seeing who it was, eased back against the dock again. A small smile crossed his face and he gave Joseph Henry a nod. It was only a brief acknowledgment, but there was recognition behind it. They did not cross paths often, but Gerald knew him well enough. He pulled a toothpick from his shirt pocket and rolled it between his teeth.

"Morning, Mr. Henry."

Joseph Henry returned the nod with the faintest tilt of his chin.

"Morning, Gerald."

He walked the rest of the way to the truck. It sat under the lean-to roof with a fine layer of dust across the fenders and hood from the previous day's drive.

He checked the load, running a hand along the boards of the bed and testing the straps and ties. A few crates of leather were stacked near the back, likely loaded at the end of the previous day. He gave one a light push to make sure it would not shift. There was no rush in him.

He climbed into the cab and settled a hand on the wheel. He pressed the clutch pedal and turned the ignition. The engine shook through the frame in a low, familiar rumble. He listened a moment as it settled into a smooth idle. He eased up on the pedal, then guided the truck out of its spot.

Gerald waited until the last moment before stepping forward, lifting the gate lever, and letting Joseph Henry roll out onto the narrow lane that led down the hill. The truck bounced lightly over the first stretch of ruts, then smoothed out as he turned onto the main road. The penitentiary walls fell away behind him.

The road wound gently between low stretches of field, then through a line of trees where shadows crossed the rutted path. The way was familiar, and Joseph Henry settled into it. His thoughts moved in quiet order, ticking through the work still to be done in the days ahead.

He needed to adjust the work rotations, getting Ugly into the turpentine detail, like it or not. He would have to do the same for Crow, though not for a few weeks yet. Jimmy or Nils would need to be shifted over as well, close enough to keep an eye on him. The still needed tending too: mash to check, vents to clear, deliveries to keep steady. And there was always the stockroom work that could not be put off.

His thoughts went back to the turpentine grounds again. He needed to get himself over there when he could, to mark the tree lines, the slope of the ground, the blind corners. Nothing difficult. Just the work that still lay ahead.

The Alton Shoe Works sat a few miles south of Lawrenceburg, in the small community of Alton near the old depot. It was not much to look at from the road, just a low wooden building set close to the Harrodsburg Pike. A faded sign hung above a wide loading door, the paint worn to soft outlines by the sun and weather. A pair of sheds and a tin-roofed lean-to stood nearby, all of it clustered within fifty yards of the rail spur. The factory was close enough to town to feel connected, but far enough out that the constant hum of stitching, lasting, nailing, and buffing machines would not disturb neighbors.

As the truck rolled up, Joseph Henry saw a few workers milling near a side entrance and crates stacked by a loading bay. He pulled alongside them. No one came over right away. That never bothered him. He waited with the engine idling low, eyes taking in the scene. He had not been to this factory before, but it was much like others he had seen.

After a moment a man looked toward the truck and called inside. Another stepped out, wiping his hands on a rag. He gave Joseph Henry a slight nod. Joseph Henry returned it in kind. The man pointed to the rear of the truck, and Joseph Henry cut the engine, climbed out, and walked to the back.

They worked without much more than small talk. Joseph Henry loosened the straps. Another man climbed onto the bed, lifted the bundles of leather, and passed them down to two others waiting below. They caught each piece and stacked them neatly behind them. When the last bundle had been moved, the first man stepped back and looked over the pile with a brief, satisfied nod. Joseph Henry wiped his palms on his trousers, and the man took a small envelope from his coat pocket. Joseph Henry accepted it, felt the weight with his fingers, and slipped it into his own pocket without opening it.

"Next time," the man said.

Joseph Henry nodded once and climbed back into the truck.

He turned the key, waited for the engine's rumble to settle, then pulled away. He drove down the lane that led back to the main road and out of town, the engine steady beneath him. He felt a calm settling in, the rest of the day ahead, with nothing tugging at him. The still was next, and sometimes that was hardly work at all. The sun had climbed higher now, warming the top of the cab. Joseph Henry rested his forearm on the window frame and let the light touch his skin. He was in no hurry.

As he turned onto the Pike, a deeper quiet built in him. It was one that had been familiar, but had gone missing for a time. He was glad to feel it again. He pressed the pedal lightly, and the truck gathered speed as the road bent back toward Frankfort.

Joseph Henry reached the still just before noon. The chill of the morning was gone, and the warm air carried the heavy scent of mash and woodsmoke, hanging close in the rising humidity.

As he pulled up toward the sliding door he saw Giles outside splitting kindling. Deacon sat on an overturned bucket near the door, rubbing a rag along a copper pipe fitting. Seeing the truck approach, he stood up and slid the door open wide.

Giles looked up toward the cab and broke into a grin. He grabbed another log and began shearing pieces off. Joseph Henry pulled the truck forward until the cab was just inside the door. When Giles finished with the log he was working on, he set the hatchet aside and walked over. He met Joseph Henry as he stepped down from the cab. He immediately noticed something in him.

"Well now," he said, "Look at you Boss. Standing straighter than a man ought to on a workday."

Joseph Henry smiled and may have even blushed. He shook his head with a brief laugh.

Giles kept going. "That was me, wasn't it? I fixed you up the other day." He tapped his chest with a thumb, a look on his face saying he was extremely pleased with himself. "That was all Giles."

Deacon snorted. "You gave him a piece of your mind? Set him straight? I must have missed the whole thing." Then he looked Joseph Henry up and down. "But the man isn't wrong, Joseph. You look like you could run the world."

He took a cursory walk around. Not noticing anything that needed immediate fixing, he walked over and checked the first fermenter, lifting the lid enough to feel the heat and watch the slow bubbling rise and fall. The mash smelled clean, the yeast doing its work. He moved from one barrel to the next in an unhurried rhythm, checking temper, noting the thickening line of foam along the edges, listening to the faint hiss of the vapor pipes above.

Deacon joined him at the third barrel.

"This one's close," Joseph Henry said.

Deacon nodded. "We'll run it tomorrow. Do you think we have time to start a new batch?"

Joseph Henry rolled up his sleeves. "I think we can squeeze it in."

They measured scoopfuls of grain, checked the boiler's water level, and stirred the first great sweep of the mash paddle into the warm vat. Steam rose around them. Deacon worked with quick movements, but Joseph Henry was slower, deliberate, as though the motion itself had its own timing. Giles drifted in after a while, tossing in a last scoop and wiping his hands on his apron.

When the new batch was near set, Joseph Henry stepped away and left Deacon and Giles to finish it. He crossed into the small office off the main room. Dust motes hung in the slanted sunbeam that cut through the single window. He pulled the stool out, sat, and laid a sheet of paper flat across the desk.

He chewed the end of a pencil for a moment, thinking about the work details that needed changing for his plans. After a breath he brought the pencil to the paper and wrote out the rotations in a clear, steady hand.

Ugly to turpentine harvesting beginning Friday (1st Friday of the month).

Crow, Jimmy, Nils to move to turpentine harvesting (3rd Monday of the month).

Joseph Henry to move to turpentine harvesting (3rd Wednesday of the month).

He paused after each name, weighing the timing, the spacing, the reasons each shift needed distance from the next. Nothing hasty. Just the pieces moving where they needed to be.

When he finished, he folded the paper once and tucked it inside his shirt. He'd submit it when he got back to the penitentiary.

He stepped back out into the still house. Deacon and Giles were talking about some trivial thing—weather, delivery schedules, who had shorted them on a grain sack last week. It was good to hear their voices filling the space. He joined them and spent the rest of the afternoon talking and working.

The steadiness in him grew as the hours passed. The quiet settled deeper.

Everything ahead of him was lining up just as it needed to.

Joseph Henry woke with the bell. It surprised him. It was rare that he was not up well before it. He had been sleeping more soundly these past days, and though it left him more refreshed, waking later unsettled his routine just a little. He lay still for a moment in the gray light, letting the familiar shapes of the cell form around him. The block seemed silent at first, then he began to hear the distant shift of boots, the faint groan of pipes warming, and an occasional cough or murmured groan from a neighboring cell.

He got Crow up and the two dressed and washed, that part of the routine unchanged. As he dried his face, his mind went back to the previous afternoon. He had taken the folded sheet of work detail changes from inside his shirt and walked it down the administrative hall behind the warden's offices. The air there always felt different, cool and a bit damp, carrying the faint smell of paper and ink rather than sweat and lime.

Boss Van's secretary, a thin woman with silver spectacles, sat behind her desk sorting ledgers. She barely looked up when Joseph Henry stepped in. He always thought she did not care much for him. It never bothered him, but it did seem he had to go through an extra step or two whenever he needed something handled.

He set the paper on the desk without explanation. The woman finished the ledger page she was working on, then placed a hand over the folded sheet. She gave a single, practiced nod and in one motion slid it beneath a stack of forms waiting for the next morning's file.

No questions. No conversation. No trace that it came from Joseph Henry at all. That was how Boss Van wanted it.

Joseph Henry had a good deal of pull and was given plenty of leeway, but Boss Van did not want it to appear that way. The changes would not come from Joseph Henry. By midweek they would be typed, stamped, and posted. The shifts would move as if by routine, nothing unusual in them.

He put on his cap, gave an ignored nod, and stepped out into the corridor.

The bell rang again, pulling him back to the washroom. Men filed out in loose order. Joseph Henry liked the order. The hallway felt brighter. The air felt clearer. He fell in with the movement, unhurried, with a steadiness that would run through his day.

The plan was in motion now, quiet and unnoticed, and past the point where it could be stopped.

He walked the corridor and stepped into the mess with the others, the sun filtering through the windows. The certainty settled again. So far, everything ahead was unfolding as it was supposed to. He filled his tray.

The days that followed moved at a steady sprint. Each morning began the same way, with Joseph Henry and Crow in the washroom, the pipes rattling above them and the echo of men clearing their throats and making small talk while they went through their morning business. Nothing in that space ever changed, but Joseph Henry's movements stayed sure, and his thoughts kept drifting toward the days ahead.

Breakfast came, and he would take his seat in the mess. The coffee tasted no better or worse than before. He drank it without thought, watching the room while he ate, noting the easy shuffles of the other men settling into their routines. When he rose, he did so without hurry and carried on forward.

Some days he reported to the maintenance stockroom. He checked tool lists, marked shortages, and wrote out the requests that needed to be sent up the chain. He moved crates to the back shelves and sorted the stray items that always gathered in odd corners. He liked the simple, methodical work well enough.

Other mornings he made the deliveries from the penitentiary. He crossed the loading area, exchanged a nod or a short word with Gerald or whichever guard stood there, and checked that the cargo was properly loaded before heading out. The roads were familiar, and so were the customers. Crates of leather. Bundles of woven goods. Boxes of finished pieces from the different workshops. He drove with one arm resting in the open window, letting the wind and quiet fields move past him.

Most afternoons he was at the still again. Sometimes he arrived while Giles was taking stock or Deacon was adjusting a fitting. Joseph Henry joined in without instruction. They skimmed foam from fermenters, tested vapor lines, and set new mash cooling beneath damp cloth. The warm air and low conversation filled the day. Giles talked more than the other two combined. The other two would let Giles go on about whatever was on his mind, only sometimes offering comments. Joseph Henry would move and work among them with a sense of calm, knowing this was really where he wanted to be.

Once or twice during those weeks he drove Boss Van's wife and daughter into town. Small errands. Nothing that took long. It was not his favorite task, but it was part of the long list of things that allowed him outside the penitentiary, part of the quiet facade that made everything else possible.

He left himself little free time, and even then he spent almost none of it in the yard. When he crossed the yard in the late afternoons, heading back to the block or toward the lower gate, he did not linger. He did not join the men at the tables or along the far wall. He simply walked through, neither inviting attention nor avoiding it, only offering a nod or casual greeting.

The rest of the days passed in much the same way, steady and without surprise. Joseph Henry kept to his work, moving between the still, the truck, and the stockroom with the same even rhythm. He heard now and then how Ugly was faring, enough to know the man was feeling every bit of the assignment. For a moment Joseph Henry thought about letting the time run longer, just to keep Ugly in it, to ensure he felt every minute of what Joseph Henry was laying on him. But there was no sense in dragging it out now. The schedule was already finished. Crow, Jimmy, and Nils were to be moved over in just a couple of days. Then that would be it. Joseph Henry felt the moment at hand.

The day before Crow was to be moved to the turpentine harvesting detail, Joseph Henry was walking through town after finishing a delivery. The sun was low over the rooftops and the long street stretched ahead of him. The sandwich shop was a block ahead. He had not eaten much at breakfast, and now it was nearing two o'clock. He was deep in thought about the next several days. A car or truck horn sounded in the distance, pulling him back. He looked up and glanced across the street for the source of the sound.

Then he saw her. Minnie.

He paused at the corner longer than he meant to. The horn had ceased, but it seemed to echo faintly in his mind, as if the sound had stopped in time. He shifted his eyes across the way, taking in the street and the people on it, as if trying to confirm what he was seeing was real. Traffic was light this time of day, only a wagon and a couple of motorcars rolling farther down the block.

She stood just outside a storefront, holding a small parcel under her arm. The afternoon sun caught the edge of her hair, turning it soft. Not quite the familiar gold he had known years ago, but unmistakably hers. She wore a simple dress, nothing fine. She looked older, of course, but in a way that struck him as right. An older that made him think of living, not burden.

Joseph Henry felt a dim smile cross his lips. Then his focus sharpened and the smile faded.

A man stood beside her. Gray at the temples, shoulders a little stooped, the posture of someone who had done farm work or spent years on his feet. He carried himself like someone capable. Something about him tugged at Joseph Henry's memory, though he could not place it. The two of them stood close enough that it looked natural, practiced. A young woman joined them from the doorway, and behind her a boy of six or maybe eight came forward. He clutched the man's coat sleeve, danced around for a few steps, then took Minnie's hand.

Joseph Henry watched the small exchange. Minnie laughed at something the boy said. The man rested a hand lightly on the child's back. The young woman said something that made Minnie shake her head and smile. It looked like a family at ease with itself. A husband and wife. A daughter. A grandson.

Joseph Henry felt a tightening in his chest, not sharp, not deep, just a quiet pull. He let it sit there. He fought off a sudden, profound sadness. He had wanted this. He wanted her to have her life. To build something after him. He had told her so. Insisted on it. Seeing it now, seeing her in the middle of it, settled right with him, but harder than he had expected.

He stood still, hands loose at his sides. No one across the street looked his way. He made no effort to conceal himself. Minnie brushed a strand of hair from her face and said something to the man. He nodded, slow, with an affectionate smile, the way someone does when they have known another person a long time.

Joseph Henry took in the scene for another breath, then looked down the street toward where he was headed. He forced himself to step forward and walked on toward the sandwich shop, resisting the urge to look back.

Joseph Henry finished his meal without tasting much of it. When he stepped back onto the street the sun was dipping behind the courthouse roofline, leaving the road in a long stretch of late-afternoon shade. The earlier moment still sat in him, like a hand pressed lightly against his chest. He let it sit there. There was no sense in turning it over any more than he already had.

He walked back to the truck and climbed in. The engine turned, then settled into its familiar rumble. The drive back to the penitentiary took him along the same quiet fields as always. He kept his eyes on the road, his hands steady on the wheel. The image of Minnie drifted in and out of his thoughts, never fully staying, never fully leaving. He allowed it a place for a few minutes, then set it aside.

The penitentiary walls rose ahead of him. The guard at the gate leaned one shoulder against a post. He straightened when the truck approached and lifted the gate lever. Joseph Henry nodded once as he rolled past. The guard returned it with the same small gesture.

Joseph Henry parked the truck beneath the lean-to, stepped out, and closed the door with a firm push. Inside the yard the evening move was already underway. Men crossing the yard, returning from one detail or another. Voices carrying low and tired across the open space.

He walked back across the yard toward the block. He knew what was coming now, knew how the next days would go. The pieces were set. A thin exhilaration ran through him. The turn was close. It was time.

He reached the steps to the cellblock and paused long enough to look back across the yard. Everything looked ordinary. That suited him.

He went inside and let the door close behind him.

Chapter 33
1929

Two trucks rolled to a stop at the edge of the turpentine grounds. Clouds hung low and colorless overhead, thick enough to mute the light, thin enough to let a fine drizzle sift through the trees. The moisture clung to everything. It beaded on the foliage, darkened the ground, gathered in the creases of the men's coats. It was not enough to be called rain, and certainly not enough to cool the air. It only added weight to the morning humidity.

They had left the penitentiary while most inmates were still in the mess for breakfast. Once the men were settled in the open beds of the trucks, one of the guards tossed in a sack with biscuits, strips of salt pork, and a few bruised apples for the morning meal. Some of the men pulled out pieces during the ride, eating in silence. Others waited, planning to take a few quick mouthfuls once they arrived, before the work began.

Joseph Henry stepped down from the truck, his boots sinking slightly into the damp carpet of pine needles. It had been some time since he had worked this detail. He breathed in, catching the heavy air, thick with the smell of sap and woodsmoke, the pitch scent that clung to clothes and hair long after a man left the woods. On their own the odors might have been pleasant, almost clean, but here they carried something harsher. In the context of the work they were pungent and unsettling. The air did not move. A man had to draw it in, hard and deliberate, as though it didn't want to be breathed at all.

He looked around at the stripped trunks of the pines rising around him, each one carved with a V-shaped wound, the bark peeled back in long strips. Resin dripped lazily into the clay pots nailed beneath the scars, slow and dark.

He looked back toward the trucks, seeing the last of the inmates climbing down in loose order, some stretching their arms and rubbing stiff legs after the cramped ride. The ground here was uneven, crossed with exposed roots slick from the damp. The humidity settled against their skin, close and unmoving. Even though they had just arrived, sweat gathered at the base of their necks.

Joseph Henry watched Crow, the last to step down. He carried himself carefully, one hand on the wagon rail, a slight smile appearing as though pleased he had kept his balance. His eyes moved over the trees, the ground, then the tools scattered near a small work shed. A few inmates muttered when they saw the old man.

"Who would do this to Old Crow?"

"Gonna break the man in two, putting him out on this."

One of the friendlier guards shrugged at the muttering. "We don't write the schedules, boys," he said, looking between the men and Crow. After a pause he added, "We'll keep him away from the trees."

Jimmy and Nils were already watching Crow, just as Joseph Henry had told them to, making sure he didn't need a hand. Crow waved them off when they stepped toward him and straightened himself, though the motion tightened the corners of his mouth.

The guards milled around the clearing with little urgency. Two had settled against pine stumps, rifles resting upright between their knees, coats darkened with the fine drizzle. One of them sat with his chin low against his chest, eyes half closed, blinking to keep from drifting off.

Another guard walked a slow line behind the trees, pacing without hurry. Every so often he paused when an inmate wandered a little off from his place. He would straighten, lift his rifle into both hands, and watch with a momentary tension, as though waiting to see whether the movement meant something more. But it never did. When the inmate bent back to his work, the guard let the rifle fall to his side again and resumed his slow path, the brief edge of alertness fading as quickly as it had come.

At least two other guards wandered the camp, occasionally disappearing into the woods to walk a deeper perimeter.

Nothing sharp held in the air. The drizzle softened the woods, softened their coats, softened even the bit of vigilance they might have shown on a cleaner morning. It was too early in the day, and too damp, for any of them to pretend at strictness. They kept their posts, but without discipline or energy, as if the forest itself had called for quiet. They had never had any trouble minding this detail, and most of them did only the bare minimum required to keep being called guards.

The guards were not responsible for the work itself. They were only there to keep the men in line and to keep them from slipping off into the woods. The labor ran on its own rhythm, the same way it always had. The inmates fell into their places without anyone needing to call out instruction. After only a short time shoulders began to tighten. Forearms burned from the constant downward pull of the iron. A man paused not because the tree was done, but because his hand would not unclench without coaxing. Then he'd pull again.

A supervisor appeared once or twice a week, but not today. The men knew what they were meant to do. They gathered the hack tools, scraping irons, and small axes from the shed and moved toward their rows as they always had. The older cuts needed refreshing, the buckets needed emptying, and the scar lines along the trunks had to be kept clean. The first iron rang against bark before all the tools were fully passed out.

The scraping iron was a short, heavy-bladed tool with a curved edge, made for cutting away the crusted bark and old resin to open a fresh channel. A man braced himself and pulled it downward in steady strokes, shaving the trunk clean so the sap could run. Each pass left a pale, wet stripe that glistened before the resin thickened and began a slow crawl downward. The handles grew slick within minutes. More than one man carried the marks, thin white lines across the forearms, wrists and knuckles where irons had slipped and scraped off the skin. It was the brand of the turpentine harvester.

Most of the trees held clay cups or pots nailed beneath the cuts, broad-lipped and heavy, meant to last through multiple seasons. The fresh resin gathered there in thick drops, hitting the surface with soft thuds. What didn't make it into the cups hardened fast in the creases of fingers and cuffs. If not scraped off before it set, it would pull skin with it later. By midday cuffs were stiff, trousers tacky at the thigh, and the sweet pitch scent had turned sour in the heat.

A few trees held tin cans hammered in place instead, dented from years of use. Their thin sides rattled whenever a man's boot struck a root nearby, and the resin ran into them with a sharper sound, like a stray rain drop hitting a gutter.

The cups had to be emptied often. If they filled too high, the sap would overflow, hardening in yellow streams along the trunk and wasting the heavy work.

New faces were put on lighter tasks until the supervisor could evaluate their usefulness. Jimmy and Nils had been given one of these, hauling empty resin pots from the shed to the tree lines and bringing full ones back. It was slow, steady work and kept them moving through the middle of the clearing, close enough that one or the other could keep an eye on Crow at any given time. Crow had been given the water bucket and ladle, a job anyone else would have loved. It was the easiest duty in the camp. Someone almost always grumbled that the man with that job had it too easy, but no one seemed to complain that it had gone to Old Crow.

Crow accepted the assignment with a nod and a quiet sort of pride. The bucket wasn't too heavy for a fit man, yet he shifted his grip twice before lifting it, as though surprised by the weight. By midmorning he paused longer between rounds, pretending to check the water level so he could steal a breath. He dipped the ladle and offered it steady and unhurried. He had not worked a particularly physical detail in years, and though he did not understand why he had been sent out, he carried himself like a man grateful to still be useful. A few men noticed the presence of the new arrivals, including Joseph Henry himself. One called over to him, half joking, half curious. "New faces here lately. Haven't seen you here in ages, Joseph. What gets you out here? Piss someone off?"

Joseph Henry paused a beat, then gave a simple answer, not looking at the man. "Checking the equipment. Quick inventory. Some of it needs repairing."

The man nodded, accepting it without question, and turned back to his tree line.

During the first short break at midmorning, the men took quick bites of another biscuit, leaning their weight against tools or stumps. The drizzle had let up, but it would be some time before things dried out. Joseph Henry noticed Ugly drifting toward him, wiping resin from his fingers with the back of a sleeve. Joseph Henry had been quietly keeping his distance through the morning, but he knew Ugly would sidle up sooner or later. When they finally ended up face to face, Ugly flicked his eyes toward Crow, still making his slow round with the water bucket, with Jimmy or Nils keeping a close distance that looked casual unless someone knew better.

Ugly gave a half smile, letting Joseph Henry know he'd seen the arrangement for what it was. He grunted, low and approving. "Smart," he said. "Keeping him watched like that."

Joseph Henry did not respond. He bent and tightened a boot lace.

Ugly watched him for a moment. Joseph Henry could see that his patience was already frayed, but he offered nothing to ease it. At last

Ugly said, "So… when does it start? I should already know that. This don't need to drag out all day."

Joseph Henry straightened, brushed pine dust from his knees, and kept his tone even. "When it needs to. Timing matters." He saw that Ugly was waiting for more. "About an hour after lunch."

Ugly shifted his jaw, only half satisfied, trying to make it seem as though he had already known the plan. Joseph Henry smiled inwardly.

The break came to an abrupt end as one of the guards tapped the butt of a rifle against a stump. The men rose and drifted back to their trees, and the break quickly faded into the slow clatter of irons scraping on bark. Joseph Henry returned to checking the tools and equipment a short distance from Jimmy and Nils.

Ugly was a few trees down, working the same line. Joseph Henry watched him for a moment. He had wanted to keep Ugly on edge as much as possible, part of the reason he was waiting until later for the two of them to act. Ugly worked, but he kept glancing over his shoulder between strokes of the scraping iron. The strokes were uneven though, more like a hack than a pull. Resin splattered where it should have run clean, flecking Ugly's arms and face. Sweat cut thin lines through the pitch on his cheeks and stung his eyes. He blinked harder than necessary and scraped again. Every minute or two he would pause and look toward Joseph Henry, or toward Old Crow, or down the tree line where the path cut deeper into the woods.

He was trying not to show it, but Joseph Henry could see it was getting to him. Ugly usually moved with an easy precision, even when things were tight. Now he looked unsettled, off his rhythm, as though the waiting itself was a raw, open rash.

A guard walked behind the row. Ugly startled before he caught himself, straightened, and resumed scraping with a forced steadiness. When the guard passed, he exhaled hard through his nose, the impatience undiminished. The man was unsteady. Not enough to break, but enough to make the hours ahead run longer for him.

Joseph Henry leaned toward Jimmy and whispered for him to smile and nod. Jimmy did, and when Joseph Henry looked back over his shoulder, he saw Ugly watching.

Ugly scraped at the tree again, slower this time. His eyes flicked toward Joseph Henry. There was a question in them, or a demand, or simply uncertainty.

Joseph Henry picked up a tin can and walked over to Ugly's tree, making like he was changing out a resin cup.

"What's the matter, Ugly? Look at you… you're about to jump out of your skin. You've got to keep it together."

Ugly snorted, forced a laugh. It came out thin. "I am together. Always together," he muttered, the second part almost under his breath. "Just no reason to keep waiting. We should already be moving, miles from here."

Joseph Henry didn't look at him. He was adjusting the tin cup beneath the cut and checking its angle though it didn't need checking. "You wanted me for a reason, Ugly. You said it yourself. You needed someone who could make things work."

Ugly frowned, uncertain for a moment. "Now I need a man who can move, who can get things moving," he said in a low voice.

"And I need a man who can wait until it is time," Joseph Henry said, not hiding a touch of impatience. His voice was steady now, quiet, but without softness. "The plan has moving parts. A set-up. Cover. Distraction." He looked up across the line. "That's why I moved Jimmy and Nils here."

Ugly's eyes narrowed and cut toward them, then back to Joseph Henry with a small, knowing smirk. "To watch Crow…"

"That too, not going to lie," Joseph Henry said, not bothering to hide it. He wiped resin off his fingers against his pants. "But mainly? Distraction. You'll see. You think I would go through the trouble of bringing both of them out here if all I wanted was to babysit Crow?"

Ugly hesitated. A pause opened just long enough to show he was considering it. His gaze shifted down the line, focusing first on Jimmy, then on Nils. His jaw worked as though he wanted to argue it some more, but couldn't find the angle or the energy.

Joseph Henry saw it and kept going. "The guards will be distracted. Trust me."

Ugly's impatience faltered. He glanced toward a guard he remembered seeing Joseph Henry speak with earlier in the morning. He exhaled hard through his nose, still trying to hold onto an air of authority. "You make it sound simple, Mister Henry." He emphasized the name with a thin edge of sarcasm. "Is it?"

Joseph Henry paused as if choosing his words. "When the time comes, it will be." He gave a faint shrug and the briefest laugh. "At least that's the plan," he added, knowing Ugly wouldn't like his amusement.

Ugly showed the irritation for only a beat, then studied Joseph Henry for another. Skepticism flickered behind his eyes, but he seemed to be fighting it. He wasn't committing to believe Joseph Henry, but he didn't deny it either. He nodded once, shallow, guarded.

Joseph Henry stepped back and turned away, brushing pine dust from his hands. "After lunch," he said again.

Ugly didn't answer, but Joseph Henry could feel the weight of his stare as he walked away.

The hours thinned toward midday. Work slowed, not from fatigue but from the way the detail always eased in anticipation of the lunch break. Irons still struck bark, though less often. Men shifted their weight more, pausing longer between strokes. The drizzle had stopped, and the sun broke through the clouds in places, leaving the woods thick and quiet, with a faint steam rising off the vegetation.

Joseph Henry stepped quietly along the tree line, giving no sign he was doing anything other than his own duties. He passed close to

Crow and gave the old man a brief once-over. Crow was sweating a little harder than the others, but his breathing looked steady. His hands didn't shake. He kept dipping the ladle and offering it to the next man down the line without pause. The work mattered. That eased something in Joseph Henry, but not fully. He found himself thinking again that Crow shouldn't have been here at all, and he faulted himself for letting it happen.

As the men made their way toward the trucks for their lunch sacks, Joseph Henry noticed that Ugly had not joined them. He was still at the tree line, eyes on a tree, working, jaw set. His scraping iron moved in rhythmic, patient pulls now. Not the choppy strokes from earlier. Something had settled in him. His movements were clipped, efficient, almost sharp. Not a man calming down, but a man *thinking*.

Joseph Henry saw no swagger in him now. Only a pressed, simmering focus. Not on the work. On something else. Joseph Henry's stomach tightened. He had felt a sure confidence all morning, but now he felt the slightest doubt thread through it.

He made a slow loop toward him, stopping at a trunk as if studying a split in the bark. Ugly glanced up at that moment. Their eyes locked. Joseph Henry gave a small nod, almost nothing, something anyone else might have missed.

Ugly saw it. He stopped scraping. For a heartbeat he held still, the iron suspended midair. Then his gaze shifted past Joseph Henry down the clearing, toward the group gathering for lunch. He looked back, a thin smile forming, not the showy one he used with the men but something narrower, colder.

Ugly was ready. But there was something more Joseph Henry decided. Ugly had landed on something, an idea, sharp enough to harden his expression. The look of impatience was gone. He had his own plan now. He was preparing himself, not for the plan he was given, but for the one he meant to take.

Joseph Henry saw all this, but forced himself not to react. He stepped closer to Ugly.

"You need to get your sack lunch," Joseph Henry murmured. "Can't break routine. You will know when to go. Head south down the hill, across the lines."

Ugly didn't move.

He stood there, the scraping iron loose in his hand. His eyes stayed fixed on Joseph Henry with a look that was both determined and mocking. Joseph Henry recognized something in it, a sense that Ugly had already decided the man standing before him was useful only up to a point, and no further. The quiet stretched out between them until it seemed to take on its own shape.

Then he spoke.

"No," Ugly said softly. "I don't think it will start like that."

Joseph Henry exhaled through his nose. He kept his posture easy, though he felt the weight of the moment settle across his shoulders. "This is the timing," he said, flat and even, as if Ugly hadn't just shifted the ground beneath them. "We move when it is time to move. Can't change things now."

Ugly lifted the iron and rested it against his thigh. For a brief instant Joseph Henry saw it differently, not as a tool but as something that could be used otherwise. Ugly stood there breathing slow, unhurried, as though he had all the time he needed.

"It starts when it is time to move," Ugly echoed. Joseph Henry's brow tensed, the smallest flicker before he forced it still.

"You go first," Ugly continued. "You take the first steps down the hill, Mister Henry. That is how I will know when to go. How I will know you are not planning something sideways."

Joseph Henry did not respond at once. The woods held a thick quiet. It felt almost surreal, as if time had slowed around them. Steam rose from the pine needles in faint threads. Farther down the line a tin can rang as a late drop of resin struck it. Neither man looked toward the sound. Their eyes stayed locked.

Joseph Henry finally broke the lock. He looked up slightly and said, slow and even, "Alright… it doesn't matter much to me. There will be a distraction. The plan…"

"I know what you told me," Ugly cut in, almost sharp. Then his voice flattened again. "I am not a fool. I go when I see you move. Not before." He said it as if Joseph Henry had not just agreed, lifting the iron an inch in a small, deliberate punctuation. "I need to see you walk first. Then I know everything is as you claim."

Joseph Henry felt a slow pulse in his fingers, a tightening he forced himself to release. The demand had the shape of paranoia, but it didn't sit like paranoia. "Alright," he said again, the word quiet.

Ugly gave a small breath, almost a laugh, but too thin to reach that far. "That is how it works now." He leaned in a fraction, close enough that Joseph Henry could see the resin flecked along his jaw, the strands of hair glued together in stiff clumps. "And you remember the bear story, Mister Henry. You understood it." He let the words settle in the humid air. "You do not forget that."

Joseph Henry held the look without blinking. Inside, something braced. Ugly wasn't drifting toward panic or disorder. A man speaking like this wasn't breaking. He was settling. Fixing himself to something firm. Joseph Henry just nodded.

"You understand what I am saying." Ugly said quietly.

Joseph Henry kept his tone flat. "I hear you."

Ugly did not move. "Say it." He turned the more disturbing side of his face toward Joseph Henry. Deliberate.

Joseph Henry felt the moment turn, felt the weight of Ugly's stare. He forced the air out slowly. "I understand," he said.

Ugly's eyes softened, not in relief but in satisfaction, as though a piece had been set exactly where he wanted it. As though Joseph Henry had been put back into position. He lowered the scraping iron, wiped his palm on his trouser leg, and nodded once.

"Good," he said. "Lunch."

He stepped past Joseph Henry as though he weren't there, moving with a careful, controlled calm. He was the one in charge again. He walked toward the trucks where the men were retrieving their lunch sacks. His shoulders straightened as he joined the line, his posture settling back into that familiar self-assured shape.

Joseph Henry watched him go, feeling the turn of it, feeling the truth of what had just settled between them. The plan was still his—he knew that. But Ugly had placed his hand on the wheel, and Joseph Henry didn't like it at all.

He stepped back from the tree and looked once down the slope where they would soon be headed. He set the moment aside, quietly, deliberately.

The next move would come soon, but it would not be simple anymore.

***

After a moment Joseph Henry turned and followed Ugly toward the truck. A line had formed at the back of the flatbed where a guard had pulled open a wooden crate and begun handing down lunch sacks, thick brown paper folded and lightly stained with grease. It was always the same, and no one expected otherwise. Inside each sack was a wedge of dense cornbread, a strip or two of cold fried fatback wrapped in waxed paper, a small raw onion, and a twist of paper holding a smear of sorghum. Simple food meant to fill the stomach and keep the men going for a few more hours.

The men settled where they could, against stumps or trees, sitting on an overturned bucket, or on a rock or drier patch of ground. They ate without much talk, teeth working through the rough fare.

Joseph Henry found a felled log a short distance from Jimmy and Nils. His mind circled the events to come. His nerves were rising, and he felt no hunger at all. He looked down at his lunch sack sitting untouched beside him and sighed. Lifting his head, he found Crow across the clearing. The old man had taken his lunch to a patch of exposed roots and lowered himself carefully. From where Joseph Henry sat, Crow's breathing looked heavier now, his chest rising in deliberate pulls, but his eyes were still clear and he kept that small, simple smile. Joseph Henry watched him wipe sweat from his brow, then open his sack with patient hands. He sniffed the onion, then took a small bite.

Not far from Crow, Ugly leaned against a trunk with his lunch sack in hand. He opened it with quick, precise motions, not impatience exactly, but a kind of guarded hunger. He tore off a piece of cornbread and ate it in small, sharp bites, chewing just long enough before swallowing. He stopped when he noticed Joseph Henry's gaze. Then his own gaze flicked to Crow, then back. Joseph Henry was not comfortable with how close Ugly was to Crow, but he nodded. Ugly went back to his food.

Joseph Henry took a breath and forced himself to rise. He walked past Ugly over to Crow and let his hand brush the old man's shoulder, not long enough to draw attention, but enough that Crow glanced up, gave a small smile, then, and went back to his lunch.

Joseph Henry turned back toward Ugly, without rushing. When Ugly saw him approach, he straightened, wiped his mouth with his thumb, and waited.

Joseph Henry didn't speak. He only gave the slightest nod. Almost nothing, but Ugly saw it. A slow smile came across Ugly's face, thin, like something stretched too far.

Around them the men were finishing their meals, folding the brown paper, dusting crumbs from their clothes. The guards pushed themselves upright and called for the men to form back into loose lines and return to their trees.

Across the clearing, Jimmy stood and brushed off his trousers, tension already in his shoulders. Nils shifted closer, the two of them preparing themselves for what they had to do.

Joseph Henry felt the moment gather, felt the coil draw tight in his shoulders. Lunch was ending. Men were rising. The next move was coming.

Ugly watched him with a flicker of challenge behind his eyes. He knew a distraction was coming, though Joseph Henry had never told him the details.

Joseph Henry gave a final, imperceptible nod.

Ugly held his stare.

And then, as the men began to drift back toward their work, the clearing started to shift with movement.

***

Joseph Henry had gone over the plan with Jimmy and Nils more than once in the past couple of weeks. They were not thrilled about spending a few days on the turpentine detail, but they were glad enough to help him and Crow, and neither man had much love left for Ugly Attics. The idea of using the two of them as part of a distraction had come to Joseph Henry only the day before their assignment was switched. He had not given explicit instructions, just the timing and the need. The two then spent the next several evenings working out the rest on their own. They only shared the details with Joseph Henry quietly on the ride out that very morning, leaning close so the guards would not hear.

During lunch the two had trouble sitting still. They kept shifting in place, trading glances, and occasionally looking over at Joseph Henry or Ugly. They thought they were passing for casual, but it did not quite land that way. Jimmy kept wiping his palms on his trousers. Nils slapped his hands away and whispered that he looked like a nervous groom meeting his bride for the first time, though Nils didn't look much calmer himself.

Joseph Henry could feel their nervous energy from where he sat. Every few moments Jimmy would inhale like he was about to speak, then stop himself. Nils rubbed at a hangnail, grimacing at it as though it were something far worse than a torn bit of skin.

The men around them began folding their sacks and brushing crumbs from their clothes. Jimmy and Nils both straightened at the same moment. Nils glanced toward Joseph Henry, looking for some sign to move, but Joseph Henry's eyes were on Ugly and Crow. He wasn't supposed to signal them anyway. The plan was simple: they were to move when lunch broke up.

Voices rose as the guards began calling for the men to get moving and head back to their rows. There were a few grumbles. Feet scuffed. Tools were lifted from where they'd been set down. The brief quiet of the meal began to thin and scatter.

A faint breeze slipped through the clearing. For both Jimmy and Nils it seemed to land like a cue. They stood and moved with the cluster of men drifting back toward the lines.

Jimmy edged a step closer to Nils, lowering his head, saying something low and private. Joseph Henry caught the posture: the way Jimmy leaned in too far, too close, almost exaggerated. Then he saw Nils stiffen, his shoulders jerk back just enough to read as being offended.

Nils straightened and said, "That so?" loud enough for nearby men to hear. He stepped forward and gave Jimmy a shove to the shoulder. It was barely anything, but he scowled as if it meant more. A few men slowed, turning to watch. Nils shoved him again, a flat-palmed push to the chest that looked more exaggerated than hostile.

Jimmy swatted Nils's hand aside, muttering something that carried just enough to sound like a grievance, though there was no weight in it. He looked around and saw several men had stopped altogether, their expressions puzzled.

He lifted his fists in a loose, uncomfortable way, elbows tucked too close to his ribs. Nils mirrored him, hands awkwardly high, as though fending off bees rather than blows. Neither man had ever been much of a fighter, and it showed. They circled once, each waiting for the other to make it look real.

Someone in the crowd let out a derisive laugh and yelled, "That the best you two can manage?"

Another voice followed. "My sister fights meaner than that."

A third chimed in. "This going anywhere? Hit him, for God's sake!"

A ripple of scoffs moved through the small crowd. Boots scuffed. Shoulders leaned in. Jimmy's ears flushed red. Nils glanced around, cheeks tight with embarrassment, then he looked back at Jimmy.

Nils gave Jimmy a small, helpless shrug, then swung an exaggerated, slow roundhouse. Nils half expected it to miss.

It didn't.

His fist clipped Jimmy nose and cheekbone. Jimmy went down hard, a clear look of surprise on his face. A few men in the crowd let out a bark, somewhere between laughter and a cheer. Nils froze, his eyes going wide. For a heartbeat he looked ready to drop to reach out and apologize, hand half-raised as though reaching for Jimmy's shoulder.

Jimmy pushed himself upright, blinking fast. He touched his nose and saw a smear of blood on his fingers. Something in him shifted. His face contorted with embarrassment, surprise, and anger all tangled together.

He lunged suddenly at Nils and the two collided in a clumsy tangle of arms. Jimmy swung wildly, catching Nils in the ribs with a glancing slap of a fist. Nils tried to shove him off, but his footing slipped on the damp needles. The two went down to the ground together, turning the scuffle into a stumbling, awkward grapple. It wasn't graceful and there was no skill to be found. It was the kind of thing you'd see boys getting into in the school yard, a lot of noise and flailing limbs.

But the crowd reacted at once.

"There you go!"

"Don't let'im get up!"

Boots shuffled and the onlookers moved into a loose ring. They leaned forward, hands on knees, watching the two thrash in the dirt. The mood brightened into a crude reprieve and burst of entertainment in the middle of the normal hard labor.

Even the guards paused long enough to look, one of them muttering something to egg it on before remembering he was supposed to stop it.

On the ground, Jimmy and Nils continued to grapple in a messy sprawl, arms slipping, boots kicking without aim. They rolled once, then again, each trying to get on top but with no real technique behind it. Fists glanced off ribs and face, not much force in them, neither knowing how to get leverage while on the ground. Their breaths came short and strained, more from the scrambling than any fury.

But it was loud. It was chaotic. And it drew every eye in the clearing.

The whole camp had drifted toward the fight like a kind of tide. Joseph Henry glanced at Ugly and found him watching the clearing, eyes cutting back and forth between the crowd and Joseph Henry. The distraction was happening and it was time to move. Joseph Henry turned and started toward the slope where the path cut downhill into the trees.

He took a few steady steps before catching sight of Old Crow at the edge of the commotion. Crow stood apart from the others, looking only at the backs of the noisy throng, not quite understanding what had pulled everyone together. When he spotted Joseph Henry passing, he gave him that small smile and nod.

Joseph Henry let the nod pass between them, then continued on, beginning his descent down the hill and across the line.

Ugly waited several beats before moving. He stood with his back to the throng, watching Joseph Henry's brief exchange with Crow, his gaze fixed on Joseph Henry's retreating back. Then, when Joseph Henry was far enough ahead, Ugly started forward in a slow, almost casual stride.

Crow had turned to watch Joseph Henry go, shading his eyes with one hand. He looked puzzled, trying to understand why Joseph Henry was heading off alone. The small smile was still at his mouth.

Ugly came up behind him without a word. He wasn't trying to be quiet. He didn't need to be. Crow's attention was fixed on Joseph Henry heading down the hill, and the noise of the crowd behind them swallowed every footstep.

As Ugly drew close to Crow, he slipped the scraping iron from his hip. The movement was quick and clean. Without breaking stride he brought it up and drove the iron squarely behind Crow's ear, a short, deliberate, brutal strike. The sound was soft and sickening. Crow folded without even lifting a hand, dropping face-first into the needles with a muted thud.

Ugly did not look down at him. He just kept walking toward the slope.

After cresting the slope Ugly started down the hill and fell into a jog. He caught up to Joseph Henry with surprising speed, slowed to match the pace, and looked over, breathing hard but smiling that thin, pleased sneer.

Joseph Henry hadn't expected him yet. The sudden presence of Ugly so close at his shoulder startled him. Ugly looked almost refreshed, as if coming down the hill had cost him nothing at all.

"Remember the bear, Mister Henry," Ugly said.

Joseph Henry felt irritation rise but kept his voice level. "I'm sure I can keep up, Ugly."

Ugly's smile widened. "Maybe. But Crow…" He tilted his head back up the slope. "…don't look so good."

Joseph Henry's expression changed in an instant. He stopped. His eyes snapped up the hill. From where he stood he could see movement: several men breaking away from the crowd around the fight, gathering around a shape on the ground.

For a moment he froze, pulled between two paths.

Then he turned and ran back up the hill.

He drove himself harder than was good for a man his age, boots slipping on rocks and damp needles, breath loud in his own ears. The climb blurred past him, just a steep rush of effort and despair. When he reached the top the scene came sharp and terrible. Crow was lying face-down, blood seeping, matted in his hair and trailing down the side of his neck. A guard knelt beside him, one hand hovering uselessly as though afraid to touch him.

The fight had broken apart instantly. Men stood scattered in a ragged ring, their earlier excitement drained away. A few were muttering. Others stared in stunned silence.

Jimmy and Nils ran toward Crow, their faces twisted with guilt and shock. Jimmy started to call out to Joseph Henry, but his voice cracked on the first syllable. Nils looked frozen, eyes fixed on Crow as if the scene refused to make sense.

Crow did not move.

Joseph Henry reached them and exhaled hard, the breath leaving him all at once. The clearing, noisy and restless only moments before, had fallen into a stunned stillness. Men stood fixed where they were, as though waiting for someone else to name what had just happened.

He stood a few paces short of Crow, unable to force himself any closer. The sight hollowed him. Crow lay still, the skin around the wound already swelling in a dark bloom. One arm was twisted beneath him. He looked fragile, broken, like a dry branch brought down by a stiff wind. Joseph Henry thought he saw Crow's chest rise shallowly, or maybe it was only him wanting to see it.

He did not kneel. He felt like he should, but he could not. His hands hovered uselessly at his sides, fingers flexing without purpose. He heard Jimmy say his name again, the voice thin and cracked, but Joseph Henry could not respond.

Something inside him sagged under the weight of the scene. A weakness he had not felt in years, maybe not since Minnie's final visit, settled over him like an old blanket. The world around him blurred at the edges. A guard shouted for the men to step back. Nils whispered Crow's name as though the sound itself might lift him. None of it broke through.

Joseph Henry's gaze stayed fixed on the old man lying facedown in the needles. Crow was supposed to be safe. Crow had trusted him. He had come out here because of him. A tremor ran once through Joseph Henry's shoulders, sharp, as though something inside him was shifting.

Then the tremor hardened.

It started as a tightness behind his shoulders, a heat that gathered and pulled everything else toward it. His breath steadied. The skin along his face drew taut, a strain that made the veins near his temples stand out. What had been grief sharpened into something far clearer and colder. The anger rose slowly, deliberate, as though it had been waiting its turn. First at the sight before him. Then at himself. Then it found its true place and settled where it belonged. Ugly.

Every man nearby seemed to sense the change even before Joseph Henry. They watched him straighten, watched the softness leave his face, watched something purposeful take over. Nils stepped back without meaning to. Jimmy's expression flickered, something like fear catching in his breath.

Joseph Henry lifted his head.

Down the slope, through the last breaks in the clearing, Ugly was nearing the tree line, slowing, glancing back as though checking Joseph Henry's progress. Joseph Henry did not care about the guard he knew was hidden down there waiting to spring on him. He did not care what the plan had been. He did not care what control Ugly believed he had held.

He drew a long breath and let it out steady.

"Ugly Attics."

His voice cracked across the clearing like a struck board. Every head turned. Joseph Henry started down the hill in long, deliberate strides. His focus narrowed to a single point. Everything else, the camp, the guards, the men behind him, even Crow, fell away.

"Ugly Attics."

Ugly paused at the shout, surprise broke across his face as he saw Joseph Henry coming. He stood frozen for a breath too long, as though his legs had forgotten the direction he meant to run. He forced himself to move, taking a few slow steps backward down the slope. But he kept his eyes on Joseph Henry, unable to look away.

Joseph Henry kept coming. It was somehow more unsettling to Ugly that he was not rushing. There was something in Joseph Henry's face now that held Ugly in place. Even from the distance between them, he seemed to see it, something he had never thought could be there. A hardness. A flare of something almost unhinged beneath the familiar calm.

Joseph Henry closed another stretch of ground. He had covered nearly two thirds of the distance in that unrushed, long gait. Then he stopped. He stood still on the slope for a long moment, breath steady, eyes fixed on Ugly.

"Ugly," he called. "The bear, Ugly. I don't have to be faster than the bear either." He gave the faintest smile, a cold thing. "Not if the bear has no interest in me."

The realization came over Ugly slowly, then his mouth parted. His eyes flicked behind Joseph Henry, then back toward the trees below, where escape suddenly seemed far less certain.

Ugly finally turned and lurched into a run, more stumble than stride, head still craned back trying to keep one eye on Joseph Henry as he moved. He managed barely three steps before he barely saw a figure step cleanly out from behind a pine. The guard filled the path in an instant.

Ugly crashed into him with full momentum. The guard barely rocked back. But Ugly's small frame bounced off him and crumpled to the needles, a strangled sound leaving him as the air punched out of his chest.

For a heartbeat he stared up, wide-eyed, shock breaking across his face. The truth landed hard. Joseph Henry had known the guard was there. He had known all along. Joseph Henry's steps had never been uncertain.

Ugly pushed himself upright with a grunt, breath ragged. Dirt clung to the side of his face. He brushed it off with the back of his sleeve, straightened his shirt, and lifted his chin as though the collision had been only an inconvenience. He looked from the guard to Joseph Henry, and the thin confidence returned to his mouth like a stain rising back through cloth.

"Well," he said, catching his breath, "I suppose that is it." He gave a small sniff and adjusted the strap of his trousers. He took a half step toward the guard as though moving into a safe zone. "No sense dragging out a lost cause." He paused and looked Joseph Henry in the eye. "Too bad about Old Crow though." His voice carried a soft, false pity. "Man's gotta watch his step. Unfortunate." He smirked, obviously pleased with himself. "Lots of rocks and sticks."

The guard looked confused at the remark, but Ugly paid him no mind.

He turned slightly toward the guard and lifted two fingers in a casual gesture. "Alright," he said, tone light, almost bored. "Time to get me then. Long day left. I am ready when you are."

He spoke as if dismissing a porter.

Joseph Henry had not moved. He stood on the slope above them, the air around him unnervingly still. His face was level and unreadable, stripped clean of whatever softness had been there before. He looked at Ugly as if looking through him.

Then he spoke. His voice was calm. Almost lifeless.

"Ugly Attics is trying to get away."

Ugly's head snapped toward him. Something real flashed across his face. Not anger. Not mockery.

Fear.

"What?" Ugly said sharply. "What are you talking about?"

The guard hesitated, uncertain.

Joseph Henry stepped one pace closer. His voice did not rise. It did not sharpen. It carried in the humid air with a kind of plain finality.

He looked straight at the guard. "He is trying to get away," Joseph Henry repeated. "You must stop him."

The guard stiffened. He looked at Joseph Henry, then at Ugly, then back again. He half raised the rifle.

Ugly saw it happen.

"No…" Ugly said, voice cracking upward. "This… I am not trying to…."

Joseph Henry tipped his head at the guard. The gesture was small, almost polite.

His eyes shifted toward Ugly's knee.

The guard fired.

The shot cracked through the trees, loud enough to send birds lifting from the branches. Ugly screamed as his leg buckled sideways under him. He dropped to both hands, choking on breath, the agony blooming across his face in a raw, unhidden wave. Blood ran through the torn fabric and down his shin.

He looked back at Joseph Henry, horror widening his stare, the truth sinking in all at once. Joseph Henry's expression remained unchanged. He did not move.

Ugly reached at the ground, tried to drag himself backward with one arm.

Joseph Henry nodded again.

The guard reversed the rifle and swung the butt down in a clean, practiced arc. It struck Ugly across the temple. The sound was sharp and final. Ugly dropped flat, all struggle gone, sprawled in the needles like a discarded tool.

***

The trucks rolled back through the penitentiary gates in the late afternoon, their engines rattling from the climb up the hill. The sun had shifted west, turning the yard into long strips of shadow. The men in the back looked worn. Their clothes were resin-streaked, damp and tacky, and a strained malaise hung over them. It wasn't common to rush an inmate back to the infirmary during a shift, let alone two, and no one understood exactly what had happened.

Joseph Henry stepped down last. He felt the shift in his legs, the hollow exhaustion that reached deeper than the hours of work. It sat somewhere behind his eyes, quiet but heavy.

Crow and Ugly had been brought back earlier. Joseph Henry had watched the truck carrying them disappear down the wooded road long before the rest of the detail had finished and packed up. The sight of it, Crow still as a bundled coat, had stayed with him. Ugly had lost consciousness not long after being shot, and Joseph Henry didn't know his condition. He didn't care much either.

Joseph Henry crossed the yard. He did not hurry, but his steps were sure. A guard called out, and the sound slid past him. His mind kept circling what had happened on the slope. Even when Ugly had pushed him off center, he had been calm and certain, until he was not. That part of him, the one that rose up cold and decisive, was not new. He had lived with the truth of his two selves for years. He was always one or the other. The quiet, steady Joseph Henry, or the other man entirely.

But now, walking across the familiar ground of the penitentiary, he felt something he had not felt before. The man who had taken those steps down the hill and the man who walked here now seemed to occupy the same place. Neither one nor the other. Something balanced between them. It unsettled him. He did not yet know what it meant.

He turned the corner near the administrative hall and nearly walked into Boss Van.

Boss Van had been striding fast, coat unbuttoned, hat in hand, but he stopped when he saw Joseph Henry's face. Whatever words he had meant to start with, anger or reprimand or something sharper, faltered. His eyes narrowed slightly, taking Joseph Henry in, studying him in a way he didn't often bother with.

"Well now," he said, voice lower than usual. "You had yourself a day."

Joseph Henry stopped. He didn't answer.

Boss Van let out a small breath, something between amusement and resignation. "When I gave you some leeway," he said, "I did not exactly picture you telling a guard to shoot a man." He gave a quiet laugh, short and without much humor. "Can't say it wasn't effective though."

Joseph Henry still said nothing.

Boss Van's expression shifted by a degree. Not soft exactly, but easier. "Sorry about the old man," he said. "Crow. Good fellow."

Joseph Henry's jaw moved once, tight. He only nodded.

Boss Van studied him another moment, then stepped aside. "Go on," he said, voice dropping.

Joseph Henry walked past him as if he were not there. The hall felt too long, the air too still. He pushed into the infirmary and paused just inside the door. The room was dimmer than the corridor, heavy with the smell of carbolic and damp linens. Cots lined the wall. Two were occupied.

Crow lay on the nearest cot, propped slightly on a thin pillow. His eyes were open, though a clouded sheen dulled them. His hair had been washed, but the bandage wrapped around his head was already stained through. His hands rested on his stomach, fingers curled in loose half-fists.

Dr. McCray stepped out from behind a curtain, wiping his palms on a towel. When he saw Joseph Henry, he stopped. Joseph Henry looked at him questioningly, a thin thread of hope behind his eyes.

The doctor met his gaze for a moment, then gave a small, grave shake of his head. Nothing dramatic, nothing said aloud, just the plain truth shared between the two men who had known each other long enough to not need the words.

Joseph Henry looked down for a moment, then approached the cot.

Crow saw him and his face brightened, faint but unmistakable. He turned his head slightly, the motion stiff. "Joseph," he said, voice thin and slurred at the edges.

Joseph Henry pulled a stool beside the cot and sat. "How you feeling, Crow?"

Crow gave a vague little shrug, the kind a man gives when he has no strength to waste on lying. "Been better," he said. "Been worse too, I reckon." His smile flickered. He shifted his hand an inch toward Joseph Henry's. "Glad you're here."

Joseph Henry just nodded, holding back emotion.

Crow looked past him toward the ceiling, as though trying to follow a drifting thought. "What… what you doing here, Joseph?" The words came soft, blurred by the injury.

Joseph Henry blinked slightly, confused for a moment, then leaned forward slightly. "I'm here to see you, Crow. Make sure you're alright."

"No… Joseph." Crow's gaze drifted back to Joseph Henry's face, searching it. "I mean… what are you doing here." He paused, breath catching in his chest. "In this place."

Joseph Henry felt something tighten in his throat. He did not look away.

Crow's eyelids fluttered once, then steadied. "Tell me, Joseph," he murmured. "Been wondering a long time."

The room seemed to lean in around them. Even the doctor paused where he stood, silent behind the curtain.

Joseph Henry sat back a fraction, breath pushing out slow. Something old inside him shifted, let go.

He met Crow's waiting eyes.

"Well…" Joseph Henry said.

Chapter 34
1887

We were walking back toward town along the creek road. We took the long way because we had the time. We had spent the day sitting in the shade near the river, eating what we brought with us and talking about small things that felt larger in the moment. Since we'd been married there hadn't been much time like that. Someone was always visiting. Work always pulling at us.

That afternoon felt borrowed. We both knew it, which made us careful with it in a strange way, like holding something that could be lost if we weren't paying attention.

She walked close to me, her arm brushing mine now and then as the road narrowed. She talked about her sister and something she'd read, and I listened. I remember thinking how ordinary it all was.

We were near the edge of town when we heard a wagon behind us. I stepped off the road with Minnie, like you do, and turned to see who it was.

I knew him at once.

Clem Ryerson. Everyone in town knew who he was. His family owned half the land worth owning. His father used to be in the state legislature. Now he was on the board at the bank. His mother ran the charity drives and led the church choir. I had never liked him. Most didn't, though few ever said it out loud. He had a way of finding whatever sore spot a person carried and pressing on it, not hard enough to draw notice, just enough to feel it.

Minnie had never had reason to see that side of him. To her he was only another familiar face, someone who tipped his hat and smiled when he passed.

The wagon slowed beside us, wheels creaking as the horse was reined in. I felt it before I heard him speak. Minnie seemed to feel it too, because she drew a little closer to me. He tipped his hat to her first, like I wasn't there.

"Afternoon," he said.

Minnie turned and smiled politely like she always did. "Afternoon."

His eyes finally settled on me, like he just noticed I was there. Not hostile. Not friendly either. Maybe… measuring.

"Didn't expect to see anyone out this way," he said. "Thought folks like you kept busier than that."

Minnie laughed lightly. "We took the long way back."

He nodded as though that explained something, then looked at her again. "Married now. Nice wedding." He paused a beat, then he went on, "It's a fine thing, a woman getting herself settled. Some do better than others though." He let that sit, then finally looked at me. "No offense meant."

I said nothing.

He leaned forward on the seat and lowered his voice, bringing it closer than it needed to be. "Course, marriage doesn't change what a woman needs. Just changes who's supposed to provide it." He gave a short chuckle.

Minnie stiffened.

His smile turned thin. "And some men mean well, but mean don't always count for much." His gaze slid back to her, slow and deliberate. "A woman notices that, sooner or later."

I stepped half a pace forward, enough to put myself between them without making a show of it. "We should get moving," I said.

He smiled at that, slow and knowing. "Of course."

He did not move the wagon though.

He leaned back on the seat, reins loose in his hands. "Funny thing," he said, looking at Minnie again. "You never know what sort of man you've tied yourself to."

Minnie's smile faltered, just slightly. "What do you mean?"

He shrugged. "Only that some men aren't built for keeping what they've got." His eyes flicked back to me. "Especially a fine woman."

I felt a shift in myself then. Not heat. Not rage. Just a narrowing.

Minnie turned to me, confused. "Joseph?" She whispered.

He smiled again, wider now. "I only mean, if things ever go poorly, it's good for you to know there are choices."

I turned to Minnie. My voice surprised even me with how steady it was.

"Go on ahead," I said. I tried to show some smile, "I'll catch up."

She hesitated. "Joseph, it's fine. We can just keep walking."

"No," I said. Not loud. Not sharp. Just final. "Go on."

She studied my face then, really looked at me. Whatever she saw there made her nod. She reached for my hand and squeezed it once.

"Don't be long," she said.

"I won't."

She walked on toward town, glancing back once before the bend in the road took her out of sight.

***

"You should apologize."

I paused after saying it, surprised by the sound of my own voice. I don't know why I offered him the chance, except that part of me still wanted him to choose differently. I could feel where things were heading, could feel myself settling into it, and I wanted one last moment where it might be turned aside.

He deserved what was coming. I knew that.

But I wasn't there yet.

He seemed as surprised as I was that I asked. A smirk formed on his face. He laughed softly, as if I had made a joke that he wasn't in on.

"For what," he said. "Conversation?"

This was not the direction he needed to go.

I said it again. I said it plainly. Like it was simpler than he understood it.

"You should apologize."

This time it sounded distant to me, like it was coming from someone else, standing across the road.

That was when his smile changed.

He leaned forward again and looked down at me, as though he had a lesson to give.

"You know who I am," he said. "You're overreaching." His voice hardened. "You should remember who you're talking to."

I was moving before he finished speaking.

I took hold of his arm through his sleeve and pulled. Hard. Harder than I intended, though that didn't matter to me anymore. I saw the surprise cross his face first, then something closer to shock as he pitched forward off the wagon. He came down awkwardly, caught himself for half a second, then lost it and rolled into the road.

He scrambled up fast, turning to face me in one motion. His face had gone red, sharp with anger and insult more than pain, though a scrape showed along his lower arm, which he brushed at without thinking.

"You son of a bitch," he said, and swung.

It wasn't clean, a bit wild, but it clipped my shoulder. It stung, but not much.

I looked at him for just a beat and saw him starting to bring his other fist back.

I hit him once. Then again.

He staggered, cursing now, breath leaving him in a startled rush. I drove him backward off the road and into the grass, away from the wagon.

He dropped to one knee and raised a hand in front of him, palm out.

I looked at him for a moment.

Then I saw him as he'd been on the wagon. The smile. The tone. The way he looked at Minnie.

Minnie.

I hit him again.

"Alright," he said, breath hitching. "St—stop... I…"

I hit him again.

He lurched forward onto his hands. The sound that came out of him wasn't a word anymore, just breath and hurt tangled together. When he tried to rise, one hand kept missing the ground, sliding uselessly through the grass.

I watched it for a moment. Then I looked at his face. I balled my hand again and stepped closer.

His eyes flicked up at me. Not anger this time. Fear. Resignation.

"You don't…" he said, breath breaking. "You don't want this."

He swallowed, tried again.

"You… you know who I am."

I did know.

I don't know whether I stopped caring, or whether it drove me harder.

I hit him again. And again. And again.

There was nothing frantic in it. Nothing wild. Each blow landed where I put it. My feet were grounded, steady. I did not shout. I did not even make a sound, except for the dull impact of fist on Clem. I moved with a quiet certainty. I don't think it had anything to do with anger anymore, and it had nothing to do with mercy.

He tried to curl in on himself. I stepped with him and kept striking. He made a sound once, short and thin, nothing that sounded human. His arms came up too late and without purpose. One slipped back down into the grass.

Then I stopped.

He lay there. Still.

I waited for something to follow. A groan. A twitch. A pull of breath. Any sign that the man was still there.

Nothing came.

I nudged him with my foot. Nothing. I knelt and put a hand on his shoulder and pushed gently. The weight of him felt wrong. Too loose. Limp. His head was turned at an angle that did not belong. One eye was swollen shut. The other was open, fixed on nothing. His mouth moved once, barely, and then I did not see it move again.

I stayed there longer than I should have, my hand still on him, waiting for him to start moving.

That was when it reached me. Not as panic. Not as grief.

As fact.

I had not meant this.

I sat back on my heels and looked at him, trying to understand where the line had been and when it had been crossed. I could see the road. The wagon. The empty stretch toward town. It all felt slightly out of focus.

Minnie was gone from sight. Thank God. That mattered. I knew it did.

I stood and walked to the horse. I patted its nose, then led it off the road and tied it where it would not wander back. I did not think about why. My hands knew what to do.

When I returned, he was still there.

I turned toward town and started walking.

Chapter 35

1929

"I walked to the sheriff's office. Ten months later, I was here in the Frankfort Penitentiary."

Joseph Henry saw that Crow's eyes were closed, but he was still listening. A faint, fogged chuckle rose from his throat.

"Yeah," he murmured. "You got him good, Joseph. He shouldn't'a messed with you and your girl."

His words slurred, the rhythm uneven. "What's that boy doin' now?"

Joseph Henry gave a faint, sad smile. "Not much these days, I think," he said softly.

Crow made a small sound, maybe agreement, maybe just air. Joseph Henry reached and took Crow's hand. Crow's eyelids fluttered once and opened. He looked at Joseph Henry, his gaze unsteady but there, aware for a final moment. His fingers twitched weakly against Joseph Henry's palm, then stilled.

He stayed there with him for several minutes, silent, his thumb resting over the old man's knuckles.

When the breathing grew shallow, Joseph Henry rose. He stood at the side of the cot for a long moment, then squeezed his eyelids tight, wetness seeping from the corners. Then he turned away.

Ugly lay on the cot across the room, half-turned, mouth slack, drool coming down from his mouth on his bad side. He snored lightly. The bandage around his thigh was dark and stiff where the bleeding had seeped through. His chest rose shallow but even. Joseph Henry didn't like how peaceful he looked.

For a moment Joseph Henry only looked at him. A familiar current began to rise, the one that would climb his spine and turn everything narrow. But it stopped halfway, as if caught in his chest.

What moved inside him now did not become the surge he had known before. It did not rush or burn. It settled, dense and contained, present but not pressing. Where it would once have broken loose, now it was simply within reach, quiet, ready. It sat beside his calmness, no longer pressing to break past it. The two parts held their ground together.

It felt right.

Joseph Henry became aware of Dr. McCray beside him when a hand settled on his shoulder. The touch was gentle but firm, meant as much to steady him as to keep him where he stood.

"The leg's pretty bad," McCray said. "If it means anything, he'll never walk right again."

Joseph Henry did not answer. The words touched nothing. Ugly lay there breathing, alive, and the sight of it felt wrong. Incomplete. There was no satisfaction in it.

He turned and started for the door.

"Joseph," McCray said behind him. His tone softened. "I wanted to say thank you. For speaking to Boss Van. For getting me in. It's made things," he paused, choosing the words carefully, "less ordinary."

Joseph Henry gave a small sound in his throat. Not quite agreement, not quite dismissal. He kept walking. He reached the doorway and stopped.

He stood there a moment.

Without turning back, he said, "That leg does look pretty bad. I think he's going to lose it."

The doctor stared at him, the words hanging in the sterile air. He looked over at Ugly, then back at Joseph Henry's unmoving back.

When he spoke, his voice had changed. Lower. Careful. The sound of a man who understood what had just been asked of him.

"Yeah," he said quietly. "That leg has got to go."

Epilogue

Not long after, Ugly was transferred out of Frankfort. Joseph Henry did not see the order. He did not hear an explanation. He never went looking for one. He only knew that Ugly was gone from the places he had once occupied. His cell stood empty. His name no longer appeared on any work lists. A few rumors moved through the men, passed low and without confidence, ranging from Leavenworth to execution.

The day after Old Crow died, McCray gave Joseph Henry a brief nod as they passed in the corridor. It lasted no longer than a step. He said nothing. Joseph Henry understood it as confirmation that what he had asked for had been done. It was a gesture small enough to be missed by anyone else, and it was the last sign of the matter he cared to receive.

Nils and Jimmy both testified to what had happened to Old Crow. They had not seen the killing itself, having been locked in their own fight at the time, but no one pressed that point. They told what they had heard, what they had understood, and what the men had spoken of afterward. It was enough. The administration did not require certainty so much as it required an end, and this gave it one.

Joseph Henry never learned what had driven Ugly so urgently to escape Frankfort. Whatever it was, it would now be waiting a long time. That knowledge brought him a small, contained satisfaction. He let the rest of it go.

After 1930, the work around the still began to thin. Enforcement of Prohibition grew uneven, and Boss Van's margins narrowed until the risk outweighed the return. Repeal had not yet come, but its approach was no longer in doubt. Boss Van began winding the operation down, selling off what he could and letting the rest sit untouched. He had little interest in dragging things out. There was not much profit left in it, and he was tired. Before long, the still was little more than an empty warehouse, its equipment stacked and waiting. Even Joseph Henry was no longer needed.

Boss Van did not forget him though. In late 1932, with no further use for Joseph Henry outside the penitentiary, he helped arrange his release. The attorney, Denton, handled it. It was done quietly. There was no hearing worth remembering and no farewell. Joseph Henry expected that to be the end of it.

Along with the papers granting his freedom, Denton slid another document across the desk. Joseph Henry read it once, then again, slower. Ownership of the warehouse and its contents had been transferred to him. The still. The equipment. Everything that remained. There were no conditions attached. No debts named. No explanation offered.

Boss Van stepped away and did not look back.

With no place else to go, Joseph Henry moved in. He knew the place, and he knew how to get it working again. And with Prohibition ending, there would be work. For the first time in years, nothing was being asked of him. What he did there would be his.

For a time, Joseph Henry was doing the work alone. As Deacon had said he would, he and Giles returned to Barbados.

Deacon had not liked what Kentucky life held for Giles, but he had forgotten that Barbados was no friend to him either. Giles was no longer a minority there, but that did not make him safer. The island was Black in body, but white in control, and the distance between those two facts was enforced openly and without apology. There were no institutions meant to absorb complaint or turn it into redress. In

Kentucky, race shaped where a man could go, how he could live, and how he was spoken to. In Barbados, it shaped whether there was any place at all for grievance to land. When men protested, there was no mechanism to answer them except force. Force was used. Things were different for Giles when he returned, but they were not better. The rules were older, the expectations clearer, and the consequences quicker and en masse.

The turning point on the island would not come until 1937. What had been mistaken for order by those in control gave way all at once. Violence came from both sides. What had been kept quiet for years could no longer be folded back into routine or explained away. People were hurt. People were killed. Afterward, things did not return to how they had been. Change came slowly, but it came, and it left behind the reality that endurance was no longer the only thing being asked of men like Giles.

He did not live to see it though. The unrest culminated in 1937, but 1933 took Giles. He was not a leader. He was not trying to change anything. He was there because he needed to work, and that was enough.

Deacon could not stay. Within months he reached out to Joseph Henry and returned to Kentucky. He was quieter than before, a step slower, as though something essential had been left behind. Joseph Henry was glad to have him back, even knowing why he had come.

Joseph Henry understood what had been lost. Giles had been a good man, careful with his work and fair in his dealings, and his clarity had helped Joseph Henry find his footing again.

Deacon never mentioned Giles, never said his name, and Joseph Henry was never one to press him.

Deacon went on. In time he married, had children, and made a life that held together, and was worth living.

In early 1937, the Frankfort Penitentiary burned. Not entirely to the ground, but enough. The fire began before dawn, somewhere in the older sections, where the wiring was brittle and the heat unreliable. Whether it was faulty equipment or simple neglect was never settled. By the time the guards understood what was happening, the fire had already moved through the wooden interiors and into the cell blocks. Doors stayed locked too long. Smoke traveled faster than help. Many men died where they stood or where they slept. When it was over, much of the prison was unusable.

The wing where Joseph Henry lived was largely untouched, sparing many he knew and called family or friends.

The state was left with more inmates than it had space or patience for and was forced to decide what to do with the men it could no longer house. Transfers followed where they could be arranged. Where they could not, early release, parole, and sentence commutation filled the gap for men serving lesser sentences or those nearing their end.

Nils, Jimmy, Dwayne, and others benefited. They were released with little ceremony and few instructions beyond where not to return. Joseph Henry stepped in and made sure they had what they needed. The still was operating again by then, modestly and without attention, and he took the men in and put them to work, heads down and hands busy.

The still did well. It did not grow large. It did not need to. It served the region quietly and steadily, without trouble. Joseph Henry had no ambitions beyond keeping it running and keeping the people who depended on it employed.

By the end of the decade, Joseph Henry was ready to stop. He had not been a young man when it started, and he was less so now. When Jim Beam purchased the operation as part of its rebuilding after Prohibition, the terms were fair and the transition clean. Joseph Henry did not argue the price. He was finished. The work passed on, absorbed into something larger. He made certain his men were taken care of, and then he stepped away without ceremony.

***

The building was the same, though it felt smaller than he remembered, or perhaps his memory had smoothed the edges of it. A different woman greeted him and offered a cup of coffee before showing him to Denton's office. The room had been pared down. Some of the books were gone. The decanter was no longer on the sideboard.

Denton sat behind the same desk. He greeted Joseph Henry without surprise, almost as though he had been expecting the visit, and indicated the chair opposite him. Joseph Henry sat.

"Give me just one moment," Denton said, looking back down at the papers on his desk. He signed one, then gathered the rest and placed them neatly in a wooden tray to the side.

He folded his hands on the desk and looked at Joseph Henry.

"It's good to see you," he said. "Things moved quickly the last time you were here. Your release, the transfer of the warehouse. I assume you've come to bring everything into order."

"Yes," Joseph Henry said.

"Well, that's sensible," Denton said.

He drew out a ledger with Joseph Henry's name on it and opened it. "Your accounts are in good order. Funds held in escrow are ready to be released, as agreed, now that your sentence has concluded. Interest has accumulated steadily. There are no outstanding liabilities."

"That's good," Joseph Henry said flatly.

Denton studied him for a moment, then nodded and turned a page. "You have deposits spread across three institutions. Bonds yielding reliably. No speculative exposure." He glanced up. "Any preference as to how you'd like this distributed?"

Joseph Henry looked up as though the question had been asked in a foreign language. "I don't… No, I don't," he said.

Denton paused briefly, then continued. "We can arrange regular disbursements. Monthly or quarterly. Or leave everything consolidated and draw as needed. If you have an institution in mind, we could also arrange a single distribution."

"That's fine," Joseph Henry said.

Denton paused again. "You'll want to consider long-term planning. Estate matters. Trusts, if you're inclined."

"I suppose."

Denton stopped turning pages.

He looked at Joseph Henry, really looked at him. The answers were there, but they were empty of intention. Denton leaned back slightly, resting his hands on the desk.

"Mr. Henry," he said, and then hesitated. "Joseph." He cleared his throat once. "Forgive me for stepping out of order, but you don't strike me as a man concerned with balances today."

"You've been handled by institutions for a long time. I expect you're not accustomed to being asked what you want."

Joseph Henry did not answer.

Denton went on, more carefully now. "You've come through a great deal of change in a very short time. Men usually feel relief at this point. Or eagerness. I don't see either."

"I'm fine," Joseph Henry said. The words came quickly. He looked down at his hands.

Denton did not challenge him. He took a breath. "All right," he said. "Let me ask a simpler question. What is it you want to do next?"

Joseph Henry opened his mouth and closed it again. For a moment, it seemed he might leave it there. Then his shoulders sank, just slightly, as though something was giving way.

"I don't know," he said. His voice was steady, but it had thinned. "I thought I did. Before." He shook his head once. "I had a plan. The still. That was going to be it."

Denton waited.

"I've got the money," Joseph Henry said. "I've got the place. But I don't know where I am." He looked up then, and his eyes were bright, wet. "I don't know how to live out here. Everything I knew is gone. The men. The routines. Even the walls." He swallowed. "That place took everything from me. After a time it gave me something back in return. Now that's gone too."

Denton listened without interrupting. When Joseph Henry finished, he looked down at his hands for several beats.

"That makes sense," he said finally. "You lived inside a structure for a very long time. Clear rules. Clear purpose. People who depended on you, and whom you depended on in return. You could see the outside regularly, but the structure was always there." He folded his hands. "Most men imagine freedom as the absence of restraint. Very few are prepared for the absence of direction."

Joseph Henry said nothing.

"You don't need less in your life," Denton went on. "You need shape." He gestured vaguely toward the window. "Routine. Responsibility. Something that asks for you in the morning and expects you back in the evening."

Joseph Henry looked down. "I thought that would be the still."

"And it may be," Denton said. "But a place alone won't do it. Work alone won't either." He hesitated, then continued more carefully. "People matter. Even when they complicate things."

Joseph Henry's jaw tightened slightly.

"You've been very diligent about your obligations," Denton said. "Including the ones you've chosen for yourself." He reached into a file and removed a thinner set of papers. "You've continued to provide support for your wife all these years."

Joseph Henry looked up at the mention of Minnie.

He shook his head once. "She's moved on."

Denton frowned, just slightly. "I don't believe so."

Joseph Henry looked up then. "I saw her," he said. "In town. With a man. There was a younger woman. Their daughter. And a young child. A grandson."

Denton listened without interruption. Then, "I see. Minnie lives with her brother. With his family."

Joseph Henry said nothing.

The memory returned to him with unexpected clarity. Minnie on the street. The man beside her. He had looked familiar. His family? Joseph Henry had walked away then, certain of what he was seeing, certain he understood.

Now it rearranged itself. The man was her brother. The young woman, the child… they were not hers.

For a moment, something like hope stirred. It was faint. It did not last.

"The papers," Joseph Henry dropped his head, then said quietly. "The divorce."

Denton nodded. "They were sent," he said. "They were received. Minnie wouldn't sign them."

Joseph Henry did not react at once. His face went still, as though the meaning had missed him on the first pass. It began to settle. Not all at once, but in pieces, each one landing after the last.

Then it was clear.

Joseph Henry looked up. His mouth curved, just barely, into that thin smile. His eyes filled. He mouthed her name.

FROM THE AUTHOR...

The Quiet Part grew from a deep attention to atmosphere, character, and the quiet forces that shape a life. My struggles with memory and focus often caused elements of the story to emerge in fragments. Ideas and images sometimes arrived before their origins were fully understood. By the time the scenes and voices took shape, their original meanings had sometimes faded.

I built this novel by rediscovering the story each time I returned to those pieces. Because of these memory challenges, I approached revision almost as an act of exploration, returning to pages with fresh eyes and finding new meaning in what I had written.

Often, I was surprised that the words had come from my own pen or keyboard. Other times it felt as though I were editing another person's work.

The Quiet Part is the result of that process. It is a novel shaped through persistence, curiosity, and the willingness to follow a story even when its beginnings have slipped out of reach.

This novel took shape over many years, and I owe thanks to those who read early drafts and offered thoughtful criticism. Their honesty strengthened the story.

I am grateful to friends who asked how it was going and expected an answer, and to those who reminded me that persistence matters.

Above all, I thank my wife for her patience and steady encouragement throughout the writing of this book, especially during the times I would place pages in front of her only to return two minutes later and ask, "Have you read it yet?"